"This is one of those series that stays with you, the type that you think about long after you have put the book down, long after it is over and way more than you should. It is the type that leaves you wanting for more because you weren't ready for it to be over and it sadly and truly, makes it almost impossible to pick up something else up afterward because you just know it won't compare with the greatness you just devoured."
--My Guilty Obsession

"*A Curse Unbroken* is a thrilling conclusion to Aric and Celia's story. I loved the danger, the action, the romance and the reveals. I have been a fan of this series from the beginning, and I was satisfied with this final installment in Aric and Celia's story...This is one of the best new series I have read, and I highly recommend it. *--Rainy Day Ramblings*

"*A Curse Unbroken* demands to be read in one, maybe two sittings, so forget the housework, sleep, and food. When you crack this open, prepare to lose yourself until it ends. I suggest unplugging and having chocolate handy. I laughed, cringed, cried, sighed, but ultimately closed the book satisfied, and spent." *--Caffeinated Book Reviewer*

"There are some scenes in this book so unique and creative that I imagine the best acid trip couldn't compare with them. Some of them are so over the top they are hilariously good... Sparkling cartwheels!"
--The Bookaholic Cat

"*A Curse Unbroken* is a fantastic installment to the series, it will keep you hooked from beginning to end and will leave you with a massive smile on your face. We get so many hints at what could be to come for the whole Weird family and I'm so glad that this series is still going strong. I definitely can't wait to get my hands on the next instalment!" *--Feeling Fictional*

"I love this series! It is funny, action filled, and filled with hot para awesomeness. This book is no exception. I think my favorite part about this series is the relationship between the sisters and in this book we got to see more into their past...the bottom line is if you are a fan of this series, you need this one and block the whole day for reading it because you won't want to put it down." *--Delphina Reads Too Much*

"Why do I love this series so much? Ms. Robson is a master at blending hilarious humor and scorching romance with her imaginative crazy action and fight scenes. I would rip the lips off any woman who camped out in front of my husband's bedroom half-naked, too. Oh, yes she did!"
--Addicted to Happily Ever After

"The most amazing book of the series by far. *A Curse Unbroken* definitely takes you on a ride that is so thrilling, action packed that you don't ever want to put the book down. Celia and Aric are so wonderful in this book that you totally root for them throughout the book, even though the bad guys are always after them." *--Books of Love*

"*A Curse Unbroken* is a modern-day book filled with magic beyond belief and I loved it. It is filled with action, mystery, romance, and dialogue that will have you rolling. Cecy has created yet another amazing installment of the Weird Girls series, and I can't say that I'm surprised! I loved every part of this book." *--The Hopeless Reader*

"This is my first book from the Weird Girls urban fantasy romance series by Cecy Robson and it will not be my last. For those readers who love witches, vampires, a large assortment of shifters, supernatural beings and quick packed drama this is a book for you." *--Sportochick's Musings*

BY CECY ROBSON

The Weird Girls Series

Gone Hunting
A Curse Awakened: *A Novella*
The Weird Girls: *A Novella*
Sealed with a Curse
A Cursed Embrace
Of Flame and Promise
A Cursed Moon: *A Novella*
Cursed by Destiny
A Cursed Bloodline
A Curse Unbroken
Of Flame and Light
Of Flame and Fate
Of Flame and Fury (coming soon)

The Shattered Past Series

Once Perfect
Once Loved
Once Pure

The O'Brien Family Novels

Once Kissed
Let Me
Crave Me
Feel Me
Save Me

The Carolina Beach Novels

Inseverable
Eternal
Infinite

APPS

Find Cecy on *Hooked – Chat stories APP* writing as
Rosalina San Tiago
Coming soon: *Crazy Maple's Chapters: Interactive Stories
APP:* The Shattered Past and Weird Girls Series

A Curse Unbroken

A WEIRD GIRLS NOVEL

CECY ROBSON

Copyright © 2015 Cecy Robson
Cover design © Kristin Clifton, Sweet Bird Designs
Formatting by BippityBoppityBook.com

Excerpt from *Sealed with a Curse* by Cecy Robson, copyright © 2012 by Cecy Robson

This book contains an excerpt from *Sealed with a Curse* by Cecy Robson, the first full length novel in The Weird Girls Urban Fantasy Romance series by Cecy Robson.

Published in the United States by Cecy Robson, L.L.C.

Ebook ISBN: 978-1-947330-25-2
Print ISBN: 978-1-947330-26-9

Acknowledgments

To Nicole Resciniti, my agent, my friend, and my lifeline. You were the first professional in the publishing world to read the first few books in the Weird Girls series. You loved them then. You believed. And now here they are for all to read. Thank you for the faith you demonstrated in the sisters and me from the start.

To my husband, Jamie, who sees my faults, weaknesses, and imperfections and still loves me anyway. About the whole moving-across-the-country thing . . . ah, yeah, let's not do that again. Love you, babe.

To my Weird Girls fans: This novel marks the end of Celia's journey for now. I think it's time to tell Taran's story, don't you? Thank you for standing by me and Celia. Maybe one day she'll forgive me for everything I put her through.

Kimberly Costa, Valerie Secker, Kristin Clifton, and Gaele Hince. Thank you for always having my back. Let's keep the magic going.

DEDICATION

To my Jamie and our babies. I'll love you forever.

Chapter One

Aric's hand skimmed over the small of my back as we strolled along the shore of Lake Tahoe. "We missed Thanksgiving together last year. We never celebrated your birthday and Christmas downright sucked without you."

The September sun warmed my face as I leaned closer against him. "We'll make up for it this year, wolf," I promised.

Aric bent to meet my lips with a smoldering kiss. I moaned softly as I curled my free arm around his neck. We'd spent so much time in bed since moving back in together. This kiss reminded me why.

He pulled back his light brown eyes smoky as he spoke. "Celia, I think it's time we start."

I thought my werewolf lover would guide us back in the direction of the house. Instead he led me around the bend and removed a folded quilt tucked between two boulders. "What's this?" I asked when he spread it along the sand.

Instead of answering, Aric pulled out a picnic basket from behind another large rock and placed it on the edge of the quilt. His dark Irish skin brightened to red and perspiration built along his crown. He hauled me to the quilt, causing me to trip over my feet. He barely caught me before I fell and lowered me to the center. "Sorry—sorry," he said, stumbling over his words. "There's some . . . stuff in there." He pointed to the basket. "Help yourself—I'll be right back."

I didn't understand what was happening and blinked back at him as he darted away. I tucked my knees against myself and waited, then waited and waited some more. The breeze from the lake pushed back my hair and stirred Tahoe's magic around me, enlivening my inner tigress and inviting her to frolic.

I paused from trying to lull her back to sleep and collect my long curls when I realized where Aric had brought me. This was the section of beach where I first saw him . . . and where his wolf side had recognized me as his mate. I let my hair slip through my fingers.

Oh my God.

I rose slowly, realizing what might be happening and wondering where Aric could be, when the sound of clanging metal had me whirling in the direction he'd disappeared. Shrill screams followed swearing. Lots and lots of swearing. My claws shot out when I recognized my sisters' distressed voices . . . only to withdraw when a snow-white wolf bolted past me wearing a dress.

That's right, a wolf in a dress. Welcome to my eff'd up reality. Have a seat, I'll pour you a cup of crazy.

The wolf tore down the beach, kicking back sand with her large paws in her haste to escape . . . my *sisters*? I watched Taran, Shayna, and Emme race after her, the skirts of their medieval dresses hiked up to their waists and the rose petals from their baskets fluttering in the wind.

"Son of a *bitch!*" Taran ditched the floral wreath on her head and her basket of petals. "Run, Celia, goddamnit, run!" she screamed.

She jetted past me in full foulmouthed glory with Shayna and Emme at her heels. The banging sound grew louder. Danny stumbled after them, the knight's armor he wore making it hard for him to maneuver his limbs. "Get back to the road!" he urged.

Four more knights charged behind him on horses . . . wild, bucking horses. I only recognized Koda because his midnight hair hung from his helmet. Horses clearly weren't taken by werewolf charm. And it seemed my wolves would never become accomplished equestrians. One by one, the horses flung them from their backs like sock monkeys. They landed against the sand in a loud clash of noise, half groaning, half laughing . . . and failing to see one horse thundering toward Emme. I dashed toward her as the large animal continued to kick.

The speed and agility that made me so formidable were hindered by spasms of pain that continued to claim me. While I ducked away from the horse's legs, and managed to yank Emme from its reach, I couldn't avoid the smack of its tail.

The horse's essence hit me like a thunderbolt and I fell into a violent seizure. The world spiraled around me, and what felt like slivers of glass raked against my skin. I clenched my jaw, trying to hold back my cries and work through the misery of my unplanned *change*.

The banging of tin signaled my knight's approach. "Celia, it's okay," Aric said. "I'm here. Just breathe, sweetness. Breathe."

It took several long minutes for my convulsions to recede and my torment to end. I rose on four very long and wobbly legs to stare down at my mate. Aric tugged off his helmet and threw it aside, reaching to stroke my face. Fear darkened his features. "Are you all right?" he asked.

I whinnied to assure him I was fine and nudged him with my nose.

He swiped at his face. "This is a disaster."

Gemini took a step forward. "Aric, just ask her," he said quietly.

My sisters and friends gathered around us. Aric let his hand fall to his side and slowly fell to his knee. For a moment, he simply stared. But when he spoke, I could sense his devotion in every word. "Celia, you have been my princess since the first time I saw you. Now, I'd like you to be my queen for the rest of our lives. Will you marry me?"

My vision blurred as giant tears leaked from my eyes and rolled down my long fuzzy face.

"Scratch once for yes, twice for no!" Bren yelled.

I thought I'd always be ready to hear those words. And there I was, a damn horse. So instead of allowing this moment to be robbed from me, I closed my eyes and took in everything that was Aric—his scent, warmth, love, and all that had brought us together. Someone threw the quilt around me as I felt my body shrink and my bare feet slide along the sandy beach.

For the first time, I managed to reclaim my human form following an accidental *change,* and I welcomed it for everything it allowed. Aric tucked the quilt around my naked skin and drew me to him, waiting patiently for me to answer. The lump in my throat tightened. After all the times I'd thought I'd lost him, was this really happening?

It took the soft graze of his knuckles against my cheek to assure me this was more than a dream. My body trembled and so did my voice. *"Yes,"* I managed.

Everyone assembled cheered when Aric kissed me, including Heidi who *changed* from her white wolf form to stand beside her mate, Danny. Unlike me and being *were,* Heidi didn't mind being unclothed. In fact, she preferred it.

Three white doves landed a few feet to our left, their loud fluttering wings demanding attention and stirring my inner beast. I broke our kiss, smiling as the little birds closed in. Aric had gone all out!

The one in the center scurried forward, leaving a small trail behind him in the sand.

"Celia Wird," it screeched.

My eyes widened as the shape-shifter posing as a dove lunged at me. Aric hauled me behind him, but the form the shifter took as it lunged was large and strong enough to tackle us to the ground.

I was crushed beneath the weight of Aric and the shifter. My lungs burned as the air was forced out. Aric yelped in pain before snarling and taking out a chunk of whatever was on top of us. A horrible crunching sound filled my ears as I fought to take a breath, but before I could panic from the lack of oxygen, the weight was abruptly lifted.

I scrambled into a crouch, my tigress eyes replacing my own as the rest of my beast demanded *out*. Aric guarded me with his massive gray wolf form. Blood dripped from his jowls, coating the dead tiger at his feet.

Aric had torn the tiger's throat out, killing the shifter almost instantly. My fingers gripped his fur. I was stunned. It had taken me, my three unique sisters, and a swarm of vampires to kill the last shape-shifter we'd encountered. Either Aric got lucky or his strength as a pureblood werewolf continued to grow.

Aric curled his body around mine and howled, *calling* all nearby *weres* to his aid as chaos erupted around us.

Two horses lay dead, victims of the remaining two shifters. One shifter had transformed into a giant eagle and was circling above us, a screaming horse writhing in its grip. The other shifter had turned into a black panther the size of a minivan. All the werewolves, including Heidi, attacked as beasts; leaping onto the panther's back and trying to force it down.

My sister Shayna wasn't a *were*, but had inherited a touch of werewolf essence from her mate, Koda. His magic

5

gave her a burst of speed. Not as fast as a *were,* but enough to join the fight. She lifted a knight's discarded sword, manipulating and sharpening the metal until it elongated into a deadly blade. She swung as she spun, slicing off a chunk of the panther's paw when it tried to slash her.

My remaining sisters hid behind the cluster of boulders. Emme stayed perfectly still, waiting for the right moment to use her telekinetic power. Taran wasn't as patient and attempted to stir flame from her hands. But her newly regenerated limb affected her command. The funnel of fire she built dwindled to flecks of embers within moments of summoning her power.

Her waning strength and control scared me, but now wasn't the time to show fear. I caught my breath and *changed* into a golden tigress, only to have Aric block my launch forward and growl. He didn't want me to fight. He wanted me safe. I couldn't blame him. He knew I hadn't fully recovered from my last fight and had permanent scars to prove it.

He growled once more before leaving me and ramming the panther at full velocity. The panther's ribs cracked when Aric connected, the force dragging him across the sand. But as tough as Aric was, the shifters still reigned as the deadliest preternaturals on earth. Injured or not, I wouldn't allow my chosen pack to fight without me.

I charged, my large form grinding to a halt as I sensed something descending toward me like a bomb. The eagle shifter had released the horse. Good grief, Pegasus he wasn't. The horse crashed down, narrowly missing me and splattering into a million pieces. Something, possibly his stomach, smacked me between the eyes and temporarily blinded me with fluid.

Emme screamed, *"Celia!"*

I bounded toward the sound of her voice. I still couldn't see and hoped I was going in the right direction. While I moved fast, it wasn't enough. The eagle's talons punctured my hide.   Despite the jolt of pain, I stretched out my claws to the earth and *shifted* him into the ground with me.

My body and his broke apart into tiny molecules that passed through the sand. My intent was to bury him and leave him to suffocate. He must have been familiar with my unique gift, because he released me before I could take him far.

When I surfaced several yards away, he was already breaking his partially buried body free and propelling toward me. Damn, he was fast. His powerful wings tilted, easily dodging the boulder Emme flung at him. I shot in the direction of the forest; if he wanted me, he'd have to work for it.

I raced across the road, luring the shape-shifter away from my group. If I could buy them enough time to kill the other shifter, the one chasing me would be easier to take on.

My ideas were always better in theory. I'd barely felt the forest floor beneath my paws when razor-sharp talons dug into my back legs and I was wrenched into the air.

Shit.

The damn shifter screeched, loud enough to stab at my sensitive eardrums. But that pain didn't compare with the pain I felt when his talons cut into my muscles and scraped at my bones. Agony claimed my entire being, each pull to my muscles growing worse and more torturous as I swung upside down. Beneath me the earth spun. I made out brief images: a river, the thickening stretch of forest, and the tops of its swiftly approaching trees.

Trees! Shit, shit, shit.

The momentum I used to avoid the pines added to my torment. I roared as the shifter jerked and dipped in awkward motions. This evil bastard wanted me to suffer before he sacrificed me to his deity. So despite the mounting pain, I swung my body hard, grabbing onto my back legs and curling into a ball.

He screeched again, soaring with erratic flaps of his wings.

The treetops smacked at my underside. It hurt, but it beat decapitation. I tried to use my free claws as weapons. It wasn't until I pulled myself into a better position that I realized why the shifter kept screeching and why we were flying so unsteadily.

Aric, my beloved wolf, must have managed to fasten his jaws to one of the shifter's wings before he took flight.

His presence gave me the strength I needed to act fast. I dug my claws into the underbelly and took a massive bite. The shape-shifter screeched again, but still wouldn't release me, so I snapped my fangs repeatedly until his blood poured into my mouth.

In a rather daring move Aric *changed* back to human and used his hands to scale up the shifter's back. Chunks of feathers rained down as Aric ripped the shifter's wing apart with his hands. I clawed and bit harder, knowing the shifter would use his powerful beak against Aric if I didn't distract him.

The shifter's screeches grew more pained when Aric snapped the bones of his wing like rotting bark. But instead of diving toward the earth, the shifter soared higher.

That's when I panicked. If he thought he would die, he'd take us with him. He tucked his broken wing and dove, sending us spiraling out of control.

Aric couldn't hold on like this. We were diving too fast. I shifted my weight and bit through the bones of the shifter's feet.

It worked. Finally, I was free!

And crashing at high velocity toward the earth.

"Celia!" Aric yelled above my roars.

I pushed my terror aside and reached for my inner eagle. Unlike shape-shifters who could command any form at will, my power was limited to creatures I'd touched, and unpredictable in the best of times. Instead of transforming into the majestic and powerful bird of prey, all I managed was a set of wings for arms and a very human body.

Good. *Lord.* I thought my nipples would snap off from the frigid breeze slapping at my body as I fought to halt my descent.

While I didn't exactly fly, my wingspan was wide enough to slow my fall. I would have fluttered down gently had Aric not howled above me. My head snapped up. The shape-shifter was corkscrewing ahead of me, his erratic motions breaking Aric's hold and flinging him off. Like a baby wren leaving the nest, I flapped my wings pathetically toward him. In no way was I graceful, but my need to save Aric made me fast. I batted my half-assed wings and naked self to him, snatching him from the air with my legs.

His face smashed against my bare and trembling body. Had my thighs not been shredded to bits, this move might have been kind of hot. But they were, and aw, *hell,* did it hurt.

I grunted from the pain and exertion it took to hold him and keep us airborne. "It's all right, sweetness," Aric said over my agonized whimpers. "You got this. Stay strong."

Aric slipped further down my bloody, sweat-soaked body. I gasped, frightened he'd fall through my legs. He tightened his arms around my waist. "I'm fine," he insisted. "Don't be scared."

His warm breath against my stomach brought me a sense of comfort, and gave me a boost of determination. But when I saw how far we remained from the ground I worried his faith in me wouldn't be enough.

I forced my wings to keep flapping, and tried to ignore the horrible burn in my legs. But I could barely focus. It felt like someone was slicing at my thighs with a machete and peeling the muscle away.

We were about twenty feet from the ground when my body surrendered to the pain. Spots danced in my vision before I lost my wings and we fell. I vaguely remembered Aric twisting our bodies just before we crashed into the shallow muddy river.

Although it was only September, the water felt like frozen icicles piercing my skin. The sting jolted me awake, but did nothing to ease the throbbing of my shredded skin.

Aric jerked violently beneath me and slowly loosened his tight hold around my head. I pushed myself up on my arms in anticipation of another attack. But it never came. Instead, I watched the shifter disappear into the distance, his damaged wing barely allowing him to fly.

Better luck next time, asshole.

My eyes quickly fell back to Aric. I gasped when I saw him. He lay with his back arched against the base of the embankment. Blood trailed into the water from where his skull had hit a large rock. His breath was ragged, but his eyes blinked open. "Are you all right?" he asked.

"Yes," I answered, reaching for him.

He shook his head, grimacing as his skull snapped back into place, but surprising me with a smile. He pushed my long hair over my shoulders. His stare wandered down my body until it locked onto my legs.

Aric's eyes widened when he caught my blood mixing with the river water. "You're not all right!" He cradled me in his arms. "Your thighs look like hamburger!"

I smiled weakly when he lifted me from the river and placed me along the edge of the bank, keeping his body close against mine. I stroked his cheek carefully. "I meant yes, I'll marry you," I told him quietly.

Aric stilled. Drops of muddy water trickled from his hair to stream along his temples. "Even after all that?" he asked, motioning with a jerk of his chin to where the shifter had disappeared.

My fingers trailed over his rough five o'clock shadow. I knew what he meant. Our union wouldn't make our lives any easier. "For better or for worse, right?"

His light brown irises flickered and that grin I fell in love with spread across his face.

"Yes, sweetness. For better or worse."

Chapter Two

"I'll leave you just where the trees thin and the forest opens to the road. You'll be close, but hidden and safe from the fight," Aric said. "I'll bring Emme to heal you and leave another wolf to guard you while we finish off the panther."

In a different world this would likely sound like an odd conversation. In mine, it was almost a daily chat.

Aric tucked me against him and charged, his bare feet racing in the direction of the beach. His body swerved around the dense pines in an exuberant rush, but he was vigilant as always and careful to keep me from harm. His injuries had likely already healed. That wasn't the case with me.

Aric fell under the spectrum of supernaturals who were hard to kill. While I had a tougher hide and could withstand more than any mere human, my inability to heal made me vulnerable and a liability. I hated it, but the last few months and my current situation were a sore reminder of that truth.

The cold river water had chilled my bones and the severity of my injuries made my head spin. I adjusted my bare skin against his, hoping his heat would help soothe me. It worked. The warmth that bonded us as mates spread through me, but it wouldn't be enough to save me. My legs grew slick against his stomach. And although I recognized that I continued to bleed, I remained unbelievably headstrong.

"Don't leave me, I can still fight," I muttered.

Aric pressed a kiss against my forehead. "Don't be stubborn. I proposed to a tigress, not a mule." He ran another few feet before stopping abruptly. "Shit. Now what?"

I tilted my head to see Emme riding Bren the wolf. Bren sprinted gracefully and effortlessly toward us, carrying the jumbled quilt in his teeth. Emme clung for dear life to the fur of his neck, her honey-blond hair sweeping behind her, and her body bouncing in less than charming motions. It was almost comical. Almost. If my legs hadn't been sliced to shreds, I may have had a giggle.

Bren *changed* back to human as he rose, dropping the quilt into his outstretched arms. Emme's fingers remained tangled in his long messy curls. He was a lot taller, and I supposed she was afraid to let go. Having a petite ninety-eight-pound blonde attached to him didn't seem to bother Bren. He walked casually toward us with Emme's body swinging like a bell behind him. "It's over," he said. "The panther's dead." His eyes widened when he looked at me. "Damn, Ceel. You look like hell. Guess that blushing bride stuff was all bullshit, huh?"

He threw the blanket over me and twisted Emme around to face him. He chuckled when he caught the humiliation scorching her freckled face and set her carefully on the ground.

Most women would've liked sliding down Bren's muscular and naked body, but most women weren't as timid as my youngest sister. "I'll heal you n-now, Celia," she stammered.

"Thank you," I said. My vision was starting to dim and I was close to passing out. So much for claiming I could still fight.

Emme touched my face and surrounded me with her pale-yellow healing light. Aric tightened his hold when a groan escaped my lips. He whispered soft wolfish sounds in my ear, trying to distract me from the sting spreading deep into my bones. When Emme finished, my fresh wounds would completely heal. Until then, my body was furious at the speed at which it was forced to mend, and punished me with painful spasms.

I didn't remember losing consciousness, but when I lifted my heavy lids, we were back on the beach and with those I most loved.

Bren circled the dead horses. The poor animals lay on their backs with their legs stuck up in the air like poles. He shook his head. "Damn, Aric. You're going to have to pay for those."

Aric ignored him. "Anyone hurt?"

Although everyone denied it, an innocent bystander might have objected. Eight *weres* I didn't know had answered Aric's *call*. By scent I could tell there were four bears, three cougars, and a werebadger. With the exception of my sisters, everyone present was naked. Blood painted their bodies and soaked the sand, and entrails dried in the sun. On a scale of nastiness, this topped close to puking digits. The humans were lucky to have this part of the world hidden from them or easily swiped from their memories with a little mojo. At that moment I wished I could have been one of those lucky humans blind to the disturbing side of our reality.

The dead shape-shifters, in their human forms, lay about thirty feet apart on the mangled beach. Heidi grabbed the leg of one and dragged it along the sand to join the other. Aric stopped just a few feet from them. The panther had been female, the tiger male. Both had their throats torn out, but the panther also had her skull crushed. My brows drew tight. "Why is the tiger dead?"

Aric lowered me to ground. He hadn't realized I was awake until then. But he did know what I meant. To kill a shifter, you have to either mutilate the heart or brain. Aric hadn't done either to the tiger that attacked us. "I don't know," he said, rubbing his sternum. "For now, I only care that Tura's dead."

"Tura?" I asked.

Aric growled. He continued to stare at the shifter as if expecting him to attack. "He's one of the oldest shapeshifters we're aware of and among the deadliest."

Yet Aric had taken Tura out in order to defend me. I tried not to shudder. Just like that, I could have lost him.

Aric sensed my fear and leaned into me to whisper. "I'm safe and so are you. I will always protect you, okay?"

"Just like I'll always protect you, too," I told him. I meant it, and I knew he meant what he said as well, but I couldn't shake the feeling something was wrong.

Aric motioned to the panther. "Who made the kill?"

Gemini stepped forward. "I did. But it required our combined forces to bring her down." He had his arm around my sister Taran, although his show of affection seemed forced.

Just a few weeks back, Taran would have been smiling up at her mate, bragging about what a badass wolf he was. But Taran was no longer the same. None of us were.

Anara was a trusted Pack Elder who allowed his hatred toward me to spiral out of control. This *monster* literally tore my and Aric's baby from my womb. Ugly scars lined my lower belly, a reminder that our baby was gone, and that we would never be able to conceive another. And while Anara's actions left me devastated and almost killed me, I hadn't suffered alone.

Anara had chewed Taran's arm off from the elbow down and devoured both of Shayna's. Shayna's werewolf essence regenerated her spirit and arms completely. Taran hadn't fared as well. In an effort to help, the Pack Omega had attempted to use Taran's mate bond with Gemini to regrow Taran's arm. No one could have predicted how freakishly Taran's magic would clash with the Pack's, but it had, and it changed Taran in a way that broke my heart.

Stark white skin covered Taran's new appendage and sickly blue veins ran down its length. While technically a healthy and functioning arm, it stood out like a clump of snow against a golden beach. For someone who appeared seemingly perfect—flawless olive skin, killer curves, and bold blue eyes—Taran didn't feel beautiful anymore. She wore elbow-length gloves to conceal her new limb and had lost much of the persona that made her the family hellcat. And now she was also losing control over her power.

Taran tucked her arm beneath her maiden blouse and placed her "normal" arm over it. In attempting to use her fire, she must have burned off her gloves. Gemini noticed, but instead of comforting her, his stance stiffened further.

Shayna glanced their way before walking to my side and clasping her hand on my shoulder. "You okay, dude?" she asked me.

I nodded and adjusted the quilt around me, my spine straightening as two runners sprinted past us. "Don't worry, Ceel," Bren said. "The broom humpers have it covered."

The scent of witch magic filled my nose, but it was faint, overpowered by Tahoe's. Taran shrugged Gem's arm off and stepped forward. "I tried to give us some camouflage, but I couldn't manage more than a few puffs of mist." She tucked her new arm deeper beneath her shirt. "Nothing seems to be working, even this close to the lake's magic."

"Don't worry," I told her. "We're going to figure this out."

Her tightening jaw informed me she didn't believe me. I hoped to prove her wrong, but now wasn't the time.

Aric furrowed his brows in Gemini's direction. "This isn't Genevieve's coven." He took a whiff of the air, a smile spreading across his face as his gaze traveled to the elevated walkway above us.

A band of witches in their sixties straddled racing bikes and waved his way. Each wore a helmet, T-shirt, and black spandex pants with "Bitches on Bikes" airbrushed across her butt. A woman with fair skin and a gleaming smile left the group, trailed by another woman who reached into her fanny pack and removed a container of salt. Together, they carefully walked down the stone steps and onto the beach while those who remained on the walkway gave the camouflaging spell an added boost of energy.

"Hello, Delilah," Aric said when the first woman reached us.

The woman nodded briefly before using her glove-clad hands to remove her helmet. She ran her fingers through her short white curls with her smile firmly in place. "Sorry we missed all the action, Aric," she said in a thick Southern accent. "But we were already down at the ten-mile mark when we heard your *call*." Her light blue eyes danced from one shape-shifter to the other. "Damn. Hadn't met up with a shifter since '86. Would've loved a little payback. Almost lost three of my girls to one, don't you know?"

Aric nodded. "I remember Dad telling me about that fight." He laughed. "He said no one could curse like that Delilah Swan."

She grinned at the compliment. "And no one still can, y'all."

I didn't know Delilah, but I liked her right away. She smiled widely as she held out her hand. "You must be

Aric's mate, Celia. So, you're the tiny little thing telling all the bad guys what fer."

I adjusted the blanket around me again before extending my hand. Although most present remained naked, they were *weres* and had spent most of their lives au naturel. I was only comfortable being bare-skinned around Aric. I shook her hand, slightly embarrassed. "Nice to meet you, Delilah."

"Celia's also my fiancée." His smile widened as he stroked my back. "She just agreed to marry me."

Delilah's gaze swept over the devastation. "After all this? Hell, darlin', it must be love." She waved to the other witch who had followed her. "Betty Sue, come here, sweet thang." The tall African American woman glanced up in the middle of drawing a ring of salt around the shifters. She passed her container to a *were* and joined us. "This here's probably the best tracking witch any coven's ever seen. Tell the young'uns what you did."

Betty Sue grinned. "The eagle shifter passed over us while we were on our way," she said. "I hit him with a tracking spell. I'll be able to trace him within a two-thousand-mile radius. But more importantly, I'll be able to warn you any time he reenters the state."

Hearing I would at least have advanced warning felt like music to my ears. My shoulders slumped with relief. While I didn't trust most of the broom humpers, some weren't so bad after all. "Thank you, Betty Sue," I said.

"And I thank you on behalf of the Pack," Aric said. Which was wolf for "I owe you."

"Consider it a wedding gift," Betty Sue said with a laugh.

Delilah pointed a finger at Aric. "And while you're at it, tell that diva, Genevieve, that if another shifter wanders back here, he's ours. We're no spring chickens, but we still have a fight left in our peckers."

Aric chuckled. "I'll be sure to tell her just that."

Betty Sue finished circling the shifters' corpses with salt. The rest of the coven joined them now that their camouflaging spell was in full swing. They nodded to the *weres,* then formed a ring around the shifters and joined hands.

Tahoe's magic stirred as they called it forth. They chanted something I couldn't quite make out, but each word pricked at my skin with its strength. My sisters and I had been wary of witches since our smackdown with them when we first moved to the area, but it wasn't their presence that bothered me then.

Shape-shifters carried the power of hell within them. While they were technically dead, I could still sense their evil surrounding us. "Don't worry," Aric murmured in my ear. "The purity of Tahoe's magic will cleanse whatever remains in the air after the coven purges the ground."

My eyes widened. "No one purged the ground after we killed the other shifter. Were we supposed to do that?" I was picturing the last nutcase shape-shifter I killed rising from the ground. It wasn't the prettiest of images.

"It's not necessary to us, but it is to the witches. Nature's sacred to them, and because of the lake's power, anything directly around it is considered hallowed ground. Their strong beliefs won't permit them to simply walk away." He rubbed at his sternum again. It was the second time I noticed him do that.

"Are you all right?" I asked him.

"Yeah. Why?"

"You keep rubbing your chest."

Aric stared down at his hand as if noticing it for the first time before letting it fall. "It's fine. Just sore from the fight."

As an Alpha and pureblood Leader, Aric couldn't show weakness. I shut my mouth, realizing I shouldn't have announced his vulnerability, especially in the presence of those outside our trusted circle.

Delilah pointed to the bodies. "Hey, Aric. What do you want us to do with them, set 'em on fire? Datonna's got some good flame."

A witch in pink spandex wiggled her flaming fingers at us to prove her point. Aric glanced at me. "Can you bury them? Shape-shifter burning carries a wretched stink. Even with Tahoe's power, it may take some time for it to leave the air."

"Ah. Sure."

He cocked his head. "You don't have to, sweetness."

He'd sensed my hesitation, but he clearly didn't understand the reason for it. I didn't want to admit how I hated touching them, especially since it seemed like such a wimpy thing to say. "No. I'll do it."

The coven watched me as I marched forward to *shift* the remains of the bodies deep into the sand. I jerked my hand back when I buried the female first. Though she was dead, I could sense her evil. Filthy. That was the best way I could describe her. And that filth seemed to try to dig its way into my skin and infect me with its poison.

Aric wrapped his arm around my shoulders as I stared at my fingertips. "What is it?"

I shook out my hand, well aware that everyone had stopped speaking and was watching me closely. "Is it—" I took a breath. "Is it possible for a shifter to contaminate you with its power?"

The members of the coven exchanged glances, but it was Betty Sue who spoke. "No. It shouldn't be. Shifters hoard their power; it makes them stronger. And nothing can pass on power once it's dead, child."

I *so* needed to hear that just then. "Good to know. Thank you, Betty Sue." I shook out my hand again and reached for the shifter Tura who had attacked us as the tiger, expecting to feel that horrible sensation again. I frowned when I touched him. I felt . . . nothing. Not one damn trickle of power.

"What's wrong, Ceel?" Bren asked.

I *shifted* Tura deep before answering, hoping that if Aric was right, Tahoe would soon swallow the remains. "Tura didn't feel like anything."

Aric closed in. "What do you mean?"

"He lacked evil—the poison I sensed in the female—it didn't seep from Tura's remains like hers did."

Everyone focused on me like they couldn't understand. I did my best to explain. "I could sense remnants of the other shifters—their darkness, even after they died. It's like some kind of nasty infestation. That's why I asked if it could infect me."

Aric turned his head in the direction of the coven. "But it can't, right?"

The coven collectively muttered among themselves. Everyone waited on edge for a definite answer. Aric gathered me to him. He wasn't happy. And neither was I. This was the day he proposed. This was supposed to be special. Instead I became a damn horse, we almost died—*again,* and now I could potentially have shifter cooties? Hells to the no.

Delilah stepped forward. "I've never heard of anything like it, but we've also never heard of anything like you, girl. If I had to guess, I'd suspect you're sensitive to dark ones."

Aric lowered his eyelids and took a breath before looking Delilah square in the face. "How certain are you?"

Betty Sue edged closer, speaking for her. "The world is changing, Aric. With your kind decimated, earth no longer has guardians to protect it from evil. And with our kind taken to breed demon lords, nature is running out of witches to care for and harvest its magic. The balance has been disrupted. The world's fighting to even the scales." She motioned to me. "Spreading the evil that caused it to suffer would be counterproductive."

Aric sighed. "So Celia's safe."

Betty Sue grimaced. "As safe as she can be considering how many evil creatures she's pissed off."

Yeah, well, they started it.

Aric loosened his hold so he could meet my face. "What did you feel when you touched Tura?"

I shrugged. "He didn't feel like anything besides loose skin and bones." My stomach twisted following my last comment. Shifter human forms were oddly thin and practically skeletal.

Danny stepped forward. "I didn't sense anything in them at all after they died. Maybe Delilah's right in that your tigress is more sentient than the rest of us."

Yet another thing to add to the "what makes Celia Wird weird" list. "If that's so, how come I didn't feel it within Tura?" I shuddered. "I can still sense this female's iniquity just like I did in the other female I killed a few months back."

Danny considered it. "Female witches traditionally have to make more blood sacrifices than males in order to be granted shape-shifting power by their deity. They tend to be more vicious and the strength of hell within them more consuming. Perhaps their darkness lingers longer as a result." He looked to Betty Sue and Delilah. "What do you think?"

Both witches nodded as did their small coven behind them. "That sounds about right," Delilah agreed.

Although the witches agreed that I was safe for the time being, Aric pulled me away from where I'd buried the bodies. "Tura's also been dead longer," he added. "Tahoe could have started breaking down his power from the moment of his death."

His reasoning concurred with the others', yet his hold on me grew more shielding. I clutched his arm against mine. I didn't want him to worry. He'd done enough of that.

Delilah motioned to the sand now clear of blood. "We did a nice job of cleanup and camouflaging, if I do say so myself. Maybe that's another reason why you're not feelin' him, darlin'."

"I guess." The painful spasms from my brutalized womb started to build again. I'd been doing my best to hide them from Aric, but my energy was expelled from the fight and from my abrupt healing. I had to work not to clutch my belly. "Can we go home?" I asked him quietly. "I need to rest."

Understanding flickered in Aric's eyes. "Gem, take over." He nodded to the group of *weres* and witches. "The Pack is indebted to you."

He knew something was wrong and lifted me back into his arms, carrying me swiftly away from the group. I was hoping Aric would be more discreet, but he'd witnessed me suffer far too many times, and after losing our baby . . .

I huddled against him. It was something I knew I'd never truly heal from. Anara hadn't wanted me to taint Aric's sacred pureblood bloodline, and he'd succeeded.

One of Gemini's wolves tore out of his human back and raced after us along the sand. Bren, Danny, and Heidi followed in their wolf forms. Bren sped ahead of us, Heidi and Danny flanked our sides. Gemini slowed to guard from behind.

Our leisurely stroll along the beach hadn't taken us far. Within minutes, we were back to the section of beach closest to the trail that led into our neighborhood. More runners jogged toward us from further down the beach. "Will the camouflaging spell carry this far?"

Aric sensed my nervousness. "No, love. But we're almost home and Bren is scouting for humans ahead."

Bren tore across the street, disappearing into the path. We followed. At the speed Aric ran it didn't take long to reach where the path ended and opened into our development. Aric ran behind the backyards. Our neighbors were few and mostly young professionals who worked late hours. With the exception of our crotchety old neighbor, Mrs. Mancuso, no one would be home at this early hour.

Aric hopped up the steps of our rear deck. The wolves stopped short by the door and sat in line. They weren't leaving. "Aric, wait," I said when he reached the door. "Please put me down."

He lowered me carefully, his eyes scanning my face. The painful spasms had receded enough that I could at least pretend that there was nothing wrong with me. I clutched the quilt against me and bent to speak to Gemini's wolf. I didn't have to bend far. At more than four hundred pounds, the wolves had almost fifty pounds on my tigress and their heads almost reached my shoulder. "We're okay, Gemini," I said, knowing that his other human half could hear me. "The wards should be enough to guard us. Go back to Taran."

At the sound of Taran's name, the wolf averted his gaze toward the backwoods, the opposite direction from where my sister waited. "Gemini . . ."

Aric placed his hand on the small of my back. "Celia, let's go inside and get cleaned up. You need to rest."

He placed his hand on the knob and muttered, *"Pace."* "Peace" in Italian was our new key that gave us access to the wards. Tahoe's head witch, the unfairly attractive Genevieve, had also granted my sisters and their wolves the power word to allow us through the wards. Only our voices could open them. It was an expensive key, but seeing how easily Anara had acquired the last key, Aric didn't mind shelling out the cash to keep us safe.

The wards buzzed then opened, allowing him through. He waited at the threshold and extended his hand, but I wasn't ready to step through. "I want my sisters home." My stare cut briefly to Gemini's wolf.

Aric understood my request. "Gemini, tell them to head back now."

The black wolf bowed his head, signaling that his human half had heard Aric's order. I thought he'd leave except then Aric turned to address our snow-white wolf. "Heidi, help escort them to the house and keep them safe."

Heidi took off like a bullet. Danny, our unique blue merle werewolf, watched her disappear.

"My apologies, Dan," Aric said when Danny whined. "I don't mean to separate you from your mate."

He hadn't given the same thought to Gemini and Taran. *"Pace,"* I muttered. I stepped into the house when the wards hummed and opened once more, permitting me access.

I waited until we were in our suite to speak quietly. "Why is he acting this way?"

Aric adjusted the temperature in the shower and pulled me in with him when I dropped the quilt away from my body. He knew I was referring to Gemini and took his time answering. "He's having a rough time with what happened to Taran." He rubbed his soapy hands over my body while I washed my hair.

Pink water swirled around the rust-colored tiles at my feet. I was bloodier than I thought. Aric leaned forward so I could scrub the muck from his thick dark hair. "Taran's having a rough time, too. It was her limb."

Aric squared his jaw as we rinsed off. When we stepped out of the shower, he reached for a towel and dried off my body while I added leave-in conditioner to my curls and scrunched them with a smaller towel. "She's his mate, and he was supposed to protect her," he said quietly.

I watched him sweep the thick cotton towel along my skin as the steam from our hot shower dissipated. His touch wasn't sexual. Not then. He meant to care for me. I knew him well enough to recognize his beast was still pacing within him, anticipating the next attack. Bathing me and showing me love through his gentle caress helped soothe his wolf. I didn't mind. Too many circumstances had forced Aric and me apart. His affection meant he was here, and promised that he wouldn't leave me. Not like before.

He reached for a bottle of lotion and warmed it with his hands before massaging it into my skin. I reached and did the same. My hands spread the lotion across his chest once I finished off his back. His supernatural skin didn't need it, and was naturally soft and silky without it, but I liked feeling close to him, too.

The back door opened. Aric's tense body relaxed when the voices of our loved ones filled the kitchen. "They're back," he said. "All of them. Even Taran and Gemini."

"I know." I heard Taran bark out a swearword before her footsteps stormed in the direction of her bedroom and the door slammed. Gemini said something about returning shortly before the front door opened and then closed almost inaudibly.

My gaze traveled up to meet Aric's. He shook his head. The quiet that stretched between us demonstrated that he didn't want to discuss the actions of his best friend and Beta. Problem was, Taran was my sister, and I didn't like what was happening between them. "What happened to Taran wasn't Gem's fault."

"He didn't cause the harm. But he was at fault for allowing it to happen." Aric knelt before me and kissed my lower belly where the scars were at their thickest. "No harm is to come to our mates." His voice tightened. "Especially in our presence."

I clutched his head against me. We weren't talking about Taran and Gemini anymore. Aric's sadness fueled mine, but I forced it back. We'd shared enough pain for the day. "We're getting married," I murmured.

He paused, and I sensed his mood lift slightly. He held tight to my hips as he glanced up at me, smiling. "You have any idea how happy that makes me?"

I was tired and hungry and sore. But I needed to show him how happy his proposal had made me. "Why don't you show me?" I purred.

He rose slowly, keeping his eyes locked on mine as I led him into the bedroom and onto our bed.

Chapter Three

The scent of bacon stirred me from sleep the next day. Everyone has their alarm clock. Bacon's mine. I smiled, picturing my inner beast bat her tail from side to side, but it was Aric's caress that encouraged me to open my eyes.

He wrapped his arm around my waist and traced a line of kisses along the sweep of my neck while maintaining the spooning position we'd fallen asleep in. I purred softly, inciting his touch by sliding my backside against him. I startled when something very hard poked my very soft parts, laughing when he did. Yes, Aric was definitely awake and very happy to find me lying naked beside him.

His tongue teased and played, licking my skin until he reached the sweet spot behind my ear. He focused his attention there, nibbling, and knowing it drove me wild. My purrs deepened and grew more impassioned, stirring his beast and causing the scent of his arousal to gather around us.

Need claimed us both, making us eager to please. I kept our position and reached between our bodies, searching until I found what I was looking for. His breath hitched when I stroked, my grasp firm, my movements sure, exactly how Aric liked it.

I had his attention, and he most certainly had mine. Voices wafting from the kitchen reminded me we weren't the only ones awake. I struggled to stay quiet, but Aric reveled in the sounds of our lovemaking. He didn't want me silent, he wanted me loud, and did his damnedest to entice me to scream.

I grunted when his hand slipped between my legs and rubbed, his fingers immediately hitting their mark. My head lolled to the side and my lids fluttered. I clenched my jaw, fighting to hush my growls, but it was useless. Aric knew where to touch me, how to touch me, *always*.

I arched against him, my body trembling with desire as he moved his fingers faster. "I want you," he groaned against my ear. "*God,* I want you so much."

He hooked his arm behind my knee, lifting it as I led him inside me. We both shuddered as he advanced. Aric was careful, pressing gently and taking his time not to hurt me. When he finished filling me, he withdrew, then pushed forward, gradually increasing his speed until the steady pump of his hips slapped against my back.

His hand clasped my jaw, turning it so my face angled to meet his. Lust glazed our stares as he moved faster. I worked not to cry out—not to thrash with my first and second orgasms—and I failed miserably.

Aric swore when I tightened around him and rocked my body harder. The fervor tensing his muscles spread along the tendons of his neck and shoulders, causing his head to snap backward when the brunt of release hit him hard. I took control, sliding him against me until he relaxed his hold and lowered his forehead to rest against my shoulder.

I watched as his fingertips grazed the spot between my breasts, slicking over the beads of sweat that had gathered. It took a moment for our breaths to slow, and when they did, it was Aric who spoke first. "Okay . . . that was one hell of a good morning," he murmured.

I laughed and turned to meet his face, only to jump up and away from the bed when I sensed something on top of him. My claws extended and my tigress eyes replaced my own.

Aric jerked up and leapt to his feet, landing on the hardwood floor in a crouch. *"What's wrong?"* he growled.

My eyes trailed over his massive bulging chest, then his powerful arms, expecting to see something more.

"Celia, what is it?"

My beast remained on high alert. She wanted to emerge, but I wouldn't allow more than the presence of her eyes and claws just then. "I think something's here."

Koda banged on the door. He was growling, too. "You all right?"

Aric kept his focus on me. "Stay by the door, but don't come in yet," he told him. He approached me slowly. "What do you see?"

I searched his face, then his body once more.

"Celia," he asked more cautiously. "Tell me what you see, love."

"I thought something was on top of you." As soon as I said it, I realized how stupid it sounded. My back had been pressed against his chest when we made love. Our close contact had allowed only minimal space between us, and certainly no room for anyone else.

Instead of easing Aric's fears, my words only fueled them. "What did it look like?"

Another wolf growled behind the door. Gemini had arrived. I turned to glance at the closed door then used every one of my heightened senses to seek out the threat in our room.

I wasn't sure what I expected to find. But we weren't alone. Something else was here.

My eyes stopped dead center over Aric's sternum. Smooth, unmarred golden skin met my gaze, but nothing more. My beast withdrew and my human eyes blinked back at Aric. My tigress pulled back, apparently confused, but assured that for the time being, we weren't in danger.

I wasn't so sure.

The anger straining Aric's shoulders spread down his arms to clench his fists, yet his voice remained soft. "Celia. What did you see?"

My claws withdrew, except the action felt forced. I hadn't been ready to lull my tigress back to sleep. My apprehension warned me that I still needed her there. Yet I could feel her curl inward and away from me.

I pushed my wild hair out of my face and tried to slow my rapid breaths, feeling foolish although I remained afraid. "I didn't see or scent anything. I didn't even feel it."

Aric gently clasped my elbows. I didn't realize I was trembling until I saw his arms shake beneath mine. "Shhh," he said quietly. "Don't be afraid. I won't let anything hurt you."

I took in his scent of water crashing over stones and allowed his presence to ease my fear.

"I must have imagined it," I reasoned although my instincts insisted I hadn't.

My attention reverted back to Aric's sternum, and I was reminded just how hard Tura had plowed into him. I skimmed the spot with my fingertips. "Are you all right. In here?" I asked.

Aric pulled me close and kissed my forehead. "I'm fine. Don't worry about me, you're the delicate one."

He was trying to make a joke, but I wasn't amused. "You could have died protecting me," I added quietly.

He stroked the side of my cheek. "Celia, you are my love. I would do anything to keep you safe."

I sighed and rested my cheek against his chest. There wasn't much I could've said, after all, I would have done the same for him. "I love you." I closed my eyes tightly. "Don't leave me, okay?"

"I'm not going anywhere," he said. "We're forever, remember?"

"Forever," I repeated quietly.

"Aric?" Gemini asked, his voice whip-sharp.

"Everything's fine," Aric said. "We'll be down in a minute."

They paused before retreating. "We sensed your anger," Koda added. "And Celia's fear."

"We're okay," Aric assured them. "I'll explain downstairs."

I heard the wolves inch from the door until their bare feet padded against the thickly carpeted steps leading down to the kitchen. They were probably confused, but didn't argue with their Alpha and trusted his judgment.

"They're going to think I'm losing it when you tell them what I didn't see and that it scared me." Crap. It sounded ridiculous even to me.

"No," Aric's voice rumbled. "They'll only care that you're safe. Through our links as mates, and their connection to me as their Leader, they're more in tune with your emotions and thoughts."

"More than before?" Aric's stiffening stance told me I was right. As his Warriors, Gemini, Koda, and Heidi were duty bound to protect Aric as their Leader and me as his mate, even at the expense of their lives. It had been that way since the night Aric had claimed me as his mate. Since then Bren and Danny had jumped on the "let's save Celia" train. I'd rather everyone disembark. Enough people had died for me. I didn't need any more blood on my hands.

"Their connection to you is stronger and their emotions more attuned since failing to save you," Aric said.

I eased out of Aric's hold, guilt adding bite to my tone. "No one failed me," I insisted.

Aric followed me into our bathroom. I brushed my teeth and slipped into a short blue sundress before he spoke again. "I know you want to believe that we didn't let you down—"

"Because you didn't!" I hissed. My abruptness surprised us both. I took Aric's hands in mine when he raised his brows. "I'm sorry . . . I'm not sure where that came from."

"It's all right."

"No, it's not," I said, meaning it. Aric and I weren't in the habit of snapping at each other. And for me to do it so easily was odd and completely uncalled for.

My fingers threaded through his while my mind tried to work through my thoughts. "Aric, enough people feel bad about what happened to me. They shouldn't, especially now that Anara is dead. Let's try to move on, okay? Hang on to what's still good, all right?"

Aric shook his head. "It's not as easy as you might think, sweetness. You're Pack as far as my Warriors are concerned. We watch out for our own, and hurt when they do." His thumbs passed over the back of my hands. "I'll speak to them about giving us space, but it's hard when my emotions amplify theirs."

I nodded. Aric, the wolves, my sisters, everyone was trying. And while they meant well, I couldn't shake the sense that they continued to walk on eggshells around me. I was a tough girl, damnit, except the last couple of months hadn't allowed that side of me the opportunity to shine through. I needed to prove to them and myself that I was still me, ready to squeeze lemon juice back into evil's eyes.

Or, well, something like that anyway.

When Aric finished dressing, we walked downstairs to breakfast. "So you didn't see or feel anything?" Koda asked, following my rather unhelpful and pathetic recap.

I munched on my seventh piece of bacon. "No. It was more like something was simply there."

"On top of Aric," Gemini repeated.

Emme sat next to him. Taran was at the sink washing a pan. She was going to scrub the Teflon right off that skillet with how hard she was working the sponge. I glanced at her before answering. "There wasn't any space between us, his body was against mine." I felt the rush of heat claim my cheeks. It wasn't as if the world didn't know we were having sex, but my comment still triggered my shyness. "But it was like something was there, trying to force its way through us."

Gemini's dark almond eyes cut to Aric. "What did you feel?" he asked.

"Nothing," he answered. "Just Celia's fear."

Gemini rubbed his goatee. "No entity of any sort, no spirits?"

"No," Aric said. "But I believe her."

Gemini nodded when he returned his focus to me. "Rest assured, we do as well, Celia."

Nice to know that my sanity was no longer in question. I'd had enough of "Celia's crazy" as the go-to excuse.

Shayna played with the edge of her long ponytail from where she perched on Koda's lap. "So, no ghosts, no spirits, no entities, no goblins—goblins aren't real, right?" she asked Koda. At his nod she continued. "So what? And is there any like, mojo detector thingy we could bring into the house? Something that can pick up anything magical we're missing just to make sure?"

The wolves exchanged glances. Shayna frowned. "What?" she asked.

Gemini leaned forward and pressed his forearms against the table. He let out a breath, but it was Aric who spoke. "It may not be a good idea at this time."

"Agreed," Koda said, his deep voice low.

Silence simmered like boiling water. Every preternatural I'd ever met always teetered on the edge of aggression. Danny, a human *turned* wolf and a passive male in general, was one of the exceptions. Gemini, who embodied Zen, was a close second, despite the viciousness I'd seen him unleash in battle. But the Zen within him was lost then. He lifted his chin. "I don't see another alternative. And regardless of my . . . situation, as your Beta I am to advise without prejudice. You need to bring her in."

Emme turned and angled her chin his way. "Who?" she asked.

Shayna released her hair, her eyes widening as she glanced at Taran. Taran had stopped scrubbing and a spark of blue flame crackled above her head.

Oh shit.

I knew who it was even before Gemini answered. "Genevieve," he said. "Tahoe's head witch."

"Fucking Genevieve!" Taran yelled for the fourth time.

She stomped around the kitchen in stiletto heels capable of skewering shrimp. In her defense, she managed to bite her tongue until the wolves left. If you knew Taran, that was one hell of an accomplishment.

"The wolves only mean to keep Celia safe," Emme added. Emme's tone was gentle. Taran's response? Yeah. Not so much.

"By using the same goddamn coven that tried to kill us when we first got here?" she screamed. "Screw that!"

"Well, technically most of the coven is new, seeing how the majority were impregnated by demons then eaten by their babies." Shayna held up her hands when Taran scowled at her. "I'm just saying, dude, it's a whole new batch of wand-wavers."

Demon impregnation and consumption by said offspring. Yup, yet another conversation that was fairly common around here.

The Tribe—super-nasties made up of demon lords and disgruntled vamps and *weres*—were responsible for the demon infestation. Thankfully, they were beaten down by those of us in the Alliance. "Alliance" was more of a polite term than anything real. In general, head witches, master vamps, and *were* Leaders didn't play nice. Too many supernatural muscles flexing in one room did not polite conversation make.

The *weres* and witches, though, had the whole obligation-to-the-world thing bonding them, usually leaving the vamps as the odd ones out. Not that the vamps cared. They had power, supermodel beauty, mattresses stuffed with hundred-dollar bills, and sex with ridiculously good-looking humans to make them feel better.

As head witch, Genevieve had frequent interactions with Aric as a *were* Leader. But during the war against the Tribe, Aric had Gemini deal with Genevieve more and more, something that hadn't fared well with Taran.

"I caught her putting the moves on him once," Taran said.

"When you say, 'putting the moves,' what are you saying, exactly?" Emme asked.

Taran reached for her elbow-length gloves to cover her hands. "It was back when Celia was living at vamp camp. I walked in on them in Aric's office. Gemini was looking up something on the computer. She was leaning against him."

"Are you sure it was, you know, definitely flirting?" Shayna asked.

Taran gave her a hard stare. "I know what I saw."

I crossed my arms. "Why didn't you tell us?"

Taran tightened her jaw. "We exchanged words—well, magic really—so she'd know he was mine and that she needed to respect that. The thing was, the flirting didn't bother me. I know females hit on my—on Gemini. And it was obvious he wasn't interested." She huffed. "He didn't even seem to notice her."

I approached her slowly, keeping my voice neutral. "So then why are you so upset he suggested that Genevieve come here?"

She held up her right arm. "A few things have changed since then, don't you think?"

I shook my head. "Taran . . . he loves you. You're mates."

"You're wrong," she said. Her deep blue eyes shimmered. "Nothing has been the same since I lost my arm. He's distant, and now I'm starting to have nightmares again."

I drew closer. When I had nightmares, it was because things were wacky in my life or I'd had bad takeout. But when Taran had them, they presented themselves as a warning.

"What have you been dreaming about?" I asked, although I was afraid to know.

"Eyes," she answered.

"Eyes?" Shayna repeated. "That doesn't sound as bad as demons tearing at your clothes." She held out her hands in surrender when Taran tightened her stance. "T, you have to admit. Those were pretty damn bad."

"But in a way, these are worse. They're dark—almost black."

"Like Tía Griselda's?" I asked. She was the crazy witch aunt who cursed us before we were born. Good ol' Tía Gris meant to harm us, but her curse backfired and gave us our "weird" powers.

Taran nodded. "Yes. Just like coals—and like you'd described them, so black, they didn't seem to have irises. And, *hell*—" She shuddered. "Just murderous."

"So were Tía Gris's, the way I remember."

Emme placed her hand carefully on Taran's arm. "You don't think Tía Gris is back, do you? I mean, if you keep seeing her eyes like you do, and if she's as powerful as our cousin Nieve claimed, is it possible she was resurrected?"

Taran looked to me. "I don't see how," I answered. "People, even those of magic, simply don't come back once killed. That said, I don't think any of us should brush off the warning if that's what it is."

"Fantastic," Taran mumbled. "One more screwed up thing in my life that I need to worry about." She stormed out of the kitchen and toward her room.

Shayna jerked her chin in the direction Taran had disappeared. "She's so not herself. What do you think we should do?"

I gathered my hair in my hands before letting it drop. "I don't know. I'm hoping these dreams are nothing, but we'd be stupid to ignore them."

"What about her and Gemini? Can we help them work things through, you think?"

I considered what to say. "I'm not sure how. He's not himself, either."

Emme played with her hands. "Does Aric say anything about Gemini's behavior?"

"No. It's a wolf thing, and a guy thing. He won't say much about what Gemini's going through except that he blames himself for failing to protect Taran."

I lowered my eyelids as one of the painful spasms stabbed at my belly. This one was worse than the last. I clutched my stomach, breathing slowly to help it recede, only to fall to my knees as a horrible pain ripped through me. *Shit.* I slumped to the side, clenching my teeth.

Our landline rang. As did my cellphone in my room, and Shayna's phone, then Emme's.

My sisters' frantic voices filled my ears. I was vaguely aware of Emme's pale light as it cocooned me.

Several long seconds passed before my eyes blinked open. Spots danced in my line of vision as the pain slowly subsided. Taran stood over me with her cellphone clutched in her hand.

"Don't tell him," I mouthed, knowing who was calling.

Shayna cradled me in her lap. She exchanged glances with Emme, who removed her hands carefully from my face. Taran spoke into the phone. "Celia's fine," she said.

"That's not what I felt," Gemini responded.

"I said she's fine," Taran answered, her voice terse. She disconnected when he tried to ask more.

The phones continued to ring as I sat up and pushed the hair out of my eyes. "It's Aric and the others."

"No shit," Taran said back.

I wiped the sweat from my brow. "Don't tell him what happened. It will only upset him."

Shayna shook her head. "Ceel, he needs to know."

"It'll only make things worse," I told her. "I'm all right. The pain comes and goes but it's getting less frequent."

"What if it gets worse?" Emme asked.

"Then I promise I'll tell him," I answered quietly. "For now, it's best that he doesn't know. He's not coping well with what happened to me and is carrying a great deal of guilt." I met Taran's stare. "All the wolves are having a hard time."

The perfect angles of Taran's stunning features softened with sadness when Emme and Shayna reached for their phones. "You heard her," Taran said. "It's best the wolves don't know what Celia's dealing with. Any of it."

Chapter Four

Aric's alarm clock rang too early a few weeks later. He let out a deep groan. I cuddled closer to his warm, naked body. My sleep had been deliciously content. A huge part of it was due to Genevieve's reassurance that no crazy evil had invaded our house. She'd scanned every inch of our home with her magic whoop-ass staff while we'd waited patiently outside. Well, except for Taran who was so furious to have her in our house, she'd left—without Gemini—and didn't return until Shayna called her to say Genevieve had gone.

Gemini hadn't tried to persuade Taran to stay, nor had he attempted to follow her.

I wasn't sure whose actions had bothered me more.

As much as their problems troubled me, I did my best to focus on the good in my life and the happiness that Aric brought me. When Aric and I first became more than bloody acquaintances who'd collided in a dark alley, I had relished his affection and his passion. My experience with males was minimal, and he was my dream come true. And yet, as sweet and adoring as he was, I could sense him holding back.

Now, after everything we'd endured, all I felt was his love.

His warmth and luscious skin had me melting further against him. A small whimper escaped my lips. "Do you have to go back to work?"

He ran his hand down the length of my back to rest on the small curve. "The world's not going to protect itself, sweetness. I wish it would, but there's too much supernatural shit threatening to pollute it."

He stared at the ceiling and rubbed at his chest with his opposite hand. The gesture he made with his hand had become a habit. For some reason it bothered me, but I wasn't certain why.

"I had a meeting with the Elders yesterday," he said, continuing. "I have to talk to you about something."

He'd gone to the Den to prepare for his return. He'd arrived home distracted, on edge, and irate enough that Koda and Gemini gave him ample space. He seemed to settle when I embraced him, so it reassured me that he'd simply had a rough day.

We'd spent the remainder of the evening alone, in peace, and in bed. "I could tell you were upset when you came home," I said, remembering. "What was wrong?"

He rubbed his chest again. "Did you ever hear of Shah?"

I groaned, dreading what was coming. "You're not talking about some hip-hop artist, are you?"

He laughed. "Oh, I wish. He or she is a sacred stone."

I had to find a sacred stone once. It sucked. I'd almost died. Sense a theme here? Hearing one referred to as him or her was something new, though. "He or she?" I repeated.

Aric pinched the bridge of his nose, but kept his smile. "Okay, this is going to sound strange."

"I have no doubt," I muttered.

He laughed again. "Shah is believed to be a living entity, considering he—I'll just say 'he' for now—is a large clear crystal. It's believed he's as old as the earth and has absorbed its power since his creation. Shah's different from other magic stones. The majority possess a moderate amount of magic that has been amplified through witchcraft or sorcery. Shah was potent from the start and has only grown stronger with the passage of time. From what I've gathered, he's also developed a personality along the way."

Okay. Definitely new territory here. "So, when someone says a person has the personality of a rock . . .?"

"He wasn't referring to Shah," Aric finished for me. "His personality borders on funny—as in, his behavior is odd and some find him humorous."

My impression was that of a rock telling knock-knock jokes, but I doubted that's what Aric was getting at. "All righty. So, where is this magic rock capable of ha-ha's?"

The smile eased from Aric's face. "We're not entirely sure. Centuries ago he was hidden away because of his power."

When someone needed to hide something because of its power, it was never wonderful news for the good guys if the bad guys discovered it. "This rock can't raise demons, can it?"

"Well . . ."

Okay, so much for hoping. I plopped my head back down on his chest. "A rock that can raise demons. That's just fantastic."

"Thankfully, it's not as simple as that." Aric kissed the top of my head. "Shah can do anything his holder wants, but only when he feels he will obtain something of value in return. So yes, if his holder wants to raise an army of brain-sucking demons, we're screwed if Shah feels he's been fairly compensated."

"The rock has a price?" It was crazy just saying it. "What could a rock want?"

Aric sighed. "Good question. That's where his personality comes in. We're worried about his needs being met and what his holder will demand of him."

I pushed up on my elbows. "Who's his current holder?"

"We're not sure yet. But we think a bunch of software geeks discovered him and have so far had their wishes granted."

"Software geeks have him—as in *humans*?"

Aric nodded like he couldn't believe it himself. I understood his reasoning. He viewed human inhabitants of the world as those in need of protection from the dark ones. Unless they were mated to a *were,* humans remained unaware of the dangers lurking in the shadows. Those humans who encountered evil did so by chance and typically died a horrid death. I'd encountered enough corpses and dismembered parts to know that for a fact.

"There's this new computer game that came out several weeks ago simply called Shah," Aric said, drawing me away from my disturbing memories. "Alliance members in charge of policing Internet chatter caught wind of it when it was first being developed. Shah's legend is infamous, but like most legends, humans hadn't given it much merit. The Alliance put the software developers on their radar, but didn't initially feel they were worth investigating."

"Because they were only human."

Aric nodded. "Yes. With no supernatural ties, no magic in their families, and no relationships with any *weres.*"

"Then, what changed?"

"These geeks discovered more details about Shah and incorporated them into the game— his last known location, what Shah does, how strong he is—more information than they should have known based on existing legend. Want to hear the kicker?"

My hand passed over his hard stomach. "Probably not."

"Since the game Shah was released a month ago, this band of geeks has already netted close to twelve million in profit—even though the game they developed isn't anything high-tech or extraordinary. From what Koda says, their marketing and promo was also minimal. The geeks set up a website and that was pretty much it."

There was so much wrong with this, I didn't know where to begin. "Tell me about the game."

"It's a rip-off of most treasure-hunter games. You pick which character you want to be and you send him or her beneath the Madiyan Kulom, a famous Indian temple and the last place Shah was believed to be. Your character fights his way through a maze until he finds Shah. Shah is replicated as a large clear crystal with an 'X' etched into the side—also another fact these geeks shouldn't know."

"Okay, then what happens?"

"That's it. 'Your wish is granted' flashes across the screen and you get ten thousand points."

Aric was right, nothing very extraordinary about this game. With technology being what it was, it actually sounded rather boring. I sat up. "You're thinking one of these geeks found the real Shah and wished for money. In exchange Shah obtained something of value. Notoriety, perhaps?"

Aric slipped out of bed. "That's what we're thinking. If the legend is true, Shah's wishes have been expended and his time is drawing to a close. He only has a few wishes left to grant before he cracks and is no more." He crossed his arms. "The last wish is what concerns me most. It's supposed to be the most significant and potentially tip the scales on the side of good or in evil's favor."

"If the bad guys get it . . ."

Aric nodded. "The good guys may never recover."

Damnit. I worked through the facts. "If these are humans who have him, do you think they'll wish for something so extreme that it would affect the world that greatly?"

"I don't know. But just because they're human doesn't make them immune to evil deeds or thoughts. And this game they created, along with the records it's breaking in sales, will assure that Shah lives on in infamy. The way I see it, Shah's been compensated well enough."

Aric was right. Considering how he was making out Shah likely considered the geeks' quest for money and fame a worthwhile wish to grant.

The thing was, Alliance members weren't the only ones who monitored chatter. The Tribe, while severely broken, still had a few devoted followers remaining. "What's left of the Tribe will want Shah, won't they?"

The planes of Aric's face tightened. "Or the shifters or some new threat. The dark ones are angry, Celia. The attack from the shifters proves they want blood and to gain an upper hand at all costs. We have to get Shah before anything else does."

Yeah. We do.

I followed Aric into the bathroom, wrapping myself in a silk robe as he dressed. Truth be told, I liked my wolf very naked. I stroked his shoulder when he tugged on his jeans. "Too bad we can't survive on our love, huh?"

He smiled and kissed my lips. "Yeah. Time to get back to work."

I tried to smile back and I would have if he didn't remind me where he was headed and what it meant. I'd grown used to Aric's constant presence. Martin, his Alpha and lead Elder, had granted him a leave of absence based on the severity of my injuries. It was another way he'd demonstrated his approval of our matehood, and a way of apologizing for the harm Anara had caused.

My hand skimmed over my belly. Martin meant well, but his good deeds couldn't erase all the damage Anara inflicted. Anara was gone, but there was still evil out there, waiting to hurt the innocents incapable of protecting themselves.

Aric was right. It was time to go back to work.

For both of us.

"I'm ready to go back to work, too," I told him.

Aric finished yanking on his dark blue T-shirt. "You don't have to. Stay home. I'll support us."

"You mean hang out, cook for you, and wait naked at the table for your return?"

Aric laughed. "You make it sound like it's a bad thing."

I tried not to laugh along with him. Aric considered himself a modern-day werewolf. When it came down to it, though, he was pretty old-fashioned. His mother had quit her job as an accountant when she married Aric's dad. She'd doted on her husband, and then Aric when he came along, making sure they had everything they needed. While Aric didn't demand the same of me, I knew he loved the idea of coming home every night to my open arms, and a hearty meal befitting a badass wolf.

"I want to work, Aric. Besides, waiting for you to come home will drive me crazy."

Aric shrugged. "If that's what you want, fine. But if it gets to be too much, stop, no questions asked."

"I think it will be okay." Or I hoped. Visions of exploding demon parts danced in my head. I shuddered and adjusted the belt on my ivory robe, careful to hide my scars. "What's going to suck is I have to travel far to chase Shah. I don't like us being apart . . ."

The scent of shock and anger hit my nose like a blast of cold air. Aric was suddenly facing me and he wasn't happy. "What do you mean, 'chase Shah'?"

I frowned. "We just discussed me going back to work. That means tracking Shah. My job is working for the Alliance and getting the bad guys."

"Don't you mean working for *Misha*?" Aric growled. "Damnit, Celia. I thought you were talking about returning to nursing!"

My frown softened only because I was trying not to cry. "You mean going back and delivering babies? Sorry, Aric, I don't think I'm strong enough to do that."

Aric rubbed his eyes before gathering me in his arms. "I know, sweetness. I didn't mean. . ." He sighed. "There are other jobs in the nursing field. If it suits you, work with Taran in the cardiac lab."

"It doesn't suit me, Aric. What does is ridding the world of evil."

"As a *were* that's my duty. You are under no obligation to be involved in our affairs."

I pulled away from him then. "How can you say that? This is my world, too."

Aric crossed his arms and glared. "Because you are my mate, my fiancée, and soon to be my wife."

"Just because I'm all those things doesn't mean you have a right to tell me what to do."

"I'm not." He held out his hands. "Can't you understand that I don't want you hurt?"

"Can't *you* understand that I'm not going to sit around catering to your every need while whatever evil creature wants Shah gets him first?"

Aric became quiet. "I don't expect you to do anything but to keep safe. That can't happen if you're back with the vamps."

He didn't consider my guardian angel master vampire a trusted member of the Alliance, even though

Misha had shielded me from danger in Aric's absence. But as much as the vamps had their own agenda, Misha included, they were the ones who'd trained me to become a weapon.

They also came through for me when it mattered.

I took a deep breath in an effort to calm my temper. "Aric, I haven't always agreed with your decisions—especially when they've pertained to Pack politics or *were* ways and tradition. But regardless, I've always tried to respect your reasoning and your sense of duty. You need to respect that when their actions fall within the Alliance agenda, and will help the greater good, my allegiance is to the vampires."

"Have you talked to him?"

Aric meant Misha and Misha alone. *Way to go off topic, wolf.* "No. He's still in Europe." I didn't bother telling him that he was actually in Transylvania trying to find a wife because, yeah, that would've earned Misha creepy points he didn't need.

"So, he hasn't mentioned anything about Shah?"

Aric could sniff lies. Why would he be asking me about Shah so soon after telling me about him himself? I frowned. "Ah, no," I said slowly. "The last time I spoke with him was a few weeks ago. You know this."

"The vamp hasn't called again?" Aric questioned me with more bite in his tone than I was used to or appreciated.

I lifted my chin, willing myself not to go all crazy Latina. "That 'vamp' helped save my life more than once. He's a friend, and I have no reason to keep any interaction with him a secret."

Aric opened his mouth then snapped it shut. He took several breaths, and then several more as if struggling to stay in control.

I watched him, stunned and confused as to what exactly had set him off. "Aric?"

He turned from me and gripped the edge of the counter, his breath growing more labored. Sweat poured from his temples as he worked to slow his breathing and extinguish his rising anger.

He was losing his composure.

And it scared me.

A low growl escaped from his lips. The veins of his arms bulged as he clamped down on the counter. The force of his grip caused the granite to snap between his hands. A crack, as thick as my finger, shot out like a lightning bolt and smacked against the edge of the sink.

Aric's entire body shook. He was seconds from exploding and tearing someone to shreds.

Anyone else would have hauled ass away from him.

But I wasn't just anyone.

I curled my arms around his and breathed, simply breathed, allowing our warmth to spread between us. "It's okay," I whispered softly. "I'm here, and I won't let anything happen to you. . ."

He growled, low and vicious, as if sensing a threat.

My eyes scanned the surroundings. Was something with us? "And you won't let anything happen to me, either."

When my voice alone was not enough to settle him, I tried to reach him on a deeper level. In my mind, I pictured my tigress approaching Aric's animal form. I saw her hurry toward his gray wolf without fear, and without hesitation, chuffing in way of a greeting.

He bounded toward her, his tail wagging, and allowed her to rub against his soft fur. But then the image was clouded with confusion. Our animal sides paused and glanced up as if searching for someone they could no longer see.

I was there with them, even though I couldn't see my physical form. But Aric wasn't with us.

He was gone. I couldn't sense him, *anywhere.*

I clung tighter to Aric's arms. I still felt him in my reality, but not in my deepest thoughts, where our connection linked us even when we were apart.

Fear filled me. "Aric? Where are you?"

He jerked from me with his eyes closed, barely managing to keep his balance. He trembled when I reached for him again and snapped his eyes open as another deep growl rumbled in his chest.

He was clearly riled and ready to attack, but as he took in my fear, his gaze softened. He approached me slowly when I stepped back to allow him space. "It's okay," he said quietly. "I won't ever hurt you. . ."

This time, it was his turn to hold me, pulling me into a protective embrace. He took in my scent, allowing the comfort I gave him to help soothe his labored breathing and tame his anger and drive to attack.

I waited a few minutes before speaking, both of us clearly shaken. "Are you all right?"

"Yes . . . I'm fine."

"I don't think you are." I did my best to explain what I felt. "I sensed your beast side and saw him with my tigress, but you were gone. None of us knew where you were."

One of the main differences between me and Aric, and his *were* species, was that their animal sides were a part of them. My beast was a part of a golden tiger's spirit that was absorbed through the magic I inadvertently possessed. She was a separate entity, which was why I could *change* part of my body without taking on her form completely. *Weres* didn't have that luxury; they were permanently linked to their beasts.

So then how could Aric have left his wolf behind?

Aric rubbed his eyes. "I don't know where I went."

"But wherever it was, your wolf wasn't with you. How is that possible?"

Aric's features tightened. "I don't know. It's never happened before. I could feel him near me, furious that I'd been robbed from him. But our connection was severed."

"So was ours," I said quietly.

Aric angled his head toward the frosted glass windows above our large jet tub. "You with Misha stirred some jacked-up emotion I wasn't expecting."

I couldn't believe this was his excuse. "Don't put this on me and Misha. You know there's nothing between us."

He stayed quiet, appearing confused.

"Aric?"

"I know," he said, sounding more bewildered. "I don't even know where that came from." He glanced down at the tile floor and swore. "I'm trying to make sense of this—all of it. I know I felt anger toward Misha, and fear about anything happening to you. Then everything faded away."

I squeezed his arm; afraid he was the one fading away. "You felt yourself leave me?"

He nodded, agreeing, but clearly upset. "From what I can make of it, my emotions seemed to trigger the separation from my wolf. It's like everything I felt magnified and taunted me until I lost control."

Aric was the most powerful pureblood *were* in known history, not some mindless beast.

"You lost control of your *wolf*?"

Aric's face darkened. "No. I lost control over my human side."

Neither of us moved for a long time.

"What's happening?" I finally asked.

"I don't know. But considering how crazy I get over anything happening to you, maybe it was enough to cause this disconnect."

"That doesn't make any sense."

Aric's deep timbre was laden with guilt and sadness. "Celia, when our son died, a part of me died with him. You'll never be the same, I know you won't, but neither will I."

My eyes welled and a painful lump claimed my throat. Aric would never know what it felt like for a mother to lose her baby. But I never considered what it was for a father to lose his child.

The connection that was briefly lost between us resurfaced and pulled us together.

We held each other for what seemed like forever. "I'm sorry," he said at last.

"I am, too."

He stroked my back. "Will you . . . will you think about staying out of this thing with Shah? Celia, I can't handle you getting hurt again."

I understood his fear, and all the incidents that had reinforced them. That didn't mean I was ready to walk away from what I knew was right. "I don't know, Aric."

He bowed his head. "Will you at least give nursing another try? If you want a thrill, try working in the Emergency Department. Maybe it will be enough to satisfy your need to help, and your desire to make a difference."

But it wasn't the same and he knew it.

Aric waited for me to answer. When I didn't, he passed his hand through his thick hair. "Just please think about it, love. I can't stomach the thought of losing you."

I didn't want to think about it. But marriage and matehood were about compromises so I nodded. "I'll think about it. But I want you to think about letting me play a role in finding Shah, too. Okay?"

"All right," he agreed, but I could hear the hesitance in his voice.

I didn't want us to part on a sour note, especially since this would be his first day away from me in a long while. So, I welcomed his kiss like the peace offering it was.

"I have a lot to do today and may be late," he said. "Will you come to the Den and have lunch with me?" He seemed sad then. "I don't want to wait until tonight to see you again."

I had planned to stop in, but knowing he wanted me there meant a great deal, especially following his outburst. "Why don't we have lunch at that small bistro?"

"That's a good idea. I'll meet you there so you don't have to drive all the way up to the Den."

"Okay." I waited a beat, considering what I needed to ask. "Will you do something for me?" He nodded. "Will you ask Martin about what happened just now? This can't be good, Aric."

"No. It can't be," he agreed.

My hands splayed along his chest when he seemed lost in his thoughts. "You don't want to ask him, do you?"

Aric shook his head. "It's not that. I just don't want Martin questioning my ability to lead. The moon sickness inflicted upon me was supposed to lead to insanity before killing me. If he thinks I'm unstable, it might cause us problems we don't need."

"I know you're finally in a good place with your Pack. But I don't want you to keep things from the Elders if something's wrong. As much as I hate to say this, they're the ones who can help you."

His hand cupped my jaw. "You're the only one who helped me last time. And just like before, we'll get through whatever comes together, all right?"

Which meant he didn't want me talking to Martin, either. I didn't want to think that there was anything wrong with him, but I couldn't ignore what just happened. I didn't promise Aric anything, at least not then.

I clutched him against me until his strong arms released me and we said goodbye. Then I watched his black

Escalade pull out of our driveway as he left to rid the world of evil without me. As if on cue, my iPhone buzzed on my nightstand the moment Aric's SUV disappeared out of our neighborhood. Agnes Concepción, one of Misha's most trusted vampires, had sent me a text.

Celia, the master has a little stone he'd like you to find.

Chapter Five

I slipped on a long, brown suede gypsy skirt that sat just below my navel, but kept the hideous red scars of my mangled pelvis hidden. The soft white cashmere sweater I wore fell just below my breasts. Aric loved this outfit because it complemented my curves and flat abdomen. I liked it because it was comfy.

I'd spent the week meeting Aric for lunch at a few local restaurants close to the Den. Today was a busier day for him and he wouldn't be able to leave the grounds. As a treat, I decided to bring him lunch and made one of his favorite meals.

I finished marinating the steaks for dinner then hauled the picnic basket filled with goodies into my new Mercedes GL550. In lieu of a ring I'd probably lose *changing,* Aric had shocked me with a new ride. My jaw had practically unhinged when I saw it, and initially I tried to make him take it back. "You're stuck with me and stuck with the SUV. Just smile and enjoy us both," he said with a grin.

"What if I wreck it?" I'd asked.

"You won't," he'd said.

"What if some giant creature tries to destroy it with me in it?"

He hadn't had an answer for that, except to have Genevieve ward the crap out of it.

The scent of Tuscan soup wafted into my nose, so did the Irish cheese I'd packed, and the Bavarian bread I'd baked the night before.

I allowed the aroma to soothe me. I needed it following my text-to-text interaction with Agnes earlier that morning.

Any more news on Shah? I texted back.

Nothing I can tell you over the phone. Get over here and we'll talk.

I can't right now.

Why? Are you and the mongrel having sex?

It took all I had to stay reasonable. *If we were, why would I stop just to text you?*

I never said you stopped. Or claimed it was any good.

Lord. Help me. *I'll be by later.*

Why not now?

I'm busy.

Having sex?

I'm not having sex, Agnes!

Maybe you should—the good kind I'm saying. You're awfully testy.

I'll be by this afternoon.

There was a brief pause, followed by: *So you are having sex?*

I conceded just to shut her up. *Yes. It's just hot monkey wolf love around here.*

I knew it! See you this afternoon.

What sucked was, out of all Misha's vampires, Agnes tended to be the most conservative one of the bunch.

Which spoke volumes.

It took me only about ten minutes to reach Squaw Valley but another fifteen minutes to climb Granite Chief Peak where the Den was located. The dirt path up the mountain was easy to maneuver with my new ride, but I didn't want to risk losing control and falling off the side.

I peeked over the nosebleed edge. *Yeah, going off the side would super-suck.*

Now that it was October, the temperature had begun to drop. But my inner furry beast kept me warm, so I let the windows down to breathe in the luscious aroma of pine. My sisters and I had traveled all over the U.S. as nurses until we finally settled in Tahoe. Out of all the places we'd visited, neither me nor my beast had ever encountered air as crisp or clean. We belonged in Tahoe; I just never realized it until we arrived.

I reached the massive wrought iron gate that led into the compound where *weres* were taught to maim, kill, and do algebra. I'd hoped Heidi was on duty so I could say hi. The last time she called, she'd invited us over for leftover horse. My sisters and I had politely declined, and I hadn't spoken to her since.

Instead of Heidi, an unfamiliar *were* hit the button and allowed me through. He didn't bother to glance my way or hide his scowl.

The way the wolf disregarded me was more than just the typical aversion; I could sense his deep underlying resentment of my presence. I wouldn't have cared what he thought if his dislike didn't extend past me. But that wasn't the case. Aric had lost respect from his kind for choosing to be with me. It didn't bother him. But damn it all, it bugged the hell out of me.

The majority of *weres* who consented to our union only did so because they believed the soothsayer Destiny's prediction: A new evil was coming, and only my and Aric's children would be strong enough to stop it.

My hand involuntarily fell to my belly. "So much for that," I mumbled.

I accelerated ahead, past the sprawling lawns to the collection of buildings that resembled more of a posh ski resort than a school.

I parked in front of one of the main buildings and was pulling the picnic basket out of my SUV when a few of Aric's students jogged by. After spending most of my life on my guard, I wasn't someone anyone would classify as friendly. Still, I tried to smile pleasantly. With the exception of a small wolf named Peter, who grinned back, the other young *weres* nodded briefly and scurried away.

I guessed I didn't do cheery well. "Hiya, Celia!" Peter said. "Do you need help with that?"

Peter had always been nice to me, but that wasn't the only reason I liked him. He was scrawny and wimpy for a wolf, but he didn't appear to know it. Despite the fact that even the first-year students towered over and outmuscled him, he trekked along without a care. I respected him for it. He seemed comfortable in his own skin, a feat my sisters and I had never managed.

While I could have carried twenty full picnic baskets and thrown Peter on top, he seemed eager to help. I smiled again and handed him my basket. "Thank you, Peter. I appreciate it."

As soon as I tucked the blanket I brought beneath my arm and grabbed my purse, he led me into one of the largest buildings, a three-story chalet with stacked-stone steps and pillars. The building served as office and sleeping quarters for the staff.

The floor and paneling were composed of dark wood, meticulously clean and polished. Pictures of famous *weres* in brass frames covered the foyer walls. Among them were photos of Aric's father and grandfather.

Aric had inherited their dark hair, light brown eyes, and strong chiseled jaw. If he had never pointed out who they were, I would have easily recognized the resemblance. Both men appeared serious in the photographs, very unlike the jovial men Aric had described.

My eyes wandered from the photos of his family to a large painting of a pack of wolves racing through the forest. With the exception of the full moon that shone brightly in the azure sky, all the colors in the painting were dark, muted, and eerily beautiful. Beneath the painting was a bronze plaque inscribed with the words *Perdere malis*—"Destroy all evil." I paused beneath the painting. My experiences in the past two years made the words more significant. I wasn't a *were,* but I could identify with their sense of duty to the earth.

"Is Aric upstairs?" I asked when Peter bounded up the steps.

"No, but I figured the lunch you brought will be safer in his quarters. You never want to leave food around a pack of growing wolves."

"Oh, okay." I hadn't been back to Aric's suite since recovering from my injuries. It was where we mourned the loss of our child and dealt with the aftermath of Anara's deceit.

The young wolves and *weres* who resided at the Den had only been given minimal information about my injuries. If Peter had known what I endured, I doubted he would have led me back to the suite.

We walked up to the third level and down the long wide corridor without either of us breaking a sweat. Each floor had been crafted of that same dark wood and designed with a more masculine feel, which was why the bright pink floral couch set near Aric's door gave me pause.

"Peter. What's that?" I asked, motioning ahead to the eruption of prissiness.

"Huh? Oh." He rolled his eyes. "That belongs to the girls."

I continued alongside of him. "What girls?"

"You know, the ones who want to have sex with Aric."

Peter continued on his merry little way while the world stopped spinning on its axis directly below my feet. *"What?"*

He answered while he fumbled with the keypad to Aric's door. "Yeah, they have a club and everything. Anyway, they got tired of standing around waiting for him so they all chipped in and bought that ugly thing." He punched in a few more numbers. "Sorry, I forgot the code," he said when the light finally flashed green.

He reached for the handle, but became distracted by my death grip on his wrist.

Anger spread through me, heating my body so fast perspiration gathered along my crown. "Just so I'm clear, there are women—who want to sleep with *my fiancé*—and they sit there" —I motioned with an accusing finger to the fucking couch— "so they can pounce on him the minute he shows?"

Peter stared down at his wrist, then back at me. "Ah, perhaps I've said too much."

I tore my eyes away from Peter and looked down the hall to where playful giggling echoed from the level below. Two of Aric's fans skipped up the steps, pausing when they caught sight of me.

Instead of running for their lives, as they very much should have, they strutted like runway models on a catwalk. Then again, runway models didn't typically dress like whores.

The one with red hair down to her elbows wore a black mesh top, no bra, and tiny black shorts. The other one, a brunette with short spiky hair and long bangs, let her open red robe sway behind so I'd have a direct view of her lacy panties and massive boobs stuffed into the matching bra.

Neither was barefoot. It seemed clear heels were the preferred footwear of *were* tramps everywhere.

I stood there with my mouth hanging open, still attached to Peter who'd begun to struggle. The members of the slut club smiled, obviously pleased by my dumbfounded reaction. They fell onto their couch, crossing their long legs and laughing.

The redhead who sat nearest to me tossed me a wicked grin over her shoulder before ignoring me completely. "So," she said to her friend. "Did you get a new car yet?"

"No," the brunette pouted. She stuck out her bottom lip in a way that made me think she'd practiced that move in the mirror about a thousand times. "But you know what they say, 'Don't have a car? Ride Aric Connor.'"

Peter dropped my basket and shot off like a jet the moment I released him. He hadn't quite made it to the second flight of stairs when bimbo number one and bimbo number two crash-landed in the foyer with their demolished love seat on top of them.

I kicked off my shoes and leapt down into the foyer after them, landing in a crouch. It was the furthest and hardest I'd ever landed. And it hurt.

But hell would freeze before I'd show them weakness.

The redhead charged. I had enough time to flip her to the ground and knock her out before the brunette tackled me. Her scent of pine and musk told me she was a werecougar. She was tough. I was tougher. We exchanged a few hard blows before I punched her in the nose and tore her pouty lips right off her face.

She screamed, a ghastly, wet scream, stopping to gape at what remained of her mouth on the floor.

The redhead came to, slamming me down chest first and wrenching my arm brutally behind my back. She would've had me if experience hadn't taught me one thing:

Ignore pain and focus on hurting the being trying to kill you.

I rolled in the direction the bitch wolf was wrenching my arm and used my free arm to ridge-hand her across the nose. That didn't stun her, but my follow-up kick to the temple did.

The lipless cougar then tried to take me out by the knees. She missed. I didn't. I kicked her with enough force to bounce her flailing body off the floor. They were both bloody, groaning, and limping when Peter raced back through the front door followed closely by the Pack Elders.

Martin was a big man. If I had to go by sight instead of smell, I would've pegged him a werebear. He was in his seventies, with the body of a thirty-year-old triathlete who preferred shards of glass for breakfast instead of Wheaties.

He scowled when he caught me holding the redhead up by the throat. She slumped to the floor when I released her then quickly scrambled to stand. She joined her friend and together they bowed to Martin and Makawee.

Martin scanned the large foyer. All that remained of the casting couch were pieces of torn fabric and splintered wood smeared with *were* blood. Broken chunks of furniture—an end table, a few chairs with missing legs, and a small cabinet—also littered the area from the throw-down.

It was a vicious catfight.

And I'd owned it.

The problem was, I didn't technically belong in the Pack and I'd fought *weres* who did, in their sacred institute. I didn't know all the rules and regulations but was fairly certain this was a big no-no.

The knowledge did nothing to cool my anger. I was *livid*. I stepped forward, not bothering to bow. "With all due respect—"

Martin cut me off with a simple lift of his hand. He continued to scowl, but now I could see his anger wasn't directed at me. "Lindsey, Dara, I warned you Aric's mate wouldn't tolerate your blatant disrespect of their relationship. Clean this mess up." He walked toward me and gave me a brief nod before continuing toward the offices located in the rear of the building. "I expect the disbandment of your group, but not before you collect monies to reimburse what you have damaged and destroyed." He didn't bother to glance back, yet it was clear his word was law.

The *weres* hurried to clean the area. The cougar paused to pick her shriveling lips from the floor and toss them in a wastebasket. Eventually, her missing pieces would grow back. I couldn't say the same if she'd torn off my face.

I stared at my red-stained hands. I was angry, yes, but my response had been cruel. I was many things. Cruel wasn't one of them.

My own voice filled my head, saying things I didn't want to hear.

They deserved it.

You should have killed them.

It's not too late.

Make them suffer.

A horrible sense of hate claimed me, but just as quickly as it came, it left me when Makawee approached. The peace affiliated with her power as the Pack Omega dissolved that awful sense of loathing and reined in my anger.

She took my hand and watched me with sad, dark eyes. "Celia, will you join me in my chambers? I'd like a word with you," she said gently.

Chapter Six

Makawee and I weren't friends. But she had always shown me kindness and was one of many who fought to keep me alive. As the Omega of the Pack, she embodied calm, nurturing magic like a second skin. So why did her touch disgust me? And why did I pull away?

Run, my inner voice urged.

"Why?" I questioned aloud.

Makawee cocked her head, believing I was speaking to her. "Forgive me, Celia, but what I wish to say is of a sensitive nature." Her attention left me to glance at the *weres* hurrying to clean. Her brows drew together ever so slightly, but it was enough to make the tramps avert their gaze and move faster.

I forced myself to speak. "All right." Although I agreed to follow her, that urge to flee poked at me. I was *afraid* to be alone with her. My thoughts, though, didn't make sense. Out of everyone, why would I be afraid of Makawee?

Because she was friends with Anara, my voice insisted.

Yes, but he betrayed her, too, I added.

Makawee paused at the entrance to the corridor that led to her office, watching me as I debated with myself.

The small smile she usually gave me was noticeably absent, while her concern was more than obvious. "Is something troubling you, Celia?"

"Um. No." Although that's what I claimed, I remained cemented in place.

"If you have another appointment, child, I'm certain we can speak at another time," she suggested.

"No." I pushed forward. "Now's good."

My speech was off, and everything felt forced. If Makawee noticed, she failed to show it. Her waist-length white hair drifted behind her while she walked, despite the lack of haste in her step. Like always, she wore an earth-tone dress, no patterns, no frills. This dress didn't even have buttons. It was a simple brown pullover with short sleeves.

Her bare feet passed silently over the dark wood. For someone who rarely wore shoes, her feet always seemed perfectly clean.

Although I'd never stepped into Makawee's office, it was exactly as I'd imagined it. Simple tones of cream lightened the otherwise dark wood, and Native American tapestries and throws of deep reds added color to the walls and furnishings.

"Please make yourself comfortable," she said, motioning to the worn leather couch. She turned away from me as she stepped into a small kitchenette.

I was glad she wasn't watching me. I had to force myself to sit, the urge to race away from her continuing to needle me.

She poured hot water from a teapot into an antique ceramic pitcher. "May I make you some tea?" she asked.

No. She means to poison you.

My eyes widened. I couldn't believe where my thoughts had wandered. My tigress typically ruled my instincts, but as I reached to stroke her, I sensed her pulling away from my caress. She didn't appear to know me. Or welcome me.

What the hell?

"Celia, would you like some tea?" Makawee repeated.

"Y-yes. Thank you," I managed.

Makawee used a small wooden tray painted with flowers to carry the pitcher, ceramic mugs, and tea supplies. She placed it on an old oak table in front of me, using care not to spill the contents. The pitcher and mugs appeared to have come from different sets, but they were pretty and complemented one another beautifully.

Makawee filled two small gold balls with loose tea, placed them in the cups, and added hot water. "How is the pain from your injuries?" she asked.

"Fine." She raised her eyebrows slightly, enough to let me know she didn't completely believe me. "It comes in spasms," I admitted. "But for the most part it's manageable and doesn't impede me in any way."

Makawee nodded, seemingly satisfied with my more honest response. "Forgive me for asking, but has your cycle returned?"

Her question caught me off guard. But I answered in spite of the emotions it stirred. "No." My cycle had always been irregular, but after how Anara had butchered me, it hadn't returned. Makawee was probably hoping I could still become pregnant.

But you can't.

You're barren.

And it's her fault.

My thoughts betrayed me, hurting me more than anything Makawee could have asked. Yet my response was uncalled for—and I couldn't stop it. I leaned back, patting my belly and smiling as I spoke. "Sorry, no future saviors of mankind growing in here," I said simply.

Then I took a sip of my tea!

Makawee's eyes widened in time with mine.

I thought I was going crazy. And maybe she did, too, but instead of calling for help or trying to restrain me, the sadness dulling her dark eyes seemed to engulf the room. "The fault is ours alone, Celia," she said quietly. "Martin and I were never blind to what you and Aric share."

They why did you keep us apart, bitch?

I clutched the arm of the leather couch and glanced around, certain someone else spoke. But it was *my* voice!

Makawee stirred her tea, unaware of my venomous thoughts and keeping her voice light as she continued. "Aric had always been strong, intelligent, and confident, a born leader. He was the envy and admiration of all *weres,* including those who had accomplished tremendous deeds in their lives. Yet there was something always missing, a piece that kept him from desiring to embrace his full potential."

The gentleness in her tone diminished my bitterness and rising hysteria. I clung to her words like a lifeline. At that moment, I knew she was the only thing keeping me grounded. "P-please continue," I begged her.

Makawee considered me. I thought I sensed her power reach out to me, which thankfully helped me settle further. It reminded me of the way my mother used to stroke my hair, a feeling so genuine and pure it almost made me cry. She smiled as if she understood, then took a sip of her tea and spoke. "The day Aric first saw you, he returned to the Den an absolute mess. He was inexplicably quiet and didn't seem to comprehend anything anyone was saying. He spent most of the day staring out in the direction of the lake, the very place he'd found you." She laughed a little. "His Warriors and students were understandably worried, unsure what ailed their implacable Leader. But

Martin and I knew; we recognized the signs. His wolf had met his mate."

When Aric expressed the depths of his feelings, he took my breath away. When others told me how much I meant to him, I mostly squirmed and blushed. But to hear it from Makawee was an entirely different experience.

Her retelling of the moment that changed my life was both humbling and a tremendous honor. She recognized that Aric loved me long before he ever told me.

I stared at my hands. Despite how touched I was, I couldn't help questioning why she told me. Instead of asking her, I simply remained quiet. Sometimes when you want someone to speak, all you have to do is wait and listen.

This was one of those moments.

"We tried to discourage him from seeking you out, once it was clear you weren't one of us," she admitted. "But destiny had other plans."

Yes. She did.

Makawee shook her head. "Celia, we never meant to hurt you or Aric. Our only intent was to protect our sacred earth as only we as *weres* believed we could. But I fear our vanity may have destroyed us all."

I met her eyes. "You think you interfered with destiny?"

"More than that. I believe we poisoned it." She let out a weary breath. "And hurt our chance to destroy the dark ones."

Yes. Well done.

Makawee examined me closely when my passing thoughts caused my eyes to widen. But then I realized that despite her apology, she would never understand what her actions, and those of the governing *weres,* robbed me of.

"I found my mate, a long, long, time ago," she said slowly, as if acutely aware of what I was thinking. "I met her in passing while visiting London." She folded her hands on her lap, staring outside the window and losing herself in the memory. "She was waiting for a bus in the pouring rain, without an umbrella or a hat, though she didn't seem to mind." Makawee chuckled, yet her laughter was filled with more sadness than any genuine trace of humor. "She probably resembled a drowned rat to anyone passing by. But to me she was the most beautiful creature I'd ever seen. It was only when she hurried onto the bus and looked out the window that she spotted me standing across the street. Our eyes met for one precious moment before the bus sped away."

"How did you find her again?"

Makawee reached for her now tepid tea and took a sip before answering. "I didn't."

I frowned. "You let her go?" I couldn't believe it. It had only taken one encounter with Aric, and I couldn't wait to see him again.

Makawee gave me one of her softer smiles. "I was to marry another pureblood that summer. Had I chased the bus like I wanted to, I knew I wouldn't have been able to fulfill my duties." Her eyes dropped to stare at her tea. For someone who would maintain most of her strength, agility, and supernatural senses until her death, she appeared so fragile then. "Our obligation to our Pack is ingrained in us from birth, Celia. It's in our blood, in our very souls. I believed only traitors and cowards abandoned their responsibilities. So, I ran in the opposite direction, leaving on the first plane out of London and returning home to marry that pureblood as promised." She paused. "He didn't want me, either, and beat me for years to prove it."

My jaw dropped open. "Makawee, I'm so sorry."

She patted my hand. "Do not fret over matters long forgotten. I killed him after the birth of our third son. He had served his purpose, just as I had mine."

This was a prime example of how *were* laws differed from human laws. *Weres* carried their own brand of justice.

I watched her take another sip of her tea when curiosity got the best of me. "Do you ever wonder what kind of life you could've had if you found your mate?" I asked.

Makawee's eyes glistened with tears. "Every day," she answered.

I didn't cry at movies. I wasn't into chick lit, but I did care very deeply and I knew too well what it was like to lose someone. "Maybe you can still find her."

"It's no longer possible, Celia. She was one of the Tribe's first victims." She ran the fingers of her wrinkled hand down her neck. "I felt it when they tore out her throat."

I stilled, wanting to cry on her behalf. But instead of tears, pitiless thoughts filled my head.

That could have been Aric.

These mongrels kept him from you.

They shoved him into the arms of another.

And sent him to war to die.

I rose and glanced around erratically, trying to understand where those thoughts were coming from. This wasn't me.

But it was my voice—my fears, my resentment, my *anger*—magnified and launching forward.

They took him from you.

They ordered him to breed.

They made him suffer.

And now you can't give them what they need.

"Celia, what is it, child?"

Run.

"I have to—"

Run.

"I need—"

Run.

My breath came out too quickly. Holy shit, I was losing it.

She wants you to suffer.

"Celia, what's happening?"

She wants you to die.

Makawee's voice drifted in and out, fighting with mine to make me listen.

Mine won.

Run!

I bolted out of her office and out of the building, crashing right into Aric as he raced toward me.

Chapter Seven

Aric's warmth, his presence, his scent—everything about him should have calmed me. Instead my brain was flooded with images of those *weres* Lindsey and Dara. As vividly as if they stood in front of me, I saw him take turns kissing them as they fondled him. I watched their hands tease and stroke the rising bulge in his jeans. I saw them yank down his waistband. I watched them open their mouths.

"Celia, *Celia!*" Aric clasped my shoulders. "Celia, what's wrong?"

My words came out in a choked sob as I wrenched away from him. "How dare you touch me!"

Aric froze before slowly approaching me with his hands out. "Baby, you're shaking. Tell me what happened."

I was briefly aware of others close by—Delilah and Betty Sue were there—Genevieve, too. Was Genevieve laughing at me?

My tears fell despite the growing crowd of *weres* and witches. "I know about the club, and about those girls who take their turns with you," I told him, not bothering to keep my voice low.

Aric frowned, more stunned at the accusation than angry. *"What?* I would never betray you—"

"Don't lie to me!" I screamed. "I met Lindsey and Dara. They sat on the damn couch waiting for you to show."

Understanding crossed his features. "Celia, I've had nothing to do with them since meeting you. Their presence insults me and disrespects our relationship. I won't even acknowledge they exist."

"But you knew about them." My body grew strangely numb.

Aric worked his jaw. "I knew they were here, but I swear I don't interact with them."

"Why didn't you tell me about them?"

"Because they don't matter."

"They matter to me." My voice cracked. "You should have told me, Aric. All of it. You didn't have to humiliate me like this."

My words struck him like a blow. He stared at me, shocked. I stormed to my SUV, ignoring the stares that followed me as I threw open my car door and jumped in. The moment I cranked the engine, I stomped on the accelerator and sped off.

He played you.

You fell for it.

This wasn't love.

Now you know.

I wiped my tears as each insecurity I'd ever felt dug a hole into my heart.

I floored the accelerator, wanting nothing more than to escape. I had to leave, get out of California. There was nothing for me here.

The gate leading out of the compound clanked shut behind another departing SUV. I was less than a few car lengths behind and had to stomp on the brakes to avoid colliding against the wrought iron bars.

The *were* guard made no effort to part the gates. Instead he stepped out of his tower and knocked on my window. I lowered it, still on edge and desperate to leave.

He looked down at me like I was something foul and beneath him, disdain deepening his scowl. "Aric says you're not to leave. He's coming."

I slipped out of the car, ready to jump the gate if I had to. "I'm not your hostage. Open the gate."

"And I'm not one of your bloodsucking pussies you can order around. If the boss says you stay, you stay, *freak!*"

It wasn't enough to be rude. Or call me names. Or insult my allies. He poked me hard in the chest to emphasize that he was bigger, stronger, tougher.

His mistake.

I glanced at his beefy finger just once before I grabbed it and twisted it. Bone crunched as I *shifted* him into the ground up to his neck. I ignored his snarls and stepped into his tower long enough to punch the button to open the gate.

"Who's the pussy now?" I hissed as I passed him, sticking one of *my* fingers out of the window.

I was turning onto the dirt path that led down the mountain when a fast-moving object thundering through the woods caught my eye. It was the same something that ran out in front of me. I slammed down on my brakes.

Mud splattered up like a wave, drenching my front windshield. I hit the wipers to find Aric panting back at me with furrowed brows. He must have run full-out to catch me. I was panting, too, from the sheer terror of almost mowing him over.

Kill him.

My head whipped to the side.

Kill him!

I turned, expecting someone to be there behind me.

Kill. Him!

I gripped the wheel. What was happening? That was my voice ordering me. My *freaking* voice.

Kill him now!

Aric swore, trying to clear his eyes of the mud caking his face. He couldn't see anything. He was vulnerable.

He deserves to die!

"No!" I roared.

Something ripped from my chest so hard, its sheer force left me momentarily paralyzed. I slumped into the seat, breathing hard.

Aric swore again, wiping his eyes with the back of his hand. He blinked back at me, trying to clear his vision, then walked around to the passenger side.

I stared blankly ahead, confused. *What just happened?* I couldn't remember anything. I didn't know what day it was, or the time. I'd come with lunch for Aric. I made soup and bread. Why was I driving away? Did we already eat?

Aric reached for the handle, trying to open the door, but the sound seemed to come from far away.

My mind tried to force its way through the fog, showing me flickers of the day.

"Celia, open the door," Aric said.

His voice was closer, but still further than it should have been. I was mad at him, right? I had fought two *weres* . . . the ones who wanted to sleep with him.

Aric tapped on the window. "Celia, please, love. We've spent too much time apart. I don't want to spend the time we have now fighting."

Wasn't I just speaking to Makawee?

I couldn't remember. I only remember the females, and Aric denying he'd been with them.

He'd denied it, right?

Aric knocked again. "Celia, please. Let's talk."

I glanced around the cabin, so confused I could barely find the switch to unlock the door.

Yeah. There were two *weres* and a club devoted to getting him in bed.

He should have told me.

Aric climbed in and angled his body to face me. "I'm sorry," he said. "I never meant to hurt you."

When I didn't answer, he realized I needed a moment. He removed his shirt, keeping his eyes on me as he used the clean side to wipe the mud coating his hair, face, and arms. "I'm sorry," he said again.

"You should have told me," I said aloud, my voice thick with tears. "To see them there waiting for you, knowing what they wanted, their bodies barely covered." I sniffed. "That was a horrible way to find out."

"I didn't sleep with Lindsey or Dara, Celia. I swear it."

"What about the rest?" He opened his mouth to object, but then shut it quickly when something or someone triggered his memory. I smacked my palm against the steering wheel, bending it slightly. "Damnit. How many of them did you sleep with?"

Aric rubbed his eyes. "Celia, don't do this."

My face flushed with my growing anger. "Don't do what? Have an honest conversation with you? Just tell me. What's the magic number? How many of these goddamn bitches have you screwed?" My breath caught. I wasn't a perfect person. I did curse, but I wasn't what most would have considered crass. Nor was I in the habit of yelling at Aric.

My heart slowed to a painful thump. *What's wrong with me?*

I tried to settle my tigress, but when I reached in to feel her, I barely registered her presence. She wasn't the one riled.

It was all me.

Aric turned from me to stare straight ahead. "I don't want to do this with you, but I won't lie to you. If you want to know, I'll tell you."

The truth was, I didn't want to know. I knew Aric had slept with a lot of girls before I came along. When he committed to me, I told myself that it didn't matter. If that was the case, why did I need to know now? "Just tell me."

He sighed. "The truth is, I don't know."

My lips parted. "How can you not know? Have there been that many?"

Aric met my stare. "Yes," he answered quietly.

Nausea claimed my belly, but it wasn't his fault. It was mine for asking.

Aric reached for my hand, taking it carefully within his grasp.

Neither of us spoke for several minutes. And it really sucked.

The longer he held my hand, the more I wanted to tell him I was sorry for asking, for freaking out, and for embarrassing him in front of his peers. My behavior seemed so ridiculous and out of character. He couldn't change his past any more than I could.

My tigress paced within me, seeking out his wolf when Aric spoke. "I was twelve years old the first time a female came on to me," he said. "I was walking up the long driveway to our property when another wolf approached me in human form. She was in her twenties." He shrugged. "I guess she was pretty. But I didn't notice females then. She said she wanted to spend time alone with me and took off her clothes. I took mine off, too, thinking she meant for us to *change* and go for a hunt."

My mouth went dry. "Did you—did she touch you?"

Aric brushed a strand of hair away from my face. "No, sweetness. My parents sensed I was near, and they didn't understand what was keeping me." He paused.

"They knew what she wanted, and they were enraged. Mom went after her—I don't think I'd ever seen her so angry. Dad held her back, but warned the she-wolf that if she ever approached me again, he wouldn't stop his mate from tearing out her heart." He pressed a kiss to my lips. "They found out later that she was desperate for a child and wanted to use my bloodline to give her one."

I sat unmoving. Aric placed an arm around me while his other hand continued to hold mine. "I didn't notice females then, and I don't notice them now. You're the only one I see, the only one I want, and the only one I'll ever love."

I wiped away a trailing tear. "I love you, too."

He pulled me against his bare chest. "I never meant to embarrass you, Celia, or mar what we have. I never dealt with the club, or whatever the hell you called them, because they weren't of any significance to me." He sighed. "I had new quarters assigned to us across campus in case we ever need them. I haven't returned to the building you ran from since the day we walked out together."

I considered what he told me. "Aric, you say I'm the only one you're attracted to. But the girls you were with after me were gorgeous. Barbara was—"

"Chosen for me," he interrupted.

"Diane—"

"Was the first to approach me after I'd been injured. I allowed her company only after I believed you'd left me for Misha. I never wanted her. I only wanted to prove to myself that I could still have someone, despite my disfigurement. Like all the others before her, she only wanted me for my heritage, my bloodline, and the prestige my name would bring her."

I stared at his chest. It was easier than meeting his eyes. My reaction seemed justified at the time—and I won't lie, I didn't regret fighting those *weres*. The way they disrespected my relationship with Aric, and how they spoke of him was inexcusable. But how I'd torn the *were's* lips from her face, my desire to kill them, and how I'd treated and embarrassed Aric wasn't me.

Misha had tempted me to bed more than once, but despite his incredible beauty, I'd always turned him down. Why? Because Aric was who I loved and wanted.

I *knew* he felt the same. So why did I react so irrationally? I should have confronted him privately . . .

Guilt and shame caused my eyes to sting with tears as I lifted my chin. "Aric . . . I'm so sorry, love."

"I am, too," he said. "About everything."

He bent to meet my lips. The awfulness of the day melted as he swept his mouth over mine. The heat between us surged and welded our bodies closer. But when his tongue flicked and teased mine, only the fire of passion remained.

I ran my hands through his hair, smearing the remains of splattered mud, but I didn't care. I needed to feel close to him.

Our kiss became more frantic and sensual. His hand slid over my breasts and I inched closer. I mewed when he pinched the centers and bucked hard against him.

Aric's growl vibrated against me. He was aroused, and knowing sent me into a tailspin of yearning. I grunted as my feminine regions throbbed, demanding his touch.

He slipped his hand beneath my skirt, skimming my inner thigh. I broke our kiss and clasped his wrist before it was too late. "Not here, wolf," I gasped.

Oh God, I wanted him. But although my tigress insisted that sex in a vehicle was no big deal, I had to remind her we were on the main road that led to the Den.

Aric glanced out the window while he worked to catch his breath. "Right," he said slowly. He pulled away slightly and rubbed his face. "For a minute there, I forgot where we were." His stare grew smoky. "I don't think I would have stopped if you hadn't told me to. It's been a lonely week without you."

"I know." Trickles of my loneliness found their way into my voice. Aric and I were typically all over each other and at times spent the day making love. That wasn't the case lately. In fact, we'd only had sex once that week. I missed his touch and the way his body moved inside of mine.

My hand slid across his chest to clasp his shoulder. "It was hard not to let you keep going. But it's just not the right place, wolf."

His focus trailed from my hand to my face. "I know. I'd rather be in our bed . . . or in the woods, up against a tree, leaves raining down on us when I take you—" He cleared his throat when my jaw dropped, but then chuckled. "As you can see, I've given this a lot of thought."

"Apparently so." I laughed, too, but my face remained heated.

My heart panged the longer I took him in, knowing we couldn't stay here. "I guess I should take you back."

Aric shook his head. "I wish you didn't have to, but I have a lot that needs my attention. Gem and I are meeting with the coven. Genevieve's had to take in more witches, since we lost too many head witches to the war with the Tribe. It's been a lot for her. I asked her to bring in Delilah and Betty Sue to help her, seeing how they used to head their own covens. It sounded like a good idea at the time."

I raised my brows. Head witches didn't play nice. "How's it sounding now?"

"In some ways still good. In other ways . . . not as good as I'd hoped. I've known Delilah forever; she's smart, spunky, and a good leader. She and Genevieve were getting along fine until Betty Sue and Genevieve started clashing. Betty Sue isn't impressed with Genevieve's ability to lead and has told her as much. But given the number of witches who are now a part of her coven, Genevieve needs her, and

Betty Sue knows it. Gemini and I are serving as arbitrators. We can't have the lower witches unsupervised. Too much can go wrong if they're left on their own."

"Like what?"

Aric passed his hand through his muddy hair. "They can go dark for one. And the last thing I need on my watch is another psycho witch running around starting shit."

I huffed. "No kidding."

Aric pulled me closer and I let my head fall against his shoulder. For all he had to do, he didn't seem anxious to leave. "I really am sorry about today, wolf. I don't know why I lost it the way that I did."

He kissed the tip of my nose, making me smile. "I can say the same about my behavior. Everything has been setting me off lately. The only time I can settle is when I'm with you, but with all this shit revolving around Shah and my duties here, it limits the time I can spend with you."

He didn't need to remind me. Aric had been coming home close to midnight every night and leaving as early as dawn. He was beyond exhausted. I'd never seen him so drained.

His fingers trailed along the ridge of my spine. "We've been through a lot to get where we are, sweetness. My best guess is that we're both more affected than we realize."

"I hope that's all it is."

He stroked my chin. "Even if it's not, it will be. You are my world. Nothing means anything to me without you."

His words made me teary. Aric kissed my eyelids before a single drop could fall. We held each other a little longer before I drove him back to the Den.

Heidi now stood on guard duty. Another *were* was filling in the hole where they must have dug out the idiot I'd buried. She waved to me and added a wink. Yeah, she knew what I'd done and didn't seem to mind one bit.

I pulled up to the main building and idled at the curb. Aric paused before getting out, appearing lost in his thoughts.

"What is it?" I asked.

Aric drummed his fingers on the armrest. "We picked up a lead on Shah's whereabouts today. We have wolves investigating now. If it proves valid, they're heading in. But if they fail, I'll have to leave for Malaysia tonight and take over the mission."

Okay . . . so not expecting that bombshell. "You'll leave for Malaysia, *tonight?*"

"If it's a dead lead, or if I can send someone in my place, I won't have to go. The problem is, the compound where we suspect Shah is hidden will require a more experienced team to infiltrate. I don't know if the team that's covering can handle it."

Which meant it was dangerous and required the most capable *weres* serving the Alliance. That would be Aric and his Warriors. "If I go, I promise to be careful and not take any unnecessary chances," he said, managing to smile. "After all, I have a fiancée to return to."

I didn't want him to go. Not only because of the danger factor, but because of everything that had been happening. Aric and I weren't at the top of our game. Our erratic behavior proved as much.

I groaned. This was the part of fighting evil that sucked. Evil didn't care if we were tired, fighting, or emotionally unavailable. In fact, it counted on it.

"All right. Just be safe and hurry back." I tried not to tear up, but it was hard. "I need you with me."

He waited a moment to see if I'd say anything more. When I didn't, he kissed me goodbye. "Don't worry, okay?"

But I would.

I considered what he said, then drove straight to Misha's house.

Chapter Eight

I tried calling Misha on his secret bat line, but no one answered. It seemed strange. He always took my calls whether he answered them directly or someone else did it for him. It wasn't a good sign when I pulled up to the main gate of his estate and found one of his vampire snipers holding a giant assault rifle . . . and dressed like a giant Teletubbie.

"What?" he asked me defensively when I continued to gawk at him.

"I take it Misha is still in Europe?"

"How did you know?"

Instead of answering him, I drove onto the massive estate, over the small bridge and around the fountain. Specks of memories from the day continued to prod me during the drive, but I couldn't seem to focus on any one event for too long. My interaction with Makawee seemed especially clouded.

I rubbed at my sternum, wondering why I was having such a hard time concentrating when I caught Tim waving at me from the front of the house. I slipped out of my SUV, debating if I was making a huge mistake in the

Aric department by coming to Misha's home without telling him. It wasn't as if I wanted to keep it a secret. I'd just forgotten to mention . . . I rubbed my sternum again. Had I mentioned it?

"Celia, what the hell?" Tim hollered.

I tried not to roll my eyes when I saw what he was wearing. My first clue that things were batshit crazy at vamp camp should have been the sniper dressed like a giant stuffed toy. But I wasn't as familiar with him and decided to give everyone else the benefit of the doubt.

Ha, ha. Silly me.

Tim shot me an impatient look before urging me forward again. I sighed and conceded; despite that he was dressed like a firefighter. A half-naked firefighter.

Sure, he had the hat, the boots, the pants, and the suspenders, but nothing else. I wasn't up to speed on what firefighters wore beneath their firefighting gear, but I was pretty damn sure it included a shirt and some underwear. And I was absolutely positive it didn't include a naked girl covered in soot strapped to their backs.

"The master has grown anxious about finding Shah. He apologizes about not being able to brief you directly, but he's busy and— What the hell's your problem?"

He was pissed that I was covering my eyes. What did he expect? The girl on his back was getting more adventurous with her feet. They fiddled beneath his loose-fitting pants in disturbing, jerking motions.

Did I mention he wasn't wearing underwear? "Tim, I'm not really comfortable with your food fondling you while we're trying to have a conversation."

"For someone mounting a werewolf every night, you're a real prude, you know that?" He motioned to his soot-covered good time. "Sunny, go to my room and wait there." I didn't look up until I heard Sunny skip up the steps. "Anyway," he said. "The master and the grandmaster want Shah found, and we believe we finally have a good lead."

"Okay, and where might he be?"

"The master?"

"No. Shah."

"It's not a real thing. It's a rock, Celia," he said slowly.

"I know, but this whole personality of his—"

"It's a rock," Tim repeated, growing more impatient. He turned to the house. "Just get your ass inside. I'll have Agnes tell you everything she knows."

On our way in, I spotted a couple of vampires dressed as Captain Hook, Papa Smurf, and Colonel Sanders. It took everything I had to keep my face neutral. A bored vampire is a naughty vampire, I supposed.

We entered the colossal estate Misha called his house and headed straight to the library. It was my favorite room in the ginormous Mountain Craftsman. Beautiful hand-carved cherry bookcases lined the back wall, and an immense fireplace at its center added to the old-world charm. But it wasn't its elegance that drew me in. It was the memories I had there with Misha. We'd had some of our best talks here, and it was the room where he and I became friends.

As soon as we entered, Agnes glanced up from the pile of old scrolls rolled out in front of her. Her lacy black bra protruded through the white shirt of her naughty Catholic schoolgirl uniform. Unlike the other vampires I'd passed, this wasn't a costume, but rather her choice of everyday wear.

She adjusted her tiny librarian glasses when she saw me. Her almond-shaped eyes had supernatural vision. She didn't need the damn things. But her meals found them sexy and I supposed that was good enough for Agnes. "We think we've found Shah—or at the very least what country it's in," she said.

"Cool. And where might he be?"

"He?" she asked.

Tim laughed and motioned to me. "Our freakier-than-hell mistress here thinks Shah should be referred to as 'he' because of *his* personality, right, Celia?" He returned his focus to Agnes, laughing harder. "Can you believe that shit?"

I grinned.

And emptied a pitcher of ice water down his loose-fitting pants.

Tim jerked away from me. "What the fuck?"

"Quit being a prick," I hissed at him. I turned back to Agnes while Tim did his best to empty his pants. "You were saying?"

She leaned back in her high-back leather seat. "First answer me this: Do the mongrels know where *he* is?"

I tried not to grumble. The Alliance had picked the name more for show it seemed. "They have a lead and are tracking him now."

She smiled. "Where?"

"I'm not sure."

Her smile widened and she exchanged glances with Tim. Like *weres,* vamps could sniff lies. "Where?" she asked again.

This time I couldn't hold back my grumbling. "Malaysia."

My news seemed to please her. She swiveled in her seat and smirked at Tim. "Told you I was right. Alert the team. We leave in an hour."

Ordinarily, her smugness would have annoyed me. But who was I kidding? We needed to find Shah. If I had to confirm suspicions in the process, I'd do it.

Tim left like a passing breeze. If not for the *squeak squeak* of his boots and the chunks of ice he tossed over his shoulder, I wouldn't have even heard him.

This time, it was my turn to smile. "Now, tell me what you know."

Agnes adjusted her glasses, annoyed. She didn't like being ordered around unless it was by Misha specifically. But Misha had given me the title of Mistress of the House. And that title came with power. Power over his undead. *Mwahahaha.*

"He's being held by Dilip Singh, the lead geek who created the videogame based on Shah's legend. Dilip was raised in India and frequently returns to visit family." She licked her tongue. "One of his last few trips was to Ajanur village—nowhere near any of his relatives, but coincidentally the same village where the Madiyan Kulom temple is located."

"Shah's last known home sweet home."

"Correct," Agnes said.

My tigress perked up. "How do you know Dilip's the one who has him for sure? Weren't there three other programmers who helped develop the game?"

Agnes played with one of her long thick braids. "He took eight people with him to Ajanur. Three were his fellow programmers like you said, one was his girlfriend, two were young archaeologists, and the two others were locals familiar with the area. Five have died since the profits from Shah's videogame started rolling in." She lifted her phone when it buzzed in a text and checked the screen. "Make that six. The first was Dilip's girlfriend, the next were his programmers. Guess who died next?"

"The archaeologists." Unlike Agnes, I didn't see this as a fun game of Clue.

"You're right," she said, barely batting an eye. "The female died first. It took Dilip longer to find the male." She tapped the screen of her phone. "But now he has. If the locals he hired aren't dead yet, they soon will be."

"What about the police?"

"What about them?" she asked.

I held out my hand. "Millions at stake. Nine people involved—eight dead—or on the to-die list. It doesn't take much to narrow down Dilip as a suspect."

Agnes leaned forward and glared at me like I was too stupid to breathe. "He has Shah, and therefore all the power he needs to keep suspicion off him, or send the police after the kid who pushed him off the swing in second grade if he wanted to." She laughed without humor. "The thing is, this fool doesn't know everything he's in for with Shah."

I crossed my arms. Agnes was having too much fun. "What's Shah going to do to him, Agnes?"

"Whatever he wants now," she sang. "Dilip's his holder, but not his master. To think he ruled over Shah was his first mistake."

"Just tell me what he's going to do," I said, growling as a result of my mounting impatience.

Agnes narrowed her eyes at my command, but told me anyway, motioning toward the stack of old scrolls. "These scriptures describe the magic worked and incidences surrounding Shah the last time he was used for personal gain. It seems he wasn't hidden to keep others from stealing him. He was being punished for being an asshole."

"An asshole?" I asked slowly.

"That's right. Basically, once Shah feels he's made a fair trade, he starts to fuck with his holder."

Okay. This wasn't necessarily a good thing for us. *"In what way?"*

"Any way he pleases. Let's say Dilip wants world domination now, riches beyond his wildest dreams." She giggled. "Or say an ice cream sandwich. Shah could choose to fill his entire house with ice cream sandwiches and nothing more."

I considered what she told me. "Shah has reached notoriety and fame because of the game Dilip created for him." Agnes nodded. "In exchange, he's given Dilip money, power, protection, and exoneration from possible murder."

"Again, you're correct," Agnes agreed.

"And now that he's fulfilled his duties, it's time for him to have fun with Dilip."

Agnes's wicked grin was confirmation enough.

A thought occurred to me. "Tell me this, does Shah have to be with Dilip at all times?"

"No. Dilip just has to be the last one to touch him to still be considered his holder."

"If that's the case, Shah could be anywhere."

"Technically yes, but Dilip's too greedy and too paranoid to leave him behind." She frowned when her laptop *swooshed,* announcing she had an email. I watched her scroll down her screen, her eyes taking in everything quickly. When she finished, she leaned back in her chair, scrutinizing me closely. "A *were* team invaded Dilip's Malaysian compound tonight. It seems they failed," she said when I didn't respond. "Their bodies were just found in a nearby river, riddled with cursed gold bullets."

I hadn't bothered to sit when I first entered the library. Now I wish I had. I felt sick. My only comfort was that I knew Aric and his Warriors weren't among those dead. I'd only left them about an hour ago.

Agnes returned to playing with her braids. "Dilip is a fool, but he's not stupid, and very much wants to hang on to what he thinks is his. One of his wishes must have been for protection against influence, seeing as he can't be hypnotized by vampires."

"He can't?" I was sort of counting on that.

She shook her head. "That was the first thing we tried. His other wishes must have included protection against his enemies, and protection against theft. This debacle of a *were* invasion proves as much."

"Yeah. It does." I released a breath. "Shah will be moved from the compound, won't he?"

"Most likely. But Dilip's still in Malaysia, so Shah must still be there, too." She tapped her fingers across the keyboard as she replied to the email. "We can keep him there with some red tape, but not for long."

"Okay. But then how do we get to Shah? We can't influence Dilip. As a human he can't be killed or tortured. And he's wished for protection against his enemies and against theft."

"But you're not his enemy, Celia. We are."

I smiled at Agnes. It wasn't a friendly grin. "You're speaking in code again, Agnes."

She lifted her long legs and placed them on the marble table, not bothering to remove her platform Mary Janes or tug down her plaid miniskirt. "How can I put this politely?"

"You probably can't, Agnes. It's just not in you." I rubbed at my chest again. God, it hurt. Why did it hurt?

"True," she agreed. "Celia, you're an oddity among us. As preternaturals we view all beings in one of two ways, friend or prey. There is no in-between for us." She shrugged. "You don't think that way, which means Shah won't technically see you as an enemy he's indebted to Dilip to annihilate."

As much as Dilip sounded like a monstrous idiot and likely a murderer, Agnes was right. I didn't see him as prey—something that needed to be destroyed or, *ew,* eaten. I saw him as something that needed to be stopped. "Okay, but Dilip still has protection against being robbed."

This made her flash me some fang. "I didn't say it was going to be easy."

I narrowed my eyes. "I'm glad you're enjoying our little sit-down, but you still haven't told me how I'm going to figure out Dilip's new hiding spot for Shah. Something tells me if I smack him around, he's going to count me among his enemies."

"He's a *nerd*, Celia," Agnes said, like it was obvious. "Everything we need to find Shah is probably encoded into Dilip's gadgets. The problem is, no one has been successful in snagging anything—Dilip's phone, his laptop, not even his damn eReader."

She removed her glasses and pegged me with sly grin. "The plan is for you to get close to Dilip. Real close. His phone should contain everything I need to gain access to his personal information and files. So even if he skips out of Malaysia, I'll be able to find him and Shah anywhere."

I crossed my arms, feeling more than a little leery. "What's happened to those who have tried to take Dilip's toys? His phone and tech stuff, I mean."

"The first seven were discovered strangled with their own intestines and missing all their fingers, The last three were never seen again." She smiled. "Good luck."

Sometimes I really hated Agnes. "Even if we figure out Shah's location, he's going to be ready for us—to protect Dilip against theft, remember?"

Agnes stood and leaned forward, placing her palms on the table. "This is where it pays to be a freak. Shah can only guard against what he knows. He knows *weres,* he knows vampires, and he knows witches. He doesn't know you, or your sisters. Your magic isn't familiar because it didn't come from the earth—nor has it existed before." She smiled. "If you play your cards right, Shah will never see you coming."

And if I don't, I could end up riddled with bullets, missing fingers, and, ah, yeah, wearing my lower intestine like a scarf. Being a hero just plain sucked.

Another phone buzzed. This time it was mine. I reached into my purse and pulled it out.

Aric had sent me a text. *I'm headed to Malaysia.*

I paused before texting him back: *So am I.*

Chapter Nine

Aric took my news as well as could be expected.

Okay. Not really.

"Are you out of your mind!" he'd yelled.

"You're going," was my awesome comeback.

Our video conference call from separate planes made it easier, but not by much. Misha was brought into the call first. The air around the private jet's cabin shifted as soon as his image appeared on the screen. The vampires stood a little straighter and adoration lit their eyes.

Aw, the bloodsucking pain in the asses had missed their master. I laughed a little. Maybe I had, too. "Hi, Misha."

It must have been chilly in Transylvania this time of year. A black turtleneck sweater covered Misha's muscular body, highlighting his gray eyes. His blond hair was longer, and draped just past his shoulders. He returned my smile. "Hello, kitten. You look well."

"Because I'm not banged-up and bloody, *yet,*" I told him.

"Forgive me, Master," Agnes interrupted, demonstrating respect she'd never managed to show me. "But the mongrels are ready to meet."

The corners of Misha's mouth lifted into one of his more wicked grins. "Put them through," he said.

The giant roll-down screen took up most of the right side of the cabin. Misha's image reduced, allowing the remaining Alliance members involved to take up the other half of the screen. Aric, his Warriors, Martin, and the witches stared back at us. No one seemed happy.

Except for Shayna. "Hey, puppy!"

She smiled and waved to Koda like it was prom night. He muttered something in wolf that sounded very similar to swearing. Shayna leaned close to me. "He's a little upset I'm joining you on this mission," she whispered.

He growled again. "Uh, he can hear you," I told her.

Aric was so angry his jaw could have ground walnuts to powder. He wasn't moving, wasn't speaking. And yet he still didn't seem as pissed as Taran when Genevieve appeared and sat directly beside Gemini. A spark of blue and white fire appeared over Taran's head. Followed by another, and another, until the whole top of her head exploded in flames.

The vampires hissed and scattered like roaches. Master vampires were immune to fire. But none of Misha's vamps were masters. I yanked off my jacket and used it to beat out the flames engulfing her head.

Taran smacked my hands away. "What the hell. I'm fine!"

Yeah . . . separate planes was probably a good idea.

I only sat because her fire was extinguished for the moment. The vamps slowly returned to their seats, giving Taran plenty of space.

"Shall we begin?" Misha suggested. He appeared calm, but I caught the questioning glance he shot my way. He wasn't aware of Taran's lack of control, or how much worse she'd become. But no way was I leaving my sister behind.

Taran had other strengths besides her magic.

Martin was the first to speak. "Ordinarily we don't permit mates together on missions. We find emotions can negatively affect strategies and outcomes." His voice served as a warning, as did his narrowing eyes as they passed along Aric, Gemini, and Koda. "But our need to find Shah is great. Club Sunba, which Dilip Singh frequents, has already been wired for communication. We'll position *weres* inside to serve as protection against any possible threat and to shadow the Wird sisters to ensure their safety. We wouldn't want them escorted from the premises without their consent."

By "escorted without our consent," Martin meant drugged, dragged, and possibly wounded.

Shayna spoke up. "We'll be inside first. Taran and I will be posing as part of the, uh, staff." She tossed me a nervous glance. "Emme and Celia will arrive shortly after to serve as um, club-hoppers, so to speak."

Shayna was a horrible liar. And about as smooth as broken glass along a sidewalk. Not a great combo when you're already dealing with irate wolves.

Aric straightened, growing suspicious. "When you say club-hoppers, what exactly do you mean?" he growled.

"I'm the one who's going to get close to Dilip," I answered before Shayna could sing like a canary. "One of the vamps on the inside is going to make sure Emme and I are brought directly to him."

Now wasn't a good time to mention Dilip was a fan of high-priced prostitutes. Or that Emme and I would be posing as them.

Aric didn't seem to fully believe me, but my answer satisfied him enough that he relaxed. "We'll have your back," he promised.

I smiled. "I know."

Martin scratched the center of his chest and addressed me. "Celia, forgive me for my request. But if you can't gain access to Singh's phone, you may have to return with him to the compound and attempt to secure it there, or locate his laptop. The rest of us—the vampires included—will shadow you there. The problem is, thus far the compound has been impenetrable to anything supernatural. If you get in trouble, I fear we may be delayed in reaching you."

"We'll find a way," Aric assured me.

I averted my gaze when I remembered the last *weres* who'd tried to gain access were all found dead.

"Don't fret none, sugar," Delilah said. "That's where we come in. We can't stop Shah's power. It's too strong. But we could probably stun it enough to get the reinforcements in, and you out." She winked. "You don't mess with a witch, don't you know."

Genevieve nodded, her stunning sapphire blue eyes radiant, as well as all that ebony hair spilling to her elbows. It wasn't fair to be that beautiful. "We'll make sure you escape if necessary," she assured me.

"Yay, team," Taran muttered.

The comment only made Genevieve smile. She didn't fear Taran. But maybe she should have.

We wrapped up the last of the details then ended the conference call. I spoke briefly with Misha before he was pulled away by a soft, sweet voice. "Forgive me, my darling," he said. "I must leave you."

I knitted my brows. "Did you find a bride?" He didn't answer. "Misha!"

He considered me. "Not so much a bride, but an arrangement."

I laughed. "You're not going to give me any dirt, are you?"

He scanned the nosy group around us. "Not now, but in time." His humor faded. "Stay strong, and stay safe," he told me.

"Don't knock anyone up" was my advice to him.

Misha laughed before the screen faded and the call disconnected. Taran stood abruptly and disappeared to the back where two small suites made up the remainder of the jet. Emme clasped my hand, whispering low. "Something happened between her and Gemini, but she won't talk to us about it."

Shayna nodded. "It's bad, Ceel. Whatever's between them. Gemini left the house right before you called. He was carrying a suitcase. I don't know if he's coming back."

"He moved out?"

Emme nodded. "That's what it looked like."

I straightened and carefully rose, not wanting to believe it. "I'll go talk to her."

I found Taran in the suite furthest away. She lay on the queen-sized bed, wrapped in a small white throw. Although her back was to me, I knew she was crying. The smell of her salty tears hit my nose before I could reach the bed.

Taran and I were tight, real tight. I knew when to push her and when to give her space. I lay next to her and waited for her to speak.

"How are things with you and Aric?" she asked.

I stared at the ceiling, ready to tell her we were fine. But that would've been a lie. "We're okay."

My comment gave her pause. "Just okay?"

"Things aren't the same lately, Taran," I admitted. "Aric's temper has been short since the shape-shifters attacked. He's irritable and exhausted all the time. I'm worried. He claims to be having trouble controlling his human half."

"Not his wolf?"

I knew what she meant. It should have been the other way around. "No. It's his human side that's giving him problems."

"You can't be serious? What the hell's his human's problem?"

I pinched the bridge of my nose. "Don't be mad. I think he's stressed about returning to his duties. The thing is, now I'm doing it, too. I wigged out—lost it completely and totally embarrassed him. I don't get that way with Aric, ever. I was so crazy at the time. But he was more upset because I was upset. He stayed reasonable when I couldn't think straight. I know we'll be okay, so long as only one of us gets loony at a time."

"I guess," she said. "It's obvious he adores you. Hell, any time you're in the same room together he can't tear his eyes off you."

Her words made me want to smile, but I held back. "The nightmares are getting worse," she said in the quiet that seemed to shroud the suite.

I almost didn't want to know. "How?"

"I can see into the eyes that haunt my dreams. As dark as they are, I can see what they see. Ceel . . . I watch Mom and Dad being murdered in their reflection every time those eyes visit my dreams."

"Taran . . . *Jesus*."

Her voice croaked. "Yeah. I know." There was more that she wanted to say, and she did, quickly abandoning the subject of our parents and how brutally they'd lost their lives. I couldn't blame her. That was one of those topics we avoided at all costs, except what she said next didn't offer me any sense of comfort. "Gemini asked me to marry him."

I sat up slowly. Like her nightmares, I could tell by her tone this wasn't good news. The scent of her misery surrounded us, clinging to the air and erasing all other aromas. "When?"

"Earlier today. He took me to the clearing that overlooks the lake. I thought he wanted to talk about some of the shit we've been going through. Instead he opened this little velvet box and asked me to be his wife."

Tears dripped from her eyes and landed on top of the comforter. "You said no, didn't you?"

"Of *course* I did. What choice did I have?" It was then Taran finally broke down. "Things have been broken between us since Anara ravaged my body. I know Gemini feels bad, I know he feels guilty. But that doesn't make it okay for him to treat me like a freak."

Taran sat up and rubbed the area between her breasts before the motion caught her attention and she stared at her gloved hand. "When we would make love, he wouldn't touch it. I'd keep it covered, but he'd cringe away."

I stroked Taran's dark hair away from her face. She often exaggerated; it was part of her spirited personality. But this time, I didn't believe she was distorting the truth. Gemini had been distant around her. He persistently maintained his gaze fixed on her face or anywhere else besides her deformed arm, and while he remained affectionate, his efforts seemed forced.

And I'd never seen him touch her affected limb.

"Does Aric avoid touching you where you were injured?" she asked quietly.

I didn't want to admit that Aric frequently caressed the thick ugly scars marring my lower belly or how he'd often kiss the area when we made love. It was his way of recognizing the pain Anara inflicted and the invariable reminder of our loss. "No," I answered simply.

"Which is why you're marrying him, and why I told Gemini to walk."

I sighed. "Taran, there has to be more to this than what you're seeing. I think you need to talk things through.

You love him. I know you do. Just like I know that he loves you."

She shook her head. "He doesn't love me. Not anymore. He loved the perfect girl, with the perfect smile, and the perfect body." When she spoke again, she was sobbing. "He doesn't want the one who's deformed, who can't control her magic, who's seconds from breaking down every time he recoils from her touch."

I pulled her to me, embracing her gently as my heart broke along with hers. "Taran, if he asked you to marry him, it's because he wants to promise you forever."

Taran quieted then. "Forever is a long time with someone who finds you repulsive."

I didn't have a response for that. When it came down to it, I couldn't excuse his behavior, just like I couldn't blame her for refusing him. I gathered her closer, hoping that with time, my sister would be all right. Something was really wrong with Taran. And Gemini was only a part of the problem.

We hit the ground running when we arrived in Langkawi. That is, if hitting the ground includes dressing up like whores. When a she-vamp held up my so-called attire for the evening, I thought she was handing me a red silk infinity scarf. I peered around her, expecting more. "Where's the rest?" I asked like a moron.

The vamp straightening my hair paused, as did the one applying my makeup. "What do you mean, where's the rest? That's what you're wearing," Agnes said, like it was obvious.

"Show her the back."

All there was to the back was a sheer mesh skirt. "Don't worry. You'll have a matching red thong and cute gold earrings," Agnes added to sweeten the deal.

Somehow, I thought the "cute" gold earrings would do little to draw attention away from my bare backside bouncing along. For the love of all that's holy, I didn't want to wear the dress. In fact, I thought whoever designed it should have been arrested and possibly flogged. But I needed to grab Dilip's attention and keep it. And I couldn't deny that dress had the power to do it.

"Crap," I muttered. "Where did you get this hideous excuse for clothing?"

Agnes frowned. "Edith Anne's closet."

Great. Edith was the naughtiest of Misha's Catholic schoolgirls. I'd probably need penicillin after wearing it.

"Celia, don't let your damn morals come between you and your mission," Agnes snapped.

"Oh, no, God forbid," I hissed, yanking the hanger from the she-vamp's grasp.

The minute I put the dress on and stepped in front of the mirror, I knew Aric would lose his damn mind—and not in a good way. The plunging neckline cascaded down to my navel, just above my scars. It took an absurd amount of two-sided tape to keep my breasts covered, seeing how the dress had no back. The skirt alone—mercifully made of solid satin in the front—covered my girl parts by mere inches.

"How the hell am I going to sit down?" I demanded.

Once more, the vamps regarded me like I was the crazy one. "It's not a dress meant to sit in, it's meant for straddling," Agnes answered, sounding all pissy.

Clearly, she wasn't referring to horses.

Emme marched into my suite in platform sandals that added five inches to her petite frame, followed by the vampires who'd helped her get ready. And, damn, what had they done to my sweet little sister?

She was slathered with makeup that took her from angelic to yeah, kind of ho-ish. And her blond wavy hair was so teased, I didn't understand how she fit through the door. As provocative as her teal booty shorts, matching bra (that actually made her look like she had boobs!) and her fishnet half shirt were, she still had on more fabric than I did.

"I can't wear this," she said. "It's positively indecent." She stopped short and practically screamed when she saw me.

"I'll trade you," I offered.

Her wide eyes took me in from head to slutty platform-sandaled toes. "Um. Never mind," she said. "I'm good."

Agnes smirked. "You make excellent whores," she said.

"Gee, thanks, Agnes."

My phone rang. I knew it was Aric and hurried out onto the balcony for privacy before answering. "Hi, wolf."

"Are you all right?"

I tried to the adjust the fabric covering my right breast, but the neckline was so wide, I ended up exposing a nipple and hurried to stick it into the right spot. "I'm fine." I cleared my throat. "A little nervous. Going undercover with anyone but you isn't really my thing."

I smiled when I heard him laugh. "I've done it too many times to count. But I agree, I'd rather be with you." He released a breath. "You don't have to do this, you know? I can have you out of the country within the hour. Just say the word."

"Aric, with the magic my sisters and I possess, we're the Alliance's best shot at finding Shah."

"I'd rather reach him another way." He swore. "I seriously can't handle this. Martin talked me down before, but the closer we get to game time, the more I'm not okay with you putting yourself in danger."

"I'm scared, too," I admitted. "But I'm more afraid of the wishes Shah has left and who he's going to grant them to."

He didn't have a response, and I could sense his mounting worry. I tried to redirect him. "Look, you're the undercover expert. Any advice?"

He thought about it. "Remember that you're playing a role. Stay in character, and you'll be fine."

The thing was, he didn't know my character spent most of her time on her knees. "Um. Okay."

He waited again before speaking. "I have to leave now. Celia . . . I have to play a role tonight, too. I may . . . engage a female, especially if she's close to Dilip Singh. Just know it's not real, okay? I don't want you upset."

I thought about Agnes's tips to get Dilip's attention and hoped he could take his own advice. "No problem. I trust you."

"Yeah?"

"Totally. Do what you have to do."

I didn't have to see Aric to know he was frowning. "I just thought after what happened at the Den . . ." he said slowly.

"Oh, that. Yeah. It's fine. Fine."

"Aric," Koda said in the background. "It's time."

"I have to go, sweetness," Aric said. "Don't worry about anything. I'll be with you."

"I know. Bye, Aric."

I hurried back into the bedroom area as Tim crashed into the suite. "We have to move—Dilip's at the club and—holy *shit!*" he said when he saw me.

I would have taken it as a compliment, if he hadn't salivated and his incisors hadn't lengthened. "You're not taking a bite," I growled. His attention swerved to my sister. "That goes for Emme, too."

His fangs withdrew. "You make a shitty whore," he said.

I smiled and marched out. "That's not what Agnes said. Let's go."

When we arrived at the club, the line of people waiting to get in ran the length of the stone-paved street and across the bridge. Bright colored lights sparkled against the ocean's surface, and I could hear the music pumping from three blocks away.

The club seemed to float, the way it extended out into the water. I focused on the gentle waves as I adjusted the earpiece I'd been given, willing myself to relax. I wasn't deceitful, and I didn't like to lie. This wasn't the best mission for me, but one I seemed the most qualified for. Although I'd planned to play a role like Aric suggested, prostitution wasn't exactly the role I was born to play. I needed help. And who better to help me than someone who spent most of her time dressed like a naughty Catholic schoolgirl?

"Okay. I can see you," Agnes said in my ear. "When Umar opens the door, walk in like you own the place and everyone present is unworthy of your snatch."

She had me until that last little word.

"Damnit, Celia. Don't make that face. I can see you from here."

"What took you so long?" I snapped at poor Umar, in an attempt to embrace my diva role. "I could have walked here in less time."

I was escorted through the velvet ropes. Most of the clubbers waiting in line were locals. But I was recognized as American. That meant I had money, or at least men willing to spend it on me.

Men, women, even the bouncers at the door stopped to gape at me. The damn platform sandals exaggerated the cat walk my tigress naturally gave me. I hoped that was the reason they stared and not, absolutely *not,* because I was flashing a nipple.

Emme followed behind me, mimicking my movements . . . until she tripped walking in and landed face-first.

"Keep going," Agnes urged. "She's not worthy of your—"

"I get it," I said through my teeth. "Just shut up and let me work."

My eyes swept the area. Talk about sensory overload. The club was a massive sea of wall-to-wall people twerking. Red lasers cut through the dry-ice fog in time with a very obnoxious house mix. People screamed for the hell of it, or to seek the attention they desperately seemed to need.

I couldn't wait to get out of there, but for that to happen I needed to find Dilip, and in this environment that was easier said than done. As much height as my platform sandals gave me, I couldn't see over anyone's head. Damnit, where was our inside man? "Agnes, I'm going to need some help here. Send in our guy." She didn't answer. "Agnes?"

"He's gone."

I played with my hair, trying not to react. "Out of the club?"

She huffed, but this time with worry. "I don't know. He's not responding."

I tossed back my long hair, straightened within an inch of its life. "Are you sure he was already inside?"

"Yes. He was just on the line with Umar. But we can't wait. Find Dilip."

That was definitely going to be a problem. As it was, I could barely see past the wall of sweat-soaked clubbers dancing in front of me. "You sure he's definitely here?"

"Yes. The mongrels spotted him walking in and are guarding all the exits."

"Okay. Ten-four," I said.

"Did you just say ten-four?"

"Oh, just cut me some slack, Agnes."

Tye, a werelion and friend, passed me. He must have been one of those positioned to guard my back. Relief washed over me. I no longer felt so alone.

I didn't think he noticed me until a deafening crash alerted me that he'd smacked right into a support beam. I glanced over my shoulder. Blood poured down his face and onto his gray T-shirt. He'd broken his nose, but he was too busy gawking at me to wipe it.

"Damn," he said.

"Shit," I muttered.

I hurried away from him, blushing. That earned me a bitchy reprimand from Agnes. "For the love of everything holy. Dilip doesn't want a fucking virgin. He wants someone to ride him until his balls dangle to his knees. Get into character or kiss Shah goodbye!"

"I'm trying," I hissed through clenched teeth.

I was moving so quickly I almost barreled into Shayna, who was carrying a tray full of drinks and wearing a small black skirt and tank. "Sorry, dude," she said, apologizing. She skipped along without so much as a glance back to a table full of men waving to her. I paused. My own sister didn't even recognize me. I must have dived headfirst out of Semi-Appropriate Street way into Slutville Lane with this damn dress.

"Celia, *move*," Agnes snapped in my ear.

With a huff, I continued forward, using my annoyance to feign superiority. The horde of clubbers parted, allowing me through. When I was well into the center of the dance floor, I spotted Taran dancing in a cage elevated several feet from the floor. A tiny pair of leather shorts, a bustier, and thigh-high leather boots made up her uniform. Black elbow-length leather gloves covered both of her arms. If girlfriend was worried about chafing in those shorts, she didn't show it. Taran wasn't simply playing a role—she was owning it.

Several men circled the cage, urging her seductive shimmies when the sharp scent of fury stung my nose. I turned in the direction of the scent. Gemini and Koda sat at a table in the VIP section. Koda leaned toward him, saying something I didn't catch.

His words to Gemini seemed to go unnoticed. Gemini was fixated on Taran, and furious at the men reaching in to stroke her legs. I knew he was moments from acting. I hurried forward to Taran's cage.

I smiled and pretended to knock. She kicked open her cage and bent forward, draping her arm around my shoulders and allowing her long dark hair to partially cover us. The men around us cheered, assuming we were kissing.

Nice. Just nice.

She spoke fast. "Both our inside contacts are dead—including the guy who was supposed to bring you to Dilip. They just found their headless bodies covered with bite marks in the alleyway."

"Vamps?"

"No. Small bites as if eaten by rats—it's up to you to get Dilip's attention. He's in the opposite corner. VIP section. Right side."

"Gemini's watching you and he's really pissed," I warned.

"I don't give a shit," she said.

She abruptly released me and grabbed the guy closest to her by the collar, kissing him hard. The kiss was brief and closed-mouth, but it was still a kiss in front of her furious mate.

"Get me a drink," she ordered. She scratched between her breasts and then returned to her seductive dance.

"Do you want a drink?" his buddy asked me as Taran's new friend raced off. I ignored him and moved fast.

What the hell? I knew Taran was playing a role, but Gem was seconds from mauling someone.

I moved in the direction Taran indicated, taking my time to get into character. I licked my lips, added more sway to my walk, and tossed my hair. "Did you get that?" I muttered.

"Yes. And now we lost Umar the same way."

My steps slowed. "I just left him."

"I know. Shah must know Dilip's enemies are here. He's trying to protect him."

"I can see that, but what's up with the bite marks?"

"Who the hell knows? Dilip must be getting more creative with how he orders Shah to kill for him."

"Asshole."

"Yes, he is. But try not to see him as such. Your magic and your intentions for the greater good may be enough to keep Shah from recognizing you as Dilip's enemy. But the more you want to hurt him, the quicker that can change. Focus on stopping him and snatching his phone and you should be okay. Maybe."

"Maybe?" I muttered.

"Just find Dilip, Celia. We're running out of time."

My tigress chuffed inside me, alerting me to Dilip's presence. Two women were already with him, stroking his body, whispering in his ears, and running their hands through his hair.

Aric was in a slightly elevated booth behind Dilip, his arm draped over a beautiful Asian woman with long perfect hair. He laughed at something she said. She giggled, too, and hooked her finger to slide between the buttons of his white dress shirt.

He didn't react to her tease. Not like he would have if those were my fingers, my touch.

He was playing a role.

It was time for me to play mine, too.

Chapter Ten

I strutted toward them. The seating was perfect. Aric was right there if I needed him, and I needed him then for what I planned to do. I couldn't seduce a stranger. Who was I kidding? But I could entice the male who made me scream and beg for more every time we made love.

The edges of my mouth lifted and my tigress growled approvingly. She wanted to lure Aric's wolf to her and encouraged me to make my steps more provocative. Those in my path parted, watching me closely. I wasn't sure if it was my tigress's surging presence that warned them to stand clear or if they realized that the almost naked woman before them was up to something. Whatever it was, they made sure I had plenty of space to work and great access to Dilip.

My bedroom eyes flashed at Aric. Dilip straightened, believing my inviting stare was meant solely for him. I swiveled my hips as the music alternated to a deep, thumping bass—a sexy and highly suggestive beat, and exactly what I needed.

Aric hadn't recognized me right away, too many scents trickling into his nose and too much dry ice masking his mate directly in front of him. He continued to laugh at whatever the woman was whispering in his ear. I smiled impishly when his attention trailed my way. His little friend might have been having fun with him, but it was time she saw who this wolf belonged to.

Aric did a double take when he saw me. For someone playing a role, he totally forgot his lines then. His eyes widened, his muscular shoulders tensed, and, and— Oh *shit*. He was pissed!

Instead of panicking, I continued to rhythmically move to the heavy beat, focusing on him. He removed his arm from his date and leaned forward as if ready to pounce. Our eyes locked. That's when I knew I had him, and that at least for the moment, he knew this dance was solely for him.

I turned and rocked my somewhat bare ass, earning me a low growl from Aric, and Koda's presence suddenly beside me. Koda yanked a pretty girl from the crowd and pulled her against his chest. She was meant as a prop— something to use so he could get close to me and not lose his cover. She didn't take it as that. She only saw a really big, frighteningly beautiful man giving her attention. She hooked her leg over his knee and ground against his supersized body.

Koda followed her, but his attention stayed trained on me. I could sense his unease with how Aric's wolf would respond, but I couldn't show fear or hesitate then. I had Dilip's attention, despite more aggressive attempts from his dates to wrench his focus away from me. I caught him smacking their hands away and yelling something I couldn't understand while I continued to play and tease.

My arms and body swayed in serpentine movements. I swung my hips, moving them as if my thighs were fastened to Aric's waist. Down toward the floor and back up. I danced, envisioning the darkness of our bedroom and him wrenching me toward him to meet my mouth with his.

The scent of his arousal flooded my senses and incited me to purr. I lowered my eyelids, his desire for me fueling my movements. My body ached as his aroma surrounded me and begged me to climb on top of him. Oh God. The fact that we'd barely had sex lately did nothing to tame my actions. I couldn't do this much longer if I was going to stay on task.

I needed Aric. I opened my eyes and tossed an invitation to bed with my stare.

At Dilip.

I turned fast enough to toss my hair behind me, hoping he didn't catch the look of repulsion spreading across my face. If I hadn't been so turned on by imagining making love to Aric, no way could I have pulled this off.

"Well done," Agnes's husky voice rang in my ear. "Oh yes. Well done indeed."

"Is he coming?" I asked.

"Hmm?"

Lord, help me. "*Dilip*. Is he following me?"

"Oh. Right. He's . . ." She swore. "No, but your mongrel is."

I glanced behind me in time to see Shayna dive on top of the girl Koda was dancing with. Koda grabbed her around the waist, trying to rip Shayna off. Shayna held tight to the girl's hair. Shayna was angry, vicious, and wild. Except that without some sort of handheld weapon in her grasp, my sister couldn't fight. Seriously. She sucked.

She and the other girl bitch-slapped each other like the end of world hunger depended on it. I continued forward toward the bar where Bren was mixing drinks and laughing his ass off. In the mirror lining the ceiling I watched Koda lug Shayna away.

The banging of metal had me veering in Taran's direction. Three very limp and bleeding humans were stuffed inside the cage Taran had been shaking her assets in. I caught a glimpse of Taran's body draped over Gemini's shoulder as he stormed toward the exit. She was kicking, she was screaming, and there was not a damn thing she could do to get free.

Bren was still laughing when he poured me a martini and slid it down the length of the bar. He stopped laughing when Emme flopped onto the stool beside me. "I can't do this. Seriously, I'm not meant for this type of work," she said. "Some guy—Buster Hyman—keeps following me around, asking me what I charge for blow jobs. I didn't even know what to say. I just sort of laughed and ran away."

Buster Hyman? Oh God. "Emme, it's okay. Just stay close."

She peered over her shoulder and ducked, totally panicking. "Good grief. Here comes Buster. What do I tell Buster?"

"That if he gets anywhere near you, I'll rip his fucking head off," Bren growled.

I don't know what shocked me more just then, the ferocity in Bren's tone or his inability to tear his eyes from Emme. She lifted her chin, her lips parting slightly as she met his face. The intensity in her expression told me either something had happened between them or something was about to.

Oh shit.

I lifted the martini and turned around. Now was not the time to deal with this. I needed to focus if we were going to survive this night. I took a sip of my drink as Aric approached. He wasn't happy, especially when I ignored him to smile at Dilip. For a human, Dilip's stare was extremely predatory. He beamed back at me, much like a cougar upon finding a plump rabbit.

Yeah. I had his attention. And I intended to keep it.

Aric leaned on the bar with his forearms. "What the hell do you think you're doing?" he muttered.

I took another sip of my martini. "Playing a role," I said, watching Dilip leave his women behind and move in my direction.

"And what role is that?" Aric asked under his breath. "A high-end prostitute?" He swore when I didn't answer. "*This* was the vamps' MO?"

"It's what Dilip likes. How else do you expect me to get close to him?" I growled under my breath.

Aric mumbled something in wolf.

Martin appeared to my left. Bren, finally snapping out of his "Emme daze," managed to pour him a glass of scotch and pass it to him. Martin tossed it back like water. "This is a perfect example of why we don't permit mates together on missions," he said. "Aric, stand down and allow Celia to do what she must."

Dilip appeared then, his plain cotton shirt open to expose his curly chest hair. My eyes scanned his pants, looking for a bulge. The only one I found was right behind his zipper. Damnit. Where was his damn phone?

Martin stepped in front of him and offered him his hand. "Mr. Singh, I'm Isaac Blake." He motioned to me. "I see you've taken an interest in my lovely Thea."

I smiled at him and ran my hand along the plunging neckline of my dress.

"How much?" he asked, without bothering to look at Martin or take his hand.

Aric snarled, gripping the edge of the bar. That was my cue to walk away from him and toward Martin and Dilip. Martin was discussing my services. Apparently, I didn't come cheap.

Dilip was only an inch taller than me. He licked his lips, his attention fixed on my breasts. "You Thea?" he finally asked, looking up.

"Tell him you can be anyone he wants," Agnes said.

"I can be anyone you want," I repeated in a purr.

Aric stepped in front of me when Dilip reached his hand out toward my chest.

"Who's this?" Dilip asked, laughing.

The wolf who'll kill you if you touch me, I obviously didn't say. I slowly inched around Aric, trying to snag Dilip's attention. "Um. My brother, Billy."

"Your *brother*?" Agnes asked in my ear.

"Your *brother*?" Dilip repeated, laughing harder. There was something odd in his laugh—contrived and unnatural—and I could sense the mounting hysteria in it.

He punched Aric affectionately in the arm. "How's it going, *Billy*?"

"I'm going to rip your heart out and eat it," *Billy answered.*

I clasped Dilip's hand, leading him away. "Billy's protective. He knows I want you. Now tell me, what do you want?"

Dilip laughed again. "I want to drink champagne as it drips from your breasts." He reached behind him as we continued to walk and pulled out a . . . huge plastic bottle of Sprite. He dropped it as if it burned, releasing my hand and whipping around. It didn't take a genius to know Shah had heard him, and that he had begun to mess with Dilip.

I forced a laugh. "Wow. Great trick. What else can you pull out of your pants?"

I almost gagged at my own damn question. Dilip's eyes widened and he jumped, reaching into his pants and pulling out a carrot, then a cucumber, and an eggplant. Each rolled away into the crowd gathering around us.

There was a way I could use this to my advantage. But I couldn't think of anything then. Produce-producing pants had that effect on me.

I ignored the zucchini and banana he pulled out next. "Should we get a drink?" I asked.

Dilip slapped his hands over his ears and scrunched his lids. *"No."*

"Celia, get him to focus on you," Agnes insisted. "You need him to focus on you before Shah makes it rain cantaloupes!"

I reached for Dilip's arm, only to have him wrench away from me. He spun in circles, yelling hysterically, "No. No. No. I own you. I fucking own you, you little bitch!"

He wasn't talking to me. As I watched, the bulge in his pants widened and squirmed. Something alive had taken up residence there. Whatever it was scurried beneath the fabric and raced down the legs of his slacks.

"No!" he screamed.

In my brief time belonging to the supernatural world, I'd seen a lot of crazy things. Ferrets spilling from some nerd's pants weren't among them.

My feet left the floor as Aric lifted me into his arms. Ferrets by the dozens raced out of Dilip's slacks, their fangs and claws tearing through the fabric. Aric knew if one of these little critters touched me, I'd fall into a seizure and unwittingly *change*. He meant to protect me, but his actions worked against us.

The clubbers screamed, shoving at one another to race to the exits. Members of the Alliance stormed in, trying to make their way forward. But Dilip didn't notice them, or the ferrets, any longer. He only saw Aric and me. The way Aric held me in his shielding embrace gave away that we were lovers.

Agnes was wrong. Dilip wasn't a fool. He looked to the sky and yelled, "Shah!"

Lightning crashed within the club. The fog lifted. And the ferrets became something more.

Small curled bodies rose, lengthening in size and bulk, their fur ripping open to reveal reptilian skin beneath.

Aric backed away, carefully lowering me and pulling me behind him.

Crocodiles standing on their hindquarters towered over us. They surrounded Dilip, whose crazed brown eyes fixed on us. "Protect me, Shah," he said. "My enemies have arrived."

Chapter Eleven

"Stay with Dilip," Agnes's voice buzzed in my ear. She was running, I knew that much. "But don't attack. Shah won't turn against you unless you attack." Said the vampire not currently facing rows of snapping, sharp-tooth-filled jaws.

"I can't fight them," I whispered to Aric. I didn't want to explain and give too much away. But he seemed to know what I meant.

"You won't have to," he promised. "We'll protect you."

But who will protect you?

More ferrets-turned-crocs appeared. *Shit.* There were at least fifty.

Growls and hisses bounced off the walls as werebeasts and vamps spread along the perimeter of the club. Aric motioned me back. The Alliance team had arrived but there didn't seem to be enough of us to deal with the plethora of creepy and hungry reptiles.

The first croc launched itself forward. Aric caught it in his arms, one hand keeping its giant mouth closed, while his other arm gripped the struggling creature in a headlock.

Dilip wasn't impressed by Aric's show of strength until Aric ripped the croc's head off with his bare hands and tossed it at Dilip's feet.

"Is that all you've got?" Aric snarled, taunting him. He wanted to keep Dilip's focus and Shah's efforts directed at him.

I knew what he was doing, but I wasn't exactly thrilled with his tactics.

A large gold wolf appeared in front of us, blocking the crocodiles from reaching us with his massive form. Martin had arrived, his lips peeling back from his sharp canine teeth.

Something sliced at the air and then Shayna was suddenly there, just as fierce and furious as before. In her grip she held a sword, the blade dime-thin, but its length as long as my leg.

With a flick of her wrist she snapped the snout off a crocodile that had taken one step forward. "Uh-uh, dude," she warned. "Some hoochie just felt up my man. Trust me when I say you want to keep your distance."

She scratched the center of her chest. Her motion caught my attention, until a strange sense of confusion claimed me all at once.

I felt myself stumble back before Aric's clasp of my wrist steadied me. "Celia can't fight," Aric said.

Everyone nodded, appearing to think something was wrong with me. Before I could make sense of anything—or realize Dilip's sudden retreat—turmoil exploded and Shah's army attacked.

The Alliance members spread out, a strong defense taking on what was clearly a formidable and overwhelming offense. Aric's wolf shielded me with his body as a giant croc jetted over us. My claws protruded and I growled, my beast demanding out. She was raring for a fight from her need to protect us. Hell, I was raring to go, too, and barely managed to keep her caged.

I wasn't sure how I was going to keep from fighting as more crocs disappeared to slither beneath the tables or pushed forward, their beady eyes rocking and taking everything in, when something hoisted me backward and into the air by my waist.

My bare butt smacked against the mirrored ceiling and I slid in circles far away from the fight. My shoes fell off my feet. I waved my limbs frantically, convinced I was going to fall into the chaos beneath me. Blood squirted up like a fountain as *weres* and vamps severed heads, and crocs snapped their jaws over limbs that failed to move out of their reach.

I arched my back, trying to turn around and stop my erratic motion as I skated around the ceiling on my ass. Despite knowing I couldn't fight, I waved my arms, struggling against the power that held me, until I realized Emme had lifted me in the air with her *force*. She dragged me around with an invisible string as she shoved back the cluster of crocodiles circling her.

Her face scrunched. She was using a great deal of strength and focus to keep me suspended and herself from harm. The crocs closed in despite her best efforts. Panic spread along her features as the crocs' grotesque bodies appeared to morph into a freak mixture of reptile and human as they walked on their hindquarters and their beefy tails swung back and forth.

I wasn't sure what Shah had made them into. I only knew they were huge and Emme so small. But although she started alone, that wasn't how she stayed. Tye and Bren sped to her side. Bren's growls amplified as he snapped his fangs over the tail of one croc and sent it sailing away from Emme. He wouldn't allow anything to happen to her, especially on his watch.

Tye's lion form and another croc collided with such force I heard Tye's front leg snap away from his chest. Instead of collapsing, he kept his footing on three legs. A snarl reverberated across the room as he snatched the croc's throat and dug in his fangs. The creature screeched in agony and shook from side to side, trying to fling Tye. Tye held tight, tearing open the croc's throat and splattering blood like a sprinkler.

The scene below me became a haze of writhing bodies, blurs of gray and brown leather skin tangled with the thick fur of the werebeasts. Shayna stood out in the mix. She blinded a croc by stabbing it in the eyes with a dagger while her long sword gutted its underbelly. Another croc's tail whipped back, knocking her legs from under her.

Koda arrived like a hound from hell, killing Shayna's attacker before it could harm her. Shayna sat on the floor, temporarily stunned. She rubbed at her sternum before she seemed to gather her senses, then she leapt to her feet.

Meanwhile, I hung out on the ceiling like a damn piñata.

The din of howls and cries surrounded me, keeping time with the beat of the house mix and the pulse of the glaring club lights. I continued to skate along the ceiling as crimson and the scent of death unraveled below me. God, it was nauseating. I could barely make out my friends and lost sight of the vamps as they raced along, their claws and fangs out, fighting and slashing into our enemy. Everyone seemed to become part of the fray except for me. I was useless.

Until I caught sight of Dilip snaking his way through the madness and back to his table. His legs bled from the scratches of the ferrets-turned-crocs and he wore little more than underwear. But he was running in the opposite direction—away from the exits. I didn't know why until he reached for his jacket and I caught the glimmer of gold from his pocket.

His phone. He'd scrambled back for his phone.

"Emme!" I yelled, pointing frantically in his direction. She was too busy tossing a giant crocodile into the DJ booth, mercifully cutting off the obnoxious beat. I yelled again as the music suddenly stopped. She nodded and tossed me in Dilip's direction.

She probably meant to lower me gently. But aim was a talent my sister simply didn't possess, and in her defense, she did have a humanoid croc trying to eat her face. I smacked against the wall and fell toward the floor.

I landed in a heap on a VIP table, but rolled onto the floor into a deep lunge—thanks to the reflexes of my inner beast and her need to hang on to our pride. I scrambled and bolted after Dilip. He was racing toward the dark hallway that led to the restrooms.

An emergency exit was located at the end of the hall. But I couldn't be sure if we had any *weres* left guarding it. I chased after him, stopping short when a black crocodile hurtled toward me with its huge maw open. I ducked left and right, away from its snapping fangs.

I dipped, barely avoiding its mouth as it took off a chunk of wall from the corner. My claws protruded. I was running out of options for survival. It dove toward me again. I sidestepped out of the way and spun, meeting it face-to-face once more.

A pathetic wolf call alerted me to Shayna's presence. Her blade came down, severing the croc's head in one clean strike. "Go, Ceel!" she urged.

I didn't hesitate and ran full-out to the long dark hall. I expected to encounter another of Dilip's protectors. I didn't expect to find Taran. My feet skidded to a halt, meeting her blank expression as she stared at me. She rubbed at the center of her chest. It was her only movement, a surprising feat given a giant crocodile had her zombie limb clenched between its teeth like a drumstick. Both seemed unaware of what was happening.

The corners of her mouth lifted right before she raised her deformed limb with the crocodile still attached. Taran didn't possess super-strength, but her arm seemed to. The creature's stiff body was parallel to the floor, appearing frozen.

Nothing could have prepared me for what Taran did next. The creature detonated in a wash of blue and white flames, shooting away from us and taking out the back wall. Charred bits of croc peppered a trail to the giant hole Taran had made with its body. She shook out her unmarred zombie arm and cracked the knuckles of her hand. "Don't you have some dipshit to find?" she asked.

Her tone was strangely hollow. But she was safe. And she was right.

I started toward the exit Taran had created until I caught Dilip's sweaty and panic-filled aroma cutting through the smell of fried croc. He'd disappeared into the ladies' room without us knowing.

The door smacked hard against the wall as I rushed in. The window facing the water was shattered, drops of Dilip's blood smeared along the edges. My feet propelled me forward and I dove straight through, landing in a roll and rising into an immediate run in the direction I heard a motor catch.

This wasn't a car. It was a boat. But it led in the same direction as Dilip's scent. I swore and ran along the dock, barely leaping into the back of the speeding yacht in time. I couldn't swim. And of course, this was my bad guy's means of transportation.

My landing, while rushed, was quiet. I sniffed the air for any more of Dilip's guards. I scented magic—old and earthy. Likely, it belonged to Shah. It poked at me, trying to figure me out. My tigress found it curious. I could feel her sit back within me, waiting for it to react so she could respond in turn. While she was alert and ready, she didn't seem on edge.

Shah didn't mean me harm for the moment. That didn't mean I was safe.

I crossed the yacht and carefully climbed the steps leading to the upper deck. Dilip was steering, his back to me. He mumbled, distracted. I rose carefully and advanced, trying to stay silent as the strong current of air whipped my hair behind me and slapped against my exposed skin.

The engine purred softly, but the wind and the splash of waves were loud where I stood. And yet I heard Dilip as his mumbles grew more audible. Not that I was loving what he had to say.

"You will kill anyone who tries to harm me. You hear me, Shah? You will kill anyone who harms me. I own you. You piece of *shit*. I own you!"

Lights flashed across the panel that curved around Dilip. I jerked as "Magic Carpet Ride" blasted over the speaker system. Shah was definitely in the house. I perked up, and so did my tigress, trying to ready myself for what came next as I closed in.

Dilip screamed when I was mere feet from him. He smacked at his belly, his cries becoming agonized and frightened. I thought Shah was tearing him open and mangling his flesh. But Shah had his own brand of torture, and it seemed this rock was done being used.

Dilip whipped around, his face bleached with terror. Beneath the skin of his belly a face appeared, singing along to Steppenwolf's classic.

Okay. Yet another thing that gave me pause.

Dilip's belly button had stretched across the length of his stomach to become a mouth, cheerily lip-syncing to the lyrics while a nose protruded from his sternum and his nipples morphed into rather animated and gleeful eyes.

As I watched, Dilip's chest hair crawled to form an Afro above the nipple eyes.

"Close your eyes, girl. Look inside, girl . . ." Dilip's stomach merrily sang.

I looked at Dilip's face—his other one—as I tried to swallow the bile burning its way through my throat. "Wow. That's quite a dilemma you have here," I managed. "Um. What say you stop this whole world domination thing you have going on so maybe Shah will give you your life back?"

Dilip answered with a high-pitched hysterical laugh that didn't belong on someone with that much chest hair. In the meantime, we were about to crash into an island at full velocity.

I shoved him aside and cut the steering wheel left, spinning the damn thing until the boat wound in crazy circles. Meanwhile, "Magic Carpet Ride" continued to blast through the speakers and apparently Dilip's stomach.

"Why don't you tell your dreams to me . . ."

This was a whole new brand of crazy I hadn't expected. Between my haphazard steering, the music, and the impromptu karaoke concert, Dilip's cries grew more hysterical. Maybe he wasn't a fan of the song. Or it could have simply been the whole there's-a-face-on-my-stomach thing scaring the shit out him.

The way things stood I couldn't help him even if I tried. Anyone who claimed sailing a boat was easy probably never had a guy with a freaky lip-syncing belly standing next to her.

By the grace of everything good, I managed to straighten the boat. I played with the fancy buttons and levers until the motor seemed to die or I somehow broke it while I tried my best to keep sight of Dilip. He may have been a shrieking hysterical human, but that didn't mean he couldn't kill me.

Near as I could see, he was hunched in the corner, laughing, then crying, then laughing again as the yacht slowed to drift with the current. It didn't seem like much time had passed from when my hands first seized control to when we eased to rock along the water, but it was plenty of time for Dilip to act.

I gasped when I abandoned the wheel and saw what he'd been up to.

He'd acquired a fishing knife and had made quick use of it. His warped smile met my face even though he continued to stab himself in the stomach. If he was in pain, he didn't show it. Maybe only the first few stabs had hurt, or maybe he felt nothing at all.

He sat with his legs outstretched in a "V" while his body fluids pooled around him. The punctures in his belly were vicious and angry, and bits of bowel poked through his damaged skin to shine against the moonlight. But even that didn't erase his disturbing grin.

Shah's makeshift face had stopped singing and disappeared, but I doubted Dilip's insane efforts to silence him had anything to do with it. Shah was furious and had meant to punish. While he hadn't harmed Dilip directly, he did make a point: Don't fuck with mystical stones.

Dilip lifted his hand, plunging the sharp point again. His motions had begun to slow and his laughter alternated with mild bursts of wheezes. But he pushed forward, using his remaining strength to puncture his belly.

I thought I should stop him—or save him—or *something*. But there wasn't anything that could spare Dilip from himself. So, I simply watched, horrified by his actions and confused by what drove him. Yes, Shah's magic drifted around us, but like me, he appeared to solely observe. He wasn't forcing Dilip to do anything. Dilip was all on his own.

Maybe Dilip had been crazy from the start. And maybe it had taken only a little of Shah's personality to drive him over the edge. No matter what, Dilip wasn't a good man. That was something I was completely sure of.

His misdeeds rivaled those of every twisted preternatural I'd ever encountered. He'd murdered those he'd called his friends for greed and for his own damn desires. As I watched the knife suddenly drop from his grasp, I was reminded that one way or another, everyone answered for their actions.

Dilip Singh died with that crazed expression frozen on his face, with no friends to hold his hand or grieve his passing. I wondered briefly if anyone would miss him. I wouldn't. And neither would the loved ones of those he'd killed.

The waves splashed peacefully against the side of the yacht before I realized his body fluids had taken on a life all their own. Blood and acid from his stomach bubbled around him, leaving the pool surrounding his body to form words along the smooth floor.

I'm not sorry, it said.

I couldn't be sure if they were Shah's words for tormenting Dilip or Dilip's for the damage he'd caused. At that moment I didn't care. More than anything, I just wanted to get away from them and him.

My body trembled as I searched my surroundings. Dilip's jacket lay abandoned in the small seating area. I passed it twice before I realized it was there. With shaking hands, I reached into his pocket and removed a gold phone covered in diamonds. I stared at it, hoping it would be enough to find Shah before someone else did.

Music continued to blast over the speakers, but the voices sang in a language I couldn't understand. I turned down the volume, feeling the need to speak. "I'm not here to hurt you or claim you, Shah. I just don't want someone else to find you and use you for the wrong reasons." I paused, thinking things through. "In fact, I don't want anyone to use you at all," I added truthfully.

I wasn't positive why I said what I did to Shah. But I felt the need to tell him he had nothing to fear from me. I leapt to the rear of the yacht, wondering how I'd get back, when trails of light zigzagged along the water.

My eyes widened. I wasn't familiar with everything witches could do, but I got schooled then. Betty Sue, Delilah, and Genevieve skimmed above the sea's surface, the small waves splashing against their bare feet and circles of green light gathering beneath them.

Behind them, a smaller boat sped forward, followed closely by a Jet Ski. I knew Aric rode the Jet Ski when my tigress urged us toward the edge of the yacht. She'd sensed his wolf, and my desire to be with the man.

I tried to wait patiently, but my urgency to distance myself from Dilip's corpse made me restless, as did Shah's scrutiny. It was as if I could feel his magic circling me, trying to figure me out.

I frowned. "Don't be rude," I told him. "Like I said, I'm not your enemy."

I couldn't be sure he believed me, but I sensed his magic withdraw in time for the Alliance members to appear. The witches arrived first, skipping onto the boat with an added boost from their power. All three wore long medieval maiden gowns, the hems dripping ocean water as they walked across the deck. All seemed anxious, their stares scanning their surroundings.

"Do you have it?" Genevieve asked, stepping forward. "Do you have Shah?"

"No. But I haven't actually looked for him here," I replied.

Genevieve took off with Betty Sue hot on her heels before I could finish. Delilah tossed me a leery glance before following. I felt stupid for not bothering to even search for him. In truth, it hadn't even occurred to me.

Aric arrived next. He cut the power of his Jet Ski and leapt onto the stern directly in front of me. He rose slowly, water dripping from his bare chest and onto his borrowed sweatpants. His breath was labored, but seemed to calm as he drank me in. "Are you okay?"

I nodded and fell against him as he embraced me. "Dilip's dead."

Aric stiffened. "Where is he?"

I motioned to the bridge. Aric linked our fingers and led me to the top. Genevieve was already there, her long ebony hair sailing around her like smoke. "Did you kill him, Celia?" she asked.

Aric answered before I could. "Those are self-inflicted stab wounds," he pointed out.

Delilah carefully climbed the steps, her eyes frowning when she found what remained of Shah's holder.

"Dilip didn't seem stable from the start," I said. "And when Shah sought a little payback, Dilip completely unraveled."

I explained what happened as Agnes fluttered onto the boat and up to the bridge. Her eyes traveled over me as she handed me my hooker shoes. I swapped the fiendish footwear for the cellphone. She smiled. "Well done, Celia."

She strutted to where Dilip lay, taking a whiff of the blood pooling around him. "Hmph. Interesting," she said. "So, who's not sorry, Celia? Dilip or Shah?"

"I don't know," I answered. "At this point I don't care." Having had enough death for the night, I hurried down the steps. Aric followed directly behind me.

Betty Sue emerged from down below. "Shah's not here." Her eyes narrowed when Agnes hopped over her head and onto the deck. "What's that?" she asked when she saw the diamond cellphone clutched in Agnes's hand.

Agnes smiled. It wasn't one of her nicer smiles. "Our key to Shah."

"And why should you have that key?" Betty Sue demanded.

Agnes stopped smiling. "Because I know how to open the lock."

Genevieve didn't appear to care. She gracefully drifted down the steps with the strength of her magic. Her motions were smooth, but the magic that enveloped her was as lethal as a field full of axe murderers. "Admit it, Agnes. Your master wants Shah for himself." She tilted her head, appearing simply inquisitive, but I could sense the challenge brewing beneath the gesture. "Or is it your grandmaster who desires the stone?"

Agnes flashed her a grin. "I don't have to tell you anything, Glinda. Besides, if ever a head witch needed more power, it's you. Face it, Genevieve, with so many inferior witches beneath you, neither you nor your coven holds the command it once did. My master, and our grandmaster? Now, *their* strength is unparalleled and will soon be unmatched. Such a shame you can't say the same." Her smile widened. "Such a shame you'll never be as good as you once were." She tossed her hair and hopped into her boat without another glance back. I wasn't sure who was more pissed, the witches or Aric.

"Let's go," I told Aric.

His gaze skipped over my body before he turned back to Genevieve. "I take it you'll handle it?"

Genevieve lifted her perfect brows. "Don't I always?" She'd answered Aric, but kept her attention on Agnes as her boat pounded against the waves and into the moonlight. Genevieve's expression appeared unaffected despite Agnes having kneed her in the magical groin. But I knew better. For all that Agnes said about Genevieve's lack of power, Genevieve still had the goods to burn her to ash with just a bat of her long lashes.

Aric watched her, but said nothing more. Instead he took my hand and led me onto his borrowed Jet Ski. I wrapped my arms around his waist and kissed the spot between his shoulder blades, my gentle contact appearing to ease some of his tension. "Are my sisters safe?"

He scratched his chest. "Yes. Taran's a little hostile, but otherwise safe."

Taran . . . what was it that she'd done that bothered me? I wrinkled my brow, trying to think, only to have my concerns quickly fade. "What about the wolves and everyone else?"

His hands gripped the handlebars. "They're fine. A few injuries here and there, but nothing fatal or that can't heal. We didn't lose any more. . ." He shook his head as if attempting to clear it, then said, "The crocodiles, or whatever the hell they were, morphed back into ferrets almost right after you and Dilip left. I've been looking for you since."

I rubbed my face against his back. The contact was meant for me so I could take in more of his comforting scent, but my actions seemed to stir us both. "How did you find me?" I asked, my eyes taking in the vast ocean. "It's not exactly a small area to cover."

"Our bond as mates led me to you," he said, his deep timbre acquiring more of an edge.

"Good," I whispered against his skin. For whatever reason, my thoughts grew cloudy, but not my need for Aric. "Are we done for the night?" I asked, well aware of the purr to my tone.

Aric stilled. "Yes. We're done."

"So, my room or yours?" I asked.

"Mine," he said, growling softly.

With that, he started the motor and propelled us forward.

His fear for me kept his conversation short. I didn't push and cuddled closer against him. The heat between us surged long before we returned to shore and back to his hotel room.

Chapter Twelve

Aric didn't speak to me, even as we crossed the lobby of the luxury hotel he'd been assigned to. It didn't bother me, especially with how close he remained at my side. I suspected his wolf needed to calm after fearing for my life, *again*. And after my experience in the club and my boat ride from hell with Dilip, the silence helped me focus solely on him, allowing his presence to soothe my tension and maybe rile something more.

My ultrahigh sandals continued to add more swing to my step, bringing me more attention than I needed or wanted.

Then again, all the eyes peering my way could have been trained on the damn dress and my exposed ass.

Aric's scowl forced everyone to steer clear, as did his possessive claim to my waist. We stepped inside the elevator. The bellhop, well, he stepped out.

Aric kept his attention straight ahead. "That dress leaves little to the imagination," he muttered.

I could hear the bite in his tone, but it did little to tame my response. My fingers trailed between my breasts. "You don't like it? Hmm. I thought for sure you would."

"Not when it jeopardizes your life," he snapped. "The vamps shoved you in that thing and made you a damn prostitute. Anything could have happened to you."

Okay. Maybe he was a little mad.

The doors parted with a ding on the tenth floor. Aric led me to his suite and unlocked it, allowing me to pass ahead of him. I strutted forward, giving him another full view of my bare backside. He may have been furious, but that didn't mean I couldn't distract him or make him feel something more . . .

He swore as I sashayed along the short hallway leading into the suite. He was fighting to hang on to his anger. But it was a fight I wanted him to lose. We'd been apart too long, and as far as our love life went . . . yeah, it needed to be recharged.

I turned when I reached the long row of glass doors leading out to the terrace. I flipped the switch that lowered the privacy screen and simply leaned against the wall, waiting for him to prowl forward.

His scent of water crashing over stones mixed with the aroma of his growing arousal, causing the points of my breasts to tighten and ache. My eyes sought his face. His sought my more intimate body parts.

Aric jerked his head up when he realized I was watching him watch me. He knew I was ready for him, but he stubbornly clung to anger.

He stopped a few feet from me. The muscles of his arms bulged as he crossed them over his massive chest and his brows furrowed deep. Damn, my mate did sexy brooding well.

He cleared his throat when he caught my smile. "Go wash that crap off your face. We need to talk," he snarled at me. Or at least he tried to.

My smile widened. "I'll make you a deal, wolf. First, I'll go wash the crap off my face—like you so politely suggested—then *we* make hot passionate love together. We'll talk later." I shrugged. "If you still want to."

His eyes widened briefly before glazing with desire. *"Fine."*

Celia, one. Big, badass wolf, zero.

I strutted into the bathroom, well aware of the extra sway to my hips and even more aware that Aric was watching. I shut the door; I couldn't wash my face fast enough. Some guys may have found all the makeup extremely sexy. But Aric didn't and that was fine by me. I was patting my face dry when Aric was suddenly there, slinking his arms around my waist.

He'd ditched his clothes. Also fine with me. "You're taking too long," he murmured between nibbles to my neck and shoulders. I tilted my head back, moaning when he slipped his hands beneath my dress and cupped my breasts with his large hands.

Aric unsnapped my halter, dropping the sides away. "You are never to dress like this again." He paused and thought about what he said. "Except for me—in *private*," he added quickly.

I rocked my hips against him. "Whatever you want, wolf."

Aric growled, releasing the dress to fall to my ankles. His fingers trailed over my skin, traveling upward to tug and tease my nipples.

I angled my head around to meet his mouth and swept my tongue over his. My efforts only added to his mounting need. He yanked off my panties in one pull.

I stepped out of them, losing my balance when his fingers disappeared inside of me. My body fell forward, my hands clasping the edge of the sink as he worked me. My mews and cries swelled his erection rubbing between my thighs. *"Aric,"* I gasped.

He curled his body over mine, quickening his motions with one hand while his other arm held tight. My knees buckled when my first orgasm jolted its way through me. I imagined Aric wanted to keep going, sensing how good his fingers made me feel. But he didn't realize how much I needed to please him, too.

I spun to face him, nipping his chin, his neck, biting him gently all the way past his navel. He roared when I fell to my knees and claimed him with my mouth. My lips fastened tight around him. There was nothing more I wanted than to turn him on and fuel the heat spreading between us. The way he fell back against the wall assured me I was—oh *yes,* very much—succeeding.

Aric lost control of any composure that remained—grunting, moaning, trying to find a place for his hands—until he lifted me in the air and placed my legs on top of his shoulders.

This time, I couldn't hold back my screams.

My back slid against the cool tiled wall while my fingers ran through his hair. I kept begging him to take me. Eventually he did, on the bathroom floor.

Aric pounded his hips against me as we slid along the length of the room. I reached out with my hands, pressing them into the wall and arching my back to keep us steady. Aric dipped his mouth to my breasts, finishing me once more on the floor, then again in bed.

He kissed me long and sweet when our fast breaths finally slowed. "You're so sexy," he whispered against my ear. He ran his fingers through my long, silky tresses. "Everything about you makes me hot. Your voice, your walk, your lips . . ." He chuckled at my blush, taking a strand of my hair to tickle my nipple with. "Yeah, that, too," he added.

I lifted my chin to resume our kiss. I loved that he was so attracted to me, but sometimes even after all our time in bed, I remained that timid kitten he'd first encountered. He smiled against my mouth. *You like me shy. Don't you, wolf?*

"I'll love you any way you are, and any way you'll have me," he answered.

Aric's fingers trailed along the sweep of my neck, then along my body, as he spoke. "It's our mate bond," he reminded me when he caught the surprise on my face. "When our emotions are heightened, I can sometimes sense your thoughts. The connection is meant to alert my beast when you're in danger. But this . . ." His fingers brushed through my hair. "This is just a bonus."

"Okay," I said. Being Aric's mate came with more than simply the title. But the more intimacy we shared, the more bonded we seemed to become. I watched my hair slide through his fingers. "Do you like it like this? Without the curls, I mean?"

Aric kissed me before answering, his taste mixed with mine so addicting. "It's pretty, sexy, but I prefer your waves. I love how wild it gets when I make love to you."

My heart thumped loudly against my chest. It wouldn't be long before round three would start between us. But instead of drawing closer, he sat up abruptly and fixed me with an intense stare I hadn't quite expected. "Let's get married, right now. We'll fly out tonight and be in Vegas by the weekend."

I rolled onto my side. "You're serious."

"Yeah, I am."

My fingers traced small circles along his chest. "Why the rush? I thought you wanted something more traditional. Not Elvis and some chapel on the Strip."

Aric ran his hand impatiently through his hair as the scent of fear overtook the room and smothered the desire between us. I pushed up on my arm, terror seizing me and causing my claws to protrude. "Aric, what is it? What's wrong?"

He faced me, his expression riddled with worry and dread. My chest rose and fell quickly. "Is there something you're not telling me?" When he didn't answer right away, I panicked. "Are you being forced to leave me again?"

Aric's eyes widened. "*No.* I promised you I'd never abandon you again." He dropped his gaze, his breath harsh. When he spoke again, something shifted in his tone. "Except there is someone who can keep us apart."

My eyes stung with tears, and rage blinded me. I wanted to race out of bed, to find this person, damnit, to make him bleed. "Who?" I demanded. "Tell me who."

Aric stroked away the first of my tears. He didn't speak for a long moment. When he did, my world came to a crashing halt. "You," he finally answered quietly. "Celia . . . if you don't want to be with me, I can't make you."

I stared at him, confusion warring with my breaking heart. "I don't understand what you're saying. You're my mate. How can you possibly think I don't want you?"

He shook his head. "You don't understand. You're *my* mate. I'm bonded to you. But that doesn't mean I'm yours."

I felt like he had slapped me. When he reached for me, I pulled away. I didn't want him to touch me. I wanted an explanation for his asinine thoughts. "Tell me what the hell you're talking about before I tear this goddamn room apart."

He let out a deep breath, glancing down before looking me square in the face. "When a *were* finds his mate, whether she's human or another *were,* there's no doubt they're true mates. Because of the curse placed upon you, you're neither *were* nor human anymore. I know your feelings for me are strong. I can sense them. Hell, I can practically touch them. But it's possible that you're meant to love another more." His tone was harsh and broken. "I never wanted you to know this, but I love you too damn much to keep it from you any longer."

Angry tears leaked from my eyes, wetting my scorching cheeks. I was livid, breaking from his hold when he tried to pull me against him.

I stood, facing the doors leading to the bathroom, working not to rip them from their hinges and fling them through the wall of glass leading out to the terrace.

When I turned back to Aric, I could barely control my voice. "After all we've been through and all we've lost, do you really think I'm meant to be with someone else?"

Aric watched me carefully, sensing my growing anger. "It's not that I don't think you care for me—"

"*Care for you?* Are you trying to tell me that I don't love you—or that I haven't loved you enough?" I stormed into the bathroom and started pulling on my clothes when he didn't answer.

Aric stood, meeting me in the doorway when I stomped out. "Celia, where are you going?" he asked, his voice gruff.

"Away from you!" I pointed my finger at him. "You're wrong, Aric. The only being who can keep us apart is you. I want to love you—it's all I've ever wanted to do. But you never let me!"

I rushed past him and pulled on my shoes. Aric tried to gather me to him. "Celia, I'm not trying to push you away."

"But you are. And it's not the first time, is it?" I accused. "Look at everything you've done since we've met to keep me away—all those times *you* walked away. That was never me, Aric. It was always you!"

I grunted with frustration when he wouldn't answer. His eyes fired with anger and his hands balled into fists at his sides. The huge lump in my throat expanded, threatening to cut off my air. "I mean it when I say I love you. I mean it when I say forever. You insult me by calling me a liar."

His frown vanished, my words demonstrating how badly he'd hurt me. Without thinking, I passed my hand across my belly. "If you don't know how much I love you by now, maybe we really shouldn't be together."

Aric froze. I left without another word, slamming the door behind me.

I broke down the minute the elevator doors sealed tight. I was still crying when I crossed the lobby. Tim waited at the bar, his meal in the form of two blondes edging closer. He abandoned them when he saw me, his steps slowing when he caught me wiping my eyes. "You okay?"

I nodded, but I clearly wasn't.

Tim didn't exactly ooze compassion. It was a lot for him to just ask how I was. He swiped at his bald head and bent to whisper in my ear. "Agnes thinks she found Shah. But she doesn't trust the witches, and she wants to leave the beasts   out for now. Can you move tonight?"

I thought about Aric back in the room and everything that he'd said.

"Yes," I answered.

Chapter Thirteen

I adjusted the straps of my tank and fiddled with the edge of my denim shorts for the millionth time. Emme checked her phone and turned toward me as the small plane carrying us over the Malaysian jungle swerved and bounced. She was looking pretty green from the ride, but it didn't stop her from speaking. "Aric just texted me again. He says he's sorry and wants to talk."

I shook my head and didn't respond. Whether it was the stress from my fight with Aric or our encounter with Dilip and his crocs, I couldn't be sure, but two waves of painful spasms had racked my body since I'd left Aric. The first I'd somehow breathed through. The second had me curling on the bathroom floor where I'd changed out of my dress. I'd managed to hide the attacks from my sisters and the vamps, but I was sure they'd return. I only hoped they'd subside long enough for me to complete my task and find Shah.

"Celia," Emme pleaded, trying to draw my attention. "He seems really upset, sweetie."

"Leave her alone, Emme," Taran said. She tucked her zombie limb beneath her shirt. "They need time apart."

She glanced at Shayna, who kept scratching the area between her breasts. "Hell, we all need some time away from the furries."

Shayna growled, or at least she tried to. Truth be told, for all the *were* blood coursing through her veins she was more puppy than predator. "I can't believe Koda has the nerve to be mad at me. He was all like, 'You jeopardized the mission, baby,'" she said, trying rather sadly to imitate his deep voice. "'It was all for show. The mission is our top priority. The mission is what's important. The mission can't be compromised. You overreacted. Blah, blah, blah. Put the knife down. Blah, blah, blah. I can't let you stab her. She was just part of the mission.' Mission, mission, mission. Well, do you know what I told him?"

"What?" the rest of us muttered.

"That next time the *mission* involved anything in his pants, to find a new Bond girl to take care of it."

This caught Taran's attention. "Did you really say that?"

"Well, no," Shayna admitted. "Mostly I just called the girl he was dancing with a tramp and walked away."

"Oh," the rest of us said.

I glanced out the window as the plane swept over the tall trees. "Do you want to talk about it?" Emme asked me quietly.

Not really. But I did anyway. "Something's not right with Aric." It pained me to say it out loud. "I've noticed a shift in his behavior since he asked me to marry him. He's so irritable toward everyone and we rarely make love anymore."

It was my last comment that struck a chord. You could say everyone knew Aric and I used to do it like wererabbits. Taran quirked her brow. "You and he don't have sex anymore?"

"Not like we used to," I admitted. "He's exhausted all the time and pretty much loses consciousness once he crawls into bed. We only made love once last week. It was nice, real nice, but I was the one who instigated it and he fell asleep immediately after."

Shayna turned around in her seat and leaned her chin against her palm. "Ceel, I'm not saying this to upset you, but even when Koda is worn out, his beast always gives him an extra boost of energy. I don't remember him ever being too tired. If anything, Puppy gets his second wind when he sees me, you know?"

"Aric used to be the same way." I glanced out the window again. "Now he's questioning whether he's truly my mate."

"You're kidding," Taran said.

That awful sense of abandonment I felt at his words reclaimed me. My sisters didn't move, waiting for me to respond. "That's what he said. And apparently what he believes. He felt he owed it to me to tell me."

"Shit," Taran said.

"Yeah," I added quietly. "Pretty much."

I rubbed at the center of my chest. The ache there was starting to get worse. I must have sprained something during my encounter with Dilip. If it didn't improve, I'd ask Emme to heal me. I sighed. Then again, it could've just been the hurt Aric caused.

Shayna tried to smile. "Aric loves you, Ceel," she said. "That I'm absolutely sure of. You didn't see him the whole time you were separated. Koda and I did. Your wolf was positively miserable without his little kitty."

"I believe you," I told her. "What I can't understand is why he doesn't believe that I love him, too. Or how lost I was without him." I rubbed my chest again. "I can't help thinking all his anger stems from his deepest insecurities . . ."

Taran shook me hard. "Celia. Celia, what's wrong?"

"Huh?"

My sisters exchanged glances, but it was Taran who spoke up. "You were talking and then it was like you checked out. You okay?"

A strange haze seemed to dull my senses and dim my thoughts. I shook my head, trying to clear it. "I'm fine . . . just tired, I guess." For the life of me, I couldn't even remember what we were talking about. But I didn't want to admit it, especially seeing how worried my sisters suddenly seemed.

"I'm fine," I repeated, trying to put more force behind my words. "Really. We just need to focus on finding Shah." That much I meant. We were anything but focused.

My hand reached to rub the center of my chest again, but then I caught myself and stopped. The pain I'd felt was suddenly gone.

Taran frowned, looking past me to Emme. "Em . . . is that a hickey on your neck?"

Emme slapped her hand over her neck. "No. It's just a bruise. I fell. Last night."

"On your neck?" Taran asked, smiling.

Shayna whirled around, pointing to her other side. "Oh! She's got one right there, too."

"No shit?" Taran laughed. "Tell me you hooked up with some hot Malaysian guy."

Emme's cheeks flushed and she opened and closed her mouth a few times before any words came out. "I can honestly say I didn't hook up with a hot Malaysian guy."

"Then who did you hook up with?" Taran demanded.

Emme shut her mouth abruptly when she caught mine hanging open. The only males I'd seen her with who weren't trying to kill her had been Bren and Tye. And she wouldn't—I mean, they couldn't possibly. He and she— *Did* he and she . . . Come to think of it, *which* he and she?

The radio crackled and Agnes's voice blasted over the speaker. "Listen up, freaks. We have three potential spots where Shah might be. One's a hotel on the east side of town close to the club we hit last night. A team is searching it now. One vamp's been blown to bits, but it was kind of an accident so we think it's a dead end. I'm with the team searching the underground lair beneath Dilip's compound. We think Shah might be here, given how many have been eaten."

Emme gasped. *"Eaten?"*

Agnes huffed. "Yeah. Can you believe it? So far, we've lost two vamps and a rogue witch to something with tentacles—"

A shrill scream cut Agnes off.

"Make that three vamps," she continued. "So, if you see any tentacles when you get to your location, run like hell. I don't know what this thing is, but *damn,* it's hungry."

None of us moved, but Taran had plenty to say. "That's your advice to us? Run like hell?"

"Unless you prefer to be eaten," Agnes sang.

Yeah. So not a fan of Agnes.

Emme leaned forward and wiped her paling face. "Good Lord," she muttered.

The pilot tilted the plane down, to begin our descent. I caught sight of an old cinderblock house with a tin roof surrounded by what appeared to be tall white grass. That must be the place. I hadn't seen anything else for miles.

The pilot veered the plane, angling it toward a clearing on the opposite side of a small patch of jungle. We'd have to cross through the dense stand of trees. But from what I could make out, it didn't appear to be rough terrain.

Shayna adjusted her ponytail just when Emme groaned again. "Don't worry, Emme," she told her. "The way I figure, if anything ever needed tentacles to guard it, it's Shah. If so, sounds like the vamps have the right place. Let's just check this lead out, give it the all clear, and go home." She grinned my way. "Celia and I have some wolves to make up with."

She was starting to feel better about her and Koda. I didn't share the same hope for Aric and me. What was wrong with my wolf?

The pilot landed in the field near an old farm. The scent of manure made me gag when the pilot opened the door for us. The moment we climbed out, he tried to climb back in. I grabbed his arm. "You're not coming with us?"

He smirked, allowing his fangs to lengthen past his lips. "Nope. Like it or not, you need me to fly your asses out of here. Can't do that if I'm eaten."

Most beings couldn't argue with that logic, but I wasn't like most. "Fine. But just so you're aware, if you leave us behind, Misha will know." I smiled. "We're besties. You're not. He'll find you, rip off your arms, then feed you to something scarier than that creature with tentacles." I released him when his fangs retracted. "Toodles."

I headed in the direction of the jungle. Shayna skipped to catch up, twirling the machete she carried to loosen her wrists. "Want me to take up the rear?"

I thought about how volatile Taran's magic had been lately. "Sure. Taran, stay behind me. Emme, you're in front of Shayna."

"Yee-ha," Taran mumbled.

She tucked her arm beneath her shirt, trying to shield it from the sun, but when we stepped into the jungle it fired up like a glow stick. She shook it hard, as if trying to rid it of its eerie glow. "Son of bitch. Great. That's just fucking great."

She waved her arm. Good heavens, it looked like a plastic light saber. My steps slowed. It reminded me of something that she'd done last night but for the life of me, I couldn't remember what. "Maybe your arm is capable of more than you're giving it credit for," I reasoned as I pushed forward. "I'm wondering if you just need to figure out how to use it."

Despite the darkness of the jungle, I caught her eyes glistening with tears. "The only thing this thing is good for is grossing out big bad beasts and chasing them away."

The hurt in her voice made me want to cry for her. "Taran . . ." was all I could say.

"Don't sweat it, Ceel. Some things aren't meant to be. No matter how bad you want them."

She needed a moment, so I let her walk ahead of me. As I watched her hug her body, I thought about what she'd said. Her words, while disturbing, fueled my need to make things right with Aric. We'd been through too much. I wasn't ready to let him go. I needed him.

And he needed me, too.

A jaguar cut along the path, growling and licking its chops. I yanked Taran back and growled louder. It lifted its paw and rushed away in the opposite direction.

That's right, kitty. In a cat fight, this tigress is going to win.

Snakes slithered around us. I could hear them sliding over the drying leaves and through the thick vegetation. Their colors made them almost invisible, but I could smell their leathery skin. Knowing where they lurked would help keep us safe.

My sisters nodded when I pointed them out, and we gave them a wide berth. Considering our walk was short, we encountered several snakes and a few frogs I was very leery of.

Taran motioned ahead with her glowing arm to where the trees thinned. When she caught herself, she tried to tuck her arm under her shirt again. "Shit," she muttered.

We walked up the incline, staying quiet, and stepped onto a field of what I still believed was waist-high white grass. The long thick stalks swayed majestically around the perimeter of the building, despite the subtle breeze.

Shayna lifted her machete, ready to clear a path. I snatched her wrist before she could bring it down. "What's the matter? The grass is too thick to walk through, Ceel."

I tried to keep my voice steady as I realized what was in front of us. FYI, I failed miserably. "That's not grass."

Taran swore and jumped back with Emme, who bit back a scream. Long white arms with sharp black fingernails sprouted through the ground, waving to us, and beckoning us closer.

Taran withdrew further. "Oh shit. Shit, shit, shit."

Shayna swallowed hard. "Well, at least they're not tentacles," she offered.

I just looked at her. Even when faced with freakish arms protruding through the jungle floor, Shayna's glass remained half full. I didn't have it in me. Neither did Taran.

"This is all sorts of fucked up," she said.

"Yup," I added.

"Maybe we should go?" Emme suggested. "The vampires are semi-reasonable beings. They would understand if we left, given the circumstances. Don't you think?"

"No," the rest of us answered.

Agnes would toss us into the ocean of arms, no questions asked. I glanced to the closest hand that waved my way and pointed toward the building. "I think Shah's inside."

"And what if he's not?" Emme's voice cracked. "Celia, death by creepy hands isn't the way I want to go."

She jumped when another arm sprouted from the ground and smacked her in the ass. I didn't appreciate the gesture. "You be nice," I reprimanded.

Emme pointed to herself from where she hid beside Taran. "Me?"

"No. Shah."

My sisters gaped at me. "Do you see him or scent him, Ceel?" Shayna asked.

"No. But I recognize his personality." My eyes homed in on the building. "He's in there. I'm sure of it."

The sea of hands applauded all at once. Maybe Shah meant to be funny, but it only raised the Freak-O-Meter that much higher.

"Aw, hell," Taran muttered. "If we live through this, I swear I'm going to need some serious therapy."

Yeah. What she said.

Another hand punched through the ground and tugged at my shorts, pointing in the direction of the old building. "You want me to come for you, don't you?"

The hand didn't have a face, but it seemed to consider me before pointing again.

Taran clasped my wrist. "You're not seriously going to do this—listen to an arm, are you?"

I sighed. "I don't think we have a choice. For whatever reason, Shah wants me in there."

"How do you know he doesn't want to kill you?"

I shrugged. "He's not mean" I thought about Dilip and his lip-syncing belly. "Well, at least not to me. I think he didn't like Dilip. He felt used."

Again, the hands applauded.

"Will you stop that!" Taran yelled at them.

That only made them clap louder.

"Be nice, Shah," I said again.

The applause subsided, but I couldn't help thinking the arms and hands were laughing at us. A hand reached out to me. My tigress chuffed. She was freaked out, too. But I took it, allowing it to pull me forward and on to the next. The hands were surprisingly warm and gentle.

"How is it, dude?"

I glanced over my shoulder at Shayna. I hadn't realized how far I'd walked until then.

"Odd, even for us, but okay. Like I said, I don't think he means any harm." I smiled at the hand that patted my hand next. "Do you, Shah?"

Shayna stepped forward. "Mind if I go through?" she asked. "Celia's my sister. I have to watch out for her." She yipped when the arms hauled her forward.

Taran and Emme stayed put. "Come on, peeps," Shayna called to them. "They're not so bad." She laughed nervously. "Not so bad at all."

Taran glared at the hands and pointed at them. "Let's get one thing straight. You will not grope me, you will not fondle me, you will not touch me. Got it?"

The hands leaned away from her, giving her space. Shah seemed to welcome us, but then something changed. I felt Shah reaching out to me with his power. It gathered around me like an invisible mist. He seemed sad, lonely. It made me sad, too.

"Do you feel that?" Shayna whispered. "I think the hands are crying."

I shook my head. "I don't think it's the hands. I think it's Shah." I met her eyes. "Shayna, I think he knows his time on earth is almost over."

My eyes stung, and Shayna's reddened. I was overcome with emotion—for Shah, for Aric and me, for everyone around me who hurt. For as powerful as Shah was, he wasn't invulnerable to death, and apparently pain.

Celia?

I stopped, and the hands ceased to pull me forward. Aric was calling out to me, using our bond.

I'm sorry, he said. *God, I'm so sorry.*

"*I'm sorry, too*," I said, my voice overwhelmed with emotion.

Come back.

"*I will*." I took in those hands. "*But I have to get Shah first.*"

The connection faded. I wasn't sure how much Aric had heard, since for the most part our contact was limited, and only triggered by strong emotion. But now wasn't the time to talk. As much as I loved him, I had a job to do. I couldn't let the bad guys get Shah and drain what was left of him.

Emme had started to make her way in, but it was a hysterical Taran that cemented me in place and prevented me from moving forward.

"I'm here for Celia. I don't want shit from you." She sniffed. "As a matter of fact, I don't want anything from anyone." The arms parted, allowing her through. "It's been hard, you know? Having the guy of your dreams treat you like you're some kind of freak—I mean what the hell's wrong with him? I'm not perfect. But I never was. I was a fool to think he'd always love me."

The air cracked and a handkerchief materialized in the hand closest to her. It offered the handkerchief to Taran, who took it and dabbed her eyes.

Okay. Some things in my world were just too twisted to be real.

I'd only taken a few more steps forward when roars alerted me that we were no longer alone. Someone screamed, and what I mistook for a large stone pitched toward me, rolling to a stop near Shayna's feet.

Our vamp pilot's head had been severed. "Run!" he screamed.

I veered around. Already knowing it was too late to flee.

Panthers emerged one by one until a line formed around the perimeter of the hands. Most were as big as my tigress form, some bigger and well over four hundred pounds. Shayna lifted her machete. "There's too many," she whispered.

My claws protruded. "I know."

"Tribe *weres*?" she asked.

"I don't think so. I don't know what they are . . . Shayna, look at their eyes."

Emme's breath hitched. She noticed the green tarry substance swirling around their irises. The lead panther froze upon seeing the limbs sprouting from the field, but then growled and swiped at the hand that tried to stroke it, slicing the veins. Shrieks echoed around us as nearby birds took flight. The hand spasmed and spewed blood like a fountain, soaking the earth and limbs surrounding it. Emme screamed, and the panthers rushed forward.

Using their claws and fangs, the panthers cut through the limbs, showing no mercy as they zeroed in on us. Taran grunted as one tackled her. I saw her blue and white flames catch when she called forth her fire and saw Shayna swing just as I charged the one gunning for me.

My claws punctured the sternum, cracking it open before I ripped out the heart. I kicked the dead creature off me and dove on the one leaping toward Shayna. I rammed it hard, and wrenched it down by its neck like a calf at the rodeo.

Problem was this calf had pointy fangs. It took all my weight and strength to snap its spine. I stood as more panthers dashed forward. Whatever these things were, they were strong, powered by magic, and too many to fight.

But Shah was there and offered a field of helping hands.

They reached up from the ground, yanking and pulling the panthers down, using their sharp nails to tear the panthers' fur from the skin and shred their muscles. The panthers howled in agony but none would retreat. Whoever was fueling them wanted us dead, and Shah for the grand prize.

Emme grunted as she flung the creatures back into the jungle, crushing their backs against the thick trunks of the tall trees. She didn't see two more panthers rushing her, but those arms did.

They pulled her out of reach then snagged the panthers by their legs. The panthers struggled, their gazes crazed and their large bodies wrestling to break free. Some arms fell limp, bones snapping, but most held tight, dragging the big cats down until they disappeared into the earth.

The arms closest to Shayna held the panthers for her so she could slice off their heads. It didn't take long for the angry arms and the rest of us to be covered with blood and black fur. I ran in the direction where Taran had vanished, punching through skulls with my fists, trying to reach her.

The smell of burning fur alerted me that she was safe. So did the flaming black ball she sent soaring into the jungle. She raised her stiff white middle finger. The rest of the hands followed suit, flipping off evil in unison.

Shayna jogged to Taran, breathing hard. She clasped a hand and tried to wrench her up, only to fall forward.

"Wrong freaking arm!" Taran snapped at her.

"Oh. My bad!" Shayna said.

In Shayna's defense, it was hard to tell Taran's and Shah's arms apart.

I carefully stepped over the arms that hadn't made it and the pieces of panther that remained, struggling to catch my breath and trying in vain not to gag. Good Lord, all I smelled was death. "Everyone okay?"

Emme's blond hair was pink from all the blood coating it. She wiped her mouth, but her hands were just as stained and only made it worse. "I think so. What were those things?"

"Whatever they were they were sent to kill us and take Shah. Come on, we have to get him and us somewhere safe."

My sisters jogged behind me to the building. "Hey? What about me?" our vampire pilot's head called to us.

"Shut up," Taran snapped at him. "We'll be back in a minute."

I stopped at the door. There wasn't a lock or a handle. I didn't bother pushing or pulling the door. It simply opened, allowing us through.

I poked my head in. "Shah?" I asked like an imbecile.

The building was about the size of a barn. The only light trickling in was from the rust-eaten holes in the tin roof. The floor was nothing more than dirt with bugs crawling along it in search of food. The blood soaking my skin attracted them and I had to kick a few away.

At the center was a large mass the size of a small SUV, perched on its bumper. A plastic tarp covered it entirely, but it did little to diminish the white light emitting from its base.

I glanced at my sisters. Shayna shrugged. "Might as well pull it, Ceel. Voilà and all that good stuff, you know?"

I wasn't sure what to expect, but I didn't fear it. I yanked off the tarp and the room exploded with light, blinding me. Spots danced in my vision before I finally made out what was in front of me.

Shah hummed, but he seemed more like a shimmering diamond than a crystal. If I had any doubts that it was him, the small "x" etched into one of the facets cleared that right up.

Taran looked from the door to Shah, and then back to the door. "Shit. How the hell are we going to get him out of here?"

For some reason, I laughed. "I don't know. Emme, can you lift him?"

She wasn't able to answer me. Shah exploded, the force throwing me backward and blinding me in a wash of white.

Chapter Fourteen

The white noise of the airplane filled my ears. I blinked my eyes open to stare at the cabin's ceiling. I yawned and stretched. Wow. That was one heck of a nap.

Emme and Shayna poked their faces into my line of vision. Taran and Agnes were next. Fear and worry riddled my sisters' features. Agnes adjusted her tiny librarian glasses, appearing more annoyed than anything.

I grinned. Damn. I felt good. My smile only seemed to freak them out more. "Oh shit," Taran said. She looked at Agnes. "Now what?"

Agnes shrugged. "I don't know."

Taran narrowed her eyes. "What do you mean, you don't freaking know?" She pointed at me. "Fix her."

Agnes met her stare. "What's your problem? Do you think I'm happy about this? The master and the grandmaster wanted Shah. All you had to do was get it." She waved her hands irritably in my direction. "Instead, now we have all this."

"She got you Shah!" Taran yelled at her.

"And now it seems Shah has her," Agnes snapped back. She glanced at me and shrugged before walking away. "Hopefully we can wrench it out of her without killing her."

"You *bitch!*" Taran said, launching herself at Agnes. Shayna and Emme held her back as she continued to struggle.

I didn't understand why everyone was so upset. I felt fan-freaking-tastic. I smiled again at my sisters, but that only widened their eyes further. "Dude, she's like, *sparkly.*"

"What?" I asked.

Emme sat beside me. She reached out to touch me but then thought better of it and pulled her hand back. "Celia," she said carefully. "What Shayna is trying to say is that, you're different."

"Aren't we all?" I giggled, but my ears filled with the sound of tinkling bells.

Emme opened and closed her mouth several times, trying to work through her reasoning. "Celia, Shah attached himself to you somehow," she finally said. "We don't know how to get him out."

"Hmm" was my response.

Emme gave up then and allowed Shayna to move closer. "Ceel. You don't get it. You're like, *totally* different," Shayna said. "Um. We're not sure what happened, but Shah like, burst into light and shot into you. Next thing we knew he was gone, and you were like, totally naked and shiny."

"Shiny?" She nodded. I laughed. "Like glass?" She nodded again, albeit more stiffly. "You've been asleep for almost a day," she said. "We got you back to the vamps and they immediately flew you out of Malaysia. The wolves tried to reach us, but we left before they did. Somehow, though, they managed to secure a faster plane. They just landed in Tahoe and are waiting for us. Misha's there, too. We should touch down in another hour."

"Misha's there? Oh, how'd he like Europe?"

No one seemed to like my question and blinked back at me like I'd gone nuts. But I wasn't nuts. I felt F-I-N-E, *fine*. Oh so fine. I tried to lift my arms. That's when I realized my entire body was restrained in leather straps.

I didn't like the feeling, and I especially didn't like the blanket covering me. I extended my claws and ripped myself free. My sisters backed away as I stretched and poofed out my silky hair. I paused and stared at my perfectly round and perky breasts shimmering back at me. Shimmering? That was new. I glanced up at my sisters and pointed at my girls. "Is this what you meant by shiny?" I asked them.

"Son of a *bitch*," Taran muttered.

Emme backed away and motioned me toward the bathroom door that had a full-length mirror secured to the back. She opened the door carefully, revealing the mirror. "This may come as a bit of a shock," she said.

I shrugged and strutted forward, feeling sexy. God, it was good to be alive. I spun, loving how the air felt against my naked body, only to freeze when I caught my reflection.

My entire body had lost any trace of color. The sparkles from the crush of diamonds encasing my form were the only things keeping me from being completely translucent. I ran my hands over my arms, breasts, and hair. Silky softness greeted me, but I was no longer the same. My hair, my eyes, my body, *everything* glimmered.

"Oh my God," I gasped.

Shayna approached me with her hands out. "Ceel, you're going to be all right—"

"I'm gor- *geous*!" I squealed and spun to stare at my round, smackable ass.

Everyone quieted, leaving me to flounce in front of the mirror. My porn-star big hair flew around me in perfect delectable waves. "Aric loves when my hair gets all messy during sex," I admitted. "Did I ever tell you that?" I asked when all they did was gape at me.

Taran slowly shook her head. "I can honestly say you've never mentioned that before."

Emme covered her mouth. "What's wrong with her?"

Agnes leaned against the door frame, her shoulders shaking with her laughter. "I think she's drunk off Shah's power." She whipped out her phone and aimed the camera at me. "Edith is going to die when I show her."

Taran stormed over and smacked the phone out of her hand, her blue eyes igniting with rage. "If my sister ends up on YouTube, I swear to Christ I'll set your ass on fire."

"Damn, you're bitchy," Agnes shot back.

"Sweetheart, you haven't seen how bitchy or murderous I can be." She pointed at me. "Does Misha know what you and your goddamn plan did to her?"

Agnes lifted her chin. "No. Celia and Shah's clashing magic have interfered with our communication system. The only message we received is of the master's and the mongrels' arrival." She shrugged. "We'll be landing in forty minutes. They'll know soon enough." She pushed off from the door frame and returned to the main cabin.

I spent the rest of the ride bouncing around the plane, so full of energy. My sisters spent it pacing and debating how they were going to tell Aric.

Aric. *Yum.* I missed my big, bad hotness.

When the plane touched down, I skipped to the door, restless to see Aric and mount him *like a bronco.* Mount him like a bronco? Hee, hee, hee. I'm so funny!

Taran, Emme, and Shayna carefully led me back and sat me down when I continued to giggle. "Celia," Emme said gently. "Perhaps it's best if you wait here a moment."

"Why?"

Taran swore. "Because the wolves may not be ready to see you."

I pushed out my perfect bosom and grinned. "How can they not want to see all this?"

They had no response other than to just stare back at me. They'd been doing that a lot lately. Hmm. What's up with that?

Shayna straightened when the cabin door opened. "Maybe I should handle this," she said.

She scrambled out of the plane right behind Agnes. Emme and Taran began to pace again. I couldn't understand why they were all so edgy. Everything was damn fine as far as I was concerned. Taran had lent me a small mirror from her purse. I smiled into it, admiring how sexy I looked. Life was good. It couldn't get any better than this.

"Celia?" Emme said softly. I stared up at her wide doe eyes. She held up a blue sundress. "Um. We were kind of hoping you could put this on."

I cocked my head to the side. "I don't think it's necessary."

"It is," she insisted. "Y-you can't exactly step out of the airplane naked."

"Why?"

She didn't seem to know and looked to Taran for help. Taran threw her hands up in the air before perking up and pointing at me. "Because you'll look even prettier in the dress. You want to be pretty, don't you, Celia?"

I smiled. I liked being pretty. It was fun. "Of course!"

Aric's snarls had me peering out the small window. "What do you mean, she's not herself? Is she hurt?" he shouted. "You said she wasn't hurt!"

I laughed and rolled my eyes. "Someone's cranky again."

Shayna glanced nervously back at the plane. "Oh, she's not hurt or anything. She's just not quite herself."

"If she's not hurt, what the hell happened to her?" Aric pressed.

"Shah sort of attached himself to Celia," Shayna explained.

Everyone outside stopped speaking. Aric swallowed hard. "What do you mean he attached himself to her?"

"We better get outside," Taran muttered. She took the dress from Emme and shoved it over my head. She sighed and shook her head. "Damn. It's not much better, but it will have to do. Come on, Emme."

I stood up and spun around in the dress. I didn't like the feel of it. It made me hot. I ripped it off and skipped after my sisters. The wolves and vampires gathered around Shayna remained quiet as they listened to her explain what had happened when we found Shah.

They seemed intrigued with her story. I didn't like it. Her story took attention away from me.

I waved, jumping up and down until I had everyone's attention. "Hey. Yoo-hoo! Hi!" I yelled.

Aside from the audible pop when everyone's jaw dropped, no one made a sound. Their eyes collectively flew open. Danny and a few of the vampires actually jumped back as I bounded down the steps.

"Holy *shit,*" Tim muttered.

I skipped up to Aric who gaped at me like he'd been slapped with a giant salami. "Hi, baby," I cooed, throwing my arms around him.

Instead of embracing me, Aric turned his head slowly to glare at Misha. "You fucking bastard," he said to him. "This is all your fault."

Misha wasn't paying attention to Aric. He was too busy taking in my sparkling physique. My nipples tightened under his scrutiny, making a soft tinkling sound as they stiffened. I looked down at them and back at him.

"How do you always get them to do that?" I asked him, smiling.

Aric had to be physically restrained from launching himself at Misha.

I stepped back and watched his Warriors struggle to hold him back. "Don't you like how I look, Aric?"

He jerked in my direction and shrugged off the wolves holding him. Slowly, he edged toward me, his brows furrowed deep. Instead of gathering me to him, he kept his distance, his troubled expression traveling the length of my body.

I smiled and spun for him. For some reason he didn't appear impressed with how my wavy hair flowed or how my breasts bounced. Instead, I only seemed to agitate him more. He turned his back and ran his hand through his hair, muttering something I couldn't quite hear.

He couldn't look at me. What was wrong with him? I was pretty, damnit.

I circled around to face him. He gave me a half-assed look right before he let loose a bunch of growls. Again, he turned his back on me. My heart sank and I almost started crying, but then I thought of the perfect solution to get him to notice me.

Cartwheels!

I placed my hands on the ground and swung my legs over one by one. I was a big hit.

"Oh!" the crowd yelled as one.

"Ho-ly, shit," Tim muttered again.

I was so happy with the response I tried a second cartwheel, but Emme stepped in front of me. Her face was beet red and horror crawled across her features. "Celia, you can't go around doing that."

I didn't understand. "Why?"

Taran grabbed me forcibly by the arm. "Because we can see *everything,*" she hissed.

Aric ripped into Misha like a wolf possessed. "She had no right being there. All you had to do was notify the *weres* where Shah was and we would've handled it. Now look at her!"

Misha ignored him, appearing more stunned by my behavior than anything Aric had to say. I smiled and gave him a small pinky wave. He threw back his head, laughing, which only infuriated Aric more.

I stormed toward Aric. I had had enough. I shoved my fists onto my hips and stamped my foot down, causing my breasts to shake. *Tink, tink, tink,* went my nipples. "Do you like how I look or don't you?" I demanded.

Aric gaped at me like I'd asked some bizarre question. "Well?" I asked. "I'm waiting."

Aric shut his mouth, which meant he didn't find me attractive. Tears slid down my perfect cheeks and fell against the tarmac in the form of small diamonds. "You don't think I'm pretty," I said.

"Sweetness. It's not that, it's—"

"You don't think I'm pretty!" I wailed.

The murmuring around us stopped. Aric struggled with what to say. "Celia, you're not yourself, love. I . . ."

"I think you're stunning," Misha said, smiling.

I turned to him, my grin returning. "You do?"

"You are the most beautiful creature my eyes have ever gazed upon."

I clasped my hands beneath my chin and bounced up and down. *Tink, tink, tink.* "What a sweet thing to say."

Aric didn't agree and tackled Misha to the ground. Several vampires jumped on top of him, causing the wolves to attack. My sisters screamed at everyone to stop over their growls and hisses. I was furious they were fighting. Now no one was paying attention to me!

Ooo. A butterfly!

I bounced away, chasing after it while I spread my arms and imitated its movements. "Fly, little butterfly. Fly, I say."

I followed it into the wooded area and over a small brook when I heard Taran screaming behind me. "Celia. *Celia*. Goddamnit, get back here!"

I pointed to my little friend. "Butterfly!" I said, continuing to run.

"Jesus Christ, she's fucking high." Taran stopped trying to chase me and leaned on her knees, struggling to catch her breath.

Aric tore after me. His shirt was ripped to ribbons and blood dripped from the gaping wounds on his chest and arms. "Celia, wait."

Something in his voice made me pause. "Hi, Aric. Why are you bleeding?" I pointed again. "Did you see the pretty butterfly—"

He snatched me in his arms before I could say anything more. "Get my ride," he growled to the wolves following him.

Bren raced ahead of us while Aric ran full-out with me back to the private airport lot. I sniffed. Then sniffed again, pressing my nose against Aric. His brief smackdown with Misha heightened the underlying musk of his aroma. I lifted my chin and flicked my tongue along his neck. Mmm. He tasted so good.

Aric stiffened in all the right ways.

Martin's truck peeled into the lot, screeching to a halt. He raced to us, his steps slowing as he neared. "What in blazes happened to Celia?" he asked.

Shayna stepped forward. "Shah went inside her somehow. We think."

Martin frowned. "Did she touch him—is she his holder?"

Shayna shook her head, making her ponytail swing side to side. "No. That's the strange part. He was as big as a car and we were trying to figure out how to move him. Celia smiled at him and *bam*. Everything exploded with light and the next thing we knew Celia was naked, and crystal clear, and all like, sparkly."

No offense, but I was getting bored. I took another lick of Aric. That was fun, so I kept it up.

Aric cleared his throat. "I should take her home, until we figure things out."

Martin sighed. "Perhaps that's best. I'll conference with the witches to see what they think." His voice trailed off when he realized what I was doing. "Is she all right?"

"Her behavior appears to have been affected," Aric ground out, his voice strained.

"Agnes thinks she's intoxicated by Shah's power," Emme added, sounding oddly apologetic. She climbed into the passenger side of Aric's Escalade when Bren slid behind the wheel.

Aric cleared his throat. "She's ah, fine. Just—we need to get her home," he added quickly. He lifted me into the backseat and buckled me in, then sat beside me and placed his arm around me. Bren cranked the engine and pulled out of the lot.

Aric sighed, holding me close. "Baby, about what I said, before you left the hotel. It was crazy, and I'm not sure where it came from."

" ' Kay." I unbuckled my seat belt and straddled him, needing another taste of him. "You smell so good," I purred. I trailed my tongue along the curve of his neck until I reached his earlobe and tugged.

Aric grunted loudly.

"*Celia*. What are you doing?" Emme yelled from the front.

The car jerked off to the side as Bren exploded with laughter.

Aric clasped my wrists when I reached into his pants. "Celia, baby, st-stop," he stammered.

"I don't want to," I told him. "And I know you don't want me to, either."

I ground my hips against his lap, arching my back so my breasts skimmed against his face and my nipples swept over his lips. Aric grunted, turned his head and bit back a low growl when my hips rocked faster.

Bren continued laughing. Emme panicked and called Martin. "Martin—It's Emme Wird. Celia is trying to have relations with Aric."

"I beg your pardon?" Martin repeated into the phone.

"Celia's trying to have sex with Aric!"

"*What?* Ah, ah, tell him to—tell him to resist."

"Aric," Emme urged, "you have to resist her."

Aric held my hips, my wrists, trying to stop me. I welcomed his challenge with more hip swivels and tongue sweeps than he was prepared for. "I can't," he groaned. "It's still Celia."

The ride back to our house consisted of Aric and me wrestling in the backseat, him trying to keep me from tearing his clothes off with my teeth, Bren laughing and struggling to keep Aric's Escalade on the road, and Emme demanding I stop my behavior. But then we were home. Aric lifted me into his arms and raced us into our bedroom, slamming the door shut.

This time, he didn't work as hard to stop me.

Chapter Fifteen

Did you ever wake up and *know* you've had sex? Lots of it? Yeah, well, that was me the next time I blinked my heavy eyelids open.

I lay on my back. Sort of. Aric's foot was somewhere near my right ear and his other leg was tucked against my shoulder blade beneath me. I shimmied until I slid out from under his leg. Most of his upper body dangled over the opposite side of the bed and our brand-new sheets were torn to shreds.

I pushed my crazy hair out of my face. The entire room smelled like sex and us. Claw marks ran the length of our headboard and a chunk of wood was missing from the footboard. Damn. Just *damn*.

I laughed, remembering some of our more creative poses. I'd wanted him so much. I was glad he finally let me have him. I was still smiling, thinking about the way we'd made love until the image of naked cartwheels flooded my mind.

My body jolted as if poked, and I scrambled to his side. "Aric?" I shook his shoulder. Oh God, what did I do? I shook him harder. "Aric?"

He flipped me onto my back and dipped his head to kiss my neck. "Ready for more, sweetness?" he murmured.

He paused and pushed up from me, his gaze softening. "Hey. You're not shiny anymore—"

"Did I do naked cartwheels in front of the vamps and everyone we know?" He sighed and carefully pulled me to a sitting position. "Oh my *God*!" I screamed. "I did, didn't I?"

Aric rubbed his jaw. "Try not to worry too much about it. Everyone there realized you weren't yourself."

I buried my face in my hands. "Kill me. Just kill me."

Aric pulled my hands from my face and kissed each one. "How can I kill my mate and the woman I love?" he asked softly.

He gathered me to him, and simply held me for a long while. His presence soothed me. At that moment, there was no doubt and nothing standing between us. So I melted against him and took it for the gift that it was.

"What happened to Shah?" I finally asked.

"I don't know. We . . ." Aric straightened. "He's right there."

I lifted my head. There on my dresser was the smaller version of what I'd found in Malaysia. Aric and I stood and walked to him. Shah was now only the size of my palm. "How did you get him out?"

Aric frowned. "We didn't. We came back here, made love over the past two days and—"

"Two days?"

Aric chuckled, his face reddening. "Yeah. It was pretty intense. I couldn't keep you off me, but in all fairness, I didn't want to." He kissed my head. "He must have separated from you after we fell asleep this last time."

"Okay. But now what?"

He shrugged. "I guess I'll take him back to the Den for safekeeping."

"Do you think he'll be safe there?"

"I don't know where else to hold him, sweetness." He turned me around, keeping a hold on my hips. "This whole thing, you fighting, you going after him. Celia, I'm trying, baby, but I can't handle you putting yourself out there and risking your life."

Just like that, the peaceful moment we'd shared was gone. I lowered my gaze briefly before meeting his face once more. "Aric, you do it all the time."

"But it's my sworn duty. Not yours."

"I may not have made an oath to earth, but I am obliged to defend it." My fingers trailed over his skin. "Why else do I have the power that I do?"

"Shayna told me about the panthers," Aric said. "If Shah hadn't decided to help you, or if he'd turned against you, I would have lost you. You wouldn't be here with me now, and I would be begging the next full moon to rise and claim my life so I could join you."

My hands covered his. "Aric, I'm not planning on going anywhere."

"Neither was Liam," he said softly.

I tried to swallow back the grief that engulfed me. No one spoke of Liam anymore. Some things were just too painful. And some people were just too young and good to die. But I knew not a day went by when we weren't reminded of his smile, or how he'd given his life to save mine.

Aric sighed. "I don't want to fight with you, or force you into a corner. But if you feel compelled to help those who need you, I want you to go back to nursing."

"I don't think that's where I'm meant to be."

"Will you try?" He lifted my chin, his eyes pleading. "Please, Celia. I just want you to try. If it doesn't work out, we'll regroup and work something else out, okay?"

I didn't say anything for a few beats. But when I spoke, I hated what I had to ask. "If I do, will you consider stepping down from your position as Leader?" The bomb I dropped loosened Aric's hold. "You don't want to lose me, but you have to understand that I don't want to lose you, either."

It took him a while to respond, and in the minutes that passed I regretted my request. Whether he'd meant to or not, Aric had forced me into a corner. But then I'd gone and done the same thing to him. "Okay," he finally said. "If that's what it will take to keep you safe, I'll step down at the end of the year."

For something that would help ensure our safety and well-being, both of us looked miserable. Aric bent and kissed my lips, then turned from me to pull some clothes out of his dresser. He'd been so willing to make love mere moments ago, before my ultimatum; now he simply seemed distant and I only had myself to blame. Guilt twisted my belly. In a thousand years I would have never expected to make such a demand. Sometimes I still surprised myself, and it wasn't for the better.

"I'd better get Shah to the Den," he said quietly. "I'll be back later; stay here and rest."

I nodded and pulled on a T-shirt and shorts.

Aric disappeared into the bathroom. When he stepped out, he was dressed in jeans and a long-sleeved T-shirt and grasped a hand towel. He stared at Shah. "Will you start applying for nursing jobs sometime this week?"

I nodded, knowing I owed him as much for what I'd just asked of him. "I'll start later today. I promise."

"Thank you," he whispered.

He reached for Shah, waiting a breath before he gathered him in the towel. "You're not going to touch him?" I asked. He didn't answer me, and wrapped Shah tighter. "Aric?"

"I don't think I should touch him."

Aric's voice sounded strangely distant. Instead of saying more he left our room with the fate of the world, literally, in his hands.

Just like I promised Aric, I started applying for nursing jobs. Based on my experience, and a glowing recommendation from my former manager, I had a job in the Emergency Department of my old hospital within days.

I called Misha and told him I wouldn't be working for him anymore. He simply chuckled and said, "We'll see."

My brief time away from the hospital didn't require a formal reorientation, but the only shifts available were nights. I didn't like being away from Aric. But he probably disliked stepping down from his Leader role even more. So, I sucked it up, and started my first shift the following week.

My preceptor from the garden of evil, Helen, handed me a tube of lubrication jelly and a pair of gloves. "What's this?" I asked.

Helen smiled and reached for her extra-large coffee. "Mr. Kelly was just brought in from the local nursing home with a heavily impacted colon. He needs you to relieve his discomfort. Get to work. He's in room seven."

Without another word, she strolled down the hall of clear glass partitions. She didn't glance back, but I had no doubt her smile remained. I clenched my jaw and tried hard to keep my fangs from protruding. With a heavy heart, and a big tube of lube, I headed in the direction of room seven.

The speaker system crackled above me. I waited to hear a code announced along with the affected department only to hear the chorus of "You Are Not Alone" begin to play. I thought someone was messing with the system and continued on, expecting the music to suddenly cut off. Instead several voices trailed in. *You're not alone,* they whispered at once, their echo seeming to come from every direction.

My steps slowed.

You're not alone, they said again, repeating the lyrics that continued to pour from the speaker system.

I pushed forward, trying to dismiss the voices as stress from starting a new job, the music playing over the intercom, and the remaining tension between me and Aric. While I really didn't believe my absurd logic, it was better than the alternatives—I was crazy or the ED was haunted. Neither appealed to me so I pushed aside the curtain to room seven and stepped in.

Mr. Kelly lay unmoving.

Very unlike the three vampires spread around his body, draining him of his blood.

Here's the thing. Too many rotten experiences throughout my life had left me edgy and defensive. I was always on guard— *always.* But hearing voices in your head *and* being told you're about to manually remove a few pounds of literal crap from some old man's rectum would have distracted even the most vigilant warrior.

The vamps whipped around, baring their blood-smeared fangs. I dropped my gloves and lube and backed away.

"Shah," they hissed.

"I don't have him," I growled back.

As if on cue Shah appeared in my hands, practically calling me a liar. My eyes widened before I was deafened by the sound of shattering glass and bending metal when the first vampire tackled me through the doorway.

The vampire was huge, well over six feet tall and probably close to three hundred pounds. In supernatural terms, it was the equivalent of being charged by a rhino. The force alone would have killed a human. But I wasn't human.

Still, the tile floor cracked beneath me along with every bone in my back.

The impact robbed my lungs of air. I couldn't breathe, and struggled to shove him off me. He rammed a gun into my temple. With the first breath I managed, the smell of cursed gold bullets overwhelmed my sensitive nose. If I'd known he was going to kill me, I could have saved him a few bucks by telling him normal bullets worked just fine on me. "Aw, hell," he said. "This bitch ain't so—"

I *changed* and bit through his wrist.

All bad guys liked to talk. It wasn't something they did in movies or in the superhero comics. It was a God-given fact. He was probably going to say "tough" or "bad" or something just as wrong. I didn't let him. Experience taught me it's always best to kill the bad guys before they're done talking.

I wasn't sure how impacted Mr. Kelly was, or if I was just grossed out by the flavor of blood, but the vampire tasted like shit. I spat out his gun-wielding hand and swatted Shah away with my paws while the other two vamps rushed me.

I roared. People screamed. A lot. A "Code Silver" was announced over the speaker system, alerting security that an out-of-control person with a weapon was in the ED. I guessed it was someone's way of trying to help. To me it just meant more people I had to keep from being eaten. The other two vamps cocked their weapons. I *changed* back to human and swept up Shah, using the one-handed vamp as a shield.

It seemed none of the vamps were the best of friends. They took aim and fired at their buddy in their attempt to kill me. I was grateful for the gold bullets just then. They worked really well on vampires. His body ricocheted against me before he exploded into ash. The large cloud gave me cover so I could scramble behind the nurses' station. I tucked Shah in a drawer and kept going, emerging on the opposite side as a tigress just as security arrived.

Apparently, our hospital used off-duty cops to patrol the halls during the night shift. I was certain that's what they were, especially when they reached for their guns and pointed them at me. My claws scratched against the tile in my haste to haul ass away from them. Although I called them about half a dozen names in my mind, part of me couldn't blame them for shooting. If I were them, I definitely would have shot the tiger first before dealing with the two guys holding guns.

I sped ahead and had just rounded the corner when a bullet took off the tip of my tail. A horrible burning pain ran the length of my body, to the tip of my cold wet nose. Security beat feet behind me, continuing to fire. I wasn't going to make it if I didn't act, so I dove and *shifted* through the cinder block wall directly in front of me.

It was something I'd never done. And with good reason. Normally, *shifting* through solid surfaces underground refreshed my body upon surfacing. Through walls . . . not so much.

Perhaps it was because the wall wasn't solid. Regardless, when I emerged on the other side my insides felt scrambled and grossly misplaced.

My human shape crashed against the cold linoleum floor, and I was temporarily blinded by the fluorescent lights. I pushed onto my side only to vomit uncontrollably.

Aric, I called to him. *Aric, I need you.*

It was hard to see. My head spun revoltingly fast and I felt like the inside of Mr. Kelly's colon. When my eyes were finally able to focus, they fell upon a pair of feet directly in front of me.

A janitor holding a mop loomed over me. "Hi," I mumbled.

He made a few sweeps at the mess next to me, but otherwise did his best to pretend there wasn't a naked woman with a bleeding ass cheek lying in front of him. I forced myself to my feet, using the wall I had just *shifted* through for support. All I wanted to do was take a second to breathe and maybe vomit some more, but the screams and the gunfire from behind the wall forced me back into action. I sprinted to the ED. I wanted to *change* as soon as I stumbled through the main doors, but my body insisted I eff off.

Security came in handy after all. They distracted the vampires by unintentionally offering themselves up as snacks. I decapitated a vampire with a jumping, spinning kick when his head jerked up in my direction. It landed somewhere near the heap of wheelchairs shoved against the wall.

My only problem was that I was still dizzy from *shifting* through the stupid cinder block, and I fell onto my already sore ass, giving the other vampire ample time to pick me up by the throat.

His hands squeezed tight. "Kill her, Edison!" the decapitated head screamed from the seat of a wheelchair.

Edison never had the chance. My body couldn't *change* yet, but I could extend the claws in my feet. They slashed him across his thighs while my fists broke through his chest and collapsed his lungs. He twisted at the last minute and I missed his heart, but I injured him enough that he released my throat.

I immediately rolled to my feet when I fell to the floor and leapt onto Edison's back when he tried to flee. I yanked his head back, exposing his throat so I could sever his neck with my claws.

And damnit all, he still wouldn't die!

Edison and his pal must have been old, *real* old. I'd rather have fought a new vampire any day of the week than take on a master or a vamp older than three hundred years.

It wasn't enough to rip out their hearts or tear off their heads to kill them. Oh no. It had to be both. So, there I was, on the floor, being bitch-slapped by Edison's wildly flailing arms while the fangs from his decapitated head sunk into my forearm.

His incisors dug deep. They scraped against bone while the blood he took from me seeped onto the floor through his severed throat. No. That wasn't nasty or anything.

I banged Edison's head over and over against the tile floor, trying to crack it like a nut. It didn't work; I was either too weak from blood loss or he had an exceptionally hard head. My luck generally sucked so of course things had to get worse. The first vamp I'd decapitated had gotten to his headless feet. He charged at me with the wheelchair that held his head. "I'll kill you!" his head hollered at me. "I'll kill you, bitch!"

If the people in the ED weren't screaming before, they certainly were then.

Chang, the martial arts master whom Misha hired to train me, had taught me a valuable lesson not learned in most strip mall martial arts studios. "If you can't rip an evil creature off of you, figure out a way to use him as your weapon." Honest to God, that was one of the first things I understood him say in his broken English. I kicked Edison's body away from me and slammed his head against the oncoming wheels of the chair.

The body pushing the wheelchair had nowhere to go because his head went bouncing across the floor. He just stood there, making it easy for me to bash through his chest with Edison's head and tear out his heart.

"You whooore. You bitp," Edison muttered through a mouthful of me. I was hurting, bleeding, and horrendously nauseated, but the name-calling really pushed me over the edge.

I protruded two claws from my fingers and poked the bastard in the eyes. He screamed, finally letting go. His head hit the floor with a sickening splat. Like an idiot he tried to use his body against me, despite having been blinded. He lifted his legs and tried a jumping kick. Not only did he completely miss me, he made it easy for me to catch his foot. My fangs snapped it off so he wouldn't bother me when I tore out his heart. Unfortunately, I hadn't noticed the poor housekeeping person hiding behind the linen cart. She peered around the cart and got smacked in the face when I carelessly tossed Edison's foot aside. Blood from his ankle trickled down her face.

"I'm so s-sorry," I stammered. She stared at me with horrified eyes, tripping over the unconscious security guards in her haste to join the terrified group huddled in the corner.

Edison continued to scream obscenities at me until I abruptly hushed him by ramming his heart with an IV pole. Silence had never been so golden. Before his fangs could completely retract, he was nothing more than a mound of ash.

My hands gripped the IV pole to help keep me on my feet. Spots flickered in my field of vision. I tried to blink them away, but it didn't work, and in a way made things worse. For a moment, my body refused to move, readying itself to vomit. When I didn't, I risked taking a step.

I limped to the linen cart the poor housekeeping person was pushing before the start of the chaos. My right butt cheek seeped blood with each step. I guessed that was the body part that made up my tail in beast form. I pulled a clean sheet from the cart and wrapped it around me. In the corner, a few feet to my right, stood a doctor, about four nurses, and twelve patients ranging in ages from a toddler with a bandaged arm to another nursing home drop-off. Everyone stared with wild, terrified eyes at my half-naked, ashy, and bloody body. And while they had stopped screaming, they were barely breathing by that point.

If I'd been in better shape, I would have offered them support or words of comfort. But I wasn't, and besides, what the hell would that have done? Judging by their now catatonic expressions, they were going to need at least two years of therapy before they could tie their own shoes.

I looked to Helen. She stood perfectly still, coffee cup in hand, despite most of the contents spilled across the front of her shirt. "Could someone get me some scrubs?" I asked in a hoarse voice.

No one moved, with the exception of the new doctor who fainted. In his defense, I did look pretty damn nasty.

It hurt to talk, but I tried again. "Please?"

Helen gave me a short nod then took a few stumbling paces toward the employee locker room. She didn't make it very far. Three more vampires came tearing down the hall. If that wasn't bad enough, a werelynx in human form followed close behind them. He was dressed like a ninja and swinging nunchucks with sharp blades protruding from the tips. Helen retreated in the time it took me to let out the mother of all swearwords.

And then the screaming started all over again.

Chapter Sixteen

Helen yelled, "Celia, do something!" and shoved me forward. I would've turned around and slapped the shit out of her if I hadn't been worried about the three crazies about to kill us. I pushed the linen cart toward the approaching vampires. But I was so weak, the toddler with the bandaged arm could've pushed it harder than I did.

The vamps didn't exactly leap out of the way of the cart in terror of me. It was more like they took a step back, exchanged glances, and, oh yeah, laughed. One said something to the others in what I believed was Portuguese. I didn't speak Portuguese; I spoke Spanish. But I understood enough to know he said something like, "*That's Shah's holder?*"

The werelynx swinging the nunchucks also seemed unimpressed. He stopped doing his Bruce Lee thing just to furrow his eyebrows at my nasty self. He shrugged, folded his nunchucks, and shoved them into his ninja belt. I guessed he felt I wasn't worth soiling his weapons when he could kill a wimp like me with his bare hands. He moved forward, only to step into what remained of Edison. When he glanced at me again, I had already backed up halfway down the hall, far from the terrified humans. The bad guys hadn't come for them. They'd come for me. I needed to put some space between us.

The ninja said something to the others while pointing to the clumps of Edison ash. The vampires' amusement faded as it became clear that yes, they had the right gal. All three of them glared at me. I held tight to the bedsheet and bolted when they charged.

I faintly remember hearing what sounded like screeching tires and something crashing through the lobby before thick fingers twisted into my hair and wrenched me back. I was thrown past the horror-stricken crowd, their screams becoming muffled when my head and back smacked against something hard.

Stars swarmed my vision and everything hurt. Goddamnit, even my eyebrows felt the excruciating jolt of my impact. I opened my heavy lids only to find that I'd lost the sheet covering me and was embedded spread-eagle into a wall.

I was bleeding, I was hurt, and I was about to get torn to pieces by three vampires and a ninja werelynx. Terror should have gripped me by the throat. Fear should have chilled my bones. Horror should have released my screams. Instead my only thought was, *Oh God, I'm naked!*

It wasn't a rational thought, but don't judge me. I'd just been thrown across a room and embedded into cinder block.

The bad guys rushed me. When mere feet remained between certain death and me, three large and snarling wolves the size of my tigress collided with them like giant rams, shoving them across the Emergency Department and away from me.

Koda and Gemini had arrived.

I lifted my chin, forcing my lolling head to straighten. Shayna skidded around the demolished nurses' station her eyes wild as she took in the destruction around her. *"Dude!"* she yelled when she saw me.

My head slumped forward, and my body tried to convince me this was a good time for a nap. But the sound of splintering glass, growls, screams, and whatever other noises accompanied an Emergency Department being demolished insisted I should stay awake and try not to die.

Shayna hopped over the debris, shock whitening her pixie face as she took me in. "I'm okay," I slurred.

Shayna clasped my left wrist and pulled. "Don't worry, Ceel. You're not alone. I'll get you out."

That was easier said than done. She had to prop her foot against the wall for leverage as she yanked. Each pull sent currents of sharp pain shooting into every nerve in my back. "Shayna, don't," I begged.

"It's okay, Ceel. You're almost out," she insisted.

No, I wasn't, and her efforts to save me were killing me. A sickening crunch filled my ears over the chaos in the ED. I hoped the sound was chunks of wall falling around me and not my crumbling spine.

From where I was rooted, I had a clear view of one of the Gemini wolves and a vampire destroying the inpatient pharmacy. The medication-dispensing robot whipped around as they duked it out. Clumps of bloody fur stuck to the windows and what appeared to be a hand crawled along the ledge.

Shayna was still trying to dislodge me when one of the robot's arms jabbed Gem in the eye. The vamp used that moment to strike. He kicked Gem through the pharmacy's glass wall. Gem landed atop shambles of metal and sheetrock. He flipped, narrowly dodging the ninja's swinging nunchucks. Gem went after him, but the ninja threw something that temporarily darkened the ED with smoke.

I coughed and gagged; whatever he'd thrown burned my lungs and throat. The smoke cleared in time for Shayna to free me from my cinder block prison.

And for the ninja to appear in front of us.

"Shayna!"

She dipped and rolled out of the way before the blade could puncture her skin.

Fortunately, she kept moving because the ninja didn't stop. Unfortunately, she released me in the process. My body felt like rubber, but I didn't exactly bounce when I face-planted into a pile of rubble.

"Ouch," I whimpered through a mouthful of dust.

It took a great deal of effort, time, and a whole lot of swearing before I could push up onto my elbows. To my left, Koda was dodging bullets from yet another vampire who had arrived. He'd killed the one who had thrown me into the wall, but that one hadn't been wielding a weapon. His howls echoed, rattling against the devastated halls, when a couple of bullets pierced his ribs.

Smoke wafted from his fur in tendrils. Koda could take being shot by gold, so long as the bullets missed his heart and brain. The screaming humans didn't have that luxury. I scanned the area, searching for somewhere to stash them.

Twenty feet to our right was the medical supply closet. There wasn't a lot of room, and the super-beasties could easily break through the keypad, but the door was constructed with thick metal and would provide protection from the barrage of shots being fired. I crawled forward, staying low mostly because I couldn't stand.

"Helen. *Helen!*" I called louder when she continued to scream. "Get everyone into the supply closet!"

Helen didn't hear me, but one of the nurse techs did. She ran to the door. It took her a few tries to open it with her trembling hands, but she managed. Another nurse urged everyone forward. They piled in, shutting the door tight behind them.

I pushed up on my legs, only to fall on my face again, narrowly missing the spray of bullets punching holes into the wall behind me. Another gun-wielding vamp had arrived because hey, why not? Collapsing into more broken glass, though horrifically painful, was the only thing that saved me.

Shit. All I could do was lie there like a very naked and oozing slug. *Aric. Where are you, wolf?*

Aric didn't respond to help me. But Koda did. He tackled the vampire like a seasoned linebacker. He may have been hurt, but he tore into the vamp and ripped him apart. Ash exploded as he made the kill. He veered, ready for more, but the ash had occluded his vision, and he didn't clear it fast enough to avoid the ninja or his lethal nunchucks.

Koda yelped when the ninja stabbed the tip of a blade into his haunches and then raked a knife across his face. It was horrible, but the attack brought Shayna racing from the opposite corridor. She lifted the IV pole and split it with her power, transforming it into two long and razor-sharp scythes.

The ninja leapt away from Koda and attacked. He wasn't afraid. He was a master of weaponry.

But so was my sister.

Shayna howled one of her more pathetic wolf calls and spun forward, spinning her scythes. The ninja hadn't expected someone so thin to be so lethal. His eyes widened when Shayna all but gutted him with her first strike. He pivoted right then left, catching one handle with the chain of the nunchucks. He brought the blade down, but couldn't avoid Shayna's kick to the groin.

The ninja recovered too damn quickly, reaching for a dagger from his belt and jabbing it at Shayna. She twisted out of reach, bringing her other scythe down in an arc. He evaded her blade and whirled back, and together they began a deadly dance of strikes and blocks. They fought like two vicious gladiators, my sister's cunning and skill leading the ninja away from Koda, giving him time to rush another vampire.

I wasn't a coward, but I was badly hurt and needed to hide from the last gun-toting vampire staggering through the rear entrance. He'd lost a foot, and yet he hobbled faster than most humans ran.

The linen cart had been pushed off to the side near the wall. It wasn't much in the way of cover, but it was my only option given the condition of the ED. I crawled through the devastation and the ick. Shards of glass and splinters of wood scraped painfully against my breasts, belly, and thighs. It took me a moment, but I finally managed to reach the small pocket of protection before the vamp noticed me.

My body gave out just when a pair of feet in bloodred platform Mary Janes stepped in front of me. The most notorious Catholic schoolgirl had arrived.

I glanced up Edith's long legs, careful not to look too closely. Edith wasn't a fan of underwear. "Hi, Celia," she said cheerfully. "The master sensed you were in trouble and sent us to help you."

"Eh?" was all I managed.

Edith hauled me up by my shoulders with ease. She tossed back her long midnight hair and grinned. "The master also sends his love," she said right before she kissed me.

That's right. Edith kissed me. On the lips. I clenched my jaw shut before she could shove her tongue down my freaking throat. My eyes were wide as I kicked out uselessly. Edith's eyes were closed as she continued what she probably thought was one hell of a smooch. I wanted to gag, having had an idea where her lips had been, but that would have granted her access to the inside of my mouth. No way in hell did I want anything of Edith's near any of my orifices.

If it wasn't strange enough having one of the Catholic schoolgirls making out with me, an odd blue haze surrounded us, and all I could think about was Misha. I thought of his gray eyes and how they softened only for me, and about that wicked smile he flashed when he was up to no good.

Then, unexpectedly, he materialized through the far wall and stalked toward us. It was hard fighting off Edith's tongue as it slid against my teeth while I gawked at Misha, flabbergasted by what the hell was happening. His black silk pants hung shamelessly low on his hips, exposing his Herculean physique, glistening with sweat. He slinked leisurely, like a serpent over the rubble, while his long mane swept off his powerful shoulders. My eyes widened as *every* part of him tensed with each step. When he reached me, he pushed my hair away from my face, and joined our kiss.

I just about had a coronary, but then Misha vanished and was suddenly inside me, building my strength and caressing everything that hurt. Including my ass.

I jumped away at the realization, flipping backward—away from Edith and the linen cart—and landing in a crouch. The strange blue haze surrounding me intensified and glowed, erasing my pain and damnit all, tingling *every* part of me.

Edith fixed her attention on my breasts. "The master will be pleased by your response," she said, smiling.

The cocking of a gun had me scrambling back toward Edith. I dove behind the cart and hunkered down, narrowly missing getting shot. Edith just stood there and tilted her head like she couldn't understand my reaction. "Edith, get down!" I yelled.

She huffed. "What's the big deal? They're only bullets."

The gun jammed, but then the vamp managed one more shot. It hit Edith right in the arm. She screamed in agony as smoke rose from her wound and black pus seeped from the gaping hole.

Edith peered at her wound and back at me. "That fucker is shooting with gold bullets!"

"I know. Get down!"

Instead of listening, Edith completely lost her shit. She looked up at the ceiling, raised her arms, and screamed. I fell back on my new and improved ass. I'd only heard her scream like that once before—when we'd found the beings who'd kidnapped and tortured her master. It was a guttural, primal, PMS type of scary scream—good for us and bad, very bad, for the vamp who'd shot her.

I snagged a patient gown seconds before she picked up the linen cart and flung it into the gun-wielding vamp. He grunted upon impact but all I could see were legs sticking out from the bottom of the cart. The cart shook as he tried to rise, but not before Edith screamed once more and launched herself on top of him.

Edith pierced her carefully manicured and deadly nails through the flaps of the cart and reemerged with the vamp's colon. She tossed the intestines and what resembled a kidney aside. I stopped watching then. Not only because I was grossed out, but because her kiss had somehow transferred some of Misha's power into me. And Lord knew I needed it then. The ED was suddenly flooded with more *weres* and vampires chanting, *"Shah, Shah, Shah,"* as if trying to locate him.

I rose, my claws and fangs protruding, and charged.

The wolves around me howled, one after the other, their *call* inciting one another to fight with great zeal. In the distance, another faint howl echoed, tugging at my heartstrings and making me want to cry. I ignored the emotions it stirred, desperate to stay alive and focus.

My claws raked across flesh and my legs kicked hard. I killed two more vamps and a werecheetah in beast form before Misha's power abruptly faded, and I collapsed.

All the injuries I'd endured and the pain that accompanied them struck me in one massive blow. I screamed; certain the agony alone would kill me.

My screams worked against me, attracting a mammoth wolverine. He thundered down the hall, landing on my limp form and robbing me of air. He would have killed me had Gemini not arrived and torn out his throat. As I lay on the floor, Gemini's twin wolves rejoined and *changed,* revealing his human form.

He lifted me from the rubble, his voice urgent. "Stay strong, Celia," he said. "Aric is on his way. . ."

Chapter Seventeen

If Gem meant "stay awake," I didn't manage. The next time I pried my eyelids open, I was in a patient room covered in a sheet. Emme's face was the first I saw. Her soft healing light faded as I felt the last of my pain recede.

"Celia's okay," she said softly.

Aric clutched my hand within both of his. I knew it was him even before I turned to look. His sweet warmth and addictive aroma alerted me to his presence. "Hi, wolf," I whispered.

He kissed my hand and leaned his forehead against it, worry and exhaustion darkening the circles ringing his eyes. He seemed tired, unusually tired. I scanned the room until I fixed on the wall clock. 3:00 A.M. It was late, but Aric's beast should have given him more energy than this.

"Son of a bitch," Taran muttered. She leaned against the wall with her arms crossed. "How the hell does this shit keep happening to you?"

Aric helped me to sit. I rubbed my face. My body was weak from blood loss and from how quick Emme's *touch* forced it to heal. My throat was also unbearably itchy, likely due to dehydration. I scratched it, for all the good it did me. "Just goes to show that hunting demons is safer than working in the Emergency Department," I mumbled.

No one found my comment funny, especially Aric. He frowned, although I could see the fear behind his apparent frustration. "I should have sensed you were in danger."

My hand fell away from my throat when I realized what he'd said. "You didn't?"

He shook his head, his anger and disappointment building around him.

"But I *called* to you," I said slowly.

Surprise smoothed away his frown. Okay, this wasn't good. Nope, not all.

Emme and Taran shuffled nervously around us. "It's okay," I told Aric, unable to tear my gaze from his. "You've had a lot on your mind." My excuse was pathetic at best. Throughout my fight, I kept expecting him to magically appear. He'd claimed me as his, and with my emotions running so high, he should have known that something was wrong.

Yet my mate hadn't felt anything. And it scared me.

Edith strutted in, beaming. "The master knew you were in danger," she taunted. "We would have arrived sooner had *weres* not been guarding the entrances." She looked at Aric. "He returned to Europe last night and yet even from so far away he realized Celia needed him. Where were you, mutt?"

"Shut up, Edith," I hissed. I expected Aric to lash out. Instead, he tightened his jaw and said nothing.

Edith shook her head with mock sympathy. "Poor little mongrel. Perhaps your love isn't as strong as you thought."

Aric stood. *"Enough,"* he snarled. "Time for you to leave."

Edith kept her smile, though her eyes had narrowed. She wouldn't leave just because Aric commanded, especially if Misha had ordered her to stay with me. I looked at her, my disappointment in Aric's absence weakening the assertiveness in my tone. "Edith, go home. I'm fine now."

She scowled. Clearly, I was spoiling her idea of a fun night. She tossed back her hair and strolled out, but not before shooting me a glance with an evil gleam over her shoulder. "By the way, the master was right. You taste delicious."

Aric straightened. "What the *hell* is that supposed to mean?"

I glared at Edith, willing her to burst into flames. She didn't. Instead she ran her tongue over her top lip and winked before stepping into the hall.

Sometimes Edith simply sucked.

"What did she mean by that?" Aric asked more forcibly. I wrestled with whether to tell him. "Celia?" he demanded.

I sighed. "Edith kissed me when I was hurt. Somehow, she temporarily transferred Misha's power into me." Aric regarded me like I'd been unfaithful. "I didn't exactly let her, you know," I added defensively. "She caught me in a moment of weakness. I was hurt, bleeding, and almost unconscious."

I stopped speaking then. In his light brown irises, I caught a flicker of anger, but his most prominent emotion was shame. As my mate, Aric should have been at my side, giving me strength. Instead, Misha had come in his place. While I could forgive Aric's absence, the guilt shadowing his features told me he'd never forgive himself.

"The master has been concerned for Celia's safety since Shah bound himself to her," Tim said. He'd walked into the room without knocking, of course. "Before he left, he transferred some of his power into Edith. He wanted her to have his strength in case Celia needed it in his absence."

"It would've been more if you'd just let me fondle you," Edith yelled from somewhere down the hall.

Tim smirked at Aric. "Good thing Celia has someone looking out for her."

Aric's jaw clenched, but when he took a step toward Tim, I clasped his arm and held him back. "Do you need something, Tim? Or did you just stop by to be a prick?"

He laughed, seemingly pleased with himself for getting a rise out of Aric. "I just wanted to know if you needed anything else before we left. All human witnesses have been hypnotized into forgetting the experience. But if you prefer that we stay to guard you, it's completely understandable given your own mate won't even protect you—"

If I hadn't been holding Aric, and Emme hadn't shoved him back with her *force,* Aric would be flossing Tim's remains from his fangs. "Just go, Tim," I ordered.

He turned to leave, but not before offering one last dig. "I'll be sure to tell the master you'll be coming back to work for him."

From the room next door, Koda howled in agony, making me jump. Through his torment, Shayna's reassuring voice remained soft. "It's okay, puppy, I'm here," she said. "I promise it'll be over soon."

"What's wrong—what's wrong with Koda?"

Aric pulled me to him. I didn't realize how fast my heart was beating until I tried to slow my breathing. The night had sucked, but it wasn't over. I couldn't shake the feeling that something was watching and waiting to strike. "Don't be scared, sweetness," Aric said. "Koda was shot in the eye. Martin is just digging the bullet out of his brain."

Oh. Is that all? My stomach did a flip-flop, and I felt faint. I could have done without that visual.

Aric eased me back down. Next to me, Emme and Taran were fumbling with some packages. Taran straightened my arm. "Hold still, Celia. I'm going to start an IV. You need fluid." She shuddered when she took in my face. "And considering your face is as white as Emme's butt, you're going to need some blood."

Aric rubbed his sternum. "You're giving her your blood?" he asked, sounding oddly pleased.

Taran stopped what she was doing. "Aric, look at her. I don't have to check her labs to realize her hemoglobin and her hematocrit are low."

He rubbed his chest. "No, you're right. Do what you can to help her."

I flinched when Taran started my IV, but it was nothing compared to the pain Koda was experiencing next door. I was glad I was horizontal when I heard something crunch, followed by the howl of a furious beast.

The small amount of blood Emme had drawn from Taran was running into my vein when Gemini prowled into the room. He'd found scrub pants to wear, but hadn't bothered with a shirt. His dark almond eyes fixed on her. "Hi," he said quietly.

Her shoulders tensed. She'd heard him yet she refused to glance in his direction. She busied herself drawing Emme's blood to give to me. While she appeared to be concentrating, I knew her enough to sense her sadness. Gem stared at her for a moment longer before speaking to Aric. "Genevieve, Delilah, and Betty Sue are here."

Taran scowled and tugged the cuffs of her long gloves upon hearing Genevieve's name. I couldn't blame her for getting upset. Her failing power, the condition of her arm, and the end of her relationship with Gemini had fractured what remained of Taran's confidence.

It also didn't help that Genevieve had the goods to make Miss Universe question her hotness. Genevieve's fair skin, large blue eyes, and long wavy black hair bordered on perfection. She reminded me of a life-sized ceramic doll, if the doll came complete with a perfect figure, elegant mannerisms, and power so strong you could taste it. We'd only interacted a handful of times, including this last time in Malaysia. But each time, her beauty gave me pause, and each interaction had been uncomfortable and memorable.

Aric's attention briefly passed to Taran before he kissed my bare shoulder. "Ask Genevieve in. I don't want to leave Celia," he said.

Gemini nodded and stepped into the hall, beckoning Genevieve forward. "He's waiting for you," he said.

She entered the room. Tonight, she'd chosen a deep purple velvet gown that brought out her eyes and delicate skin. Gold ribbons crisscrossed at the bodice, making her breasts appear fuller despite her lithe frame. Part of her hair was up in a twist, while the rest dangled in perfect waves around her cheeks. The yellow talisman typically affixed to her long staff dangled from a chain around her neck. Save for Halloween, most people would have looked ridiculous in this getup. But most people weren't Genevieve.

I rubbed my face and tried to smile. Good thing I don't look like hell or anything.

Genevieve's eyes widened when she caught sight of my oh-so-attractive and blood-smeared appearance. "Hey, Genevieve," I muttered. "What's new?"

She smirked at me as Delilah and Betty Sue filed in. "Not much," Genevieve said. "But it seems like you've had quite the evening." To Aric she said, "How can I help?"

"You've seen the mess outside?" he asked. Genevieve nodded. "I need you to clean it."

Genevieve smiled. "Considering you wouldn't permit my coven to guard Shah, it's going to cost you."

"You've already made it clear to me and the Alliance that you're not in agreement with this decision.

But for the time being, that's where he'll stay. . ." His voice trailed off when I stiffened against him. "Celia, what is it?"

I was hoping he wouldn't ask me, especially in front of everyone else. "Shah's here," I admitted.

"What?" everyone asked at once, although Taran threw in a few swearwords for emphasis.

I pushed my hair from my eyes. It was then I realized it was caked with body fluid. I dropped my hand away and tried to wipe it on the sheet. "I don't know. He just appeared."

Genevieve raised an elegant brow. "Why do you keep referring to Shah as 'he'?" she asked.

It seemed Genevieve, like many others, continued to see Shah as an "it." "Because that's what *he* is," I answered, growing impatient.

I watched her, Delilah, and Betty Sue as if someone had nudged me to pay attention. "He appeared in my hands when the first group of vamps arrived. They seemed to think I had him—or at least seemed to feel he'd appear to me if called."

"And did *he*?" Betty Sue asked, although it seemed more like an accusation.

"Yes. He did." There was no sense in lying, but I wasn't loving Betty Sue's presence all of a sudden.

Delilah glanced nervously between me and Betty Sue. "Where's Shah now, sugar?"

I adjusted the sheet against me, wrestling with whether to disclose his whereabouts. I had no claim over Shah, but I couldn't help but feel a sense of duty to him.

"Celia?" Aric asked, his eyes scanning the group. "You have nothing to be afraid of, just tell us where he is."

That's what Aric thought, except I couldn't ignore the strange unease that filled me and whispered a warning. I finally spoke, mostly because I didn't think I had a choice just then. "I shoved him into a drawer at the nurses' station. He should still be there."

"You were the last to touch it?" Genevieve asked. She didn't sound as accusing as Betty Sue. That didn't mean I liked her question.

"Well, yes, but it wasn't intentional. He appeared in my hand—" And like magic, Shah materialized in my open palm.

The witches, wolves, and my sisters gathered around me. Instinctively, I pulled my hand back as if any one of them could snatch him from me, including Aric.

Genevieve met Aric's stare. "It would seem Shah remains bonded to Celia. How is that possible?"

Aric lifted his chin. "Good question, especially since Makawee was the last to touch him."

"Are you certain?" Delilah asked.

Aric squared his jaw, but it was Gemini who spoke. "Yes, both Aric and I were present when Makawee held him and placed him in a special stronghold." He tilted his head slightly. "Or are you questioning my and my Leader's integrity?"

There was an underlying growl to Gemini's tone, but considering Delilah was a non-*were,* she seemed to bare her teeth despite her smile. "We would never question Aric's loyalty, shug."

"Good," Gemini answered, meeting her stare and forcing her to drop her gaze.

Genevieve cleared her throat. "Perhaps given the circumstances, Shah should reside with me."

Taran scoffed. "Oh yeah. Brilliant idea. I'm sure you can't wait to get your hands on him, too."

Emme groaned as Taran's magic sizzled around her. Genevieve surprised me by smiling gently, yet her surging power told me she wasn't far from acting.

"Shah's not going with you or anyone else," I told her. I glanced at Shah and stroked my thumb over his smooth surface. "Go back to Makawee's stronghold." I could feel everyone watching me when Shah just lay in my palm. I sighed. "Please, Shah," I told him.

From one blink to the next he was gone. And damn, didn't that piss the witches off? Betty Sue stormed out. Delilah tossed me a wary glance before following. Much to Taran's obvious displeasure, Genevieve stayed put.

Genevieve considered me carefully. Her expression wasn't harsh, but her magic surged nonetheless, prodding me as it strengthened.

"Genevieve," Aric warned. "If you have something to say, say it. Otherwise, take care in how you question my mate's allegiance."

The magic poking me withdrew. Genevieve bowed her head. "Forgive me, Celia, I meant no disrespect."

"Ah, sure," I said slowly. Perhaps I should have taken offense to Genevieve's supernatural probe, but I understood her paranoia. Something was off.

Don't trust them, a soft voice urged. I didn't react until the second half of the warning. *Or the wolf.*

Aric caught me when I practically fell off the bed. "What's wrong?"

I scanned the room certain someone was there. Everyone gathered glanced around before all attention returned to me. "S-sorry," I stumbled over my words. "Emme, stop the transfusion, Taran's blood is done running in."

She clamped off the tubing and switched out the bag of blood. "Sorry," I said again. "It's been a long night."

No one could argue against that. Genevieve nodded slowly before addressing Aric. "You were saying you needed this mess cleaned up?" she asked.

"Yeah, did you bring your broom?" Taran snapped.

Aric pinched the bridge of his nose. Genevieve surprised me by smiling. "How much is it going to cost?" he asked her.

Genevieve kept her smile on Taran when she answered. "Ten thousand, plus unlimited use of the property you acquired from the Tribe for the next two years."

"Which property?"

That was when she looked at Aric. "The one in France, of course."

Aric scoffed. "What the hell are you going to do with a castle, Genevieve?"

"Even witches need a vacation home, Aric."

Aric stroked the small of my back as he thought matters through. "You can have fifteen thousand and unlimited use of the castle for the next six months. After that it will be sold to help the *weres* who lost their families during the war."

"Done," Genevieve said. "Although, I would have done it for twelve, even without the castle," she said on the way out. She paused and looked to Gemini. "When you're done, I'd like a word with you."

Gemini rose at Taran's glare, watching her with a weary expression and more sadness than I could bear. "I'm done," he said.

Chapter Eighteen

Shayna hurried in about an hour later. I hadn't realized I'd fallen asleep until I noticed the time. "Koda's all fixed up—holy Moses, Ceel, you're the color of Emme's butt!"

Once again, Emme didn't appreciate the reference and crinkled her brow. That said, I didn't doubt Shayna's brutal comparison.

Taran stood and opened up the clamp wide so the last of Emme's blood could finish flowing into my vein. Between them, they'd given me the equivalent of a unit of blood, but as Aric helped me to sit and the room tilted, I was certain it hadn't been enough.

Shayna rolled up her sleeve. "Should we try some of mine next?"

Emme shook her head. "Shayna, I don't think that's a good idea. With Koda's werewolf essence streaming through your system, it might be dangerous for Celia."

Shayna shook out her sleeve. "Okay, but I'm wondering if it might give her the boost she needs. We all have the same blood type, minus the totally hairy howler within me, I mean."

Shayna meant well. That didn't mean I was desperate enough to give her blood a try.

Aric smiled and rubbed the center of his chest. "Why don't we take some supplies home with us?" he suggested. "We can always try it tomorrow if you remain weak, honey."

It was strange to hear Aric call me "honey"—while sweet, it wasn't something I remembered him ever calling me. What was even stranger was how eager he seemed for me to receive Shayna's blood. "You want me to do this?" I asked slowly.

He rubbed at his chest again. "I only want you to be well, my love."

I stared at him for a beat before leaning against him, once more needing to feel close to him. God, what was wrong with me? I couldn't shake the fear that he was drifting away. "Can we go home? I want to get out of here."

Aric swept me up in his arms. "Of course, sweetness," he whispered. I was embarrassed that he had to carry me, but it was either that or stagger through the halls like a drunken fool.

The gleaming brightness of the ED gave me pause when we stepped out of the treatment room. So did its condition. All the destruction had not only been repaired, but everything appeared brand spanking new. The floors shone as if freshly waxed and the glass partitions gleamed.

Genevieve stood at the end of the hall, speaking to Gemini as she passed a wet towel along her flushed face. Betty Sue and Delilah stood on either side of her, sweating profusely and dabbing their faces with handkerchiefs. Repairing this war zone must have exhausted them.

The older witches had changed out of their street clothing and into long maiden-type dresses similar to Genevieve's. Maybe the dress was required when casting a cleanup spell as powerful as this, but their clothing did nothing to enhance their natural beauty. And, as much as I had initially liked them, both seemed more like wannabe witches than the powerful enchantresses I'd first met.

Gem still wasn't wearing a shirt. He crossed his muscular arms as he listened attentively to the witches. I noticed Genevieve taking him in with more than professional interest. I also sensed Taran's rising anger when Genevieve made a comment that caused him to chuckle.

Gem must have sensed the snap, crackle, and F-you surge of Taran's dwindling power because his head whipped around in our direction.

"Easy, Taran," Aric said quietly. "The last thing anyone needs, especially Celia, is another throw-down." He cleared his throat. If he meant to draw attention from Taran's swearing, I doubt he succeeded. "I'm taking Celia home. Gemini will see to your payment on the next business day, Genevieve."

She smiled and nodded. Betty Sue, not so much. As Aric's mate, I felt like I should also say something and hopefully placate the witches. "Thank you for your help. If I could ever return the favor, please let me know."

Betty Sue rolled her eyes and stormed away with Delilah hot on her trail. Genevieve's talisman glimmered when she called after them. "My sisters, I have not dismissed you."

Betty Sue's steps involuntarily slowed, but then she wrenched free from Genevieve's hold in a magical pull that snapped back in our faces like a rubber band. Delilah whirled with her hands out when Genevieve's magic gathered in a roar that shook the building.

"Don't do it, shug," Delilah warned. Her stare cut my way. "Betty Sue's just riled seeing how there're those around us who can't be trusted."

Aric and the Warriors answered the insult with growls loud enough to rattle the glass panels. Delilah ignored them, then she and Betty Sue vanished in a crack of lightning strong enough to rival Genevieve's power.

I rubbed my weary eyes. *Great, more Celia Wird fans. Pretty soon, they'll start their own club.*

Genevieve turned back to us, a small frown creasing her forehead yet somehow making her appear more lovely. "Forgive my sisters' rudeness, Celia. With your permission, I'll have them make a formal apology when you're feeling better."

"It's not necessary." I glanced over at Taran, who was scowling at Genevieve. "If you'll excuse us, I need to go home."

"Of course," she said, bowing her head slightly.

Gemini stepped toward Taran. "May I walk you out?"

"No," Taran answered. "Heaven forbid I'd interrupt your good time." She stomped away with more attitude in her step than I'd seen in months—head in the air and hips swaying in a way that told me we'd all better keep our distance. Emme followed hesitantly behind her, but not before stealing a worried glance over her shoulder.

Gemini watched her exit the ED, his brows knitting tight. "Just give her space," Aric told him. "In time, she'll find her way back to you."

My gaze cut to Aric. Despite everything Taran claimed Gemini had done, Aric seemed to feel that Taran had caused the rift between them.

"I'm not so certain," Gemini told him. He continued to stare ahead even though Taran was no longer in sight. It seemed Aric wanted to say more, but instead he carried me out of the ED and into the lot, carefully placing me within the safety of his Escalade.

Aric kept his arm around me on the way home. Aside from telling me the wolves would bring my car back, he didn't say much. He carried me up to our room when we arrived and turned on the shower.

All I wanted to do was crawl into our bed, except when I caught my reflection in the mirror, I realized it was definitely a bad idea. My hair was matted and caked with blood and bits of fur. Black ooze from Edith's injury drew a line from my right shoulder down to my breast. And don't get me started on the thick layer of blood and ash painting most of my body.

Crap. How am I even alive?

"What happened to you tonight, Aric?" I asked as I continued to stare in the mirror. I'd been afraid to ask him for fear that he'd feel worse, but now that we were alone, I needed to know.

Aric's eyes swept over the disgusting glop shellacking my body before finally settling on my face. "I couldn't sleep without you," he said quietly. "I'd gone downstairs to watch TV, trying to pass the time before I could visit you on your break. I was damn restless, but never once did I sense that you were in danger." He rubbed hard at his face, frustrated. "If it weren't for Gemini's *call,* I'd still be sitting in the family room like an idiot."

"Oh" was all I could manage.

He shook his head as his anger built. "I don't know what's happening to me, or to us. But I don't sense our bond like I used to. It's *killing me,* because I want it to be there, and it's not."

His light brown irises shimmered. I'd seen Aric cry a few times. Those moments were rare, but riven with sorrow worthy of his tears. Despite my putrid odor and the lingering scent of Genevieve's magic, I could scent his rising fear. It enveloped us, threatening to choke us and rob us of the future he'd promised.

My eyes stung with tears. Aric believed he was losing his connection to me. And I couldn't be sure he was wrong. Whatever plagued him was affecting us on a level I couldn't understand. I didn't have to be a being of magic to sense it.

"Aric . . ."

A single tear slid down his cheek, forcing me to avert my gaze. I'd always hated seeing others cry, even those I didn't know, partly because it was never a luxury I could afford.

Then I'd met Aric.

Without actually saying so, he'd given me permission to cry and, without meaning to, had often been the cause of my grief. But these weren't tears over the loss of our child, our friend, or our relationship. These were tears of the unknown, and his recognition that something had come between us.

I placed my hands over his. "I don't know what's happening, either, wolf," I said, my voice cracking before my own tears began. "But I promise you, we'll see it through together."

Aric yanked me to him, holding me close. I wrapped my arms around him, burying my face in his chest. "Celia, I love you. I would give you my soul if it meant sparing your life. No matter what happens—or what this is—you have to believe I love you. You are my life, sweetness."

"O-okay." I wiped my eyes and looked at him. "For better or for worse, right?"

He released a breath and managed a small smile. "For better or for worse," he repeated.

Aric released me slowly only to snatch me into an embrace when I swayed backward. "Shit," he said, lowering me to the edge of our whirlpool tub.

"I need to lie down soon," I said, trying to blink away the spots dancing in my vision. Aric stripped out of his clothes and tugged off the patient gown I wore, careful to maintain his hold on me. He lifted me and carried me into the shower, supporting me with one hand as he washed my hair before lathering my body with soap. I watched his expression while his hands swept over my breasts, legs, and bum. He wanted me. I could tell by the way his body reacted against mine, but he didn't take things further. And despite how weak I felt, part of me wished he had.

Aric dried me with a towel and massaged my skin with lotion. He meant to care for me, and protect me, yet his contact further stimulated his desire. He turned and tied the towel tight around his waist. But there was no hiding his need, even through the thick cotton.

When he turned to me again, he wouldn't look at me directly. I supposed he was embarrassed. I didn't fault him; we often made love following a shower, and yet he seemed disturbed by his body's response.

"Shit," he muttered.

I lowered my chin. If I could've managed, I would have spared him by showering alone, yet I sensed his yearning to feel close to me and perhaps make amends for his absence.

Aric carried me to bed, helping me yank on a pair of panties before slipping one of his T-shirts over my head. My body shivered, suddenly unbearably cold. "Baby, you're freezing," he said.

He pulled me under the covers, wrapping us with the heavy down comforter as he gathered me to him. My teeth chattered uncontrollably. God, I couldn't remember ever feeling so cold. I blamed my still-wet hair, the coolness of the room, and my blood loss, but I didn't panic. I was sure that the comforting heat that surrounded us as mates would warm me and ease the chill.

"Hold me," I begged him.

Aric stopped moving. "I . . . am," he whispered.

Despite the cold that continued to rack my body, it was his words that froze me in place. That familiar surge of heat never came.

The warmth between us was gone.

Chapter Nineteen

My fear that our connection was severed kept me awake for a long while. It was only when Aric's natural body heat warmed me that my body stopped shaking and I surrendered to sleep.

Aric didn't sleep. I knew that for a fact. Sometime around dawn, I woke up when the bright sunlight trickling through cracks in the blinds hit my face. Aric's fingers stroked my curls, just as they had when I first fell asleep. He blinked back at me with tired, bloodshot eyes ringed with shadows.

Thick scruff lined his jaw and deep frown lines etched his forehead. He was worried for us. Well, so was I. Regardless of what I'd said, I was scared senseless.

"I'll cover the windows," he told me quietly.

I clung to his waist when he tried to rise. "Stay with me," I mumbled, my body begging me to keep still.

"Sweetness . . ."

"Please, wolf." I adjusted my position, just enough so that the brightness wouldn't bother me. Almost immediately I returned to sleep.

I wasn't sure what time it was when I finally woke up. I only knew it was late in the morning. My legs felt rubbery and my gait was unsteady at best, but I managed to reach the bathroom and freshen up. I also managed to down two full glasses of water.

When I returned to the bedroom, Aric hadn't budged from his spot. He usually woke when I left his side. And while under other circumstances I wouldn't have given it much thought, too much had happened. I needed to act. I slipped into a pair of shorts and carefully stole away to our finished basement.

I moved quickly, hurrying past our three treadmills and row of workout equipment lining the wall. In addition to the gym, the basement had a small bar tucked into the corner. I edged around it, but I was scrambling faster than my body was ready for. I had to grasp the edge of the bar before I landed on my ass.

Carefully, I eased my way onto a bar stool, taking a moment to rest against the bar before reaching for our landline. As I tried to remember the number I needed, I felt what could only be described as a nudge. Although I wasn't sure how, I knew who was there even before I lifted my head.

Shah sat between a bottle of tequila and an unopened bottle of scotch. I sighed. "What are you doing here?" I asked, even though I realized he wouldn't answer.

I glanced over my shoulder, paranoia setting in. "You shouldn't be here. It's not safe."

Shah remained still as, well, stone. "I'm serious. I think you're better off in the stronghold Makawee created for you." Again, he didn't move. Maybe he knew or understood something I didn't. For a giant crystal, he'd more than proven he wasn't stupid. "Okay, buddy. If you don't want to be there, I won't make you go. You can stay close to me if you'd like, but I need you to hide, okay? I'm not sure what will happen if the wrong person or thing touches you, and you've been used enough."

A creak by the steps had me whipping around. I half-expected some evil creature to be slithering its way toward me.

But no one was there.

And yet I still sensed that I was being watched.

I reached to gather Shah just in case, but he was gone. His absence gave me comfort, in a way. Given my circumstances with Aric and all the trouble that found me last night, Shah wasn't safe anywhere near me. I only hoped that where he was, he would be. "Thank you," I whispered.

My attention returned to my task at hand. I took a breath and made a call I hoped I wouldn't regret, unable to shake the feeling that I was betraying Aric. But he and I needed help, and I didn't know where else to turn.

"Aric?" Martin's deep baritone said in greeting.

"No, it's Celia Wird."

I wasn't sure why I threw in my last name. It wasn't like Aric's Alpha didn't know who I was.

"Soon to be Celia Connor," he added gently. When I didn't say anything more, concern dripped into his tone. "You're not well, are you?"

"Not really," I answered, unable to keep my voice from shaking.

"Gemini filled me in on your condition. Perhaps Makawee could aid you in your healing."

"It's not that," I said. "I need to talk to you about Aric." I paused, suddenly uncomfortable with what I had to say. It was only because of my desperation to help my wolf that I finally spoke. "Things have been different between us since he proposed. They're strained—his anger, mine, and our insecurities seem to be eating us alive." My gaze dropped to my opposite hand. My nail beds were practically bleached from my blood loss. "We share a certain warmth between us," I said, trying to keep my focus. "I'm sorry, it's a good thing, but hard to describe."

"I understand this heat you're referring to." His voice faded. "I shared it with my mate; it's something fairly common among *weres*." He waited when I said nothing more. "Is it fading?" he finally asked.

I bit my bottom lip before answering. "It's gone," I admitted.

The silence was so pronounced on the other line, it was clear that I hadn't blessed him with good news.

"It was still there when Aric arrived at the hospital last night," I continued. "But when we went to bed, I didn't feel it anymore. Nor did I feel it when I woke up beside him. Do you think it could be related to his prior moon sickness infection?"

"I don't know," Martin answered. "There's not much we know about the infection because no *were* aside from Aric has ever survived it. The combination of your bond, your rare magic, and Aric's strength is the only plausible explanation for his recovery."

"And what if he hasn't fully recovered?" My heart clenched the more I thought about it. Moon sickness drove *weres* to murder anything in their path while slowly and painfully deteriorating their nervous system. "Could he be getting sick again?"

Wherever Martin was, he was pacing. I could hear his feet crossing a large room. "If he is, I'm confident you can see him through it, as you did before. But if you can't, you need to inform me at once."

My jaw involuntarily clenched. "So you can kill him and put him out of his misery?"

I wasn't being overly dramatic. That was the order the Elders had given when Aric was cursed with the disease.

Martin's tone softened. "No, Celia. Aric has proven his strength. And now, with young Daniel's power being revealed, I have faith we can save him. Whether it's moon sickness that plagues him or something else we've yet to unearth."

I dropped my forehead into my hand as a wave of nausea caused me to sway. "Then if it's not moon sickness, what could be happening?" I managed.

"I'm not sure. However, the effect Aric's condition is having on your connection concerns me. Celia, it should be impossible to weaken or sever a bond without your consent. Try to reestablish it, any way you can."

For a long time, I lay on the worn leather couch beside the bar, thinking about what Martin had said and trying to make sense of what was happening. But every time I had even a small inkling, my head would spin and muddle my thoughts.

The front door opened and closed upstairs before several pairs of feet padded into the kitchen. "Fried chicken or ribs?" Shayna asked.

"Chicken for dinner," Koda answered. "Ribs for tomorrow, and you for dessert."

Shayna squealed like she always did when he lifted her for a kiss. She giggled when they broke their kiss. "Puppy, Emme's watching."

Koda laughed. "No she's not, she's got her eyes closed."

"Don't mind me," Emme said, likely blushing.

I forced myself to sit, waiting for a moment until my vision cleared enough to stand. With feet that felt way too heavy, I trudged up the stairs and into the kitchen where my sisters were putting away groceries.

Everyone stilled when they saw me. "Hey," I said.

Koda rushed to my side and clasped my shoulders. He probably thought I was going to keel over. He was probably right.

"Damn, you look like shit."

"And a good afternoon to you, too," I answered, trying to force a smile.

Koda glanced over my shoulder then turned back to me, frowning. "Where's Aric?"

"Upstairs."

"And where were you?"

"Downstairs," I answered like a dork.

Aside from demons and their offspring, Koda was hands down the most intimidating individual I'd ever met, and that was when he was in a good mood. He narrowed his eyes. "What were you doing in the basement without him?"

"Ah, nothing."

"Nothing?" he asked, clearly annoyed that I was lying. His stare demanded an explanation. I wasn't a wimp, but I definitely pitied Koda and Shayna's future children then. God forbid they'd miss curfew without a good excuse.

"I'm going to go and check on Aric." Koda wouldn't release me. "You know, and make sure he's all right?" said the freakishly pale girl who hung out in the basement. "So, I'm guessing you should let go of me." I groaned when he wouldn't. "Come on, Koda. Don't give me a hard time."

Shayna edged her way to us and pried his hands from me. "She's not feeling well, puppy. Let my sister be with her mate."

The term stung me. Koda must have felt it, because the tension eased in his stance and he acknowledged me with as much kindness as his scary beast could muster. His gaze and that of my sisters burned hot against my back as I made my way to the stairs. I tried to move as normally as possible. For the most part I managed not to stagger or pitch backward down the steps. Except my body was pissed at having to walk up from the basement and buckled as I opened the door to our bedroom.

"Aric," I called, just before a swirl of spots clouded my vision.

I never hit the floor. Aric caught me. He carried me to the bed and yelled for Emme. And while I panted heavily and could feel my jugular throbbing, my brain managed to keep me conscious.

Everyone raced into the room, including Taran, who must have been hiding out in her bedroom. Emme touched my face with her small hands. She closed her eyes, but she didn't surround me with her soft yellow light. "There's nothing to heal," she said quietly. "Celia either needs three weeks of rest to recuperate or another transfusion."

The last thing I wanted was to be confined to a bed, waiting for my body to regenerate its normal blood volume. Something was wrong with Aric, and the super-nasties wouldn't stop until they found Shah. Nope. Bed rest was so not an option. I rolled onto my side and met my perky sister's face. "Shayna, you need to give me your blood."

Chapter Twenty

Aric wasn't happy when Koda told him I'd been lurking in the basement. Seriously, those were the big guy's exact words. "Remind me to kick your ass when I'm better," I mumbled, to which he actually grinned.

Okay, maybe that wasn't an ass I would easily kick.

The only thing that saved me was the pathetic state I was in. "You shouldn't have left our room without me, sweetness," Aric told me, frowning. "You could have fallen down the stairs in your condition."

"Sorry, love."

I was sorry for worrying everyone, but at the moment I was more terrified of what was going to happen to me. Aric had phoned Danny to come over while my sisters prepared to transfuse Shayna's blood into me. Aric said Danny should be present in case Shayna's werewolf blood needed to be "tamed."

Nice. Just *nice*. My suggestion seemed like a reasonable one at the time.

Danny arrived along with Bren. It was strange having everyone in our bedroom, and the wolves kept exchanging tension-filled glances.

"Don't worry, sweetie," Emme said as she secured the IV to my arm. "We have diphenhydramine ready in case you have an allergic reaction to the blood."

"And epinephrine if we need to restart your heart," Shayna said. "Not that we'll need it, dude," she added quickly when she caught my horrified expression.

I looked around in time to see Taran hide an antiquated pair of defibrillator paddles behind her back. *What the hell?*

"Do you think we'll need the cage?" Bren whispered to Koda.

"We'll see how she does," Koda muttered.

When they realized I'd heard them, Koda averted his eyes while Bren feigned a grin and gave me the thumbs-up.

I started searching for the nearest escape route. "Maybe this isn't a good idea," I said. Hell, the world had saved itself long before I'd ever showed up.

"Don't worry, Ceel. You're fine." Shayna pointed upward. "See, my blood's already transfusing."

I took in the makeshift IV pole Shayna had constructed out of old wire hangers with her gift. Sure enough, drops of blood were already running into the chamber.

"Do you feel okay, honey?" Emme asked me gently.

I nodded. I did feel pretty good. In fact, I felt great! It was almost as if I could feel my red blood cells increasing in numbers and new blood circulating throughout my body. I sat up in bed and watched in awe as my sunken thin veins widened and plumped while my pallor dissipated and my golden skin tone returned.

Werewolf blood good.

My muscles relaxed, like after a good stretch. I felt young and energized. I smiled at my loved ones gathered around the bed. They smiled back.

At first.

Almost in unison their smiles faltered. "What?" I asked, feeling something brush against my arms. When I looked down, I realized my hair was growing. It spiraled past my elbows, to my waist, and kept going.

"Maybe you should stop the transfusion now," Danny suggested.

Shayna reached for the clamp, but I snatched her wrist, keeping her still. "Relax," I said, followed by a spurt of maniacal laughter. "Everything's fine."

Our stares were locked, and while I was smiling, Shayna's eyes widened in apparent alarm.

"Stop the transfusion, *now*," Aric said.

Taran dropped the defibrillator pads and scrambled around Shayna. I took hold of her wrist with my free hand before she could touch the tubing. My jaw clenched, my fangs protruded, and a deep growl built in my throat. "I said, everything's *fine*."

"Oh *shit*," Bren said.

The wolves exchanged brief glances before they pounced on me all at once. Time went into fast-forward. I don't know exactly what happened. My mind only recalled a lot of grunting, hissing, and growling. I realized the hisses and growls had come from me when an invisible hand pushed against my chest. My eyes closed from its comforting feel. Whatever it was shoved me with feather-like softness until my back made contact with something flat and solid.

I pried open my lids. I had ended up with my back against the ceiling . . . floating. Below, the wolves were sprawled on the floor looking like someone, maybe me, had knocked them on their asses.

Aric blinked back at me in shock. In his left hand he held the IV tube and bag of blood. I looked at my arm and grinned. Although Aric must have used enough force to cause a deep gash when he pulled the catheter, my injury was healing on its own. "Cool," I said a little too psycho-like.

"Dan," Aric said slowly. "Why is Celia flying?"

"Ah, she's not flying. I think Emme's *force* is holding her up."

"I'm not touching her, I swear," Emme mumbled, sounding defensive. Her hands were clamped over her mouth as she stared at me. Damn, she looked terrified, but I guessed I didn't help matters when I began spinning on the ceiling like a super-sized top.

"Everything's fine," I said again. "Can I have some more blood?"

"No!" everyone yelled back.

"I meant the *force* in the blood you gave her last night, Emme," Danny explained. "Shayna's blood must have amplified your magic in it."

"Aw, hell," Bren said. "She's got Taran's blood, too. You don't think she's going to start exploding things with fire like she did last time?"

I stopped whirling around. "Only if you make me mad," I answered, throwing in another nutso laugh.

Everyone stilled. *Geez, I was only kidding.* "The vamps are right," I said. "You guys have like, no sense of humor."

"Taran," Aric muttered through clenched teeth. "Put her to sleep."

She nodded, but not before releasing a bunch of swears. It took some doing on her part before her irises could bleach to white and her power could spark. Soft tendrils of blue and white mist emanated from her core and slithered like snakes in the air toward me.

"Ah, ah, ah," I said, just before spinning like a freaking pinwheel.

And just like that it was naptime for my sisters and wolves.

I watched them sleeping contentedly for a while, but then my fingertips began to itch. I felt the need to climb a tree like my tigress would in the jungles of India, to feel wood scratch beneath my claws. Lucky for me, Tahoe had the perfect forest-like atmosphere my inner kitty needed.

While I didn't know how to control the bit of power that Emme's blood gave me, I did give it my best try. Since I continued to hover over the bed, I thought it would be the perfect place to land. I cleared my mind and concentrated on releasing the energy keeping me up.

Everything would have been fine had I just tucked in my arm. I landed hard and dislocated it when it banged against the foot of our sleigh bed.

No sooner did I sit up than my arm popped back into place. While it did hurt, there was a warm, invigorating sensation at the site that gave me an added boost. Had I been fighting the extra energy would have empowered me to keep going.

So I kept going, all the way out the window.

My swift punch knocked out the screen so I could climb out. It was a chilly late October afternoon, but the strong breeze enlivened my beast. My claws protruded from my fingertips and toes, helping me climb the side of our house and onto the roof. I stretched at the top. The shingles felt cold against my bare feet. I jogged in place, enjoying the bouncing sensation against my soles. While it felt fantastic to move, I had a lot of pent-up energy that willed me to act, to seek out evil, to go after anything that sought to taint this magnificent world.

"Celia Wird! What are you doing up there?"

I got my wish.

Mrs. Mancuso, my elderly neighbor from the Planet Yardstick Up Your Ass, was outside planting mums along her front walkway. She threw down her garden tools and stood, scowling. When we first moved in, I actually felt sorry for her. She lived alone and had neck skin dangling to her knees. It soon became apparent that she was alone because she was simply too miserable to be around.

Mrs. Mancuso narrowed her beady rat eyes. "I always knew you were smoking crack. I'm calling the police. You're going to jail, Celia Wird. You and your drug-dealing sisters!"

I didn't kill her, though my tigress tried to convince me it would be one less evil entity besmirching the world. Instead I did what any decent being with werewolf blood coursing in her veins would have done. I dropped my shorts and mooned her. "Smoke this," I said, slapping my ass.

Full-out cackling from the front lawn had me pulling up my shorts and peering over the roof's edge. Taran was rolling on the damp grass in hysterics. Her arms were clutching her sides and she was kicking her stiletto-clad feet in the air. Danny and Emme simply stared, their expressions frozen in shock.

Emme dropped the keys she was holding on the grass. "Oh my goodness," she whispered.

The front door was thrown open. Koda and Shayna ran out. "Shit!" Koda yelled. "Aric, she's on the roof!"

"What?" Aric said from inside the house. He sprinted outside with his cellphone clutched in his hand, eyes wide. "Never mind, Heidi," he said into the phone. "We found her."

Bren rushed out, dragging a set of thick shackles. He tucked the chains behind his back and grinned. "Hey, Ceel. Come on down, I want to talk to you." To Koda he muttered, "Get the cage."

"Celia, don't panic," Aric said. "I'm coming up."

"I'm not panicking," I answered, unsure as to why everyone was acting funny. The restlessness I felt was quickly increasing. I had so much energy that my body couldn't keep still. I jogged in place at full speed while pumping my arms erratically. Aric paused briefly to watch me before soaring onto the porch roof and scaling the side of the house. Next door, Shayna was rather unsuccessfully attempting to calm Mrs. Mancuso.

"Get away from me, you whore," Mrs. Mancuso snapped when Shayna approached her with her palms out. For someone over eighty, Mrs. Mancuso was extremely agile. The old hag leapt through her yard like a newborn fawn and reached for her garden hose. Like Vin Diesel, albeit with way looser skin, she pointed her weapon and fired, spraying the crap out of Shayna.

It was then Taran stopped laughing.

"Son of a bitch, woman. What the hell's wrong with you—?"

Mrs. Mancuso was a woman possessed. She must have been waiting and plotting for years to use her gardening tools and supplies against us. She doused Taran with water while simultaneously pelting her with flower bulbs. Danny and Koda stepped in. Danny was taken out almost immediately by a handful of potting soil to the eyes. Koda went after her next. I didn't see what happened because Aric grabbed me in a tight bear hug and pulled me away from the ledge.

"Bren, open the cage!" he yelled.

"Baby, what are you doing?" I asked. Before he could answer, my body began to convulse.

Shah, a voice demanded.

Shah, it said louder.

Shah! it screamed.

Aric tightened his hold. Instead of comforting me, it made me loopy and I shook more forcibly. My vision whirled in a blur and my breathing rate went into overdrive. I was trapped, like a cornered beast. And my inner tigress didn't like it one bit.

I grunted and growled, the energy inside me boiling over. "Let me go, Aric," I pleaded. "I need to run, I need to run."

"Celia—"

"*I need to run!*" I screamed.

Aric released me and I immediately jumped off the roof. I briefly saw Mrs. Mancuso wave two angry middle fingers at me before I tore down toward the lake. Aric sprinted after me, with Danny hauling ass behind him.

"Celia, stop. Let Dan touch your skin!" Aric yelled from behind me. "We need to figure out what's wrong."

I couldn't stop. Every cell in my body was imploring me to go faster, but I did manage to slow down enough for Danny to catch up to me. He grabbed my wrist as we continued to run. Other than a slight popping noise in my ear, I didn't feel a thing. "Celia's okay," Dan said, gasping. "She just received too much of Shayna's blood."

"You *think?*" Aric growled.

"The effects feel like they're deteriorating as she runs," he said, releasing me. "Just let her go, she'll burn it off."

I sped off then, and *damn,* did it feel good to increase my speed. Aric picked up his pace and joined me. "I'm okay, Aric. Check on the others. I'll be back as soon as I can."

"I'm not leaving you," he said. "The others can take on Mancuso alone." He thought about it. "Maybe."

Well, let's hope.

We cut through the path leading to the road. We crossed it quickly and hurried onto the beach just when it started to rain. My bare feet hit the cool sand, moving fast. Shayna's blood was amazing. I couldn't remember feeling so alive.

I thought I'd run a few miles and then turn around, but I kept going long after we passed the five-mile mark. My physical endurance seemed unstoppable. We reached the seven-mile mark at full speed and yet my legs had no desire to slow down.

Aric dutifully ran next to me despite the thunder, lightning, and hailstorm that had begun. It wasn't until we ran another mile, however, that Aric and I began talking. "I mooned Mrs. Mancuso."

Aric's head whipped around to me before he let out a laugh. He coughed some as well. I assumed it was hard for him to pant and guffaw at the same time. "Taran's essence in your system probably had something to do with it," he said, gasping.

I groaned. "Why couldn't I have just acted like Emme? You know, blushed a few times and called it a day."

"Because Taran's blood is more dominant," he answered, continuing to laugh. "My guess is that Shayna's wolf side responded more to Taran's aggression."

We ran another three miles before I finally relaxed enough to turn back in the direction of the house. By the time we were almost to the path that led back to our neighborhood I'd slowed my full-out run to a fast walk.

Aric reached for my hand the moment we stepped onto the path. I gasped when that wonderful heat between us returned full force. He stared at our entwined fingers, and we slowed to a stop. He breathed a sigh of relief and smiled, a sense of peace appearing to envelop his entire aura. "It's back," he said.

My grip tightened. "I know."

Twilight was quickly approaching. Our porch light flickered on as we reached the front walkway.

Shayna and Koda glanced up from where they lay sprawled on the couch. "You okay, Ceel?"

"I'm fine," I said, this time meaning it.

Aric gathered the hair that dangled to my knees and pressed a kiss to my forehead. "She just needed to burn off some energy."

Koda laughed. "No shit, she did."

"Where is everyone?" I asked.

"Emme took off with Bren after he talked Mrs. Mancuso out of suing you for public indecency."

More than anything, Emme's decision to leave with Bren caught my attention. "Did Emme and Bren say where they were headed?" *Please don't say to bed. Oh, please, please, please.*

"Not really. She said something about helping him out in his apartment." Shayna cocked her head. "Why are you looking at me like that?"

"Oh. Sorry." I cleared my throat, but it did little to clear the disturbing images racing through my head. I loved Bren. I truly did. But Emme had been lonely since Liam left her and his death practically destroyed her. My little sister was vulnerable. I only hoped Bren realized as much. . .

"What about Danny and Taran?" I asked, struggling to come back to the moment.

"Danny left. He needed to get back to the lab." She made a face. "Gemini stopped by to make sure we were okay. He and T got into a bad fight and she left. I tried calling to check on her, but she's not answering her phone."

I played with my hair, hating what was happening between them. "She probably needs some time alone. I think the least we can do is give her space."

"I know," Shayna said, her voice quiet. She rose and motioned to my hair. "What are you going to do with all that hair, Rapunzel?"

"Donate it," I answered at the same time Aric said, "Keep it."

He tugged on it, smiling. "All right, but it could have been fun."

Shayna grinned and quickly braided my hair. She had Aric hold the end while she skipped into the kitchen and used her gift to transform a wooden spoon into a sharp pair of scissors. In one motion she cut the braid. She played with my ends, smiling. "If you want, I'll even them out, maybe add a few layers?"

"Tomorrow, okay?" I glanced at Aric as he continued to speak quietly to Koda.

"Do me a favor, Koda," he said. "Go to the Den and ask Makawee to check on Shah."

Koda frowned. "Why?"

Aric rubbed his chest. "I don't think he's safe there. I think he's better off here, with us. If she's agreeable, ask her to give him to you, but don't touch him directly."

Koda leaned back on his heels. "You're sure about this? After all the shit that went down last night?"

"It's clear Shah wants to be with Celia, and I'm not certain the Den is the best place for him."

Koda nodded slowly. "I don't agree, Aric. But if this is what you think is best, I'll leave right now."

Shayna shoved my braid into a giant sandwich bag and skipped to Koda's side. "I'll go with you, puppy. Maybe we can pick up some dinner on the way."

Any wariness that remained in Koda seemed to vanish when Shayna wrapped her thin arms around his big bulging one. He bent to meet her lips. "Okay, baby."

Aric kicked off his shoes and led me upstairs when they left. He shut the door and stripped out of his shirt, taking a moment to push his long hair away from those tantalizing brown eyes. "Do you want to take a shower?" he asked.

His chest continued to rise and fall in steady motions and drops of perspiration or rain glistened against the hard muscles of his chiseled torso.

"Later," I answered before I pounced.

It seemed I still had some energy left after all.

Chapter Twenty-one

I rolled onto my side sometime later, blinking with my tigress eyes to make out the images in our dark room. Aric had left our bed. My hands pressed the sheet over my breasts as I sat up. I frowned. The house seemed unusually quiet. Yes, my family was out, but it was more than that. Something was different in our bedroom, as if all life had vanished.

I slipped out of bed and pulled on a pair of panties. "Aric?" I called, although something within me insisted he wasn't there. I sat on the edge of the bed and waited for—I don't know— sound maybe?

Heavy breathing behind our closed bathroom doors had me sighing in relief. I smiled. Aric was there, I wasn't alone. "I thought you'd left," I said.

His breathing stopped, cut off as if with the flip of a switch. Something in the quiet riled my beast and sent her on high alert. Her agitation poked at me, making me uneasy. I tried to settle her as best I could, reminding her that Aric was with us, when Shah suddenly materialized on my dresser.

My eyes widened. He shouldn't have been here. I shook my head at him, trying to get him to leave. My tigress warned against announcing his presence. I listened and mouthed to Shah that it wasn't safe for him here.

From one breath to the next, he was gone. I pushed the hair out of my eyes and returned to bed, keeping my attention on the closed double doors. Once more, only silence greeted me. "Aric? Are you all right, love?"

Aric pushed open the doors. Moonlight trickled in from the skylight behind him, shadowing his face. I didn't give it much thought and edged away, making room for him beside me. "I'm starving. Let's order takeout, okay?"

I turned and reached for my cellphone while I waited for him to answer, then scrolled through my list of contacts. "The bar and grill down the road should still be open. Do you want something from there?"

Aric crawled under the covers without speaking. There was something different about him, but I didn't initially know what. His large hand came to rest on my hip. "Not now," he murmured in an unusually deep voice.

I thought he wanted to make love, but instead of his gentle teases and strokes that usually preceded our intimacy, he slapped his hand over my scars and yanked me to him. I startled, clasping his wrist when he moved his hand aggressively south.

I dropped my phone. "Aric, stop. You're hurting me." He wrenched free from my grasp and grabbed my breast, squeezing it hard. Fear and shock warred within me, blinding me to what was happening. I struggled to shrug him off, but his hold on me tightened, and his motions grew more demanding, forcing me to submit.

He rammed his hips against me. "Aric, stop—*stop!*" My breath lodged in my throat. At once I realized his scent was completely gone and so was any trace of warmth. A cold chill swept down my body, making my stomach lurch.

This isn't Aric.

I fought against his hold. His teeth clamped down on my neck, piercing my skin with all the aggressiveness of a hungry beast upon his prey. Warm fluid trickled down my neck. "Shut up!" he growled when I screamed.

Even through a mouthful of blood, I knew the voice was not his.

My legs kicked out savagely at his shins. His bone snapped beneath my heel. He grunted, but instead of releasing me he wrapped his injured leg around both of mine and clasped his hand over my mouth. I could barely breathe, the force of his hand bruising my lips.

I couldn't get enough air through my nose. My breaths had quickened to racehorse speed, and my heart threatened to explode from the rush of terror. I tried to *change* and break away, but my tigress was gone.

He held me with just one arm while his other hand released my mouth only to grab at my breasts brutally. I let out a choked sob. *"Aric, no!"*

He flipped me onto my back, landing so his knees pinned my arms. I was screaming and crying, knowing I was about to be raped. I knew this, and that thought hurt more than the pain against my arms and the swelling bruises to my breasts. My cries grew hysterical. I fought and kicked, bucking hard, and still I couldn't get free.

He released a horrid growl and pulled back his fist. Everything slowed, allowing me to meet the wretched cruelty in his eyes. He looked like Aric, but there was nothing of the real him left. And although I knew this, I reached out, hoping to find a trace of my wolf locked within this shell.

"You told me you'd never hurt me," I choked. "You told me you loved me."

He stilled with his fist in the air, closing his eyes and his mouth tight. There was a deep rumbling in his chest, like lava building within a volcano. Whatever this thing was, it was about to erupt. I needed to escape, yet I remained too helpless to move.

His head jerked hard to one side then the other, forcing his neck to the point of breaking. A growl mixed with a curse escaped his lips while a turmoil of emotions flooded his face—sadness, guilt, gut-wrenching fear, but most of all primal fury.

When I was sure he'd kill me, his face whipped back to meet mine. Sweat dripped down to his chin, and just as abruptly as he'd attacked, he withdrew, stumbling from the bed and backing into the corner.

I scrambled to the floor panting so hard I thought I'd pass out. "A-Aric?"

He swiveled his head from side to side in an awkward gesture that told me he still hadn't regained control. "Run, Celia," he rasped. *"Run."* He searched the room as if something else was there, until he faced me once more. "You need to go—do you hear me? *You need to go, now!"*

Tears trickled down my face. Without turning my eyes from his I reached for the robe at the foot of the bed. I slapped at the silky fabric several times, before my trembling hands could finally lift it. I continued to shake as I pulled it on, terrified to be naked. "No. I won't leave you."

Aric reeled fast enough to make me jump. His hand gripped our leather chair, crushing the frame with the strength of his grip. "Go," he urged. *"Go!"*

The tendons and muscles stretched along Aric's broad back, straining and threatening to sever his spine. He was in agony. Something was tearing him in half.

I covered my mouth with my hand, knowing I should leave; yet I couldn't force my feet to run. He needs us, my tigress insisted. He needs *you.*

My entire body shook violently as I inched my way to him. Every rational thought should have sent me bolting from the house. But I couldn't leave him, and neither could my tigress. My fingers quivered as I reached to touch him, but just as my skin skimmed over his, Aric catapulted through the window.

Glass exploded in his wake and there was a loud thud as he hit the ground below. A sharp burning sensation filled my lungs as I took my first full breath. For a moment, my body simply swayed in place and my vision seemed to double. Somewhere deep within me, my tigress roared, snapping me out of this cloud of confusion.

The breeze from my shattered picture window beckoned me toward it. I peered over the damaged wood of the sill to find Aric on the front lawn seizing violently, his body illuminated by the light streaming from the living room window.

I leapt from the bedroom window onto the thick grass just as Koda's and Gemini's screeching cars pulled up to the sidewalk. Koda and Gem raced out growling with all the ferociousness of hell itself. Their eyes wandered to me as they scrambled to Aric's side. "What happened?" Koda asked. His tone was low, vicious, deadly—making it clear he was seconds from slaughtering.

I couldn't answer. Shayna had sprinted to my side as I watched Aric convulse. Nothing made sense, nothing was right. *Jesus Christ,* what was happening?

My quickening breaths burned my chest. "Ceel?" Shayna shook my shoulders, her voice shrill. "Celia, what happened to Aric?"

I took in her familiar aroma, trying to gather comfort from it to speak. Koda and Gemini spoke in a rush, either to me or to Aric, I wasn't sure who. It took all I had to concentrate on Shayna's quaking voice. "Oh God, Ceel. What happened to you?" She tried to close my robe, but I wouldn't allow it and wrenched away from her.

There was another screech of tires and the quick footsteps of others running toward me. Emme and Taran were suddenly there, muffling their screams. Strong arms fell upon my shoulders; I yelped and jumped away, crying into my hands.

"Celia," Gemini's normally calm voice rang out ferociously. "You need to tell us what's happening so we can help Aric." He took a step toward me at the same time I took another step back. *"Celia,"* he said more insistently. "Who attacked you?"

I buried my face further into my hands and released several choked sobs. Shayna wrapped an arm around me. "She's going into shock!" she yelled.

It was true; I was losing it. Just like I had the time we thought he was dead. I couldn't allow myself to fall back into that darkness. Aric, or whatever was left of him, was in danger.

"Celia, tell us who attacked you," Gemini growled.

While I couldn't speak through my sobs, I did manage to point . . . at Aric.

All eyes that had been watching me turned to Aric in time to see him arch his spine with enough force to crack it. Every vein in his body rushed violently to the surface of his skin as if trying to rip through it. Black fluid pulsed along each branch. Whatever had infected Aric was forcing its way through his system.

I completely fell apart. Aric's body was being ravaged and there was nothing any of us could do. Koda was yelling something to Gem when what sounded like every bone in Aric's back crunched. He collapsed, his head falling limply to the side. He wasn't moving, he wasn't breathing, he was . . .

I scrambled to his side, where Koda had remained. My knees sunk into the mud, the grass beneath and around him torn up by his violent thrashing. I wanted so badly to touch him, but being so close to him brought all my fright back in one nauseating rush. I couldn't stop shaking; I was going to be sick.

"Aric. *Aric*. Wake up! Breathe, damnit. *Breathe!*" Koda said, shaking him.

Behind me, I could hear Emme crying softly. Gemini was on the phone with Martin, speaking fast. "Don't let either one of them out of your sight," Martin's deep baritone ordered. "I'm coming."

Aric's face turned from blue to gray as the sickly black fluid shoved its way through even the smallest capillaries of his face. My cries strengthened, and I began to scream. *"Wake up, baby. Please, wake up!"*

Aric's eyes remained closed and his chest failed to rise. He was dying while I watched, and it ripped my soul apart. I forced my hand to touch his chest. I barely brushed his skin when a cloud of smoke in a silhouette of his body rose above his still form. The image was Aric's perfect double in shades of black and dark gray—every hair, every muscle, every feature, outlined to reflect his unmoving twin below. I watched it with wide eyes until it disintegrated into the night.

Like a strong gust of wind, Aric's clean aroma filled the night air. He let out a pained roar and his eyes flew open, latching onto me. The intensity of his stare cemented me in place. No one moved, but then Aric lurched forward, reaching for me.

I stumbled away before he could touch me. The wolves hauled him back, sensing my fear.

Deep remorse and sorrow etched lines into his face. *"Sweetness,"* he pleaded. "I'm not going to hurt you. I just need to hold you."

Anguished tears dripped from my eyes. He was back. My Aric was back. I tried to step forward only to fall and land in Taran's arms. "You son of bitch!" she screamed at him. "What did you do to her?"

Emme tried to close the front of my robe, like Shayna had before. I looked down, confused as to why until I saw what they saw—what everyone saw. *Oh God.*

My breath caught in my throat. I should have realized I was completely exposed, but I was blind to anything but Aric's suffering. Bruises shaped like long fingers painted my breasts, revealing the marks from the assault. What was worse was the angry red handprint over my thick scars.

Horror fell upon me like a landslide of boulders until numbness forced its way forward, claiming me. My panties were torn, the thin lace barely enough to keep the sides together.

I folded the sides of my silk robe closed and crossed my arms, hugging my body. Everyone knew I had almost been raped. And everyone believed it was at the hands of the man who told me he loved me.

Thick tears fell down my face, mixing with the blood that continued to seep out of my neck. Emme said something about needing to heal me, but my gaze had returned to Aric.

He tried forcing his way to me, yet the wolves held strong. *"Celia,"* he begged. "It wasn't me. It wasn't me, sweetness."

"Aric," Gemini warned, his tone tight. "Leave her alone. You're scaring her."

Aric stared back at me with eyes that implored me to tell them all that I wasn't afraid of him. But at that moment, I still was, despite knowing he wasn't technically the being who attacked me.

Taran didn't seem to care. Every whisper of hair along my arms stood on end as she gathered her magic. A crowd of concerned neighbors, including Mrs. Mancuso, had arrived to investigate the cause of the commotion. Taran was trying to alter their memories. Yet I suspected she wasn't far from turning her power on Aric.

I vaguely remember Emme and Shayna taking me into the house. They led me back to my room, but I didn't want to return to where I'd been attacked.

"I-I don't want to go in there," I stammered. "I'm scared," I admitted.

Shayna and Emme paused. "It's okay, Ceel. You're not alone," Shayna said quietly. "Emme, take her to your room and heal her. I'll run in and get you something to wear."

I showered in the bathroom that connected Emme and Shayna's rooms as soon as Emme healed my wounds. I had a good cry as the water sprayed down my skin, needing to unleash one last time as all the impurities of the assault were washed away.

Aric and the wolves shuffled downstairs where they were waiting to speak to me. Their voices, while muffled, carried all the strain and anger from the incident. I knew I had to face them and explain what had happened. But sweet heavens, I so didn't want to.

I stepped out of the shower and dressed in the yoga pants and long-sleeved T-shirt Shayna had brought me. For a brief instant, I simply stood there, until a familiar nudge had me looking toward the vanity.

Once again, there was Shah. I went to him, staring down, but careful not to touch him. An odd pull had me edging closer. He wanted me to take him. I shook my head. "I'm not your holder, no matter what you say."

The pull increased. "You don't owe me anything, Shah," I said. "And I think you've been abused enough." Suspicion made me glance over my shoulder toward the closed door. "Look, I don't know what's going on, but I do know you're not safe."

You're not alone, multiple voices said.

I whirled around. Nothing was there except for me and Shah.

You're not alone, the voices repeated, seeming to come from every direction.

"Shah . . . you need to go, bud," I whispered.

I waited for him to vanish then stepped into Emme's room. She and Shayna sat on her bed. Taran waited by the door. I knew they'd heard me crying in the shower. They looked as good as I felt. Shayna wiped her nose as she struggled to hold back her tears. Emme was crying into her hands while Taran leaned against the door frame with her arms crossed, appearing ready to kill. All of us had been abused in foster care; my experience with Aric had opened up old wounds.

My cellphone buzzed on the bureau. "It's probably Misha again," Taran said. "He keeps calling, wanting to talk to you. We told him you were safe, but he insists on speaking with you directly."

I picked up the phone. "Hello?"

"Taran told me you were attacked by that mongrel," Misha hissed on the other end.

I tugged on the edge of my T-shirt, trying to cover myself more. "It wasn't like that, Misha."

"I am in flight from Paris. My family will escort you to my residence, where you will be safe until my arrival."

"It's not necessary, Misha, I—"

"Yes, it is," Misha ground out. "I felt your terror. I felt your pain. And I felt it all at the hands of that mongrel."

"It wasn't Aric, Misha. And I'm not going anywhere—"

"*Celia.*"

"Misha, something is happening. I'm not sure what it is, but Aric wasn't who hurt me." I put an extra push into my tone. "I assure you, Aric wasn't the cause."

"I'm not so certain."

I let out a shaky breath. "I am. Look, as soon as I know more, I'll call you. In the meantime, be safe. I'm not sure what we're dealing with here."

"Very well. But know this, if that mongrel harms you, the treaty between my kind and *weres* will end, and we'll deem his actions a declaration of war."

He disconnected, and for a moment all I could do was stare at the screen. Shayna inched her way forward. "The Elders are downstairs. Bren's there, too. They want to see you. Are you up for it?"

I nodded. "We need answers and we need to get to the bottom of this."

My sisters nodded in unison and started to move toward the door when I stopped them. "Just. . ."

"What, dude?" Shayna asked quietly.

"I need some space from Aric. I don't think I'll be able to focus if he's too close based on what's happened."

"I'll make it clear he needs to keep away," Taran answered in a dark voice that gave me absolutely no comfort.

I met her square in the face. "I don't want more trouble, Taran. Like I said, it wasn't Aric that attacked me. I'm only asking for some distance between us."

She didn't respond other than to glare. I rubbed my arms as if cold and left the room with my sisters following closely behind me. We walked down the back stairs and into the kitchen. Shayna slung her arm around my shoulders as we reached the edge of the granite-topped island. Emme and Taran walked forward to stand slightly in front of us. With the exception of Aric, who paced restlessly, all the wolves were seated at the table.

They stood when it became clear that this was as close as we'd approach. Aric stopped pacing and prowled toward me.

Taran blocked his path. "Back off, Aric. Celia needs her space," she told him flatly.

Aric's anger seemed to intensify, yet he nodded and joined the wolves at the far end of the table. Bren swore and scratched at his beard as he took me in. "Damn, Celia," he said. After scrutinizing me closer he left the table and stomped toward me. He pulled me away from Shayna, thereby declaring he was taking over bodyguard duty.

Aric released a threatening growl. I knew his beast was troubled and was determined that he, and not Bren, should be the one protecting me. Except Bren was no submissive wolf and answered his Alpha's growl with one of his own.

I squeezed Bren's arm, keeping my voice firm. "Stop it. Both of you."

Martin's tone demonstrated the strength of his position as Elder. "Aric, rein in your temper. You're upsetting your mate."

Aric backed away from the head of the table, closer to the sliding glass doors leading out to our deck. It was as far away as he could get from me in the room. And I hated it.

For a long time, no one said anything. Finally, Aric spoke. "I should be the one at your side, Celia. It should be me keeping you safe."

His voice was laced with anger and exhaustion. Taran's was all ire. "That's a laugh, considering you tried to rape her!"

Aric went ballistic. He smashed his fist through the table and split it down the center. It took all the wolves to stop him from speeding toward Taran. "I would never hurt her and you fucking know it!"

His face darkened to purple and all the muscles strained beneath his tight blue shirt. He remained seconds from releasing his beast. I lurched forward, but Bren hauled me back. Aric saw me trying to reach him and attempted to barrel his way to me.

"No," Martin warned. "For the time being, you must keep your distance."

Although I didn't want to, I stopped fighting to reach him. Aric refused to succumb and continued to ram his way to me. Makawee stepped between us and placed her hand on Aric's head. There was a faint howl of wolves and Aric collapsed to his knees, breathing hard. It was only then that the wolves released him. They continued to watch him their guard vigilant.

Gemini closed the distance between him and Taran, although he remained watchful of Aric's movements. "Aric *called* us," he told her. "He *called* us and told us Celia was in danger and that we needed to protect her."

Taran pointed an accusing finger toward Aric. "How do you know it wasn't all a setup—so he could kill you, too?"

"Taran," Koda said, his tone just above a snarl. "You didn't hear his *call*. *We did*. He was howling at us, desperate to save Celia."

Aric rose slowly, his stance rigid. "I wasn't in my own body. My wolf and I were being forced out as we slept. I woke up disoriented and stumbled into the bathroom. It was then I knew something was inside me." He spoke through ragged breaths and met me with savage eyes. "I saw . . . I saw everything that was happening to you. Somehow, I shoved my way back in, but I barely had any control." His jaw clenched tight. "I tried to break my own neck. When that didn't work, and I was close to losing what hold I had, I threw myself out the window."

My hands fell to my sides. I remembered how his head had snapped so forcefully from side to side and how he had so suddenly vanished.

He let out a breath, trying to soothe his anger as his hands balled into fists and his eyes shimmered with regret. "I fought that spirit inside of me with everything I had, Celia. You have to believe that I could never hurt you. . ."

He couldn't finish, but I knew what he meant. I could sense his disgrace and shame as if it were my own. This time, no one could keep me from him.

Aric snatched me into his arms when I shot forward, the scent of his clean aroma and the heat from his body easing my remaining fear. He whispered soft wolfish words, comforting my tigress. I didn't understand the words, but understood the vow within the soft tones. He would protect me, even if it cost him his life.

No one moved for a long while, giving us moments we needed. Melancholy replaced the tension in the room. I understood why. Just because Aric and I were holding each other, it didn't mean we were safe.

"Gemini, phone Genevieve," Martin finally said. "We need the help of a witch."

Taran stiffened as she watched Gem tap the screen of his cellphone. The moment Gem was done explaining what had happened, Genevieve's normally serene voice grew urgent. "Get out of the house— *get out of the house now.*

Chapter Twenty-two

Despite the careful inspection Genevieve had performed several weeks back, she was convinced that something possessed our home. When we stepped out onto the front porch, the Catholic schoolgirls were waiting to escort me to Misha's house.

Oh goody.

I refused. They insisted. The wolves growled. The vampires hissed. Eventually the good Catholics let me leave, but only because both Elders were present and at least for the time being, they knew better than to break the treaty signed between their kinds.

We ended up at the Hyatt in Incline Village. Emme, Taran, and I shared a room. And while we were all on the same floor, Aric was in his own suite, as were Koda and Shayna.

Gemini stayed behind at our house to wait for Genevieve and a few members of her coven. He said she'd refused Delilah and Betty Sue's help. I knew they weren't getting along, but to flat-out refuse them struck me as odd.

Bren had insisted on staying in our room, but Martin reasoned that it wasn't a good idea and sent him home. "Based on the evening's events, Aric's inner beast is feeling especially protective," Martin explained outside of our room. "Young Brendan, being an unmated wolf, is seen as competition."

Emme turned away from us, strangely upset, except I couldn't offer her comfort just then. Instead, I addressed Martin. "But Bren and I are only friends. Aric knows this."

Martin glanced up at Aric, who waited down the hall. He'd been ordered by Martin to keep his distance until we knew for sure what was happening, and that the entity that had possessed him could no longer seize control over him. Aric obeyed, but had refused to leave me. Martin scrutinized me with compassion. "I realize what you're saying, Celia. But this is one of those moments when you can't reason with a wolf." He tilted his head. "Be safe. If you need me, we'll be at your home waiting to see what Genevieve's coven uncovers."

We watched him disappear into the elevator. With a huff, Taran stepped into our room with Emme directly behind her. I tried to follow, but Aric called out to me. "Celia, wait." I looked at him. He seemed so far away even though only a few feet separated us. It wasn't right not to be with him. Damn, we'd already spent too much time apart. I wasn't sure what he saw in my expression, but it was enough to upset him. "Good night," was all he said.

"Good night," I mumbled.

Shayna came to see me a few minutes later, carrying roses. "They're from Aric. He wanted me to tell you that he loves you and that he's really sorry."

"Sorry he tried to rape her or sorry for beating her up?" Taran asked.

Anger surged through me. "Shut up, Taran," I snapped.

Her initial shock turned to fury. "What the hell is your problem? I'm trying to stick up for you. We're all better off without these damn wolves messing up our lives—"

"Enough," I hissed, shoving my face into hers. "Do not put the shit you're going through with Gem back on us."

We glared at each other. In the end, Taran's bitch was no match for my tigress. She averted her gaze and snatched her purse from the dresser. "Screw this," she said, stomping toward the door. "Screw you, too, Celia."

"Taran, don't go," Shayna called after her. "We don't know what's happening."

Taran slammed the door behind her. I slumped to the bed exhausted. I didn't like fighting with her. And I knew she was angry about my assault. But she was also hurting from her own turmoil and it had begun to cloud her judgment.

Emme sat next to me. "She'll be back. I'm sure of it."

I didn't agree. Taran was angry and feeling alone. I could relate. Aric was my fiancé and we weren't even allowed in the same room together. For heaven's sake, how much more drama could there be in one night?

I propped myself up on some pillows and glanced at the flowers Shayna had brought. She'd filled an ice bucket with water and placed the bicolored pink and dark red roses inside. They were gorgeous and yet they made me sad. Aric didn't owe me an apology. Something else did. And that something would pay if I could get my hands on it.

I stood abruptly and tried to prepare for bed. It was three in the morning when I finally crawled under the sheets and almost six when I crawled back out. I couldn't sleep, haunted with the memories of my past abuse and the assault. Every time I closed my eyes, I relived what I had been forced to endure. The memories were graphic and brutal. I recalled every detail—the lighting in the room, the smells, the sounds, and the horrible feeling of helplessness.

I brushed my teeth, threw on a sports bra and shorts, and left to check out the first-floor gym. When I opened the door, I found Aric sitting against the wall opposite my room.

He stared back at me with sad eyes encircled with dark shadows. It was him—really him; his aroma of water crashing over stones greeted me with tremendous warmth.

I forced my hand from the door handle and sat against the wall across from him.

"Hi," he said quietly.

"Hi, wolf."

He pulled a knee forward to lay his forearm over it. "I couldn't stay in my room," he said. "I needed to know you were safe."

A single tear slid down my face. "Thank you," I whispered.

Aric inspected me closely. "I don't want to ask, but I need to know. Are you afraid of me?"

He could have scented my fear from down the hall. My gaze dropped to the carpet. Gold diamonds trailed along the dark burgundy loops. "It's not that I'm afraid of you," I answered honestly. "But I am afraid of what this entity could do through you. Your soul wasn't who hurt me, but your body still did."

He lowered his head. "I hear what you're saying," he said quietly. "Damn, Celia. What's going to happen to us?"

Aric was a mess. Hell, I wasn't much better, but I would be damned if I was going to let anything destroy what still existed between us. "Nothing," I answered him. He looked up at me, unsure what I meant. I swallowed the huge lump in my throat. "I'm not leaving you, Aric. We just need to stop this thing." I didn't want to elaborate, knowing it would only upset him further, but I felt he should know. "Listen, what happened last night brought up a lot of bad stuff from my past. I thought I was over it, but now it's haunting me and keeping me awake."

Aric was suddenly sitting next to me. I startled, surprised. I'd only just blinked. "I'm sorry," he said quickly. "Don't be frightened. My wolf is just going crazy without you . . . and so am I."

I knew what he meant. If it was up to my tigress, she'd be leading us back to his room. "I know."

His stare seared into mine. "Whatever it takes, whatever I have to do, I'm going to stop this thing. Nothing will keep me from taking you as my wife."

Aric's words made me smile through my tears. Despite my reservations and fears, I knew he loved me, and that no matter what, I wasn't alone. I leaned my head against his shoulder when he draped his arm around me. His heat stroked gently against my skin. After a few deep breaths of his scent, my eyelids drooped, feeling heavy. His presence brought me a sense of calm so strong, I fell asleep against his shoulder.

For a long while there was only darkness . . . until the screams began.

I woke abruptly, unsure what was happening, in time to see Aric racing down the hall toward Shayna and Koda's room. I bolted after him as the screams grew louder and more distressed.

Aric smashed through the steel door like it was made of thin packing foam. Almost immediately the metallic scent of blood filled my nose. We scrambled toward the bedroom and toward the shrieks to find Koda on top of Shayna, forcing her down to the bed.

Blood soaked the sheets and smeared the walls. I'd barely registered what was happening when Aric tackled Koda to the floor.

I leapt onto the bed, reaching for my sister, who was splattered with blood. "No!" Koda growled. "It's not Shayna!"

Koda's warning came too late. I stared down at my chest where the blade of Shayna's sword had disappeared.

Chapter Twenty-three

I don't remember much of anything. Everything came in bits and pieces. Aric was screaming for Emme. Shayna was sobbing. And there was pain, lots of sharp, aching pain drilling through my chest and into my back. I remember feeling cold and damp and so alone.

You're not alone, the voices whispered.

"Baby, stay with me," Aric pleaded. "Emme's here. She's going to help you."

I knew Emme was there, I heard her scream before I felt the familiar touch of her small hands against my face. I sort of recalled her soft yellow light before everything turned black.

Gradually, light trickled in and I found myself in a dark room with Ray and Joe, the boys who had hurt us when we were in foster care.

"We've missed you, Celia," Ray said.

I scanned the room I'd been forced to stay in. Sickly green paint covered the plaster walls. There were no doors, no windows, no escape. My heart pounded into overdrive, forcing adrenaline quicker through my bloodstream.

"You're not real," I bit out through clenched teeth. "You're dead, you're *dead*!"

Joe stood and pointed to the opposite corner. "No. They are."

On the floor lay my mother and father, their bodies pumping the last of their blood through giant holes in their chests. Surrounding them were the gang members who'd shot them, their sawed-off shotguns raised and pointed at me.

You're not alone, voices said.

The men, all of them, closed in.

You're not alone, the voices repeated.

But I wasn't listening. I was whirling around, searching for a way out.

The men moved in a flash, pulling me to them. I drove my clawed hands into faces and kicked out with my legs. But my strikes went right through them while their brutal hands raked along my body.

"Celia," Aric begged. "Please look at me, baby."

I was huddled in a corner shaking and crying. My chest and stomach were drenched with blood. Aric knelt a few feet away with his hand outstretched. Koda was holding Shayna as she sobbed uncontrollably, blood covering them both. Emme wasn't crying, but she appeared ill and unusually pale.

"I'm so sorry, Ceel," Shayna whimpered. There was something in her voice that told me she meant it for more than just stabbing me.

I tried to stand, but my legs fell out from beneath me. Aric clutched me against him, his own chest heaving with rage and frustration as I wept.

Emme inched her way to my side when I finally started to settle. "It was Ray and Joe. W-wasn't it?" she stammered. "And those men who killed Mom and Dad."

I nodded, unable to speak. I stared at the wallpaper's cream and yellow pattern and the edges of the burgundy curtain. The colors mixed in a swirl from the last of my tears. Crying sucked. I hated to cry. And I'd done more than my share in the past year to last a lifetime. I tried to form words, to say something—anything.

Stupid consonants and unrecognizable syllables spilled out of my blubbering lips, but no actual words took shape. I finally gave up and stared at the bland kaleidoscope of color that swam in my vision. It wasn't until the numbness set in that I was finally able to speak.

"How did you know?" I asked Emme.

Emme's voice was disturbingly shaky. "I saw them hurting you." She briefly closed her eyes. "And I saw Mom and Dad. But I also saw you here, in front of me. You wouldn't wake up even after I healed you. It was only after you looked at Aric that everything stopped."

I didn't remember looking at Aric, and I definitely didn't remember how I ended up in the corner, but then again, I couldn't comprehend anything that was happening. Several of Misha's vampires clamored in the hallway, working their mojo on everyone passing by on their way to breakfast.

I stole a glance at Aric. "I don't know what's happening."

His eyes were narrow with fury. "I'm taking you back to the Den. It's the only place I think you might be safe."

Might be safe?

Tim stormed in along with Agnes, Edith, and Liz. "The master wants Celia with him," he said.

"Do you think I give a shit?" Aric growled back. "She's staying with me and that's all there is to it."

Growling and hissing erupted. "Stop it," Emme insisted. "Do you think your bickering is helping?"

I wiped my eyes and stood. Aric helped steady me. "I'll go to the Den," I said quietly. My eyes cut to Shayna. "I just hope it will be enough."

Aric led me to the door, snarling when the vamps blocked our path. "Celia is coming with us. Get out of the way."

"Tim, *move,*" I ordered.

He glanced at the Catholic schoolgirls, nodding stiffly to allow us through.

"Damn, Celia. You all look like shit on a cracker," Agnes hissed.

I scowled at her, but in a way I was grateful. I'd rather be pissed off than scared and helpless. I tightened my hold on Aric when he and Koda growled at her in challenge.

Liz put down the nail file she'd been using on her protruding fingernails and glared at them. "You hairy beasts can growl all you want, but Celia never bled around us." She thought about what she said. "Well, at least not *that* much."

Aric snarled and yanked me closer to him. His protectiveness amplified the warmth stimulated by our bond, immediately easing my remaining distress. He breathed deeply against me; he had felt it, too. "Come on, sweetness. Let's get you out of here."

The vamps followed us into the hotel parking lot and tailed us when we pulled out. I cuddled closer to Aric, fighting to stay awake. My body and brain had had their ass kicked and all they wanted was sleep. But I was too afraid to close my eyes and return to that room where the worst of my memories waited.

Aric kissed my head, grateful for the closeness we were sharing. When we crossed into Nevada, he questioned Koda. "What happened in your room before we got there?"

Koda took his time answering, likely disturbed about everything that had transpired. For as big and strong as he was, he wasn't made of stone. It killed him to see those he loved suffer. "Shayna's scent disappeared when we were sleeping. At first, I thought she had left the bed.

But when I felt her body in my arms, I knew something was wrong."

Shayna turned around, her eyes red and swollen. "It was like what Aric said, Ceel. Something pushed me out of my body." She took a few breaths, trying to control her fragile emotions. "We ordered room service and left the empty tray on the bedside table. I woke up, looming over the bed, and watched my own body reach for the knife on the tray and form it into a sword." She stared back at Koda. "It *knew* how to use my power—whatever this thing is, it knew. I forced my way back in somehow, but I couldn't stop that thing from hurting you." She started to cry again. "I can't believe I stabbed you!"

Koda slipped his arm around her. "It wasn't you, baby," he said softly.

"Koda was stabbed through the stomach before we arrived," Aric whispered.

Shayna buried her face in her hands. "It was trying to pierce through his testicles!" she wailed.

Everyone in the car fell stone still. *Oh shit.*

Koda slipped his arm away from Shayna's shoulders. He gawked back and forth from Shayna to the road. I supposed she hadn't mentioned that little tidbit before.

"How did you get rid of it?" I asked as Koda veered onto the gravel road leading up to the Den.

She shook her head. "I didn't. Aric did. He touched me and I felt it move. It was like he was shoving it out of me."

I looked up at Aric, who simply nodded despite the fear that riled his beast. He stroked my cheek with his thumb when I pressed my lips to his. "I thought it had killed you," he admitted when I pulled away. "My wolf went after it while my human side remained with you. It was my beast who remembered how to fight it and knew how to force it from Shayna's body."

Koda watched Aric through the rearview mirror. "I didn't think it was possible for our halves to separate like that," he said.

Aric stroked my arm. "Neither did I."

The vampires followed us into the Den. When the *weres* refused to allow them in, Agnes cited diplomatic courtesy under section twenty-two of the Alliance agreement. I figured she would find a way in without using brute force. Agnes was annoying at best and an all-around pain in the ass, but she was also one of the smartest dead people I'd ever met.

We entered the large meeting room in the main building. Aric held my hand as we crossed the dark wood floors. The building was empty of students. I welcomed the quiet. Having a bunch of kids gawking at their Leader's fiancée covered with blood was not my idea of fun.

I kept my focus ahead to the cluster of supernatural elite waiting for us. Some I recognized from Liam's funeral most I didn't know. Taran waited beside Bren, who had been ordered by Koda to track her down and drag her back to the Den.

She leaned against the paneled wall with her arms crossed—scowling at Gemini, who stood between Genevieve and a few members of her coven. Again, Betty Sue was noticeably absent. This time, though, Delilah was present. She shook her head when she saw me, probably wondering how I was still alive. This had to be the sixth attempt on my life since we'd met.

Taran only stopped glaring when she realized the condition we were in. Koda and Shayna were smeared with dried blood and surprise, surprise, so was I. Her annoyed expression was quickly replaced by alarm as she raced toward us. "Son of a bitch. What the hell—?"

Aric hauled me to him as a tremendous funnel of blue and white fire spiraled from Taran's core, aimed directly at us. His blood-curdling howl echoed in my ears as my back slammed against the hardwood floor and the force of the blast propelled us across the room.

Aric's lifeless form slumped on top of me. I choked out a scream from the smell of his sizzling and smoking flesh, the pungent odor stinging my nose.

"Taran!" Gemini roared.

Fireballs crashed around us like meteors, splintering and cracking the wood as pained screams bounced against the high walls. Some shrieked in torment, others growled, readying to attack, while countless more were abruptly silenced.

Taran was gone. The entity had claimed her and it had complete control over her power.

Chapter Twenty-four

Blue and white flames bathed the ceiling in a giant wave, eating through the wood and plaster with a heat so extreme my tears bubbled against my face.

I squirmed from beneath Aric, knowing he was badly hurt. I needed to save him and escape with him from this inferno. He groaned in agony as I dragged him by the shoulders just when a huge beam broke from above and punctured the floor.

Aric grunted and snarled, wobbling forward and pinning me against a wall. *"No!"* he muttered.

I thought he was in pain from being moved so carelessly until his face twisted into that sadistic being who'd assaulted me. Aric's muscles continued to roast, but his underlying aroma had once more disappeared. He lifted me from the floor in his vicious grip, his heartless eyes drilling into mine.

My body tensed, expecting his blows, only to have him abruptly release me. He punched both fists through the wood paneling and into the wall, sending dust and bits of wood raining down on my head. His pained expression met mine. "Celia, *run*," he said in his own voice.

I blinked twice before scrambling away. I didn't know where to go. Most of the room was on fire and everyone was focused on Taran, who'd been backed into a corner. Her eyes were wild with fear, but she was all Taran. "For shit's sake, back off," she yelled at them. "It's me, damnit— *it's me*!"

Aric collapsed to his knees, his back resembling a blackened piece of meat—dark and crumbling, and falling away in pieces. I couldn't run. He needed help.

I rushed to his side only to have Bren block my path. He grabbed me by the throat and wrenched me off the ground. "Going somewhere, my pet?"

My long hours of combat training were the only thing that saved me. I didn't think about Bren my buddy. As far as my body was concerned, he was the enemy and I was done with being prey. I rammed my claws into his eyes and followed up with a ridge hand across the bridge of his nose.

He dropped me, but at once I was thrown against the opposite wall by the might of Emme's *force*. She cocked her head, annoyed. "You're not going anywhere," she rumbled in a deep voice.

The pressure of Emme's power squeezed my entire body—crushing my breasts, stomach, and limbs. Martin appeared out of nowhere and snagged her arm in his powerful hold. The moment his skin touched hers, she choked and collapsed, hysterical. The pressure was taken off of me and I landed on the floor.

Martin stalked away from Emme and toward me with a voracious smile that promised my death. I was his next meal. The entity had found another home.

Oh. Shit.

The last time I'd taken on an Elder, things had definitely not gone my way. I rushed to my feet, ready to run like hell, only to have Martin fall on his hands and knees and release possibly the deepest, most inhuman growl I'd ever heard. Every hair on my body stood on end. I seriously thought I'd collapse from the raw hatred in his tone. He shuddered once and looked back at me with his familiar eyes—now wide with disgust.

A wolf leapt in front of me, baring his teeth inches from my throat and forcing me to look away. I punched him hard in the snout and rolled away, narrowly avoiding his snapping jaws. With a primal scream Agnes torpedoed forward, her long deadly nails and fangs exposed.

She slammed into the wolf, tackling him in midair when he lunged at me. With ferocious ire she punctured his jugular, biting down into his bone. Her attack, while in defense of me, worked against us. More wolves joined the fight, forcing the vampires to retaliate.

I ran forward to stop them, only to be stabbed through the thigh by one of Shayna's knives. I roared and grabbed at my leg, falling to my knees and making myself an easy target. Another blade struck my left clavicle, just missing my throat. Sharp pain burned through my flesh.

I was still screaming when Aric caught the next knife by the hilt and another dagger a foot from my head. That didn't make sense—Shayna *never* missed. It wasn't until I saw Makawee standing over her that I realized she'd somehow forced the dark being out of my sister.

Aric whirled around to face me with the knives still in his hand. "Celia—"

The scent of sex and chocolate collided with that of water crashing over stones. Misha had arrived and he was *pissed*. He attacked Aric, forcing him into a burning wall and pummeling him in a blur of fists.

Fire engulfed vampires like a match to rice paper, but Misha was a master. The fire caught on the fabric of his suit but dissolved when it reached his flesh. I tried to stand, only to crumple and dig the knife in my thigh deeper into my femur. I screamed for Misha to stop. He ignored me and continued to unleash his wrath.

Aric, while injured, was a Herculean Alpha male. It didn't take long for him to fight back despite his crippling injuries. The strikes and blows tolled like boulders against a cement bell– deep, hard thuds—stone against stone.

Martin and Makawee charged them. They would have been able to subdue Aric, but not Misha—especially when his remaining vampires left their own brawls to aid their master. Another wolf lunged at me, his open maw revealing his deadly fangs. Koda threw him to the ground by the throat.

They fought while I yanked the knife lodged in my thigh and used it to gut another charging wolf. Her intestines spilled out like wet noodles. I wasn't trying to kill her, just subdue her enough to get away. I scrambled up to meet Taran face-to-face. I only wish it was really her.

I staggered back from the pressure of the magic she'd begun to build when Genevieve bellowed, *"Basta, smetti!"*

An eruption of gold-colored magic flung us across the room, extinguishing the flames eating their way through the building. Instead of lessening now that the fire was contained, the chaos only soared.

Aric and Misha continued to throw down and so did their kind. I tried to stand, only to slip in a pool of my blood. Taran curled up into a fetal position, crying. I forced myself up on my arms and tried to raise my head when my arm was snatched out from under me and I was yanked into the air. I was suspended several feet from the floor by my wrist. The entity had claimed Emme once more.

She strolled toward me, smiling wickedly through Emme's sweet face. "I like the way you scream," it taunted.

My fingers were crushed, sending an electric charge of pain through me. I should have wailed, roared, something. But I couldn't. A horrible numbness infected my body. I thought I was going into shock, but then images from my past shoved their way into my consciousness.

Myriad versions of my dead parents crawled along the floor naked, reaching for me as blood and pus oozed from their mouths. "Celia, pretty Celia," my mother cooed.

Everywhere I turned I saw them, their freak forms urging me to look at them, to see their suffering. The versions of my father wouldn't speak. They mumbled incoherently, their dead eyes full of tears and their stark white hands batting at my feet. My body shook from my terror and another section of my arm was crushed while my zombie-like parents tugged on my legs, begging me to listen, to see them, to save them.

I was dying. And I no longer cared. Anything was better than this.

My vision began to fog when I caught Genevieve limping toward me. She leaned heavily on her long staff to support herself, her presence parting the sea of my dead parents' forms. Her once beautiful milk-white skin blistered and swelled an angry red and her regal gown was nothing more than burned rags clinging to her body. The being infesting Emme turned to her and laughed. "Do you want to play, too, witch?" it asked.

Genevieve held nothing but focused fury. Her approach lured the creature's interest away from me. I should have used the distraction to my advantage, but the continued whimpers and tugs from my parents kept me still and released my grief.

Emme took a step toward Genevieve, and that was when Genevieve demonstrated why she was Tahoe's reigning head bitch. She raised the long staff above her head and slammed it into the floor. *"Basta, demone. Basta!"* she screamed.

A whirlpool of bright gold swirled from Genevieve's staff, rippling out like water catching a skipping stone. The magic struck Emme, drawing an ear-piercing scream that crumbled the damaged fragments of wall.

I fell into Aric's arms, his body saturated with his and Misha's blood. The dark silhouette of Emme hovered above us, grumbling in fury. "Death," it promised, pointing to my heart.

Aric's chest rumbled against me. His growl matched those of the wolves and the hissing vampires who formed a protective arch around us. I would have liked to join their anger. I didn't, choosing to burrow into my mate. With a thundering blast, the entity broke apart, dissipating in the air.

Aric rushed me outside onto the terrace. The cold air slapped at my skin and made everything hurt more than it already did. "Celia," Aric said softly. "It's okay, baby. You're safe now."

You're not alone, those haunting voices said to me again.

I jumped, which caused the stabbing pain in my arm to soar. "Shit," I muttered, bracing it closer to my body.

"Celia, try not to move, and let Emme heal you," Aric said.

I nodded in Emme's direction, although she seemed apprehensive about drawing near. "It's all right, Emme. I know it wasn't you." My voice was unbelievably hoarse. Pain, torture, and dead parents begging you to help them could really screw with someone.

Aric's hold strengthened as Emme realigned my bones and sealed my stab wounds. I thrashed as the agony of her mending was almost as bad as the torment the entity inflicted. I slumped against Aric's chest when she was done, breathing heavily.

Genevieve loomed over us her voice weak. "Aric, is there any way this spirit has obtained a taste of Celia's blood?" The color drained from his face. "Aric," she insisted. "This is important. I need to know."

He let out a pained breath. "It bit her when it was first inside of me."

The only sound I could hear was that of my racing heart, trying to recover from the speed at which my sister healed me. Everyone waited in deafening silence for Genevieve to speak. "By ingesting her blood this dark creature has acquired a portion of Celia's soul. With it, he can possess anyone she's connected to—you, her sisters, and anyone in your Pack. He knows all her fears and all her secrets." She sighed. "If he can't kill her using one of you, he'll drive her insane and force her to kill herself."

I thought about what Genevieve said. The way I was feeling . . . it didn't seem like insanity was too far away.

She edged away when Aric unleashed a deadly growl. "He won't kill her. I'll stop him."

Makawee stepped forward. "I'm not sure if you can, Aric," she said quietly. "Anyone with a soul who is connected to Celia can be used as a conduit. As your mate, the Pack is linked to her as well."

"But I'm strong enough to fight it—"

"As are Makawee and I," Martin interrupted. "But you've seen how fast that thing moves. In the time it takes us to force him from one body he moves to another vessel and continues to go after Celia. We succeeded this time, next time we may not be as fortunate."

Aric trembled against me, but it wasn't from fear. My wolf was seconds from exploding with rage.

You're not alone, the voices called out again.

From the corner of my eye, I caught a trickle of light. "Aric, put me down please," I whispered.

Aric reluctantly complied. I could sense his hesitation to release me and his urgency to ensure my safety. Yet I couldn't remain at his side just then. I walked to where Shah had perched himself on the ledge of the stacked-stone terrace, a strange dullness lifting from me and my ears filling with an old Irish lullaby the closer I drew: *Too-ra-loo-ra-loo-ral. Too-ra-loo-ra-li.* The song intensified in volume giving me the clarity I hadn't known I'd been missing. My eyes widened when I realized what had happened. I whipped around. "It's Tura—the shape-shifter. He's the one behind all this."

Chapter Twenty-five

Everyone who'd been so enraptured by Shah's sudden presence ignored him to focus fully on me. "What do you mean, it's Tura?" Delilah was clearly already starting to doubt my sanity. "His body lay at Aric's feet, shug."

"His body lay there." I faced Aric. "But that doesn't mean he was dead."

Shayna gripped the hilt of her dagger as if anticipating Tura would suddenly appear. "I thought those things gave up their souls in exchange for the power to take on any form. If his shell remained empty, and it didn't have a soul, wouldn't that make him dead?"

Everything seemed to make sense all at once, yet it did nothing to settle my fears. My voice shook. "He does possess the power to take on any form. That's why I think the form he took was Aric's."

I was hoping everyone would dispute my claim—or at the very least call me nuts. Hell, after what I'd been through, they owed me as much. But their tightening faces told me I was onto something. So did the invisible nudge Shah gave me. Makawee strolled in his direction, but Shah vanished and materialized in my hand when Shah felt she'd stepped close enough.

Makawee tilted her chin and folded her hands over her belly. "What else does he tell you?"

"Excuse me?"

"Shah is speaking to you, Celia," Martin said. "In his own way he's communicating. Can you feel it?" he questioned Aric.

Aric nodded and lowered his head. He'd felt Shah's power as well, but appeared to be occupied reaching his own conclusion. "When Tura lunged at Celia, I felt something stab me in the heart. I dismissed it as the brunt of the impact. Now, I'm not so sure." Aric narrowed his eyes at Misha when he suddenly appeared at my side and pulled me toward the rear of the terrace and away from him. "What the *fuck* do you think you're doing?" he growled.

A thrum of power emanated from Martin's clasp to Aric's shoulder. But Martin might as well have been patting his head for all the effect it had on Aric. Martin's eyes widened. Aric brushed aside his über-powerful Elder's mojo like a pesky bug.

Aric propelled himself toward me. The power of the Pack slammed in our faces and the howl of wolves echoed in all directions. It took Aric's Warriors and the Elders' combined power to hold him back. My grip to Shah tightened as Misha's vampires created a barrier between us.

"Do you not hear yourself, mutt?" Misha hissed. "If Tura did somehow take over your form, he's been leaching your power and invading your Pack long before you tasted her blood."

His gaze cut to me. "Celia's blood only sealed the connection and made it that much easier for Tura to control you."

Nausea churned my stomach. "My sisters' blood was in my system from the transfusion." I met their blanching faces before my attention fell to Aric's horrified expression. "Misha's right—if anything we gave him better access. That's why you were so agreeable to have me receive Shayna's blood—it wasn't what you wanted, it's what Tura needed to solidify his link."

Another nudge from Shah told me I was right. Jesus, that's the reason Aric had been so tired, confused, angry, and . . . "Shifters feed off of pain, fear, and insecurity, don't they?"

Makawee's lips had formed into a firm line. "Yes. Celia . . . the day we spoke in my quarters, you weren't quite yourself."

I thought about my heightened jealousy of and vicious response to those *weres* who had wanted to seduce Aric—and why he'd started to question my love for him— and why he'd been so different. I also remembered the voices turning me against Makawee and inciting my paranoia. The other night, in the shower following my attack at work, it wasn't Aric who was aroused. It was Tura. My suffering had given him some kind of perverse pleasure.

My eyes locked with Aric, and in his stare, I knew he realized what I did. All this time, it had been Tura causing the problems between us. That bastard had infected our sacred connection and the love that bonded us.

"Have you been confused, Celia?" Makawee asked. "Or forgetful perchance?"

"Both," Aric answered for me. His anger was so severe his body involuntarily tightened as if ready to attack. "And so have I."

"I have, too," Emme admitted quietly. "Since I went to Malaysia."

"Shit," Taran muttered. "Same here."

"Me, too. Since going there, I mean," Shayna said.

"I felt it, too," Martin agreed.

It was his confession that frightened me the most. "Why didn't you come to me?" Makawee questioned.

"Every time I began to sense something unusual, I would easily dismiss it." Martin squared his jaw. "Or it seemed Tura would dismiss it for me."

Aric stared off to the distant mountains. "Was it an ache in your chest that didn't seem to belong?"

The look of dread we all shared told him he was dead-on. For as strong and heartless as this shifter was, he knew to cover his tracks by muddling and manipulating our thoughts and memories. I felt so stupid, but as the tension around me soared, I knew I wasn't alone.

Some days simply sucked beyond reason.

"It makes sense," Gemini growled. "Weeks had passed since the shifter attack, giving Tura time to feed off your power and grow stronger. It also gave him an opportunity to learn your strengths and weaknesses, and to test your connections to those you're linked to by taking turns invading their bodies." He rubbed his goatee irritably. "As Misha suggests, the blood he stole from Celia was the catalyst to solidify his control."

It must have taken a lot for Gemini to agree with Misha, but there was no time to be petty. My head throbbed when I clutched Shah closer to me. "He wants Shah." I scoffed when everyone simply stared. "That's why Shah has refused to stay in Makawee's stronghold. He knew Tura could invade any one of you and become his new holder."

Aric muttered a curse, and ran a hand through his hair. Around me, no one seemed able to keep still. There was something more to Tura's presence that seemed to rile them. I'd learned enough not-so-fun facts for the day. Yet it seemed there was more crappiness to be had. "Aric, what's happening?"

"There's something you should know that could explain Tura's yearning to destroy you," he said, the anger surrounding him rising. "The shifter you killed several months ago was known as Cara, 'the face.' She was one of the deadliest shifters . . . and Tura's mate."

"Of course she was Tura's mate," I said, sensing my bullshit meter reach its limit. "Of course."

"Celia—"

"This is ridiculous!" I screamed, cutting Aric off. "How many other ways can one person get completely screwed? The goddamn shifter has possessed you and everyone I love—revenge for his mate, I presume—even though that crazy bitch of his came after me first." The vamps took a collective step back, recognizing I'd completely lost my shit. "Can't for once one of these bastard bad guys cut me a break? Can't for once I just be safe?"

I didn't really expect anyone to answer, but I needed to unleash then. It was either that or cry, and I was done with that.

The thing was, I understood what it meant to be mated, and as a result understood Tura's drive. Had anyone harmed Aric, I'd make them suffer, too. Except knowing this didn't offer one shred of comfort; it only made me fear what was to come.

Possession by shifter, no means to stop him, and no means to know when he'd strike next. Damn. Seriously *damn*.

"Celia," Aric said, his deep timbre and ire snagging my attention. "It doesn't matter who he is. I'll make sure he's reunited with his mate soon enough."

But at what cost? My thumb traced over Shah, the motion helping to lessen my hysteria and sort things through. "Tura could have forced any one of you to send those vamps and *weres* after me. That's how they found me in the ED."

Shayna shook her head. "But Shah wasn't there with you—he was already in the stronghold. At least, that's as far as everyone knew."

"Unless Tura knew something you didn't," Makawee reasoned. "When Shah attached himself to you, Celia, Tura knew or at least felt that link."

Misha lifted his chin. "If Shah attached himself to Celia, can Tura take Shah's power or use Celia as his holder to obtain what he wishes?"

Our unease swelled and the world seemed to stop spinning, waiting for Makawee's response. She considered me, frowning ever so slightly. Genevieve and Delilah limped forward, stealing glances at Makawee as if they understood what was happening. "You don't consider yourself Shah's holder. Do you, child?" Makawee asked.

"No," I answered truthfully. "For all that Shah's a rock, he's a being with his own thoughts and feelings. I've felt his pain and I know he hurts. I have no business owning or claiming something so human."

For the first time, Aric's eyes softened. Even if I hadn't spoken aloud, he knew me well enough to know I'd never force an innocent to do something against his will. To me, Shah was simply that. "Had anyone else found Shah, things would have been disastrous," he said.

Delilah didn't seem to hold my beliefs in the same regard. "But if you declare yourself as Shah's holder, you could wish all this away, shug."

"Or give Tura full access to him," I countered.

"You don't know that," Genevieve said.

"I think you're wrong," I told her. "I'm better since Shah attached himself to me. He's helped me without asking, but only because I haven't asked."

"That doesn't make any sense," a *were* standing behind Aric said. She averted her gaze when Aric glared at her.

"It does to me. I don't think—" I paused to glance at Shah. "—scratch that. Tura can't force me to attack someone else, but like Genevieve said, he can still infect my mind. I'm seeing things. Bad things from my past . . ."

"We'll stop him," Aric ground out. I imagined he had an inkling of what I was referring to.

"And how are we going to do that?" Taran asked. "Look, this Tura guy isn't screwing around." Her eyes became bloodshot when she pointed at me. She was trying not to cry, but her tears were seconds from releasing. "I saw what he showed Celia. And even though the images were clouded, I'll remember them for the rest of my life." Her voice trailed off and at first, I thought she wouldn't say anything more, yet something in her mind clicked as the severity of our situation appeared to hit her all at once. "I've been dreaming of Griselda, the aunt who cursed us— well, of her eyes technically. The image in the reflection replays the murder of our parents—the way I imagine she watched it unfold."

"She was there that night?" Aric asked me.

I was the one who'd found the gang members who broke into our tiny apartment standing over the bodies of our parents. "I don't remember seeing her or scenting her," I told him. "I only remember the men who killed our parents."

"Celia, I don't remember seeing Griselda either," Taran agreed. "But I can't help wondering if this is all connected somehow."

"How can it be?" Gemini asked quietly. "You said Griselda was dead."

Taran wouldn't look at him when she answered, choosing to wipe some of the soot from her cheeks instead. "That's what we were told. But let's face it, my nightmares are only this strong and graphic when something is trying to warn me. Considering everything that has happened, I can't pretend like this is all some sort of coincidence."

"I'm starting to see those eyes you speak of, too," Emme said almost inaudibly. "I have since our return from Malaysia."

"I started seeing them a few nights ago," Shayna said. "They were blurry at first, and I didn't know what they were." She shrugged. "Now I guess I do."

"Shit," Taran muttered. "Why didn't you say anything? That's how my dreams started, and look at what they've evolved into. This is so messed up!"

"T, calm down," Shayna said, despite that her voice carried her fear so clearly. "I thought I was just dreaming them because I'd been thinking of you."

"Well, I guess you were wrong," Taran answered, her tone frigid. She was terrified. We all were. I thought we should give her a moment, but Genevieve didn't share my thoughts.

"What is your conscience telling you, Taran?" Genevieve asked her.

"I don't know. If I did maybe we could figure out a way to kill this thing before it kills someone else!" She pulled away from Gemini when he reached for her. "Don't," she snapped. "Just figure out a way to stop this freak before it's too late."

Misha hooked my arm and led me back to him. "Until you do, Celia stays with me," he said, his voice absolute.

Aric moved toward him. *"Like hell."*

Misha's vampires hissed. Aric's Pack growled. It was just a banner day all around. A faint howl tickled my ears as the Elders used their magic to subdue the wolves. Aric was the hardest to control, but eventually they managed to hold him.

"If Tura can only possess those with a soul *and* a connection to her, Celia will be safer among those without one," Misha continued as if uninterrupted. "My *call* isn't enough to link us."

"What about your blood exchange with her?" Aric accused. "You've taken more than your share in the past, leech."

"As a master, he would still have to establish a tie through her. No such bond has been established so she is safe in his presence." Martin didn't seem happy about what he had to say, but he wouldn't lie, especially if it meant sparing my life. "Aric, for Celia's well-being, you have to let her go."

Aric turned away from me. It was then that I noticed his horrible burns were healing. Bits of crispy flesh flaked off, revealing fresh skin beneath. I cringed, knowing how much pain he was likely enduring, but also knowing he'd never demonstrate it, above all in the presence of the vampires. What I would have given then to steal him away and care for him.

My attention drifted to the vamps when they sneered. Aric had to let me leave with them, and they knew it. Tura could find me anywhere and strike at any time. That didn't mean every part of me didn't want to stay with Aric or that I appreciated their smug responses.

Shah insisted I wasn't safe. Not with Aric, not with my sisters, not with my friends. For all that he was or wasn't, I trusted him. And although I didn't quite trust the witches, there was something I needed to ask Genevieve. "Do you have any idea how to destroy Tura—for real this time?"

She seemed surprised I hadn't already left the world of the sane, given the circumstances. "I'm not sure how to kill him, without killing who he possesses and even then, at the speed in which he moves, he'll likely invade another vessel." She considered me. "However, I may be able to block his entry into your sisters at least for a time . . . and perhaps spare them from your dark memories."

At this point, I'd take anything I could get.

She leaned on her staff. "Tura may have feasted on

Aric's power, but it wasn't enough to grant him a corporeal form. He'll need another host. Keep Shah close, and trust no one. If Tura does get Shah, he'll be unstoppable."

Chapter Twenty-six

"Celia," Makawee said quietly. "While I understand that Shah has offered some protection against Tura, it doesn't mean you're safe from yourself. If Tura knows your fears, he'll manipulate them and create new nightmares which could force you to harm yourself."

"I need to stay with her and protect her," Aric insisted.

"You know that's not possible." Martin's words were phrased as a statement, but I recognized the order for what it was. So did Aric, and if he wasn't furious before, he was then. He stormed to the edge of the terrace, drilling his fists into the stone ledge, trying to rein in his wolf.

Aric didn't want to hear any more about how Tura could easily invade my mind or possess him and those we loved. He simply wanted to keep me safe. Instead he had to wait helplessly while this asshole drove me insane. I watched him, not believing how ridiculously shitty our situation had become.

"It's time to depart," Misha said.

It wasn't like I could argue. I strolled to where Aric waited. As I walked, I whispered to Shah still clutched in my hands, "Hide." He vanished before I reached Aric.

For a moment, I simply stood beside him, wanting to feel close to him yet very aware that everyone was watching our every move. "I have to go, wolf."

"I wish you didn't have to," he answered, his jaw tight.

"Me too, love." I lowered my voice. "Tura can cage my beast. I'm losing her and I'm not sure I can get her back."

He wasn't happy about my news. "Maybe you're just unfocused because of the severity of our situation."

I shook my head. "I'm losing her, Aric," I repeated. "If she leaves me completely, I'll be left defenseless." It didn't seem right to dump news like this—not even on him, but I couldn't stop. "I need you to find a way for us to stop Tura. Baby, I won't be able to do this alone."

Aric gently lifted my hands and kissed them. "Listen to me, Celia. Whatever happens you need to believe you're not alone. I *will* find a way to help you. In the meantime, you have to find a way to free your beast. Tura can't keep something so strong away from you—just like he can't keep me from you." Those intense light irises flickered back at me, warming me in all the right places and giving me strength to keep from breaking down. "I'll be with you soon. I swear I will."

I nodded and pulled away at Misha's approach. Aric met his gaze. "I'm entrusting you with her life. If *anything* happens to her on your watch or you use her to gain Shah, no treaty in the world will stop me from killing you."

"Celia will be safer with me than with you." The corners of Misha's lips lifted, revealing his infamous wicked grin. "But I suppose you realize as much, mongrel."

"Misha, please don't," I said when Aric growled. I stood on my toes and kissed his chin, calming him, but realizing that at least for now, we needed to separate. "I'll call you later. Okay, wolf?"

I walked away at his nod, my head pounding from the stress. The vamps flanked my sides as I passed my sisters. I meant to say goodbye, but the fear claiming them made it hard for me to even meet their eyes. They thought they could hurt me and they were right. Unlike Aric, they didn't have the ability to force Tura out. They kept their distance, which hurt me more than I dared to admit.

Like Aric, my sisters had always believed me stronger, tougher, and smarter than I actually was. This was another one of those moments, and they were counting on me to pull through. I wanted to give them hope and assure them we'd triumph. Yet I couldn't while I knew that which made me strong was leaving me.

I never knew exactly how to reach out to my tigress; I simply did. It was natural, like breathing. Yet although my lungs continued to work, I could feel her fading and I wasn't sure how to keep her with me.

I frowned as we rounded the corner and a thought occurred to me. Although Tura had prevented my *change* when he'd forced Aric to attack me, I hadn't felt my tigress pull away so severely until Shayna stabbed me . . . and sent me into that hellish nightmare. Was Tura somehow caging her within my dream?

You're not alone, the voices said again.

I shook my head. The brink of insanity wasn't for wussies.

We passed a window of the demolished building as we hurried up the incline. It gave me a good view inside, although I wished I hadn't looked. Bloody ash smeared the walls where some of Misha's family had met Taran's fire. Broken glass shone like diamonds against the bright noon sun as it streamed in through the chunks of missing roof. Some of the *weres* who were cleaning up stopped what they were doing just to glare. I averted my face, not really blaming them for hating me just then.

Misha's driver started his Hummer limo at our approach. Another vampire opened the door, allowing Misha and me to climb in. We were followed by the three vampires shadowing us, and two more who seemed to appear from nowhere.

Edith sat beside me, eyeing up my blood-smeared neck, stomach, and leg. She licked her lips. "Can I have the leftovers?" she asked. "I never did get breakfast."

"Take your fangs and shove them up your ass," I snapped. "And if you so much as lick the air around me, I'll throw you out the damn window." In my weakened state, no way could I take on Edith. But she didn't know that and waning strength or not, I wouldn't put up with her asinine behavior.

"You're so testy," she claimed. "You know what your problem is?"

"Supernatural freaks of nature are trying to kill me, again?"

"No—well, I guess in all fairness that's part of it—I think the big picture is you're not having enough sex."

"Edith. Please stop speaking."

"I'm only trying to help. . ." Her voice faded at Misha's subtle yet reprimanding glare. She flipped back her dark hair. "Forgive me, Celia. I spoke out of turn."

"You always do, Edith," I muttered. I leaned back into the seat and tried to settle. I was quiet the whole ride to Misha's estate. He spared me from talking by making a few business calls to France and Russia, speaking perfectly in both languages. I concentrated on how easily his tongue slipped over the most complex-sounding phrases. It was better than worrying about what was to come. Liz entertained herself by filing her nails while Tim was on his phone setting up their "meals."

"Make that two blondes for the master." His attention cut my way. "And a brunette. The master is ravenous after making Aric Connor beg for his life."

I narrowed my eyes at him. He smiled. Oh yeah, this was going to be fun.

When we reached the grand compound, Misha led me to the guesthouse, while the others hurried inside in anticipation of their lunch. "You are welcome in the main house as always," he told me.

I smiled at him. "I think I'm better off here."

He considered his words. "I will have my family guard you at all times. As always, you have nothing to fear here."

"With the exception of the last time when the Tribemaster attacked, ransacked the place, and made us all his bitches."

He threw back his head, laughing. "Perhaps you are correct." His humor faded into a small smile. "Although our lives have begun to take separate paths, I'm glad to have this time with you now."

"Misha, you're my friend. That won't change so long as you respect my relationship with Aric."

"I believe you ask too much of me," he said quietly.

I struggled, trying to find the right words. Sometimes, I felt my attempt to be Misha's friend was a tremendous disservice to him.

"You will find everything you need in your suite," he continued. "Should you lack anything else or desire the superior lovemaking only a master vampire like myself can provide, please phone the house."

And sometimes I wanted to smack him. "Er. Thanks."

Misha was still laughing when he left.

I strolled around the 1,500-foot first floor trying to think of anything rather than the ass-kicking my life had taken. Bloodlust vampires and werewolf attacks had forced

Misha to renovate and redecorate. The honey wood floors had been sanded and polished and the walls had been freshly painted gold with white trim to match the comfy white couch. Where a giant picture window used to overlook the garden, French doors now led out to a new brick patio. The accent wall opposite the flat-screen television was a deep rust color, while the throw pillows and blankets were in different shades of brown and gold. What gave me pause, however, were the pictures of Misha everywhere.

They weren't your average catalog style poses, *oh no*, not my favorite vampire. The best way to describe these pictures was that they mimicked something out of *Rolling Stone*. Case in point: the black-and-white 10 x 12 of him standing naked while he strummed the guitar resting over his unmentionables. The jerk didn't even play guitar, although I doubted anyone else would care about his lack of musical talent.

I tipped the frame so it faced down, only to roll my eyes at a profile shot of him on the mantel. And was this one ever a doozie. Misha stood shirtless in black leather pants and black boots, holding a giant bow and arrow aimed at a naked blonde. She knelt on a bar stool with her hands cupping her breasts and an apple in her mouth. I wasn't qualified to interpret art, but by the way her eyes were closed and her head was thrown back, I had the strange feeling the apple and the arrow depicted more than Misha's ability to shoot arrows. That one got flipped, too.

The third was another black and white, with Misha portrayed as "The Thinker." It appeared to have been taken outside in the garden. He sat on a large stone surrounded by a multitude of flowers. From the flowers emerged hands . . . lots and lots of hands from women tempting and begging him to choose them. If I knew Misha, they had all gotten their wish.

They reminded me in a way of Shah's makeshift limbs poking from the ground. I laughed when the hands in the pictures applauded, mimicking Shah's in that field. I glanced around, realizing I had company. "Where are you?"

When I returned my attention to the photo, Shah lay beside it. I lifted him. "You like to have your fun, don't you, kid?"

I carried him with me when I entered the bedroom suite to shower. Not only did I find my cellphone, but some clothing in my size. Misha was an overly sexed and usually inappropriate being, but he did have a heart and a way of being kind that was unmatched.

After showering I called Aric. He answered on the first ring. "Are you okay?"

I placed Shah on top of a throw pillow beside me. "Not really. This whole situation is so messed up." I didn't bother telling him how even bathing was becoming taxing. My arms felt weak just lifting them to shampoo my hair. It would have made him feel worse and more stressed about finding Tura.

"I promise you I'm going to make Tura pay for what he's done."

There was an underlying bite to his tone. "Did something happen when I left?" His silence answered for me. A horrible feeling swept through me. "Aric, are my sisters okay?"

"Tura made Emme and Shayna attack each other. The Elders and I fought to separate them, but he kept jumping back and forth between us as if playing a game."

"Oh my God. Are they okay?"

"They're fine, and safe, and that's how they'll stay. I promise."

I tried to erase the image of Shayna and Emme going after each other. They were so close. "How did you stop him?"

"He jumped into Bren while Koda was seeing to Shayna's injuries. Tura tried to send him after Emme before she could finish healing, but Bren was able to fight his hold and keep from hurting her."

Holy shit.

Aric continued to speak, seemingly unaware of the significance of Bren's response. Something was definitely different between Bren and Emme. "Genevieve is trying to throw something together to help them. But anything she can conjure will only give us a slight delay . . . and Taran is resisting any help from her."

"Fabulous." My head fell against the pillow. Shah appeared on my belly. I stroked him and tried to calm myself. "Doesn't she understand Tura gained all his initial power by making hundreds, if not thousands, of blood sacrifices? He was deadly to begin with and now that he's drawn from your strength, I have no clue how we're going to stop him." I let out a frustrated breath. "Taran has to let this thing with Genevieve go. At least for the time being."

"But she won't. Hell, as pissed as Taran is, I'm waiting for her to take a swing. She flat-out refused Genevieve's help, called her an opportunistic twit, and told her she didn't trust her or her coven."

I slapped my hand against my forehead. "She called her a twit?"

"No."

"No?"

"No, sweetness. She called her something close to it, but you're my mate and I won't use that word around you."

I groaned, realizing what he meant. "How did Genevieve take that?"

Aric paused. "She told Taran she's sorry she feels that way, and only means to help."

Once more Genevieve took the high road thereby making Taran look like the psycho jealous ex. I couldn't be sure if Genevieve was really that refined or that cunning. Either way, my loyalty remained with my sister. "Okay, vulgar name calling aside, I can't really blame Taran for being angry. That said, for now, the witches are the only ones who can help us. I'll talk to her. Hopefully, I can reason with her."

"Yeah. Hopefully." We spoke a little longer but neither of us were ever ones for small talk. "Try to rest," he finally said. "You'll need your strength to fight Tura when the time comes."

"Okay," I said quietly. I wouldn't admit that I was scared to close my eyes and dream.

"Goodbye, sweetness," he said.

"Goodbye, wolf. Call me tonight if you can."

"I will, I promise."

I disconnected and headed into the kitchen where Agnes sat cross-legged on the counter licking a lollipop. On the table was a tray full of homemade fried chicken, along with biscuits, mashed potatoes, corn on the cob, coleslaw, and a gravy boat filled to the rim with hot brown goodness. Misha's chef knew a way to a girl's heart.

"What's the rock doing with you?" she asked, motioning to Shah.

"He just appeared," I explained, feeling defensive.

"You didn't call it—him." She rolled her eyes. "Whatever."

I tucked him into the pocket of my sweatpants. "No. And my favorite color is blue. Anything else you want to know?"

Agnes frowned when the bulge in my pocket vanished. Shah was gone again. "What does the rock want from you, Celia?"

I shook my head. "He doesn't want anything. I think he's lonely."

Her frown deepened. "Just when I think you couldn't be more of a freak you surprise me."

"I aim to please, Agnes." I edged around her and took my first bite of chicken. Her bitchiness had no effect on me. I was all about comfort food. She sat there, watching me as I reached for the bowl of potatoes to dip my chicken into. "Agnes, what's your problem?"

"You don't get something for nothing, Celia." She motioned to my empty pocket. "Just remember that."

I took a biscuit and popped it on my plate when Agnes left. Shah appeared on the table the minute she slammed the door behind her. I smiled. "Believe it or not, she's the nicest of the good Catholics."

Over the next several days, I spoke to Aric briefly, and my sisters even less. The nightmares brought on by Tura had begun to plague them, despite the damn protection necklaces the witches had fashioned. It was as if he'd take his turn pushing us to our breaking point, dangling us over the cliff of no return before releasing us and forcing us to cling to whatever remained of our sanity.

"I don't know how long I can keep doing this," I admitted to Aric. It was morning, and I'd spent yet another night awake.

"There has to be something we're missing—or something obvious he's blinding us from seeing."

I wiped my eyes. I was so tired from lack of sleep they burned. "When you figure it out, be sure to tell me."

"Celia . . ."

I hadn't shared my nightmares or Tura's mind screws. They were too disturbing to relive. But I couldn't deny what was happening to me. "I think I'm losing it, wolf."

Aric swore. He could hear the desperation in my voice, just like I could hear the worry in his. "You have to stay strong, sweetness. We're working tirelessly to figure this mess out. From what Dan has gathered in his research, if Tura doesn't have a host, he won't be able to survive—no matter how much strength he's leached from me. That alone should be enough to kill him."

But for now, he had his choice of hosts, bouncing among the countless *weres* in Aric's Pack when he wasn't busy invading our dreams. *Bastard.*

"The witches have developed a spell that could stun Tura if he attempts to claim another body," he added. "The problem is, given Tura's power, the spell isn't strong enough to bring him down, nor does it last long enough to corral him. Genevieve thinks she may have something more potent, but such magic takes time to perfect and solidify."

"Time I don't think my sisters and I have, Aric."

"I know, sweetness. But we're getting closer. Hang in there. For me, *please.*"

"I'm trying." I didn't mean to be so negative, but there was a reason sleep deprivation was an effective form of torture. Tura was breaking me, and I didn't know how to salvage the pieces. "Given your power, and the amount he's taken, I don't know how the coven's magic will be enough."

"He may have fed from me and taken his share, but he can't hold on to me—not like before. I can force him out with the strength of my beast, just like Koda and Gemini did when Tura invaded their bodies earlier in the week."

The problem was, for as lethal as Koda and Gemini were, they didn't have the strength to force Tura out fast enough. Emme called me crying after helping to heal a cluster of students they had mauled before they had finally forced Tura out.

"Seek out your beast for comfort, Celia," he said when I grew quiet. "She's strong and will help you through this."

"Aric, my tigress is completely gone. I can't find her anywhere within me."

"It's not possible," he insisted.

"I couldn't even open a can of spaghetti today, wolf. It's as if my strength has completely vanished."

He swore and seemed to be pacing. "Let me come over. Maybe I can help you find her or draw her out from where she's hiding."

"It's not a good idea, love. After Tura invaded those *weres* from your Pack yesterday and sent them after me, Misha has ordered his vamps to kill any that enter his compound." It had taken everything I had in me to convince Misha not to rip their heads off.

"It shouldn't be like this."

"I know, but for now it is. Try to find a way out of this soon, okay?"

"I will," Aric answered, although I could hear the concern in his voice.

I disconnected after I told him I loved him and rolled onto my side. I placed Shah back on the throw pillow and stroked the top of his smooth surface. The gesture for some reason made me smile. I couldn't help thinking that maybe he liked the attention. "Let me know if anything scary shows up hell-bent on killing me—or if the Catholic schoolgirls knock on the door wanting to play BDSM Twister, again." It wasn't a joke. When Edith showed up yesterday, I could barely understand her through her ball gag.

Shah didn't respond, of course, but I had the feeling he was laughing.

I rolled onto my back again. I didn't mean to fall asleep. I only meant to rest. But as I stared at the ceiling, wishing like hell I could be with Aric, my body surrendered and I couldn't fight the exhaustion any longer.

I woke in the bedroom Aric and I shared, wearing a lacey pink nightie with rosettes on the trim that Aric had given me a few weeks back. From my iPad, "Wherever You Will Go" played over the sounds of the filling bathtub.

There was a splash followed by Aric's satisfied moan. He beckoned me in a gruff voice. "Are you coming, sweetness?"

I stopped trying to make the bed. The sheets were a mess following a night of passion. I hugged the pillow in my hands and took a whiff, relishing our combined scent. The aroma accelerated the aching need filling my body. "Yes, love," I whispered. "I'm coming."

Our bathroom was constructed in alternating shades of brown and rust porcelain tile. The sinks and whirlpool tub were white and all the fixtures brushed nickel. Two overhead skylights and a large frosted picture window allowed natural light to filter in. It was typically a bright room.

But it wasn't then.

You're not alone, the voices said.

I charged in the moment the metallic scent of blood struck my nose, screaming at what I found. Bright crimson liquid pooled everywhere, saturating the thick white bath mat lying beside the tub. The faucet continued to run, spilling more of Aric's blood onto the floor.

His glassy eyes fixed on me. He was still alive, despite the deathly white color bleaching his skin. I raced to him, slipping on the blood that continued to seep from the edge of the tub.

I reached beneath his arms and tried to pull him out.

You're not alone, the voices repeated.

My strength failed and Aric sank into the tub of thick blood. I thought he would drown in it. Half my body fell in as he submerged into what seemed to be an endless bottom. I couldn't see. I could only feel him slipping further from my grasp as my lungs demanded air.

Somehow, I managed to hook my arm under him and drag him out. I hauled his body out of the tub, falling with his upper body clutched against me. Aric sputtered out a mouthful of blood, wheezing and unable to take a full breath.

"Baby, don't leave me," I pleaded. *"Please,* I'm begging you, stay with me!"

He responded by shoving his mangled wrists into my face. I choked on the cry that ripped through my chest. He'd bitten through his own flesh. Blood and small chunks of skin spilled out of his mouth as he spoke. "You were gone too long," he gasped. "I couldn't live without you."

In my arms, I held my mate as he died.

You're not alone, the voices echoed.

I screamed, knowing they were wrong . . .

I woke up covered in blood, sobbing into Edith's breasts. I scrambled away from her and to the opposite side of the bed. But she wasn't looking at me, her gaze was completely homed in on Misha, whose crisp white shirt was soaked red. Agnes and Tim were trying to help him from the floor. For some reason, they could only position him on his knees.

Tim shot me an accusing glare. "Master, did she harm you?"

My balance gave out and I stumbled out of the bed. Some of Bren's favorite swearwords flew out of my mouth as I literally crawled across the floor in my urgency to reach Misha. The dream had left me shaken, but the reality that I had somehow hurt him terrified me more.

The vampires hissed at me. "Oh, shut up!" I snapped.

I ignored their increasingly dangerous growls and slumped directly in front of Misha.

He gawked at me, horror sharpening his features. My hands gently touched his face, arms, and chest, searching for injuries. "Are you okay—?"

Misha grabbed my forearms and turned them to reveal my bloody arms. I almost screamed. Tura had manipulated me into slashing my own wrists. Misha wasn't covered in his blood. He was covered in *mine*.

His stare drilled through mine, the power of his hypnosis claiming me almost instantly. *"Leave us,"* he murmured.

I vaguely recalled the sound of doors shutting quickly as the vampires made their mad exit. My hands pushed against his chest, allowing me enough space to watch Misha's incisors lengthen. I was glued where I lay. A low growl built from the pit of my stomach when he leaned closer. "Misha, *don't*."

"Trust me," he rasped through his fangs.

Chapter Twenty-seven

I woke on a cold stone floor in an old rustic cottage. Outside, snow crept up to the edges of the window. The room was small, dimly lit by a few candles. Tiny flames flickered from the burning twigs carefully placed inside a crumbling fireplace. Next to the hearth a young woman with dark blond hair and tired gray eyes sat in a wooden rocking chair, sewing a quilt with shaking hands. A flimsy shawl covered her shoulders while a thin wool dress draped the rest of her emaciated form.

Every few stitches, she glimpsed nervously toward the door. Close to her feet sat a boy about ten. He polished a pair of large, black, official-looking boots, although he wore only rags. His face was smeared with ash and dirt. He was hungry. I didn't know how I knew, but I did. I also knew who he was. His mother didn't have to speak his name.

You're not alone, the voices whispered.

I stood and crossed the small space to kneel beside the boy. Beneath his tattered clothes, I could see how malnourished he was. He had the same gray eyes he would have as a man, although they lacked their usual luster . . .

and resolve. Wisps of his blond hair escaped from a battered wool hat that was clearly too big for him. I tried to brush his greasy hair from his eyes. He rubbed at the spot where I'd touched, leaving a smudge from the polish behind. He didn't see me. Not that it surprised me.

Outside a horse galloped to a stop and whinnied. Someone had arrived. Judging by the sound of Misha's and his mother's rapidly beating hearts, he wasn't welcome. Misha's mother abruptly stood. The quilt slipped from her lap and onto the cold floor. She didn't bother picking it up, she was too busy staring at the door as heavy footsteps neared. It was cold in the house, but you wouldn't have known it by the way her face glistened with perspiration. Misha didn't glance up. He continued to concentrate on polishing the boots, although his own hands had begun to tremble.

A man entered the house wearing a thick wool coat and boots exactly like the ones Misha polished so meticulously. He was tall and heavy with a thick black beard. He threw a cloth bag onto the floor. I could smell the bread and cheese inside it. Misha's stomach growled. Yet he made no move toward it nor did he bother to thank him.

The man smiled at the woman. She didn't smile back. She stared with dead eyes at the floor. It bothered the man. He huffed and snatched her elbow then dragged her to another small room with a curtain for a door. For a moment, Misha stopped his work. When the deep grunts of the man and the muffled whines of his mother began, Misha resumed his work.

Misha scratched the soft brush feverishly over the boots, focusing hard on making the leather shine. A small tear slid down his face, streaking his dirt-smeared skin. I sat beside him and gathered him in my arms, trying to shield him from what was happening. But there was no protecting him from what was happening. Not then.

The heavy grunts continued in the other room, causing Misha's brushstrokes to grow more frantic. Anger filled, but I managed to keep my voice soft. "Listen to me, Misha," I whispered. "One day, you will be one of the most powerful beings in existence. One day, others will beg for your mercy."

His eyes widened and he looked up slowly. He couldn't see me, but he could hear me, so I continued. "You will have strength, and wealth, and power. So much power no one will dare hurt you." I swallowed hard as I watched the tears of disbelief trickle down his face. "And if anyone is foolish enough to try, I will be there to stop them."

From the room next door, the large man emerged carrying the pair of filthy boots he'd worn into the house. He threw them down at Misha and snatched the freshly polished ones from his hands. After examining them closely he put them on and left. It was not until the horse galloped away that Misha's mother returned to the rocking chair. She tried to smooth her hair before retrieving the quilt from the floor and resuming her sewing. When Misha started to clean the filthy boots she finally spoke.

Normally I didn't understand a word of Russian, but I did then. "Leave that for now. You need to eat, my son."

Misha turned in the direction I waited. Although I still didn't believe he could see me or feel my touch, I hugged him tightly and kissed his tear-streaked face. "It's okay. Eat. I swear to you, your time will come."

I awoke embracing Misha. But he was no longer a little boy and we were no longer in the past. We sat on the comfy white couch of the guesthouse.

I stared into his familiar strong gray eyes, feeling strangely at peace. "What did you do to me?"

Misha kept his arm around my shoulders while his right hand stroked my hair from my face. "I was in the parlor entertaining a business associate when I sensed your fear. I thought you were being attacked. We arrived to find you piercing your wrists with your fangs."

"My fangs?" He nodded. Oh hell, Aric was right. My tigress was still with me.

"You would not respond to the sound of my words or my touch," Misha said. "It was only when you met my eyes that you stopped." He dropped his hand, his voice dripping with regret while his face only demonstrated anger. "I saw everything that has ever caused you pain— *everything*. I felt it and experienced it all at once."

I gaped at him with wild, horrified eyes. *"How?"*

"In returning my soul, you have given me unimaginable power. Some gifts I have learned to control. Others unveil themselves as my spirit permits. I used what I've learned to share the darkness of my own past."

At first, I didn't know how to respond, sadness throbbing mercilessly in my chest. "But *why*?"

He skimmed his fingers gently down my face to rest on my chin. "Because of who you are. I knew that in sharing my suffering, you would abandon your own to come to my aid."

My attention fell to my wrists. In addition to giving me a glimpse into his past, Misha had managed to heal me.

"How is it that death has not claimed you?"

"That's a good question." I shrugged. "For the most part, I've been lucky, I guess."

Misha laughed without humor. "Luck? No one is that fortunate, my darling. Your cunning, strength, and magic have certainly played roles in saving you." His voice quieted. "Only your beauty, which brings me to my knees with the force of a tidal wave, can rival the power within you."

I edged away from him, his words making me uncomfortable. I didn't belong to him. Despite our current situation, I very much remained Aric's mate. I owed it to him to remind Misha as much and although there were many ways to respond to his words, at the top of my list being run like hell, I resorted to making bad jokes. "You're only saying that because I'm sitting here covered in blood."

"No. I'm not," he added almost silently.

"Misha . . ." I inched away from him and tucked my knees against me to create space between us. Misha may have felt what he felt, but thankfully he didn't press. In the silence between us, I considered his words.

Misha was right. I had left my own misery behind to help him—and I'd do it a thousand times over if he needed me—yet that didn't explain why I felt better. Not only had my spirit been rejuvenated by the trip into his memory, but physically, I also felt stronger. "Why am I no longer weak or bleeding?"

"I used the healing power of my essence to mend your physical form. It is not a power I can use freely," he added. "Tura has left your soul battered, and thus it is more vulnerable to intrusion. When you return to your former self, I will no longer be able to assist you in such a manner."

"Okay," I said slowly. "Thank you."

Misha kissed my forehead before standing. "Lunch will be ready in an hour. Will you join me?"

I closed my eyes, relishing the peace that bathed my soul before answering, "Yes."

Misha gave me a small smile. "Very well."

I followed him out, but clasped his hand before he could leave. I wanted to say something poignant. The brief moment of tranquility he gave me could have possibly saved me from plunging into darkness. How do you express gratitude for something like that? I searched for the right words before finally saying, "Misha . . . thank you for being my friend."

Misha raised my hand and kissed it. I half-expected to catch traces of that terrified little boy somewhere inside him, but there was nothing left of that boy in the man who stood before me. His eyes were sharp with intelligence, arrogance, and control. He appeared omniscient, as most everyone saw him. I almost asked what happened to that man who had made him and his mother suffer, but I wasn't callous enough to question him.

Misha stopped, considering me before stepping into the garden. "Your words inspired me, Celia," he said. "I killed him the next time he sought the company of my mother. I sliced his throat with the same knife we used to cut the bread he brought us."

With that little bombshell, he entered the garden and disappeared toward the house. I started to shut the door when the speaker system that connected the guest and main houses crackled. Once more the Eagles began to sing "You Are Not Alone."

You're not alone, the voices whispered again, bouncing along the walls from every direction.

I covered my ears, swearing as the voices repeated themselves. So much for thinking Misha had saved me from going nuts.

You're not alone, the voices insisted.

My head snapped up as I realized who was speaking to me.

You're not alone, they said once more, over the sound of the Eagles' harmony.

"No . . . I'm not alone," I said aloud. For a moment I couldn't move. When I finally did, I tore after Misha.

My bare feet slapped against the fresh snow falling on the slate walkway. I ignored the biting cold and the sting it caused my feet. "Misha, *Misha!*" My voice was lost, drifting away as the wind pushing its way toward the lake howled along the path. "Misha— *Misha!*"

I raced through the garden and was almost to the stretch of lawn leading to the house when he whirled and caught me in his arms as I stumbled forward. Vampires emerged from every direction, circling us protectively in anticipation of another attack.

Misha gripped my arms, his fierce stare taking in our surroundings in a glance. "What is it?" he asked.

I could barely get the words out, my body once more drained of its strength. "I know how to stop Tura."

Chapter Twenty-eight

We gathered everyone at the Den, *weres,* the vamps, the witches, too. Honestly, I didn't trust anyone, not then. Thankfully, those who mattered seemed to trust me.

Aric and I watched each other from opposite sides of the clearing where we'd congregated. I didn't want to risk damaging any more Den structures. The last two buildings I'd played a role in demolishing surely were enough. As I looked at him, all I wanted to do was rush into his arms. And I would, if I could somehow pull my plan off.

"I don't like this," Genevieve said. "Celia, I wish you would just tell us your thoughts and explain your strategy." Her magic and that of Delilah's and the rest of their coven circled the perimeter, but she kept her attention on me.

"She doesn't have to tell you shit," Taran answered for me.

Her response infuriated Genevieve's coven and earned frustrated groans from Gemini and Aric. Taran *so* didn't care. When Genevieve did little more than raise her eyebrow, Taran responded by flipping her off with her gloved hand.

I tried to keep my eye from twitching and failed miserably. Forget that Taran despised the very snow-covered ground Genevieve seemed to glide over. And forget that there was a body-jumping psychopathic shapeshifter using our power against us. Taran was severely sleep deprived. And a sleep-deprived Taran was scarier than hell.

Dark circles ringed her eyes and those of Shayna's and Emme's. The dreams haunting them made them afraid to fall asleep, so like me, they'd done their damnedest to stay awake, severely impacting their health and moods. They wouldn't look at each other, and although only ten days had passed since I'd last seen them, it was obvious that they'd lost a significant amount of weight.

I stepped toward the center of the circle. "Everything will make sense once it happens, but it may take a while so be prepared to act." My eyes cut to Delilah. "Remember how you told me you wanted a little payback when we first met?" She nodded. "If this works, you'll get your wish."

I nodded to Misha, who did little more than blink before every vampire in his keep, along with his mystics, who took point behind each *were* present. That move was as popular as you might imagine. "What's this?" Martin demanded as the *weres* around us growled.

"A small assurance to keep Celia safe," Misha answered for me. "None of your Pack will be harmed—unless, of course, Tura chooses to invade their bodies and turn them against Celia."

"No one will be killed," I shouted over the increasing growls. "In the event of an attack, the vampires are only to force the invaded *were* into submission."

"Unless they try to kill us first," Edith added with a smile.

Edith was no help and "submission" wasn't the best choice of words. I was dealing with a bunch of "doms" after all.

Aric, for as angry as he was, seemed to understand, and thankfully backed me. His steely expression halted the *weres'* increasing ire and he didn't hesitate to join me when I motioned him forward. I took his hands in mine, hoping like hell I wouldn't break down. "What are you thinking?" he asked, lifting my hands and brushing his lips against my knuckles.

"That I really want this to end, so I can be your wife."

His gaze softened as mine blurred. He traced his thumb over my ring finger. "My name will go here where it belongs, just like I'll claim yours as mine. No matter what happens I'll be your strength, just like you've always been mine."

My stare traveled to my ring finger as Aric continued his caress. During the marriage ceremony a pureblood *were's* name was magically traced onto his mate's ring finger, signifying their union and their eternal love. In exchange his mate could receive the same. It was something Aric and I had planned to do, and we'd still do it if I could get us through this. "I love you," I told him.

"I love you, too," he said back. "Celia, whatever happens, you have to believe that together, we are unstoppable."

A wolf yelped, steering our attention away from each other. Tim lay across Bren's body.

He'd broken Bren's neck to stop him from attacking us. *Shit*. The stupid stunning spells the witches had crafted weren't having any effect. "Tura's here," I said, quickly.

Another roar, another sound of bone breaking, followed by two more yelps, and then another. Aric backed away from me as he scanned the perimeter. Agnes jumped on a werecougar bounding toward me, bringing him down.

"Go, Celia," Aric urged. "We're out of time. Do what you have to—"

He tackled Danny in wolf form. I cringed when Aric forced him down. I motioned my sisters toward the center of the circle. They rushed to me. "Taran, put us to sleep."

"*What?* Are you out of your goddamn mind?"

More and more bodies were being invaded. Tura skipped from one to the other, moving faster, and drawing closer to me, forcing the Elders and the vampires to scramble to protect me.

"Taran, put us to sleep, *now!*" I yelled. Shayna and Emme began shaking. They didn't want to go to sleep. They knew their nightmares awaited them. "Taran, *please!*" I begged her.

Her tearful blue eyes took in the growing chaos; the *weres* were healing quickly, their beasts awakening enraged and turning on the vamps who'd harmed them. The coven scattered, trying to flee from the rows of snapping fangs and deadly claws. "Son of a bitch," she muttered. "Ceel, I hope you know what you're doing."

I didn't. Not really, but I had to try. "I love you," I told them as Taran's blue mist enveloped us. Emme and Shayna collapsed at once, Taran quickly followed. My body wobbled as Aric forced a giant grizzly bear into the thick snow. "Come to me when I *call,*" I managed to slur.

The flicker in his eyes told me he'd heard me, but then it switched to something dark and sinister. Tura had claimed my wolf once more, sending him barreling toward me as I crumpled to the frozen ground.

You're not alone, the voices whispered.

Something tickled my cheek. I woke up in the bedroom of that tiny apartment we used to live in. I batted at the roaches crawling across my face and those making their way up my legs, knowing things were about to get way worse. The roaches stayed put, my gestures seeming to have no effect on Tura's mind games.

You're not alone, the voices whispered.

I rose from the beat-up mattress as more roaches swarmed me. They seemed to be everywhere, crawling from every crack in the wall, every buckle in the linoleum tile, and from behind that old mirror our mother would brush our hair in front of. They sought me, their tiny antennae eager to probe my flesh and find a break in the skin where they could crawl beneath and feast. I slowed my breathing as best I could, trying to shove away my fear even though by now, I was completely covered with roaches.

A blast from a shotgun, followed by another, echoed from the other room. I meant not to react, but I did anyway. In our tiny living room, Tura was reenacting my parents' murder. Because, I imagined, the other times I'd been forced to relive it hadn't been horrifying enough. My body trembled as I worked to calm my racing heart. I had to go into that room. I knew I did, but not until something insisted that I turn around and see who lay in bed.

Tears burned my eyes as I saw the corpses of my sisters being devoured by roaches. It was bad enough to see them being eaten, but to see them as they had been as children made it that much more painful. "You're an asshole, Tura," I said aloud, then turned away from my sisters and walked into the living room.

You're not alone, the voices repeated.

"I know," I said, my voice gaining an edge. "My sisters are always with me."

My declaration caused the roaches to die on my flesh and fall away in clumps with each step I took. The gang members were there as I expected, their sawed-off shotguns trained on me as they loomed over my parents.

Once more, I saw the gaping holes in my beloved mother's and father's chests, their hearts spilling the last of their blood. This time, as much as it hurt, I ignored them. I glanced around, searching—knowing she had to be there. My eyes took in the small living room where only the pullout couch that served as my parents' bed and a small TV would fit. I ignored the men taunting me.

"They deserved to die, *puta*," one of them told me. "Just like you do."

"Look how they bleed," another said as he struck my shoulder. "Do you like the pretty color?"

My gaze traveled to the small kitchen even as my parents' corpses pulled my hair and shirt, trying to draw my attention. I did my best to ignore them, needing to find who I was looking for. She had been there with us the night of the murder. She had kept us safe. My eyes searched the room several times. I cried out with relief when I finally spotted her, sitting in the corner licking her chops.

Aric was right. My tigress hadn't left me. She simply needed me to believe that I could find her, and that nothing could pry us apart. "Come on, little kitty. We have to get Emme first."

My tigress bounded toward me, tackling me so hard that I barely kept my footing. It was as if she'd vanished, but my protruding claws made it clear she was with me. I needed her when I caught the first of Emme's screams. But the men didn't want me to leave. They jumped me at once, not expecting that I was ready for them.

I slashed one with my claws directly over his jugular. His blood spurted, splattering my back while I wrenched the shotgun from another man and used it to bust the skulls of the men who'd killed my parents.

My parents stumbled toward me in their zombie-like forms. "You're dead, and you're at peace," I told them. They froze before staggering with their arms out, their hands opening and closing as if pleading with me not to leave them. It took all I had not to cry when I heard their bodies collapse on the floor as I tore out the door.

Joe and Ray met me in the dark corridor. Without hesitation, I shot Ray in the face and tore Joe's head off. I tossed it behind me, forcing myself to ignore what I'd done and who they were to me, and keep on task. "*Emme. Emme, where are you?*"

Her screams seemed to come from every closed door lining each side of the corridor. I wrenched open the closest ones to me. "Emme, I'm here. Tell me where you are!"

Her shrieks were suddenly silenced before she yelled at the top of her lungs. *"Celia!"* I took off at full velocity, barreling through the furthest door on the right to find Emme in her nightmare. She lay naked on the floor, her limbs pulled outward. A swarm of vampires punctured her veins and arteries, draining her blood as her dead ex-lover stroked her face and hair. Liam had no eyes, and pieces of his skin hung from him in strips.

Tura was going to burn in hell for this. And I would get him there.

Tears soaked Emme's face and her eyes pleaded for me to help her. "Don't be afraid. You're not alone," I promised, wiping my cheeks with the backs of my hands.

I didn't speak again until I killed the vampires feeding from her and wrenched her away from Liam's hold. She sobbed into her hands when Liam tried to follow her, his hands reaching to play with her hair. "He's gone, Emme. You have to leave him here." I clasped her wrist and pulled her away from Liam and into the hall, screaming for Shayna.

Emme's clothing returned the moment we left the room. Her wild eyes swept up and down the endless hall only to return to the room we'd just abandoned. "Liam's hurt," she said. "We have to help him. I-I can't leave him. . ."

I shook my head. "He's already gone, honey. And where he is, I swear to you he's whole."

Although she cried, she nodded and stepped away from the door. "Now, I need you to concentrate. Tell me where Shayna is."

She opened her mouth to argue, but then she veered in the direction I'd come from, and pointed. "There. She's down there."

I didn't hear Shayna, but Emme did. "Show me," I told her.

If Emme was afraid, she didn't demonstrate it then. She sped down the hall, cutting right to a dark corridor and then left into another. She flung open the first door, yelling Shayna's name.

Leathery wings slapped our faces. Demon children the size of infants with hideous yellow fangs flew around us, their beady red eyes glowing in the darkness and drool dripping from their mouths. There were so many, I could barely see in front of me. "Shayna. *Shayna!*"

"Ceel, help me!"

With a primal scream, Emme scissored her hands out, parting the flock of winged demons with the might of her *force*. Shayna writhed on the floor, the demons stripping the muscle from her bones. She lifted her head, terror gripping her face. "Get up, Shayna," I told her. "You need to get up!"

Emme lost it upon finding our sister. She let loose her rage and the extent of her power, tearing the demon children in half and crushing their skulls. Shayna squirmed, forcing her upper body up and clasping her mutilated hand tight in mine. I wrenched her to her feet, calling to Emme as I rushed Shayna out the door.

Shayna's hands slapped against her limbs and belly, disbelief clouding her features as her body became whole. Emme followed us into the hallway, her cheeks flushed with anger and effort. "Where's Taran?" Shayna asked.

I yanked the doorknob free and passed it to Shayna. "I don't know. Find her."

As Shayna ran, calling for our remaining sister, the knob elongated into a sharp deadly spear. "Taran, we're coming. We're coming, T!"

It wasn't until we rounded another corner and Shayna kicked open a moldy door that I heard Taran. I'd been brave and tough, but I positively froze when I met Anara face-to-face. The Elder who'd robbed me of my baby loomed above us in his humanoid wolf form with my sister tight in his grip.

Taran dangled in the air, sobbing as Anara crushed her zombie limb between his monstrous fangs. Her skin had completely bleached, her eyes had sunk into her skull, and sickly blue veins branched out across her body. And yet that wasn't the sole cause of her torment. She may have been blind, but her attention was trained on the far corner of the room where Gemini and Genevieve were making love. It wasn't just sex they were sharing. Taran could have handled that better. The way Gemini held her, and the way Genevieve met his stare, more than a physical act was taking place.

I wrenched away and forced myself in Taran's direction, knowing I should act, knowing she needed me to help her fight Anara. But his presence impeded my movements and it was our younger sisters who reached her first.

Shayna raced forward, grunting as she punctured Anara's chest with her spear. He roared, releasing Taran to slump on the floor. Emme sprinted forward and lifted Taran with her *force,* away from the swipe of his deadly claws.

Anara roared again, ripping the spear from his chest and dropping on all fours. The thing was, this wasn't Anara. It was Tura, it was all Tura. And now that I had my sisters, I had to *call* for the owner of the last remaining voice.

"Aric!"

The voices haunting me were right; I wasn't alone. I had my sisters, and now my mate arrived in a blast of white light.

Aric's giant gray wolf form soared into Anara when Anara snapped his fangs inches from Shayna's throat. My sisters realized what was happening and lunged forward, beating on Anara and yanking at his fur with their bare hands—even Taran, whose grisly appearance melted away with each strike.

Shah materialized in my palm when I opened my hand. He had no voice of his own, and no real way of speaking. But he had sent the voices to me so I'd know how to fight. And now he wanted to fight, too. I ran forward, leaping into the air and bringing Shah down against Anara's snarling face.

The entire room exploded, sending me gliding along the snow, right in the middle of the *were-* vampire smackdown taking place on Den grounds. They stopped their onslaught. But it wasn't because of me, or my sisters, or Aric sprawled in all directions.

It was because Tura in his corporeal tiger form had materialized before us and he wasn't pleased with what I'd done. With roars and hisses that shook the ground, every preternatural rushed forward and attacked. Even the witches aimed their magic at Tura. They wanted him to die.

Except for one.

Chapter Twenty-nine

Delilah's eyes morphed from their light blue shade to that murderous coal black. Her talisman shimmered as she held out her hand and called forth her power. Shah, who had fallen mere inches from my hand, scooted across the ravaged field and into Delilah's hand.

I scrambled forward. *"No!"*

Tura's giant paw crashed down on my chest when I tried to lurch to my feet. He held me down until Aric's beast form snapped his bone at the joint. I shoved the limp paw away and bolted down the mountain to where Delilah had disappeared.

The sweeping branches of pines smacked against my face. Delilah glided around the trees with her power, circling the pines and trying to muddle her scent.

She was fast, but so was I, and my tigress demanded blood for her betrayal.

The ground rumbled beneath my feet when I'd almost reached her. Roots as thick as arms broke through the frozen ground, reaching for me. I cut left and right, trying to avoid the tangle of roots while Delilah thickened the barricade to slow me down. I knew what she was doing;

she was buying time to build her magic and lock her claim on Shah.

The wall of threading roots grew taller and denser. But if she didn't think a tigress could climb, she was dead wrong.

My front claws protruded; as did the ones at my feet. They punctured my shearling boots, shredding the leather and helping me scale the wall. I flattened against it as Delilah spat a curse, quickly followed by another.

One sliced into my shoulder, releasing a stream of warm blood. It burned as it cut down to the bone, but the pain I felt only fueled my rage. I reached the top of the wall where she was levitating and pounced, bringing her down to the ground with my weight. I *shifted* before we hit the frozen earth and surfaced in time to watch her speed away and back toward the clearing.

I sprinted after her. In the distance I heard Tura's agonized roars. The good guys were tearing him apart. But if Delilah was returning there, instead of fleeing, it was for a reason. And the reason surely wasn't good.

"Aric!" I called. *"Delilah's headed right toward you!"*

Stakes speared out of the ground, puncturing my foot. I screamed, but managed to keep my wits and fall to the side, avoiding the field of stakes blocking my path. With a grunt and an even louder swear, I yanked the stake imbedded in my foot and backed away, racing along the rows of stakes with my bleeding foot until I found a section narrow enough to *shift* through.

I surfaced in front of the last of the stakes. Lightning struck as I hobbled in the direction of where the fight had begun. The sound that followed was unearthly. A screech, like hell's fury itself, cut through the forest, forcing the sweeping firs to bend away from its rage.

My attention shot upward to where Delilah floated over the treetops screaming an incantation in Spanish.

Particles of gray mass shaped like the silhouette of a tiger soared upward, despite the leaping *weres* in beast form snapping their jaws at it and trying to bring it down.

The fangs failed to connect, likely because what remained of Tura was quickly dissolving into the air. But what remained was important enough for Delilah to seek. In other words, we were screwed if it reached her.

I broke through trees and into the clearing, stopping short between Aric's wolf form and Misha. Both were injured and bloody, but that didn't compare to the rage cloaking their auras. "She's offering herself as a vessel for Tura," Misha hissed.

"Why?"

"To absorb what remains of him, combining her power, Shah's, and that of hell itself."

Of course, because we weren't screwed enough.

Genevieve wasn't having it, and neither was her coven. The women circled Genevieve, who raised her staff and aimed their collective magic at Delilah. *"Muori!"* she yelled, throwing the ultimate death curse.

A thin current of gold light as bright as the sun shot through Tura's dissipating shape and right at Delilah. She blocked it, using Shah to absorb the curse and rebound it. Everyone scattered, but not everyone survived. A *were* and several witches fell dead while two of Misha's vampires exploded into ash.

Aric and I edged around the cluster of boulders he'd dragged me behind. "Goddamnit," he yelled, his now human form pulling me to him.

Tura had just reached Delilah when Genevieve screamed another spell. *"Separa!"* She was trying to keep them from joining. Her hold didn't last, but it didn't have to. It was long enough for what remained of Tura to dissolve into the breeze.

Delilah screamed and raised Shah over her head, calling his power and hers. She was crazed with fury, and determined to make us all pay.

She thought Shah now belonged to her. I wasn't so sure and I sprinted out into the open to find out. I ignored the pain from my injured foot as I ran and dodged the death curses Delilah flung like beads. When I reached the clearing's center, I stretched out my open palm. "Shah!" I screamed.

Shah materialized in my hand. I clutched him to me as Aric tackled me and rolled us away from a massive death curse that caved in the ground where I'd stood. He wrenched me behind a stand of trees in time to see Taran charge forward and launch a funnel of blue and white fire from her zombie limb. Delilah fell shrieking when Taran's blaze struck her core. She slammed to the ground, the protective shield she'd gathered around herself the only device that spared her bones from breaking and saved her from sudden death.

What remained of the coven pounced on her and subdued her with their power. I didn't move right away, too stunned that we were alive and shocked that Shah had actually come to me. I supposed I was right; the little guy was done being used. "Thank you, Shah," I told him quietly.

Someone tossed Aric a pair of sweatpants. He yanked them on, his stare trained on Delilah as he then led me forward. Two witches held her by her wrists with their magic, allowing Genevieve to glide to her and easily yank the talisman from her neck. Genevieve whispered something over the stone, crumbling it to dust, then dropped the simple metal chain to the ground.

We watched Genevieve step back and point her staff at Delilah. *"Rivela,"* Genevieve commanded. *Reveal.*

My sisters gathered around me, their anger escalating as Delilah's deep wrinkles faded, her plump form thinned, and her hair darkened as black as her stare, falling in waves to her shoulders. She couldn't have been older than me. But that wasn't the only problem, and my sisters saw it, too. The witch before us was an exact twin of the one we killed during a bloodlust epidemic raging through Tahoe.

Everything seemed to slow. "What the hell?" I rasped. I looked back at Taran, who initially met my face with shock. But then something changed in her expression, almost at the same moment it changed in mine.

It was then my world as I knew it unraveled.

And I realized exactly why.

Taran stumbled forward, her eyes shimmering with rage and clarity that caused a fear I'd never seen in her. She locked her stare onto the witch's murderous eyes—their color so dark, they appeared absent of irises. "Are those similar to the eyes from your vision?" I asked, my voice shaking.

Tears streaked Taran's face, and she nodded. She knew I understood. But the revelation, and the weight of its significance, did nothing to spare us. It lashed out like a whip and caused me to break down. Aric wrapped his arm around me. He didn't realize why I wept. No one did except for my sisters. "You're the daughter of the aunt who cursed us? Aren't you?" I asked the witch.

Koda relinquished his hold on Shayna and stormed forward, wrenching the witch up by the throat before she could speak. "Answer her," he growled before flinging her to the ground.

The witch clutched her throat, spitting up blood. The other witches didn't care; at Genevieve's order, they hauled her back to her feet. Magic streamed from Genevieve's staff. "I believe you owe the Wird sisters an explanation."

If Genevieve's magic didn't force her to speak, Aric's protective hold over me made it clear he'd get her to confess by any means necessary. "I am Rosaliana, daughter of Griselda," she said, raising her chin. "And sister of Perladina, whom you robbed me of."

"We could say the same," Taran snapped. "After all, your fucking *mother* had our parents killed!"

Taran was in hysterics when she turned to us. "Those *were* Griselda's eyes haunting my dreams." She swallowed hard. "Do you know what this means?" she asked me, although she already knew the answer.

I nodded, fighting to hold back my tears so I could speak. "Griselda was the one who sent those men to kill us. But they found Mom and Dad first." I released a breath. "That's why you could see Mom and Dad's murder in their reflection. Griselda was the one behind it all along."

Taran lost what remained of her composure. Gemini hauled her to him. She didn't fight him, clinging to him as she broke down. Koda gathered both Shayna and Emme, his hulking body trembling from the strength it was taking to hold back his wolf. Bren and even Danny had to be subdued by the Elders. "Let her finish speaking first," Martin whispered tightly.

"You weren't supposed to live!" Rosaliana accused, her voice quivering as her focus traveled to my sisters and me. "All of you were supposed to die. The evil is coming, and he must be allowed to come!"

"No," Genevieve said quietly. "Celia and Aric's children will be strong enough to stop him, just as Destiny herself has proclaimed."

Genevieve didn't know I couldn't bear children. But I wouldn't admit that now, especially if it meant granting Rosaliana even a shred of peace.

"She needs to die, Genevieve!" Rosaliana screamed at her. "They all do. The darkest one has promised unimaginable power to anyone who stops them."

Genevieve's perfect face remained impassive yet deadly. Aric was all ire. He released me and prowled toward Rosaliana.

Genevieve intercepted him, placing her staff firmly on the ground in front of him. The base of the staff stirred with pulses of magic and ripples of gold smoke swept along the dirt. Her eyes sparkled, not with their typical wisdom and beauty, but with something darker, deadlier. In a way it seemed wrong for someone so lovely to look so dangerous.

Her voice remained calm, but her magic screamed for vengeance. "No, Aric. Rosaliana is my responsibility. She dies by my hands."

Rosaliana's head dropped as she shrieked with rage.

Aric ignored her and shoved his face into Genevieve's. It may have seemed odd for Genevieve to appear so deadly, but it wasn't for Aric. My wolf did lethal well. A hideous growl built from Aric's core and rumbled like the angered Greek gods of ancient myth. "She orchestrated the torture and attempted murder of *my mate* and her sisters. It's my damn right to kill her. I will kill her, and if you get in my way—"

I tore Rosaliana's arm off her body, just like I would a leg from a well-done turkey. The bone snapped cleanly from her shoulder and the muscles and ligaments ripped like wet paper. She screamed. Loudly. The witches who were holding her stepped away, fast.

Blood splattered like a sprinkler as I literally beat her with her own goddamn arm. With each blow I thought of how she caused me to relive my abuse and experience Aric's death. Her gurgled screams annoyed me. The pain I inflicted couldn't possibly compare to Shayna's blade piercing through my sternum.

Why was she yelling? Had she smelled her mate's skin burn at the hands of her sister's magic? Had she witnessed her sisters' torment? Had she experience their nightmares?

No. I had. I'd suffered. And so had those I most loved.

How dare she try to crawl away when I couldn't escape Emme's telekinetic grip around my throat or the countless attacks from those I trusted. Because of her, I was almost raped by the man I loved. Because of her, I feared my lover. Because of her so many had perished.

After a few more blows, my weapon became useless. There's only so much you can do with a severed limb once all the bones have been shattered. Besides, I'd tired of her screeching. I tossed the arm aside and punctured her sternum with my claws.

My methodical actions surprised me. It was as if I was performing a simple task like dusting. But instead of spray, wipe, spray, wipe, I separated her rib cage with my hands and ripped out her heart without bothering to glance at her face. It beat one time in my hand before I tossed it over my shoulder.

Rosaliana's heart landed with a wet thud by Genevieve's feet. Genevieve stiffened. To her credit she didn't so much as cringe, although I could tell she very much wanted to.

I wiped my hands as if they'd been merely coated with dust. "There. That settles that."

Genevieve's mouth dropped open. Aric crossed his arms. He watched me closely but said nothing. My freak-out disturbed them both. Not that I could blame them; that was a bit mental even for me.

I stormed away then, away from the clearing and toward the forest, stomping along the snow with more noise than my feet had ever made. I continued walking through the dense trees until I came upon a tiny brook. I fell into it on my hands and knees, weakened, exhausted, and disturbed by my actions.

The water was ice cold, yet surprisingly refreshing. It felt good to feel something other than pure, unadulterated hate. As much as my life had sucked, I never truly hated anyone until Anara forced his way into my life. Since his death, I'd absolutely convinced myself I could never hate so deeply again . . . then Rosaliana and Tura came along.

Who else would come?

I washed my hands and face and stared at my reflection in the water until the tiny fragments of Rosaliana's tissue and bits of clotted blood polluted the clear brook. When I finished, I sat on the edge and hugged my knees. My jeans were soaked with water, blood, and God only knew what else. Yet I ignored the chill of the approaching night.

It was a long while until I actually allowed myself to think. I had survived. Again. But although my inner beast was a cat, I didn't believe I had nine lives to live.

The sun had set when soft steps pressed into the snow behind me. I knew it was Genevieve even before my nose caught her scent. She moved like a graceful swan in water, despite the rough terrain of mountain. "May I sit with you, Celia?"

My jaw clenched tight. "You don't have to ask. It's not like I'm going to rip your arms off or anything."

"Yes. Of course not," she answered slowly, if not nervously.

Genevieve used an elegant hand to tuck her long velvet skirt beneath her, though she kept a firm grip on her staff. When she saw that I'd noticed, she laid it beside the small boulder where she sat. It was a polite demonstration of trust, more out of courtesy than the actual belief that I wouldn't eat her. I had frightened her. Hell, I had frightened myself. But sometimes a girl couldn't help but to wig the fuck out.

"I want to apologize to you for what happened." She sighed. "There's been a tremendous upheaval within my coven since the war. By taking in more witches who have lost their Leaders, power struggles have caused a lot of needless bickering."

"Like with you and Betty Sue?"

She quieted for a moment. "Yes, but I see now that Rosaliana had likely played a role in that, too."

Yeah. She probably had. "Where's Betty Sue, do you think?"

"She's dead, Celia," Genevieve answered. "Aric sent a team to her house. They found her buried in her garden. My guess is she discovered her old friend wasn't her old friend at all."

"So the real Delilah's dead, too?"

Genevieve's focus dropped to the stream. "She has to be. Rosaliana couldn't have taken on her identity without killing her. And in taking a pure witch's form, she was able to mask her own darkness." She clasped her hands. "We don't know when it happened. But it was definitely before she came across you the day of the shifter attack."

I didn't argue. Nothing with the supernatural was ever a coincidence. "They were working with each other from the start."

"Yes. She must have created a spell to allow Tura to leave his form. I believe Tura meant to invade your heart and kill you, but the ability Rosaliana granted him allowed him access to Aric when Aric took the blow meant for you."

In saving me, Aric had given Tura life, power, and access to all of us. At the very least, the asshole owed us a thank-you note. "Rosaliana showed up after the attack just to make sure I was dead, didn't she?"

"That's what we've concluded." She looked at me then. "I'm sorry. I should have discovered Rosaliana regardless of the mask she wore long before you and everyone else suffered."

I blinked a few times. She seemed sincere. "Okay."

She raised her eyebrows elegantly, the same way she did everything else. *"Okay?"* she asked. "You can't be serious?"

I fixed her with a hard stare. Although I suspected it alarmed her, she didn't wince. "What else do you expect me to say? Until recently, I've tried to avoid the supernatural world. I don't know the rules. *Am* I supposed to kill you?" Genevieve remained quiet, leaving me with the impression that maybe I had that right. I muttered a swearword under my breath. "You weren't the cause of all this, Genevieve. I accept your apology, just leave things at that."

She nodded. We sat in silence for a while. I stared at the peaceful brook, now illuminated by a full moon. I wondered how some places could always remain tranquil while in others chaos forever reigned. It surprised me when Genevieve's delicate hand squeezed my shoulder. Her smile was small, pleasant, and that lovely sparkle had returned to her eyes. "You know, Celia. If your sister didn't hate me, I imagine we could be friends."

But she does, so we can't. I gave Genevieve the once-over. At first glance, anyone in the mystical world would assume she was a vampire. Her skin was flawless, her body perfect, her face heartbreakingly beautiful. She was strong, intelligent, ethical, and kind. I couldn't blame Taran for feeling threatened by her. On my best day, I couldn't match her on her worst. And that annoyed the hell out of me. "You were homecoming queen, weren't you?"

She grinned despite my irritated tone. "Prom princess, too. What about you?"

I scoffed. "Everyone hated me. I was constantly in detention for fighting."

Genevieve hugged her knees and cocked her head slightly. "And yet here you are, engaged to the class president, the most valuable player, and the captain of the football team all rolled into one."

She tried to give me a compliment, but her words only made my eyes sting. I glanced at my nails, still stained with blood. "Yes . . . but sometimes I don't know how."

She placed her hand over mine. "I do," she said softly.

About a hundred feet away, the almost silent footsteps of a predator treaded through the darkness. From behind a stand of trees the class hunk stepped out. I rose and hobbled toward him, noticing for the first time the bloody footprints I'd left behind. Yeah, I might have been a tad easy to track.

As I limped, Shah appeared in my hands. He'd left me when Aric had embraced me during Rosaliana's big reveal. Genevieve followed, noticing Shah almost instantly, but failing to reach for him. I stopped directly in front of Aric and showed him that Shah was with me. He stroked my cheek with his hand, although that was probably still bloody, too. I couldn't stop my voice from shaking. "I'm tired, and he's not mine to keep. Will you come with me so I can hand him to Makawee? She's the only one I trust to look after him."

Aric bent and kissed my lips. "Nothing could keep me from your side," he whispered.

Emme rushed to me after I handed Shah to Makawee, but not before I told him goodbye. He'd helped me realize how to lure Tura out of hiding, and as much as he could, he'd been my friend.

Emme healed me, but my filthy condition and demolished clothing kept us at the Den a little longer. Aric led me to his new quarters and into a hot shower. We took our time bathing and holding each other before we finally stepped out.

The mystery behind my parents' death and the bull's-eye we'd been marked with had left me raw. I needed the intimacy and security that only time alone with Aric gave me. When he and I made our way down the grand staircase and into the foyer below, I was wearing the spare set of clothes Shayna had brought me from the room assigned to her and Koda. They were there, and so were Bren, Emme, Taran, and Gemini, although once again, Gemini appeared to be keeping his distance.

He sighed as he left Taran's side and approached us. "Shah's power has abandoned him. He is no more. The Leaders of the Alliance would like a word with Celia."

Aric narrowed his stare. "Why?"

"Why do you think?" Taran hissed. "They're convinced you took their last wish."

At once the Leaders piled out of the room to our far left. Aric met them with a growl that shook the room. "You insult my mate and the woman who saved us by calling her a thief!"

Uri, Misha's master, stepped forward, his phony gentleman persona absent in his rage. "We don't fault Celia, after all, with so much power in her grasp, temptation was surely hard to resist."

"And yet I did," I countered. Misha met my stare with a sharp expression clearly meant as a warning. He didn't want me to offend Uri, the other grandmasters, or the *were* and witch elite who had arrived. But I did, my sisters' gathering presence driving me to do so. "And where were any of you, when your clans, covens, and Pack members were out there dying and trying to bring back Shah? You didn't want to get your hands dirty. Then again you never do. All you wanted was to reap the rewards like always."

Aric wound his arm around my waist and gripped my hip in a show of unity, just as my family closed into a circle they'd formed around us.

"Despite our lack of involvement, you owe us the truth," an unfamiliar head witch ground out. "Shah's last wish was proclaimed to be the strongest and most significant of all. The one that could tip the scales on either the side of good, or in the dark ones' favor."

"Are you deaf, Broomhilda?" I shot back. "I didn't wish for anything!"

What seemed like Aric's entire Pack appeared in front of us, shielding us from the encroaching supernatural elite. I thought Aric's growl had summoned them, but it wasn't until Martin stepped forward that I realized it had been him. "You know Celia speaks the truth—you can scent it and you can feel it. And now that you know you may evacuate our premises."

Everyone piled out slowly, leaving only my closest allies in the spacious foyer. I exchanged brief glances with my sisters. Their shattered expressions and silence demonstrated their pain. They were seconds from breaking down, and there wasn't a damn thing I could do to spare them from their misery.

Aric escorted me into a small parlor when he sensed my rising anger. He knew damn well that after everything that happened, and all that my sisters and I had discovered, my tigress and I needed space to keep from attacking Uri, that witch, and anyone else who had the nerve to question my loyalty.

He shut the door for privacy and led me across the room and out to a small terrace. "It's okay, sweetness. They're just angry because they never had the opportunity to use Shah for their own selfish gains." His deep timbre remained calm, yet I could sense his angered beast looming within.

I knew he was right, but his warmth and support did little to settle the frustration tearing its way through me. I was about to ask him to take us home when someone entered the room.

Makawee carefully shut the door behind her and walked toward us, her steps causing only a whisper of sound. She stopped just in front of me, the edges of her deep brown eyes crinkling when her thin lips curved into a smile. "What did you wish for?" she asked me quietly.

Her question surprised me. "Makawee, I'm telling the truth, I didn't ask Shah for anything."

Her stare traveled down the length of my body before returning to fix on my face. "May I?" she asked, extending her hand.

I hesitated before nodding, unclear and wary of her intentions. She placed her hand tenderly over my belly, barely grazing the surface of my blouse. Her gentle smile widened the longer her hand remained in place. "You may not have asked him, Celia, but in exchange for showing Shah kindness, he gave you what you most wanted."

Aric's grip to my hip tightened, otherwise he failed to move. I couldn't move at all.

Makawee nodded. "You're pregnant, Celia. You're carrying Aric's child."

Epilogue

The feel of the powdered sand between my toes brought me a sense of calm, as did the aroma of the salty sea air and the spray of roses and Fijian flowers that made up my bouquet. "It's time, Ceel," Shayna said, her eyes and those of my sisters shiny with tears.

When Bren began to thrum the first chords of "Into the Mystic" on his guitar, I knew she was right. One by one, my sisters left me to walk down our makeshift aisle, looking stunning in their simple slip dresses that matched the turquoise ocean water.

In the bright clear sky, werehawks and wereeagles patrolled, beating their powerful wings against the current in a majestic aerial dance. Heidi was in charge of security and had arranged to have weredolphins and weresharks patrol the waters. I never knew any sort of *were* marine life existed. And although I found it bizarre, I refused to complain. If it took Flipper the Dolphin and friends to ensure that Aric and I could exchange vows without chaos and bloodshed, I'd gladly accept their help.

My hand stroked my belly. I thought the simple appliqué of rosettes cascading from the bodice and to the

A-line skirt of my strapless wedding gown would camouflage my pregnancy, but although I was certain that I wasn't far along, my scars had vanished and I'd begun to show.

Only two weeks had passed since learning that Aric and I had conceived, but he refused to wait any longer to marry me and that was fine by me.

Bren's deep voice reached a crescendo, my cue to step out from the small stand of palm trees and onto the beach. The small group assembled rose, temporarily obstructing my view of the groomsmen: Bren, Danny, Koda, and Gemini, the best man. But as much as I adored them, there was one wolf in particular I couldn't wait to see.

The breeze swept my long hair and my cathedral-length veil behind me in time for me to catch my first view of my groom.

Aric wore light tan tuxedo pants with a crisp white shirt and nothing else. He didn't need anything else. I didn't think it was possible for any male to look more spectacular. His eyes were smoldering, his body strong, his face handsome.

And he had chosen to be mine.

As I smiled at my mate, all the fierceness he normally carried as a Leader of his kind couldn't compare to how he watched me then. He held my gaze as if my life and that of our child depended on it. I wanted to run into his arms and never release him.

Aric was my destiny; more than ever, I was sure of it then.

He bowed his head and pinched the bridge of his nose as I neared. When he looked up at me again, a single tear streaked down his face. I smiled through my own tears when I reached him.

"Hi, sweetness," he said quietly.

"Hi, wolf."

I passed my flowers to Taran, allowing Aric to take my hands in his.

Makawee stepped forward. "You may begin your vows," she said.

Aric grinned, the gesture lighting his magnificent eyes. "The first words I ever spoke to you were in the form of a question. I asked you what you were." He laughed. "You growled at me and made it clear that you didn't owe me an explanation."

Those in attendance busted out laughing. "Not my Celia," Bren muttered.

My cheeks reddened, although I held on to my smile as he continued. "What you should have told me was that you were my sun that rises in the morning and the moon that makes me howl at night. That you were more than I ever wanted, needed, or desired in a mate." His deep voice lowered. "That you would take my heart every time you'd leave my side, and that your smile would bring me to my knees. That's what you should have told me, because that's precisely what I've known from the first moment I saw your beautiful face. I love you, Celia. And I will love you for eternity."

Tears slid down Aric's face. He'd stolen my breath with his words, but somehow, I managed to speak from my heart.

"You weren't supposed to love me," I told him, my voice shaking. "You were never supposed to come into my life. Demons, *weres,* vampires, and traitors aside, you have turned my world upside down from the first moment I met your gaze." I tried to steady my breath. "You catch me when I fall, and have risen with me from the ashes of death and despair. With a touch of your fingers, the scent of your being, a look from your eyes, I am whole. You weren't supposed to love me," I said again, my own tears falling. "But I am blessed because you do. I love you, Aric, and I will love you for eternity."

We finished our vows as the sun began to set. Aric bent to meet my lips, one hand curled around my waist, the other traveled to my belly. In his kiss and gentle hold, he swore to protect me and our child from harm. As I realized the fate that awaited our little one, I prayed we would both be enough.

Something was coming. And the world was counting on our baby to save it.

Reader's Guide to the Magical World of the Weird Girls Series

acute bloodlust A condition that occurs when a vampire goes too long without consuming blood. Increases the vampire's thirst to lethal levels. It is remedied by feeding the vampire.

Call The ability of one supernatural creature to reach out to another, through either thoughts or sounds. A vampire can pass his or her *call* by transferring a bit of magic into the receiving being's skin.

Change To transform from one being to another, typically from human to beast, and back again.

chronic bloodlust A condition caused by a curse placed on a vampire. It makes the vampire's thirst for blood insatiable and drives the vampire to insanity. The vampire grows in size from gluttony and assumes deformed features. There is no cure.

claim The method by which a werebeast consummates the union with his or her mate.

clan A group of werebeasts led by an Alpha. The types of clans differ depending on species. Werewolf clans are called "packs." Werelions belong to "prides."

Creatura The offspring of a demon lord and a werebeast.

dantem animam A soul giver. A rare being capable of returning a master vampire's soul. A master with a soul is more powerful than any other vampire in existence, as he or she is balancing life and death at once.

dark ones Creatures considered to be pure evil, such as shape-shifters or demons.

demon A creature residing in hell. Only the strongest demons may leave to stalk on earth, but their time is limited; the power of good compels them to return.

demon child The spawn of a demon lord and a mortal female. Demon children are of limited intelligence and rely predominantly on their predatory instincts.

demon lords (*demonkin*) The offspring of a witch mother and a demon. Powerful, cunning, and deadly. Unlike demons, whose time on earth is limited, demon lords may remain on earth indefinitely.

den A school where young werebeasts train and learn to fight in order to help protect the earth from mystical evil.

Elder One of the governors of a werebeast clan. Each clan is led by three Elders: an Alpha, a Beta, and an Omega. The Alpha is the supreme leader. The Beta is the second in command. The Omega settles disputes between them and has the ability to calm by releasing bits of his or her harmonized soul, or through a sense of humor muddled with magic. He possesses rare gifts and is often volatile, selfish, and of questionable loyalty.

force Emme Wird's ability to move objects with her mind.

gold The metallic element; it was cursed long ago and has damaging effects on werebeasts, vampires, and the dark ones. Supernatural creatures cannot hold gold without feeling the poisonous effects of the curse. A bullet dipped in gold will explode a supernatural creature's heart like a bomb. Gold against open skin has a searing effect.

grandmaster The master of a master vampire. Grandmasters are among the earth's most powerful creatures. Grandmasters can recognize whether the human he or she *turned* is a master upon creation. Grandmasters usually kill any master vampires they create to consume their power. Some choose to let the masters live until they become a threat, or until they've gained greater strength and therefore more consumable power.

Hag Hags like witches, are born with their magic. They have a tendency for mischief and are as infamous for their instability as they are their power.

keep Beings a master vampire controls and is responsible for, such as those he or she has *turned* vampire, or a human he or she regularly feeds from. One master can acquire another's keep by destroying the master the keep belongs to.

Leader A pureblood werebeast in charge of delegating and planning attacks against the evils that threaten the earth.

Lesser witch Title given to a witch of weak power and who has not yet mastered control of her magic. Unlike their Superior counterparts, they aren't given talismans or staffs to amplify their magic because their control over their power is limited.

Lone A werebeast who doesn't belong to a clan, and therefore is not obligated to protect the earth from supernatural evil. Considered of lower class by those with clans.

master vampire A vampire with the ability to *turn* a human vampire. Upon their creation, masters are usually killed by their grandmaster for power. Masters are immune to fire and to sunlight born of magic, and typically carry tremendous power. Only a master or another lethal preternatural can kill a master vampire. If one master kills another, the surviving vampire acquires his or her power, wealth, and keep.

mate The being a werebeast will love and share a soul with for eternity.

Misericordia A plea for mercy in a duel.

moon sickness The werebeast equivalent of bloodlust. Brought on by a curse from a powerful enchantress. Causes excruciating pain. Attacks a werebeast's central nervous system, making the werebeast stronger and violent, and driving the werebeast to kill. No known cure exists.

mortem provocatio A fight to the death.

North American *Were* Council The governing body of *weres* in North America, led by a president and several council members.

potestatem bonum "The power of good." That which encloses the earth and keeps demons from remaining among the living.

Purebloods (aka *pures*) Werebeasts from generations of *were*-only family members. Considered royalty among werebeasts, they carry the responsibilities of their species. The mating between two purebloods is the only way to guarantee the conception of a *were* child.

rogue witch a witch without a coven. Must be accounted for as rogue witches tend to go one of two ways without a coven: dark or insane.

shape-shifter Evil, immortal creatures who can take any form. They are born witches, then spend years seeking innocents to sacrifice to a dark deity. When the deity deems the offerings sufficient, the witch casts a baneful spell to surrender his or her magic and humanity in exchange for immortality and the power of hell at their fingertips. Shape-shifters can command any form and are the deadliest and strongest of all mystical creatures.

Shift Celia's ability to break down her body into minute particles. Her gift allows her to travel beneath and across soil, concrete, and rock. Celia can also *shift* a limited number of beings. Disadvantages include not being able to breathe or see until she surfaces.

Skinwalkers Creatures spoken of in whispers and believed to be *weres* damned to hell for turning on their kind. A humanoid combination of animal and man that reeks of death, a *skinwalker* can manipulate the elements and subterranean arachnids. Considered impossible to kill.

solis natus magicae The proper term for sunlight born of magic, created by a wielder of spells. Considered "pure" light. Capable of destroying non-master vampires and demons. In large quantities may also kill shape-shifters. Renders the wielder helpless once fired.

Superior Witch A witch of tremendous power and magic who assumes a leadership role among the coven. Wears a talisman around her neck or carries staff with a precious stone at its center to help amplify her magic.

Surface Celia's ability to reemerge from a shift.

susceptor animae A being capable of taking one's soul, such as a vampire.

Trudhilde Radinka (aka *Destiny*) A female born once every century from the union of two witches who possesses rare talents and the aptitude to predict the future. Considered among the elite of the mystical world.

turn To transform a human into a werebeast or vampire. Werebeasts *turn* by piercing the heart of a human with their fangs and transferring a part of their essence. Vampires pierce through the skull and into the brain to transfer a taste of their magic. Werebeasts risk their lives during the *turning* process, as they are gifting a part of their souls. Should the transfer fail, both the werebeast and human die. Vampires risk nothing since they're not losing their souls, but rather taking another's and releasing it from the human's body.

vampire A being who consumes the blood of mortals to survive. Beautiful and alluring, vampires will never appear to age past thirty years. Vampires are immune to sunlight unless it is created by magic. They are also immune to objects of faith such as crucifixes. Vampires may be killed by the destruction of their hearts, decapitation, or fire. Master vampires or vampires several centuries old must have both their hearts and heads removed or their bodies completely destroyed.

vampire clans Families of vampires led by master vampires. Masters can control, communicate, and punish their keep through mental telepathy.

velum A veil conjured by magic.

virtutem lucis "The power of light." The goodness found within each mortal. That which combats the darkness.

Warrior A werebeast possessing profound skill or fighting ability. Only the elite among *weres* are granted the title of Warrior. Warriors are duty-bound to protect their Leaders and their Leaders' mates at all costs.

werebeast A supernatural predator with the ability to *change* from human to beast. Werebeasts are considered the Guardians of the Earth against mystical evil. Werebeasts will achieve their first *change* within six months to a year following birth. The younger they are when they first *change,* the more powerful they will be. Werebeasts also possess the ability to heal their wounds. They can live until the first full moon following their one hundredth birthday. Werebeasts may be killed by destruction of their hearts, decapitation, or if their bodies are completely destroyed. The only time a *were* can partially *change* is when he or she attempts to *turn* a human. A *turned* human will achieve his or her first *change* by the next full moon.

witch A being born with the power to wield magic. They worship the earth and nature. Pure witches will not take part in blood sacrifices. They cultivate the land to grow plants for their potions and use staffs and talismans to amplify their magic. To cross a witch is to feel the collective wrath of her coven.

witch fire Orange flames encased by magic, used to assassinate an enemy. Witch fire explodes like multiple grenades when the intended victim nears the spell. Flames will continue to burn until the target has been eliminated.

zombie Typically human bodies raised from the dead by a necromancer witch. It's illegal to raise or keep a zombie and is among the deadliest sins in the supernatural world. Their diet consists of other dead things such as roadkill and decaying animals

Read on as the Weird Girls saga continues with *Sealed with a Curse,* the first full length novel in The Weird Girls Urban Fantasy Romance series by Cecy Robson. The excerpt has been set for this edition only and may not reflect the final content of the final novel.

A Weird Girls Novel

By

CECY ROBSON

Chapter One

Sacramento, California

The courthouse doors crashed open as I led my three sisters into the large foyer. I didn't mean to push so hard, but hell, I was mad and worried about being eaten. The cool spring breeze slapped at my back as I stepped inside, yet it did little to cool my temper or my nerves.

My nose scented the vampires before my eyes caught them emerging from the shadows. There were six of them, wearing dark suits, Ray-Bans, and obnoxious little grins. Two bolted the doors tight behind us, while the others frisked us for weapons.

I can't believe we we're in vampire court. So much for avoiding the perilous world of the supernatural.

Emme trembled beside me. She had every right to be scared. We were strong, but our combined abilities couldn't trump a roomful of bloodsucking beasts. "Celia," she whispered, her voice shaking. "Maybe we shouldn't have come."

Like we had a choice. "Just stay close to me, Emme." My muscles tensed as the vampire's hands swept the length of my body and through my long curls. I didn't like him touching me, and neither did my inner tigress. My fingers itched with the need to protrude my claws.

When he finally released me, I stepped closer to Emme while I scanned the foyer for a possible escape route. Next to me, the vampire searching Taran got a little daring with his pat-down. But he was messing with the wrong sister.

"If you touch my ass one more time, fang boy, I swear to God I'll light you on fire." The vampire quickly removed his hands when a spark of blue flame ignited from Taran's fingertips.

Shayna, conversely, flashed a lively smile when the vampire searching her found her toothpicks. Her grin widened when he returned her seemingly harmless little sticks, unaware of how deadly they were in her hands. "Thanks, dude." She shoved the box back into the pocket of her slacks.

"They're clear." The guard grinned at Emme and licked his lips. "This way." He motioned her to follow. Emme cowered. Taran showed no fear and plowed ahead. She tossed her dark, wavy hair and strutted into the courtroom like the diva she was, wearing a tiny white mini dress that contrasted with her deep olive skin. I didn't fail to notice the guards' gazes glued to Taran's shapely figure. Nor did I miss when their incisors lengthened, ready to bite.

I urged Emme and Shayna forward. "Go. I'll watch your backs." I whipped around to snarl at the guards. The vampires' smiles faltered when they saw *my* fangs protrude. Like most beings, they probably didn't know what I was, but they seemed to recognize that I was potentially lethal, despite my petite frame.

I followed my sisters into the large courtroom. The place reminded me of a picture I'd seen of the Salem witch trials. Rows of dark wood pews lined the center aisle, and wide rustic planks comprised the floor. Unlike the photo I recalled, every window was boarded shut, and paintings of vampires hung on every inch of available wall space. One particular image epitomized the vampire stereotype perfectly. It showed a male vampire entwined with two naked women on a bed of roses and jewels. The women appeared completely enamored of the vampire, even while blood dripped from their necks.

The vampire spectators scrutinized us as we approached

along the center aisle. Many had accessorized their expensive attire with diamond jewelry and watches that probably cost more than my car. Their glares told me they didn't appreciate my cotton T-shirt, peasant skirt, and flip-flops. I was twenty-five years old; it's not like I didn't know how to dress. But, hell, other fabrics and shoes were way more expensive to replace when I *changed* into my other form.

I spotted our accuser as we stalked our way to the front of the assembly. Even in a courtroom crammed with young and sexy vampires, Misha Aleksandr stood out. His tall, muscular frame filled his fitted suit, and his long blond hair brushed against his shoulders. Death, it seemed, looked damn good. Yet it wasn't his height or his wealth or even his striking features that captivated me. He possessed a fierce presence that commanded the room. Misha Aleksandr was a force to be reckoned with, but, strangely enough, so was I.

Misha had "requested" our presence in Sacramento after charging us with the murder of one of his family members. We had two choices: appear in court or be hunted for the rest of our lives. The whole situation sucked. We'd stayed hidden from the supernatural world for so long. Now not only had we been forced into the limelight, but we also faced the possibility of dying some twisted, Rob Zombie–inspired death.

Of course, God forbid that would make Taran shut her trap. She leaned in close to me. "Celia, how about I gather some magic-borne sunlight and fry these assholes?" she whispered in Spanish.

A few of the vampires behind us muttered and hissed, causing uproar among the rest. If they didn't like us before, they sure as hell hated us then.

Shayna laughed nervously, but maintained her perky demeanor. "I think some of them understand the lingo, dude."

I recognized Taran's desire to burn the vamps to blood and ash, but I didn't agree with it. Conjuring such power would leave her drained and vulnerable, easy prey for the master vampires, who would be immune to her sunlight. Besides, we were already in trouble with one master for killing his keep. We didn't need to be hunted by the entire leeching species.

The procession halted in a strangely wide-open area

before a raised dais. There were no chairs or tables, nothing we could use as weapons against the judges or the angry mob amassed behind us.

My eyes focused on one of the boarded windows. The light honey-colored wood frame didn't match the darker boards. I guessed the last defendant had tried to escape. Judging from the claw marks running from beneath the frame to where I stood, he, she, or *it* hadn't made it.

I looked up from the deeply scratched floor to find Misha's intense gaze on me. We locked eyes, predator to predator, neither of us the type to back down. *You're trying to intimidate the wrong gal, pretty boy. I don't scare easily.*

Shayna slapped her hand over her face and shook her head, her long black ponytail waving behind her. "For Pete's sake, Celia, can't you be a little friendlier?" She flashed Misha a grin that made her blue eyes sparkle. "How's it going, dude?"

Shayna said "dude" a lot, ever since dating some idiot claiming to be a professional surfer. The term fit her sunny personality and eventually grew on us.

Misha didn't appear taken by her charm. He eyed her as if she'd asked him to make her a garlic pizza in the shape of a cross. I laughed; I couldn't help it. *Leave it to Shayna to try to befriend the guy who'll probably suck us dry by sundown.*

At the sound of my chuckle, Misha regarded me slowly. His head tilted slightly as his full lips curved into a sensual smile. I would have preferred a vicious stare—I knew how to deal with those. For a moment, I thought he'd somehow made my clothes disappear and I was standing there like the bleeding hoochies in that awful painting.

The judges' sudden arrival gave me an excuse to glance away. There were four, each wearing a formal robe of red velvet with an elaborate powdered wig. They were probably several centuries old, but like all vampires, they didn't appear a day over thirty. Their splendor easily surpassed the beauty of any mere mortal. I guessed the whole "sucky, sucky, me love you all night" lifestyle paid off for them.

The judges regally assumed their places on the raised dais. Behind them hung a giant plasma screen, which appeared out of place in this century-old building. Did they plan to watch a movie while they decided how best to disembowel us?

A female judge motioned Misha forward with a Queen Elizabeth hand wave. A long, thick scar angled from the corner of her left jaw across her throat. Someone had tried to behead her. To scar a vampire like that, the culprit had likely used a gold blade reinforced with lethal magic. Apparently, even that blade hadn't been enough. I gathered she commanded the fang-fest Parliament, since her marble nameplate read, CHIEF JUSTICE ANTOINETTE MALIKA. Judge Malika didn't strike me as the warm and cuddly sort. Her lips were pursed into a tight line and her elongating fangs locked over her lower lip. I only hoped she'd snacked before her arrival.

At a nod from Judge Malika, Misha began. "Members of the High Court, I thank you for your audience." A Russian accent underscored his deep voice. "I hereby charge Celia, Taran, Shayna, and Emme Wird with the murder of my family member, David Geller."

"Wird? More like *Weird*," a vamp in the audience mumbled. The smaller vamp next to him adjusted his bow tie nervously when I snarled.

Oh, yeah, like we've never heard that before, jerk.

The sole male judge slapped a heavy leather-bound book on the long table and whipped out a feather quill. "Celia Wird. State your position."

Position?

I exchanged glances with my sisters; they didn't seem to know what Captain Pointy Teeth meant either. Taran shrugged. "Who gives a shit? Just say something."

I waved a hand. "Um. Registered nurse?"

Judging by his "please don't make me eat you before the proceedings" scowl, and the snickering behind us, I hadn't provided him with the appropriate response.

He enunciated every word carefully and slowly so as to not further confuse my obviously feeble and inferior mind. "Position in the supernatural world."

"We've tried to avoid your world." I gave Taran the evil eye. "For the most part. But if you must know, I'm a tigress."

"Weretigress," he said as he wrote.

"I'm not a *were*," I interjected defensively.

He huffed. "Can you *change* into a tigress or not?"

"Well, yes. But that doesn't make me a *were*."

The vamps behind us buzzed with feverish whispers while the judges' eyes narrowed suspiciously. Not knowing what we were made them nervous. A nervous vamp was a dangerous vamp. And the room was bursting with them.

"What I mean is, unlike a *were*, I can *change* parts of my body without turning into my beast completely." And unlike anything else on earth, I could also *shift*—disappear under and across solid ground and resurface unscathed. But they didn't need to know that little tidbit. Nor did they need to know I couldn't heal my injuries. If it weren't for Emme's unique ability to heal herself and others, my sisters and I would have died long ago.

"Fascinating," he said in a way that clearly meant I wasn't. The feather quill didn't come with an eraser. And the judge obviously didn't appreciate my making him mess up his book. He dipped his pen into his little inkwell and scribbled out what he'd just written before addressing Taran. "Taran Wird, position?"

"I can release magic into the forms of fire and lightning—"

"Very well, witch." The vamp scrawled.

"I'm not a witch, asshole."

The judge threw his plume on the table, agitated. Judge Malika fixed her frown on Taran. "What did you say?"

Nobody flashed a vixen grin better than Taran. "I said, 'I'm not a witch. Ass. Hole.'"

Emme whimpered, ready to hurl from the stress. Shayna giggled and threw an arm around Taran. "She's just kidding, dude!"

No. Taran didn't kid. Hell, she didn't even know any knock-knock jokes. She shrugged off Shayna, unwilling to back down. She wouldn't listen to Shayna. But she would listen to me.

"Just answer the question, Taran."

The muscles on Taran's jaw tightened, but she did as I asked. "I make fire, light—"

"Fire-breather." Captain Personality wrote quickly.

"I'm not a—"

He cut her off. "Shayna Wird?"

"Well, dude, I throw knives—"

"Knife thrower," he said, ready to get this little meet-and-greet over and done with.

Shayna did throw knives. That was true. She could also transform pieces of wood into razor-sharp weapons and manipulate alloys. All she needed was metal somewhere on her body and a little focus. For her safety, though, "knife thrower" seemed less threatening.

"And you, Emme Wird?"

"Um. Ah. I can move things with my mind—"

"Gypsy," the half-wit interpreted.

I supposed "telekinetic" was too big a word for this idiot. Then again, unlike typical telekinetics, Emme could do more than bend a few forks. I sighed. *Tigress, fire-breather, knife thrower, and Gypsy.* We sounded like the headliners for a freak show. All we needed was a bearded lady. I sighed. *That's what happens when you're the bizarre products of a back-fired curse.*

Misha glanced at us quickly before stepping forward once more. "I will present Mr. Hank Miller and Mr. Timothy Brown as witnesses—" Taran exhaled dramatically and twirled her hair like she was bored. Misha glared at her before finishing. "I do not doubt justice will be served."

Judge Zhahara Nadim, who resembled more of an Egyptian queen than someone who should be stuffed into a powdered wig, surprised me by leering at Misha like she wanted his head for a lawn ornament. I didn't know what he'd done to piss her off; yet knowing we weren't the only ones hated brought me a strange sense of comfort. She narrowed her eyes at Misha, like all predators do before they strike, and called forward someone named "Destiny." I didn't know Destiny, but I knew she was no vampire the moment she strutted onto the dais.

I tried to remain impassive. However, I really wanted to run away screaming. Short of sporting a few tails and some extra digits, Destiny was the freakiest thing I'd ever seen. Not only did she lack the allure all vampires possessed, but her fashion sense bordered on disastrous. She wore black patterned tights, white strappy sandals, and a hideous black-and-white polka-dot turtleneck. I guessed she sought to draw attention from her lime green zebra-print miniskirt. And, my God, her makeup was abominable. Black kohl outlined her bright fuchsia lips, and mint green shadow ringed her eyes.

"This is a perfect example of why I don't wear makeup," I told Taran.

Taran stepped forward with her hands on her hips. "How the hell is *she* a witness? I didn't see her at the club that night! And Lord knows she would've stuck out."

Emme trembled beside me. "Taran, please don't get us killed!"

I gave my youngest sister's hand a squeeze. "Steady, Emme."

Judge Malika called Misha's two witnesses forward. "Mr. Miller and Mr. Brown, which of you gentlemen would like to go first?"

Both "gentlemen" took one gander at Destiny and scrambled away from her. It was never a good sign when something scared a vampire. Hank, the bigger of the two vamps, shoved Tim forward.

"You may begin," Judge Malika commanded. "Just concentrate on what you saw that night. Destiny?"

The four judges swiftly donned protective ear wear, like construction workers used, just as a guard flipped a switch next to the flat-screen. At first I thought the judges toyed with us. Even with heightened senses, how could they hear the testimony through those ridiculous ear guards? Before I could protest, Destiny enthusiastically approached Tim and grabbed his head. Tim's immediate bloodcurdling screams caused the rest of us to cover our ears. Every hair on my body stood at attention. What freaked me out was that he wasn't the one on trial.

Emme's fair freckled skin blanched so severely, I feared she'd pass out. Shayna stood frozen with her jaw open while Taran and I exchanged "oh, shit" glances. I was about to start the "let's get the hell out of here" ball rolling when images from Tim's mind appeared on the screen. I couldn't believe my eyes. Complete with sound effects, we relived the night of David's murder. Misha straightened when he saw David soar out of Taran's window in flames, but otherwise he did not react. Nor did Misha blink when what remained of David burst into ashes on our lawn. Still, I sensed his fury. The image moved to a close-up of Hank's shocked face and finished with the four of us scowling down at the blood and ash.

Destiny abruptly released the sobbing Tim, who collapsed on the floor. Mucus oozed from his nose and mouth. I didn't even know vamps were capable of such body fluids.

At last, Taran finally seemed to understand the deep shittiness of our situation. "Son of a bitch," she whispered.

Hank gawked at Tim before addressing the judges. "If it pleases the court, I swear on my honor I witnessed exactly what Tim Brown did about David Geller's murder. My version would be of no further benefit."

Malika shrugged indifferently. "Very well, you're excused." She turned toward us while Hank hurried back to his seat. "As you just saw, we have ways to expose the truth. Destiny is able to extract memories, but she cannot alter them. Likewise, during Destiny's time with you, you will be unable to change what you saw. You'll only review what has already come to pass."

I frowned. "How do we know you're telling us the truth?"

Malika peered down her nose at me. "What choice do you have? Now, which of you is first?"

Photo by Kate Gledhill of Kate Gledhill Photography

Cecy Robson (also writing as Rosalina San Tiago for the app Hooked) is an author of contemporary romance, young adult adventure, and award-winning urban fantasy. A double RITA® 2016 finalist for *Once Pure* and *Once Kissed*, and a published author of more than twenty novels, you can typically find Cecy on her laptop writing her stories or stumbling blindly in search of caffeine.

www.cecyrobson.com

Facebook.com/Cecy.Robson.Author

instagram.com/cecyrobsonauthor

twitter.com/cecyrobson

www.goodreads.com/goodreadscomCecyRobsonAuthor

For exclusive information and more, join my Newsletter!

http://eepurl.com/4ASmj

CPSIA information can be obtained
at www.ICGtesting.com
Printed in the USA
LVHW030851260821
696089LV00006B/346